SOMETHING WICKED

SOMETHING WICKED

David Housewright

MINOTAUR
BOOKS
NEW YORK

Special thanks to Kayla Janas, Keith Kahla,
Alice Pfeifer, Alison J. Picard, Emily Polachek,
and Renée Valois for their assistance in writing
and publishing this book.

First published in the United States by Minotaur Books, an imprint of
St. Martin's Publishing Group

SOMETHING WICKED. Copyright © 2022 by David Housewright.
All rights reserved. Printed in the United States of America.
For information, address St. Martin's Publishing Group,
120 Broadway, New York, NY 10271.

www.minotaurbooks.com

Library of Congress Cataloging-in-Publication Data

Names: Housewright, David, 1955– author.
Title: Something wicked / David Housewright.
Description: First edition. | New York: Minotaur Books, 2022. |
    Series: Twin Cities P.I. Mac Mckenzie novels; 19
Identifiers: LCCN 2022000927 | ISBN 9781250757012 (hardcover) |
    ISBN 9781250757029 (ebook)
Subjects: LCGFT: Novels.
Classification: LCC PS3558.O8668 S58 2022 | DDC 813/.54—dc23/
    eng/20220114
LC record available at https://lccn.loc.gov/2022000927

Our books may be purchased in bulk for promotional, educational,
or business use. Please contact your local bookseller or the Macmillan
Corporate and Premium Sales Department at 1-800-221-7945, extension
5442, or by email at MacmillanSpecialMarkets@macmillan.com.

First Edition: 2022

10   9   8   7   6   5   4   3   2   1

FOR RENÉE
AS ALWAYS

By the pricking of my thumbs,
Something wicked this way comes.
Open locks [to]
Whoever knocks!

William Shakespeare
Macbeth, Act 4, Scene 1

ONE

Jenness Crawford's voice trembled with rage.

"My grandmother was murdered," she said. "I just know it."

Nina Truhler had been sitting comfortably behind the desk in her office, pleased to hear from her friend and former employee. Only now she was standing, one hand resting on the desktop for support, the other pressing her cell to her ear.

"What?" she said. "When?"

"Just over a month ago."

"You're just telling me this now?"

"There's nothing you could have done. You couldn't even have come to the funeral. There wasn't a funeral. Just a private memorial, her ashes scattered over the lake. Then the will was read. Well, not really read because everyone knew what it said, my parents and uncle and aunts. Tess had discussed it with them when she wrote it, what she wanted done, but now they're meeting with a developer and I don't know what to do."

"Wait. Jen. Go back. You said your grandmother was murdered?"

"I'm convinced of it but no one will listen to me. The police chief, the one they hired from Minneapolis, she said I was distraught. Yes, I'm distraught. Someone murdered my grandmother and now they're trying to steal the castle."

"Are you sure?"

"Nina, yes, I'm sure."

"What can I do?"

"I need—I need a favor."

"McKenzie?"

"I'm hoping he'll help me, but I wanted to ask you first before calling him because—because of what happened the last time he did a favor for a friend. Getting shot . . ."

"He's okay now."

"Is he? Nina, I know you don't like it when he does these things . . ."

"What can we do?"

You'll notice she said *we*.

"Can you come down to the castle?" Jenness said. "I've reserved one of our cabins for you and we still observe all of the COVID protocols so there shouldn't be any danger."

"Yes, Jen. We're coming. We're coming today."

At least that's what Nina told her friend. What she told me later was somewhat less dramatic.

I was watching baseball, a rare Minnesota Twins–Chicago Cubs afternoon matchup, and thinking what a difference a year makes. Last September I had my choice of baseball, men's basketball, women's basketball, hockey, and soccer games, all of the seasons overlapping. When the coronavirus reached the U.S. earlier that year, hockey and basketball were shut down midseason and it seemed as if baseball and the WNBA would be canceled altogether. But the NHL, NBA, WNBA, and MLS were allowed to continue their seasons in protective "bubbles"—no one from the outside world was allowed in for fear of infecting the players and staff. One NBA player who snuck out to visit a strip joint—he said he went there for the chicken wings—was suspended from his team and tossed out of the bubble until he completed a ten-day quarantine to make sure he wasn't contagious.

Meanwhile, baseball played a sixty-game schedule followed by playoffs in empty stadiums with players, coaches, and staff forced to follow strict safety protocols. Those protocols came into question when players in the Marlins and Phillies systems tested positive early in the abbreviated season. Only the rules and player discipline held and the season continued.

At its very best, sports provide an entertaining distraction from the trials and tribulations of everyday life and in those days the misery index had climbed to nearly catastrophic heights. COVID-19 was infecting millions of Americans and killing hundreds of thousands of us, the economy was in freefall with unemployment and business closings pushing toward Great Depression numbers, protests and social unrest were sweeping the nation, and a frighteningly dysfunctional government seemed incapable of doing anything that didn't make matters worse. Was it any surprise that dentists at the time reported an alarming increase in the number of cracked and fractured teeth in stressed-out patients who ground their teeth mostly at night?

Now we were moving forward—or at least as far as the threat of COVID variants would allow. Sports had settled into their normal seasons, with an unlimited number of fans in attendance reminding everyone why they were played in the first place. There were plenty of people at the ball game I was watching and if it had been played at Target Field instead of Wrigley, I would have been with them.

I was checking to see when the Twins would return home when Nina walked into the condominium we shared in downtown Minneapolis. She dropped her bag next to the coatrack near the door, hung up her blazer, moved to the sofa where I was sitting, sat next to me, and pulled my arm around her shoulders.

"Who's winning?" she asked.

"Top of the third, no score yet," I said. "What are you doing here?"

"I live here, remember."

"No, you sleep here. You live at Rickie's."

Rickie's was the jazz club located on Cathedral Hill in St. Paul that Nina had named after her daughter, Erica. Like nearly all of the restaurants and clubs in Minnesota, Rickie's had taken a life-threatening hit because of the virus. Many closed, some forever. Only Nina had a large parking lot. She built a stage inside an enormous tent that she fitted with a custom heating system. She arranged socially distanced tables for parties of two and four in front of the stage. And she turned the rest of the lot into a drive-in, people watching the musicians from the safety, if not comfort, of their vehicles while listening to a simulcast on their radios, her waitstaff providing curbside food service. On select occasions, she hosted acts in her upstairs concert hall that had been reconfigured to provide full-restaurant service to about thirty percent of the customers she usually served. Plus, she sold pay-per-view tickets to live streams of acts staged not only at Rickie's but also clubs around the country like the Blue Note.

None of these efforts had produced anywhere near the revenue she had enjoyed before the pandemic, though. Just breaking even every week became a Herculean task; Nina was forced to lay off fifty percent of her kitchen and waitstaff. It shattered her heart to do it. Yet she had remained standing and now her business was approaching pre-COVID levels.

'Course, it didn't hurt that she had a rich husband.

At first Nina had refused to accept my help.

"I don't need your money," she said.

I tried to explain that it was "our" money, only she wouldn't listen. This precipitated the longest, loudest, and most emotional "discussion" we'd ever had. See, a couple of decades earlier, Nina had escaped an abusive marriage and, with her infant daughter in tow, had built Rickie's from scratch. Alone. To accept help from someone, to even admit that she needed help, was painful for her.

The argument started at about ten at night. At around one in the morning I finally convinced her that "We're in this together, remember? For better, for worse, for richer, for poorer, in sickness and in health, remember?" I also reminded Nina that she was the one who had neglected her business to sit by my side for nearly three days while I was lying in a coma in a hospital bed with a bullet in my back; who had pretty much dropped everything to help me recover and rehab myself back to some semblance of normal. "I don't recall any talk of what was yours and what was mine back then, so . . ."

At some point, I can't remember exactly when, we fell into each other's arms, mostly from exhaustion. Nina whispered, "I'm going to pay you back."

"I can hardly wait," I told her at the time.

Now Nina was snuggling closer against me on the sofa. I was fast losing interest in the baseball game.

"We need to get out of here," she said.

"Get out of where?"

"Here, here; this place."

Nina waved her hand. Our condo was located on the seventh floor with a spectacular view of the Mississippi River where it tumbled down St. Anthony Falls. Which was another thing about having a wealthy husband—Nina didn't need to bring any money home for us to continue living in the style to which we had become accustomed; she could afford to plow all of her income into her club. We were very, very lucky and we knew it.

"You're right," I said. "It's a dump."

"We need a vacation. When was the last time we went on a vacation, anyway?"

"We were going to Italy for our honeymoon."

"Then they were pounded by COVID-19."

"And then the U.S. got pounded."

"Then my business went to hell. And you got shot."

"But now your business is healing, I'm healing, and the borders are opening."

"I still don't feel comfortable getting on a plane."

"Fair enough," I said. "So, where can we go that doesn't require using our passports or air travel?"

"I was thinking Redding."

"Redding, California?"

"Redding, Minnesota. Specifically, Redding Castle on Lake Anpetuwi near the border with South Dakota. I was chatting with Jenness Crawford this morning. You remember Jen."

"Sure. How is she?"

"Fine. You know after she left Rickie's, what was it? Fifteen months ago? After she left, she took a job working for her grandmother at the castle. Her grandmother passed . . ."

"Oh, no. From the virus?"

"I don't think so. Anyway, Jen runs the place now."

"Good for her."

"She invited us to visit," Nina said. "I said yes. I hope you don't mind."

"Not at all. If I'm not mistaken, the place is supposed to be pretty spectacular."

"Let's find out."

"When would you like to go? Next week?"

Nina patted my knee.

"It'll take us what? Thirty minutes to pack?"

Three hours later the GPS in my Mustang directed us up a long and narrow road cut through a dense forest to a large rock. The words "Welcome to Redding Castle 1883" were carved into it. Beyond the rock was a clearing. In the middle of the clearing stood an enormous building that looked less like a castle than an English country house, something you'd imagine finding in the rich countryside just a few hedgerows from Jane Austen's place. It was bathed in a golden light; the late afternoon sun was at the perfect angle to beautify its two round turrets, tall gables, huge windows and balconies, some facing the forest; others with a spectacular view of the sparkling blue water of Lake Anpetuwi.

I stopped the car along the road to gaze at it. I remember the exact words I spoke to Nina—"Geez, look at that."

"It was built in 1883," she said.

"Yeah, I got that from the rock."

"I think the rock was added later."

I glanced at Nina. Normally, she was the one who became excited by what was old and distinguished and beautiful. Instead, she looked as if there was something on her mind.

"It's been in the Redding family all these years," she said. "Jenness is a Redding on her mother's side; Redding was her mother's maiden name."

"Okay."

We parked among a dozen other cars in a lot on the far edge of the clearing next to a barn painted in the same earthy brown and reddish beige colors of the castle. There were eight small cabins also scattered along the perimeter of the clearing, each in a different earth tone; each built with a clear view of the castle as if there was nothing else to see. I slid out of the car and stretched. Nina remained inside for a few beats. When she finally emerged, she stared at me over the roof of the Mustang that, incidentally, she had given to me for my birthday about three years ago. Something in her expression made me stare back.

"What?" I asked.

"I'm sorry," she said. "I should have told you. I don't know why I didn't."

"Told me what?"

A voice called to us.

"Nina," it said. "McKenzie."

The voice belonged to Jenness Crawford. She was half walking, half jogging down a narrow cobblestone path that wound from the castle to the parking lot. She surprised me by wrapping her arms around my waist and hugging me, an act that would have been unthinkable a year earlier; that some people were still reluctant to engage in, vaccines be damned.

"Thank you, thank you for coming," she said. "I'm just so glad that you're here."

"I gathered that."

"Thank you so much for agreeing to help me."

I'm proud to say that I didn't hesitate for a single beat.

"What are friends for?" I asked.

Jenness spun toward Nina. It gave me a chance to give my wife that look—you know the one I mean.

Nina opened her arms for Jenness. The two women embraced. They could have been mother and daughter if Nina had given birth when she was twelve.

"Nina, thank you," Jenness said.

Jenness was one of those people who smiled with her eyes. She was clearly delighted that we were both there.

"What should we do first?" Jenness asked. "Should I show you the room where my grandmother was killed?"

Grandmother? Killed? my inner voice asked. *Nina, what have you gotten us into?*

"Why don't we check in, first," I said. "Let Nina and I get settled and then we'll talk."

"Yes, yes, of course," Jenness said. "Don't worry about checking in, I already took care of that. You're in the James J. Hill Cabin."

It was a log cabin with a stone fireplace on the far side of the clearing and the Empire Builder, as Hill had been called during his lifetime, mostly at his own insistence, never set foot anywhere near the place. Hill had been the CEO of the Great Northern Railway. For a short time in the early 1880s, he and John Redding had been partners, mostly in secret because Hill's name was synonymous with all that was evil among many who knew it. Together they built railroads from the town of Redding northeast to St. Cloud, west to Watertown, South Dakota, and southwest to Sioux Falls, South Dakota. As far as anyone knew, Hill had never visited Redding Castle, but what the hell? At least that's what Jenness told us as we crossed to the cabin nestled against the forest wall. Jenness carried my bag because it was the lightest. I carried both of Nina's bags. I was grateful that she only took thirty minutes to pack. God knows what she could have managed in a full hour.

"Did you guys eat?" Jenness asked. "Don't worry about it. Meet me on the patio in, say, a half hour. There'll be a buffet."

Nina and Jenness hugged some more, Jenness left, and Nina closed the door. I set her bags on the round rug spread in front of the fireplace. The cabin wasn't much more than a single room except for a tiny bathroom hidden behind an oak door. The ground floor was furnished with a small table with two chairs, a tiny refrigerator, microwave, and coffeepot. A rocking chair and an old-fashioned stuffed chair with matching love seat faced the fireplace, plus a hot tub built for two and designed to look old-fashioned was located beneath the staircase. The stairs led to a loft with a queen-size bed and a low V-shaped ceiling.

"This is cozy," Nina said.

"Lucy, you have a lot of 'splainin' t' do," I told her.

"Who's Lucy?"

"From the old Lucy show. Lucille Ball? Are you telling me you never saw reruns of *I Love Lucy*?"

"No."

"It ran in the fifties."

"A little before my time."

"She was always doing something crazy and her husband would put his hands on his hips and say 'Lucy, you have a lot of 'splainin' t' do.'"

"Why would he talk like that?"

"He was a Cuban bandleader."

"So, he couldn't speak proper English?"

"It was a bit."

"It's those kinds of stereotypical depictions that fuel discrimination . . ."

"Don't change the subject."

"You're the one who brought up Lucy."

I placed my hands on my hips.

"Nina," I said. "You have a lot of explaining to do."

"I'm sorry."

"Jen's grandmother was killed?"

"That's what she said."

"When?"

Nina repeated the content of the phone conversation she and Jenness had earlier that day.

"Why didn't you tell me?" I asked.

"You're angry."

"No, not really."

"I don't blame you. I'm the worst kind of hypocrite."

"I wouldn't say worst."

"You were shot because you were doing a favor for your friend and I practically begged you to stop; screamed at you to stop. And now I volunteer you to do a favor for my friend."

"If Jenness had called me first . . ."

"That's not the point."

"What's the point?"

"When you were shot—that was very hard on me."

"Imagine how I felt."

"McKenzie, c'mon."

"It happened. We move on."

"I get that, only when Jen called this morning . . . I wanted you to help her but I didn't want to ask you to help her. That way if you get—hurt again, I can always say 'Don't look at me. I'm the one always telling him not to do these things.' I'm such a coward."

"Hey, no one talks about my wife like that."

"McKenzie . . ."

"Besides, you've always been there for me when I do these things, so . . ."

Nina turned her head so she could look directly into my eyes.

"Forever and always," she said.

"Well, then . . ."

We found Jenness sitting at a small, ornate metal table on a large patio built between the castle and Lake Anpetuwi. She was gazing out at the lake while she sipped from a wineglass. The sun had nearly set, giving the still water a dusky orange color and making the patio's granite tiles seem as if they were on fire. There were five couples lounging on the patio along with Jenness, each sitting at a nearly identical table, all of them watching the sun, a few shading their eyes with the flat of their hands. None of them spoke.

Finally, the sun dipped below the horizon and a few moments later the lake was cast in dark shadow.

"I never get tired of that," a woman said.

Conversations, paused by the glorious sunset, resumed. Music, which had been muted during the sunset, was piped in through camouflaged speakers; soft jazz evenly divided between vocalists and instrumentals. A man who looked like a model for a Big & Tall clothing line stood and went to the buffet set out on a long table near an open door that led to the opulent dining room inside the castle. He filled a small plate by the light coming through the doorway and the castle's enormous windows.

Jenness smiled brightly as Nina and I mounted the stone steps leading to the patio. We were late by twenty minutes and I was thinking of a good excuse to give her, only the way Nina and I were holding hands, or perhaps it was the expression on our faces, made Jenness roll her eyes and shake her head.

"Get a room, you two," Jenness said.

"Good evening to you, too, Ms. Crawford," I said.

Jenness stood and gestured at the buffet.

"I bet you're hungry after—anyway, you should eat. Can I get you something from the bar?"

We placed our orders and Jenness disappeared into the dining room even as she slipped her mask on. Nina and I filled our plates at the buffet and retired to a small table near where Jenness had been sitting. As we began eating, an older man emerged from the dining room and lit a fire in a smokeless firepit in the center of the patio. He stepped back inside just as Jenness returned carrying a tray loaded with our drinks. She set them in front of Nina and me, and reclaimed her table.

Jenness removed her mask.

"What do you think?" she asked.

Nina jabbed a fork at a cup filled with sticky toffee pudding.

"You stole my recipe," she said.

"I did not."

"You. Stole. My. Recipe."

"Not really."

"No, really."

"Nina, it's a homage," Jenness said. "On our menu it reads 'a Rickie's favorite.'"

"Besides," I said.

"What?" Nina asked.

"If I'm not mistaken, you stole the recipe from that pub in Oxford the last time we went to England. What was it called? The White Horse?"

"I didn't steal it. It was given to me by the cook. Delightful man."

"It was given to an enthusiastic, grateful, and high-tipping tourist, not to mention flirtatious."

"I wasn't flirting."

"I don't think they knew you were going to put it on Rickie's dessert menu."

By then a woman had approached our table, halting a discreet distance away. She was about sixty and very attractive in an I-spent-an-enormous-amount-of-time-and-money-to-look-this-good sort of way.

"Excuse me," she said. "I didn't mean to eavesdrop."

Probably that's true, I told myself. With social distancing and mask-wearing during the pandemic, people had been forced to speak much more loudly than normal to be understood and some of us were still learning to lower our voices, again.

"Did I hear correctly—you own Rickie's?" the woman added. "Rickie's in St. Paul?"

"I do," Nina said.

"I love that place. Your food, oh my God, and the music. We used to go there at least a half-dozen times a year."

"Used to?"

"We haven't been back since the virus. You haven't closed or anything?"

"We're doing okay."

"So many great restaurants closed—Bachelor Farmer, Pazzaluna, Butcher and the Boar, even Izzy's Ice Cream. Jenny!" The woman turned toward Jenness. "You never told us you had famous friends in the restaurant business."

"Hardly famous," Nina said.

"So introduce me," she said.

Before Jenness could speak, though, the woman spun to face Nina again.

"I'm Olivia Redding," she said.

"Nina Truhler."

"I'm Jenny's aunt."

"Oh?"

"Like I said, I love Rickie's. How do you know Jenny?"

"She used to work for me."

"As a waitress?"

"She was a manager."

"A manager? At Rickie's?" Olivia smiled at Jenness. "Well, look at you."

"Aunt Olivia, you know I have a degree in hotel and restaurant management from the University of Minnesota, right?"

"Of course, dear. You're doing such a wonderful job running this place, too, aren't you? Oh, but I have to go now. Can't leave your uncle alone for a minute." She turned yet again to Nina. "Will you be staying with us long?"

"For a couple of days, anyway," Nina said.

"I'm sure you'll enjoy your visit. There's so much to do and it's not like you can stay in your room and just watch TV."

"I noticed that," I said.

Olivia glanced at me like I was a fly that had landed on her salad.

"Yes, well, Nina, I hope we can chat again, but I must go now. Rickie's, my, my, my . . ."

Olivia pivoted and crossed the patio to her table. It was her husband who had helped himself at the buffet when we first arrived. He was now working on his third plate by my count. While she was slender, his size suggested that three plates was a snack.

Jenness leaned toward us.

"Livy hates it here," she said.

The man who had started the fire in the firepit had returned with a tray filled with candles burning inside dark glass candleholders. Jenness sat back and waited while he set one of the candles first on our table and then hers.

"Mr. Doty," she said.

"Miss," he replied.

When he retreated back inside the castle, Jenness leaned toward us again.

"How could she hate Redding Castle?" Nina asked.

"We offer fishing and water sports; canoes and kayaks and hiking trails and cross-country skiing. My cousin Maddie has a chance to make the U.S. Olympic team; she and some of her teammates have been training here for years."

"I don't understand."

"Nature. Fresh air. Liv thinks it's unhealthy. I'm not kidding. Deer and fox and beaver and eagles and hawks and the occasional coyote—this is a woman who goes to Las Vegas three times a year. Her idea of wildlife is a blackjack dealer. She wants to sell this place, I know she does."

"Who owns it?" I asked.

"Since my grandmother was killed, all the Sibs do."

"Sibs?"

"Siblings. Tess had five children: my two uncles, two aunts, and my mom. According to her will, they all share equally in everything."

"Tess?"

"I called her Grandma every day of my life until I went to work for her last year and then she told me to call her Tess. She said it was more professional. When she died . . ." Jenness closed her eyes and took a deep breath. For a moment I thought she might start crying, yet when she opened them again they were dry. "I called her Tess but I was always thinking Grandma."

"How was she killed?" I asked.

"I don't know," Jenness said.

"Who discovered the body?"

"I did. Me and Mrs. Doty did. Actually, Mr. Doty was the first to see her."

Lucy, you have a lot of 'splainin' t' do, my inner voice said.

"Tell me what happened," I said aloud.

"Tess had failed to come down for breakfast. She always ate at seven thirty A.M. sharp. Always. Only she didn't appear in the dining room for breakfast, so Mrs. Doty went to her room."

Jenness leaned back in her chair, twisted to her left, and gestured at a balcony near the corner of the castle. The large window behind the balcony was closed and the drapes drawn, yet enough light escaped to illuminate the iron railing and two chairs.

"That was Tess's room," she said. "Mrs. Doty pounded on the door but Tess didn't answer so she called me. I knocked, too. We have keys to all the rooms, of course, only the door was locked from the inside—we have dead bolts for the safety of our guests. I had to call Mr. Doty. We decided there was no way to break down the door, so I had Mr. Doty get a ladder from the barn and use it to climb to the balcony. The window was unlocked. He opened it and saw my grandmother in her bed. She looked like she was sleeping, he told me. Instead of trying to wake her, he went to the door and opened it. I went to the bed and tried to wake Grandma, only she was gone."

"I'm sorry," Nina said.

"A policeman, he wasn't talking to me, he was talking to the new chief; he said 'She woke up dead.' My grandmother woke up dead. What the hell does that mean?"

"Something cops say," I told her. "People often die in their sleep, Jen. Most will tell you that's the best way to go. Die in your sleep in the arms of a beautiful woman." I was looking at Nina when I said that last part. She didn't so much as grin. "Anyway, their loved ones find them and they call 911 because what else are they going to do? Police respond and when asked later what happened, they say 'So-and-so woke up dead.' It's not meant to be insulting. Just a way to deal with something they have to deal with every day."

"Only my grandmother didn't die in her sleep."

"What did the police say?"

"They—they disagree."

"The medical examiner?"

"I don't know, I haven't spoken to her, but, McKenzie—Tess was killed, I know she was."

"What makes you say that?"

"When I arrived last year, the castle was failing financially. It was failing for a number of reasons. I can tell you about that if you want to hear. I can tell you what I did to stop the bleeding, too. Things I learned in school; what Nina taught me. How we started turning it around even during the pandemic. Just a couple of months ago, Tess told me that she had changed her mind; that she wasn't going to sell the castle after all. Let's keep it in the family, she said."

"Your grandmother was planning to sell Redding Castle?" Nina asked.

"The castle needed a lot of work, still does; a lot of renovations. Our reservations were declining and so was our restaurant traffic. Plus, none of the Sibs were interested in running it after she was gone so Tess decided that maybe it was time to sell and she started talking to developers. Only I was willing to run it, wanted to run it, and after she saw the changes I was making, she took the castle off the market."

"What was she going to sell the property for?" I asked.

"I heard as much as four million dollars, only I don't know how accurate the figure was."

"That's a lot of money," Nina said.

"Only Tess didn't care. You can't take it with you, she said."

"How old was your grandmother?" I asked.

"Eighty-seven. I know what you're thinking. You're thinking she died of old age in her sleep. Only that's an awfully big co-incidence, don't you think, Tess talking about selling and then deciding not to sell and then dying before she could do anything about it? I remember"—Jenness pointed at me—"listening to you at Rickie's talking about one of your cases. I remember that you said that you didn't believe in coincidences."

"I didn't say that."

"Yes, I remember."

"I said I don't trust coincidences. Except, Jen, they happen all the time. That's why Merriam-Webster's has a word for it."

"McKenzie . . ."

"Jenness," Nina said. "You said over the phone that 'they're trying to steal the castle.' You meant the developers, didn't you? Yet it's your uncles, your aunts, even your mother that are talking to them."

Jenness nodded.

"What you're telling us now—do you honestly believe that someone in your family actually murdered your grandmother, their mother, for the money they would get for selling Redding Castle?"

"Maybe."

Wow, my inner voice said. It's been done before, I reminded myself, but *wow.*

"Okay," I said aloud.

"Will you help me?" Jenness asked.

"That's why I'm here."

"What should we do first?"

"I want to take a look at your grandmother's room," I said. "Then I'll have a chat with the police and ME; take a look at their official reports. After that we'll see."

Jenness stood abruptly.

"All right," she said.

"Tomorrow, Jen," I said.

She hesitated before regaining her seat.

"I suppose that would be best," Jenness said. "Tess's room— that's where Olivia and my uncle Ben are staying now. Big Ben Redding they call him."

I glanced across the veranda to where Ben and Olivia were sitting. There was a lot of height and breadth to him; if you met Ben on the street you'd might think he was a heavyweight boxer or an action-movie star. His wife was a foot shorter and about one hundred and fifty pounds lighter. She looked as though he could drape her around his neck like a scarf.

"I'll have a lot of questions," I said.

"I can't speak for the Sibs," Jenness said. "Can't make them talk to you. I've instructed my staff to answer any questions you care to ask, though."

"How many people do you have working here?"

Jenness took a deep breath and said, "We used to have twelve, but because of the virus I had to cut the number to eight" with the exhale. "We hope to add more staff as we increase prof- itability."

Nina nodded as if she felt Jenness's pain.

"I'll do what I can," I said. "But, Jen, no promises."

"I understand. It's just the Sibs, other people, they think I'm being selfish trying to keep this place as it is and I suppose I am. Only Redding Castle—it is Tess. It's all the Reddings then and now. It's represented who we are for one hundred and thirty-eight years. To bulldoze it for a big payday—what does that say about what we've become?"

I had already bounced my head off the loft's low ceiling twice before I wised up enough to sit on the corner of the queen-size bed as I undressed. Nina crawled up behind me and kissed the scar on my shoulder where the shrapnel had sliced into me when a bomb blew up a friend's truck. She kissed the collarbone that had been fractured when I leapt out of a two-story building to avoid getting blown up by another bomb and nuzzled the top of my head where they had drilled two dime-size burr holes to relieve the epidermal hematoma that had occurred when I was nearly clubbed to death. At the same time her fingers danced over the hole in my back where I had been shot.

"When we first met you had such a beautiful body," Nina said. "Now look at you. You're all nicked and gouged like a piece of old furniture."

I glanced over my shoulder. Nina was wearing her black hair short again. Her startling silver-blue eyes were clear and bright; if she had gained so much as a pound since we met, I hadn't noticed.

"Yet you still remain as beautiful as the rising sun," I said.

"Nice line. Thank you for this, by the way. Thank you for helping Jenness."

"I don't know how much help I'll be. My first inclination is to side with the cops. We'll see."

Nina sprawled on her back and opened her arms to me.

"C'mere," she said.

I crawled up next to her.

"In baseball they call this a day-night doubleheader," I said.

"McKenzie, do me a favor. Shh."

TWO

Redding Castle was just as glorious at sunrise as it was at sunset. I studied it for a few minutes, marveling at how its many windows shimmered under the brilliant light before carrying a mug of coffee up the staircase to the loft bedroom. There was a small skylight built into the V-shaped ceiling and I opened it. Afterward, I grabbed Nina's foot beneath the duvet and gave it a shake.

"Rise and shine, sleepyhead," I said.

She opened one eye, stared at me for a moment, and then closed it again.

I wiggled her foot some more.

"Wakey-wakey, honey."

Nina kept both eyes closed.

"Who talks like that?" she asked.

"I let you sleep as long as I could."

"What time is it?"

"Six forty-five."

Her eyes snapped open.

"What is wrong with you? Who gets up at six forty-five?"

"People who go to breakfast at seven thirty."

Nina gave it a few beats.

"Jenness, I forgot," she said.

Nina closed her eyes again.

I swept the duvet off her. She lunged forward, grabbed the edge, and pulled it back up.

"Don't do that," she said. "It's cold."

"You know, for most people these are normal weekday hours."

"I'm not normal."

"I noticed that about you."

"It's why I built a jazz club," Nina said. "So I wouldn't have to get up before noon."

"You usually get up way before noon."

"Not at six forty-five in the goddamn morning."

"Do you kiss your daughter with that mouth?"

Through the skylight I could hear voices.

"See what you've done," Nina said. "You made me swear."

"Shh."

I moved to the skylight.

"I almost never swear," Nina said.

"Shh."

I listened hard.

"I don't see why not," I heard a woman say. "I like it here. Don't you like it here?"

"You're not listening," a second woman said.

The way the skylight was built, I couldn't see the ground; had no idea who was speaking.

"I am listening," the first woman said. "You're just not making sense."

"I'm not going to let that—that cousin of yours ruin a good thing."

"But Redding Castle is a good thing."

"You might not think so if suddenly you don't have enough money to train and compete properly."

"I'll be fine, Mom. You know that."

"You wanted to run before going to school," the second woman said. "Are we going to run or not?"

"I'll run really slow so you can keep up."

After that I heard nothing.

Nina was sitting up in bed, wide awake now.

"Hmm," she said.

Breakfast was served on the patio.

"We still encourage our guests to eat their meals outside or in their rooms," Jenness said. "Some insist on eating in the dining room. That's okay. Last year, though . . . because of the state's social-distancing mandates, we had to remove nearly two-thirds of our tables. We tried to serve our guests in shifts so we'd have as many tables open for outside restaurant customers as possible. Even so, we lost so much business. We did better with curbside and delivery than I had expected; especially considering how far we are from town. Still . . . we're operating at nearly full capacity now, but we haven't been able to make up our losses."

"There're things you can try," Nina said. "Optimizing the menu; replacing underperforming options with high-popularity, high-profit-margin dishes, that sort of thing. Raise prices."

Jenness held up her hand; her thumb and index finger were set about an inch apart.

"Only there's so much you can do before you start affecting customer satisfaction," she said. "Before you trigger traffic declines."

"Discounts and promotions? Bundling meals, upsells?"

"I'm willing to try anything and please, Nina, I'm open to suggestions and not only for the restaurant. One of the reasons we survived the pandemic is because of the lake and the forest. During the height of the virus, travelers felt safer spending time outdoors compared to enclosed spaces. Meeting and event space, outdoor dining, green spaces for socially distant gatherings—we have that. We've always had that. Only that advantage isn't as strong now that the bigger hotels and resorts are starting to regain their popularity. And winter's coming. In Minnesota, winter is always coming. We barely survived the last one."

While they were talking shop, I glanced up from my eggs Benedict to see two women dressed for jogging move across the patio to a small table. Jenness saw them as well and gave a wave. The older woman ignored her. The younger woman waved back as if she and Jenness were great pals who hadn't seen each other since summer vacation.

"Who are they?" I asked.

"Carly and Madison Zumwalt," Jenness said. "Carly is my aunt. She's the youngest of Tess's children. In fact, she's twelve years younger than my mom who's the next youngest. I heard my uncle say once that she had been a great surprise to my grandparents. Zumwalt is the name of her first husband. She's been married three times. After her last divorce was finalized about eight, nine months ago, she changed her name back to Zumwalt."

"Why not Redding?" Nina asked.

"Because Maddie's name is Zumwalt and as a junior at Redding High School she won the Minnesota State Cross Country Ski Championships by thirty-seven seconds and then went to Duluth and won the CXC Junior Cup by twenty-three seconds, which made her a mortal lock to make the Midwest Junior Team, which gives her a good shot at the National Junior Team, which could eventually lead to the U.S. Olympic Team."

"And Carly wants to bask in her daughter's glory," I suggested.

"Jesse Diggins was twenty-seven when she won the United States' first ever gold medal in cross-country skiing at the Olympics in South Korea. Maddie is seventeen. She has plenty of time to get stronger. She could pull it off. She really could."

I stared at the young woman for a few beats, checking out her long slender legs and long slender arms until she glanced at me and I averted my eyes. I assumed a cross-country skier would require a lot of leg strength, a lot of arm and shoulder strength, yet nothing about her body seemed overdeveloped. She looked to me like someone who *ran* cross-country and I was willing to bet she could run for hours without even breathing hard. It made me regret how out of shape I had become.

"Carly wants to sell the castle, too, doesn't she?" I said.

"How'd you know?" Jenness asked.

"I'm a semiprofessional investigator."

"We heard them talking outside our window this morning," Nina said.

"Hey, hey, hey," I said. "Jen's going to lose all respect for me if you start giving away my secrets."

"It's not a secret," Jenness said. "Carly told me herself that she wanted to sell the place; told me on several occasions. Told me this morning, in fact. I get it, though. The others grew up here; played in the forest, played on the lake and in the house. Anna and Big Ben built honeybee hives in the forest behind the General Oglesby Cabin . . ."

Who the hell is General Oglesby? my inner voice wondered.

"My grandparents used to serve the honey it produced in the restaurant; sold jars of it to our guests. Redding Castle Honey. I'm hoping to revive it. Anyway, while the other Sibs grew up here, Carly merely grew old, if that makes any sense. She didn't really have anyone to play with. Think about it. Big Ben was a senior in high school the year she was born; Anna was a sophomore. Mom was in middle school. From what I've heard over the years, Carly was treated less like a sister than a child the others were forced to babysit. She resented it, too. Still does."

"Tell me how this is going to work," I said.

"The Sibs have to vote on everything involving the estate. Simple majority wins. I have my mom's vote. Carly is against me. That leaves my uncles Ben and Alexander and my aunt Anna. I need two of them to see things my way."

"Ben is married to Olivia," Nina reminded us.

"That doesn't mean he'll take her side," Jenness said. "Big Ben—how do I say it? Ben is his own man."

"Good for him," I said.

From her expression, I didn't know if Nina agreed with me or not.

"They're going to meet with a developer, meet her here; the one from town who seems to be the most interested in making an offer for the property," Jenness said. "Then we'll see."

"When?" I asked.

"Friday. Today's Tuesday. I have three days to find a way to save Redding Castle."

After breakfast, I asked to see the room where Tess Redding's body was found. Jenness led Nina and me through various rooms, up staircases and along corridors while reciting facts and figures about the castle as if she were a tour guide: 18,000 square feet spread out over two turrets and four floors; eighteen guest rooms—the ones located at the top of each turret were the most in demand and therefore the most expensive to book—twenty-two fireplaces including one in each guest room, plus the enormous fireplace in the lobby-slash-sitting room; eight cut-glass chandeliers; ninety-foot reception hall that the Sibs had once used as a playroom and was later transformed into the restaurant dining room; elaborately carved oak and mahogany woodwork everywhere.

"The actual castle with the two turrets was constructed in 1883 by my great-great-great-grandfather John Redding," Jenness said. "It was enlarged and redesigned by his son Douglas in 1912 and then redesigned again into a hotel and resort by my great-grandfather Steven after World War II. He's the one who added the eight cabins along the perimeter. My grandparents Joseph and Tess added the restaurant in 1968. The entire property amounts to just over forty-eight acres, including five acres of lakefront."

There was also an art gallery where we stopped briefly to admire paintings by Frederic Remington and James McNeill Whistler as well as a half-dozen illustrations by the legendary editorial cartoonist Thomas Nast. In addition, the gallery contained a Steinway & Sons grand piano that was at least a century old. Nina was clearly more impressed by the piano than the paintings. She ran her hand across the black finish.

"Incredible, isn't it?" Jenness said. "The artwork, the antiques; a lot of them date back to long before 1883. John was an extremely wealthy man and he wanted everyone to know it so he collected a lot of stuff, most of it shipped in from New York and Boston. There's a copy of a book in every guest room and cabin that narrates the history of Redding Castle. You should read it."

We left the gallery and continued a short distance down the second-floor corridor until we reached Tess's room.

"I'm next door," Jenness said. "We were the only members of the Redding family who actually lived here. The Sibs and their families will visit from time to time; Christmas at the castle is always a big deal. Only no one else has lived here since Carly was married for the first time."

"What about staff?" I asked.

"Mr. and Mrs. Doty have the cabin next to the barn. They've been with us since, God, I don't know. Since before I was born, anyway. Everyone else lives in Redding."

Jenness knocked on the door. While we waited I asked, "Did you hear anything the night your grandmother died?"

Jenness's body language suggested that she wanted to give a different answer than the one she was stuck with.

"No," she said.

"Did you see anyone lingering about the corridor?"

"No. There are only two guest rooms on this floor and they're both on the far side of the castle, so there shouldn't have been anyone near here."

"Staff?"

Jenness shook her head and knocked some more.

"Is there any other way to get up here besides the stairs leading from the lobby?" I asked.

"Yes." She pointed at what to me looked like a wall at the end of the corridor. "We call it the servant stairs."

"Show me."

Jenness moved to the wall where the corridor ended and pushed against it. There was a discernible click and the wall swung open like the door to a bathroom medicine cabinet. Jenness pulled the door all the way open and I saw a white staircase spiraling downward.

"Where does it lead?" I asked.

"The kitchen."

"Any other stops?"

"No."

"Does anyone know about this?"

"Everyone who's ever worked here."

"The family?"

"Sure. It's not a secret. I mean it looks like one—a secret

passageway. We don't tell the guests about it, but we use it to get up and down without going through the lobby."

"Are there any security cameras?"

"Not on the staircase. Just the lobby, the restaurant, and the parking lot; that's all."

We closed the doorway.

"When did your grandmother go to bed?" I asked.

"Ten o'clock. Sharp. Tess liked schedules. Everyone here worked to a tight schedule. Including me. The restaurant closes at nine; the bar would stay open as long as there was anyone to serve but that's rarely past nine thirty, ten. Tess would supervise cleanup and then she would go to bed."

"You said her door was locked. Did she always lock her door?"

"I have no idea. It never occurred to me to ask."

"Do you lock your door?"

"Yes."

"When did you go to bed?"

"Not long afterward. Usually, I try to catch the news and Stephen Colbert before going to sleep. Not quite the same lifestyle as when I worked at Rickie's and we used to have a quick bump before going home at around two."

"You have a TV?"

"I have a computer." Jenness smiled at Nina. "Tess didn't like TVs. Well, that's not necessarily true. It was just that she was very keen that the castle always maintained a nineteenth-century vibe. We use computers in the office, the restaurant and reservation desk, of course, but they're deliberately tucked away so that guests aren't able to see them. Tess was fine with providing Wi-Fi for the same reason—it can't be seen. As for the electronics that guests brought into the castle, whatever they use in the privacy of their rooms was their own business, was how Tess looked at it.

"First thing I did was upgrade the system. During the pandemic, people weren't traveling as much as they used to but when they did, they tended to opt for longer stays; tended to work from their rooms. It was as if they just had to get out of their own houses; one of the reasons we've been nearly full every day starting last February even before they began widespread vaccinations. Fast Wi-Fi and practical workstations—even now that's a deciding factor on where many travelers stay, especially those hoping to blend a little work with a little play."

"I knew you were smart when I hired you all those years ago," Nina said.

Jenness knocked once again. Instead of waiting, though, she pulled a ring of keys from her pocket and unlocked the door.

"Olivia?" she said. "Ben?"

There was no answer. Jenness stepped inside, holding the door for Nina and me.

"They said something about going into town together this morning," Jenness told us. "I just wanted to make sure."

"Do they live in town?" I asked.

"No. They live in Edina."

Edina being one of the ritzier suburbs of Minneapolis, my inner voice reminded me.

"Mom and Dad live in Redding and so does Carly," Jenness said. "Uncle Alex and Eden live in Mankato; they both work for a nonprofit dealing with social justice issues. They'll be here later today. I put them in the cabin next to yours. Anna teaches at Southwest Minnesota State University in Marshall; only forty minutes away yet she visits us least of all. The castle is all booked up so she'll be staying with me when she arrives Thursday, which is fine. Gives me a chance to work on her."

We stepped deeper into the room. The first thing I noticed was the ornate brick fireplace surrounded by dark carved wood. There was an antique clock on the mantel above it and a painting of several women laboring in a field that reminded me of Monet hanging above that. Open doors on each side of the fireplace revealed a bathroom and a walk-in closet.

The first thing Jenness noticed, however, was the king-size bed with carved mahogany posts and a canopy against the wall opposite the fireplace. She stared at it for several beats.

"Everything was moved out of here after Tess died; almost immediately after she died." Her voice was just above a whisper. "All of her personal possessions; clothes, photographs, her toothbrush. Why do people do that? My mother; Aunt Anna came up from Marshall to help, too. Do they think we'll process our grief quicker if there's nothing to remind us that someone we loved actually lived here? Laundry in a hamper, books on the nightstand, a half-empty bottle of shampoo? The Minnesota United Football Club scarf she used to wear even when it was eighty degrees outside? Jesus."

Nina slipped her arm around the younger woman's shoulder and gave her a hug.

"I'm all right," Jenness said. "No, actually I'm not. I'm all cried out, though. Listen, I have things to do. Like I said before, we're understaffed, so I've been helping with the housekeeping. If you don't need me . . ."

"Can I help?" Nina asked.

"Stripping beds and wiping down bathrooms is a little below your pay grade."

"I'd like to help."

"Nina . . ."

"Please."

Jenness stared at her former employer and for a moment I thought that she was mistaken; that she wasn't all cried out.

"Take orders from me?" she said.

"Oh, like I haven't done that before," Nina said.

"Thank you."

They held hands the way even the closest hetero male friends never do.

"Do you need anything, McKenzie?" Jenness asked.

"I'm good."

"Well, come on then." Jenness pulled Nina through the doorway. "Toilets don't scrub themselves."

I closed the heavy door after them and locked it with the dead bolt and unlocked it and locked it again, as if repeating the process would tell me something. It did. It told me that the damned thing was nearly impregnable.

Whoever killed Tess, if she was killed, could not have entered through the door, my inner voice told me.

"Who would've thought it?" I said aloud. "An honest-to-God locked-room mystery."

I turned my back to the door and leaned against it, my arms folded across my chest. Inserted into the wall directly across from me, about midway between the fireplace and the bed, was a large window. Beyond the window was the balcony Jenness had pointed out the evening before.

"Or maybe not," I said.

I didn't know whether it was a recent building code thing or not, but these days to gain access to a balcony, like the one Nina and I had in our condominium, you needed to open a hinged or sliding glass door and step out. Back in the day, however, access was often through a large single-hung window. You would push up the bottom sash and climb out. That's the way we crawled onto a balcony at the Hotel Provincial in New Orleans and at a B and B in Vieux Quebec, the historic neighborhood of Quebec City. And that's how I slipped onto the balcony of Redding Castle.

Looking up, I had a nice view of the tops of many trees. Looking down I could see the wide L-shaped dock that jutted into Lake Anpetuwi and the canoes and kayaks that were tethered to it. And the concrete steps that led down the steep hill from the castle's patio to the lake. And a wooden fence that ran along the top of the hill for the length of the property to keep careless visitors from tumbling down the bank. I didn't pay much attention to any of that, however. I was more interested in the drop from the balcony to the ground. About fifteen feet, I decided.

I streamed a scenario in my head: The killer hid in Tess's room. He killed the woman, waited until the castle quieted down, crawled onto the balcony being careful to close the window behind him, jumped, and ran off. I had made a similar leap myself three years ago to escape a bomb. 'Course, I had badly sprained an ankle, shattered my collarbone, and suffered a concussion, but I had landed on a motel's asphalt parking lot with plenty of force. There was grass beneath the balcony.

Really, McKenzie? my inner voice asked.

"It's possible," I said aloud.

What else is possible?

I climbed back inside the room.

It was absurdly neat and I wondered if that was the result of Jenness Crawford's housekeeping staff or just the way Big Ben and Olivia Redding lived. I checked the walk-in closet. Hangers and the drawers of an ancient bureau revealed about as many clothes as you might expect a married couple to pack for a five-day trip.

I examined the ceiling and the walls, rapping on them with my knuckles. Afterward, I dropped to my knees and inspected the hardwood floorboards. I did the same thing in the bathroom, running my fingers over the slate tiles. Following that, I closely examined the fireplace and the walls of the main room. I even moved two stuffed chairs that had been arrayed in front of the fireplace so I could look beneath the round rug they were resting on.

I was searching for another secret passageway and, yeah, I know that sounds silly, like something out of one of the lesser Agatha Christie novels. Except Nina and I had stayed at a 160-year-old B and B in Lanesboro, Minnesota, that actually did have a secret passageway leading from an upstairs broom closet to the downstairs dining room, although it wasn't much of a secret considering how happy the owner was to show it to us.

I found what I had expected to find—nothing.

What else is possible? my inner voice asked again.

I carefully scrutinized the window that led to the balcony. It did not have a lock.

I slipped back onto the balcony and leaned against the railing. I looked straight down and quickly backed off because of a familiar feeling of panic that the sight had generated in my stomach. See, I've had this thing about heights since I was a kid and jumping from high places hadn't helped any. I didn't even like to climb stepladders, I reminded myself.

To which my inner voice replied, *You big dummy.*

I found Mr. Doty inside the barn, its large doors open to the sun. There were no animals inside, unless you counted the twenty-two-horsepower riding lawn mower he was tinkering with.

"Help ya?" he asked.

I placed Mr. Doty in his early seventies. He was tall and thin with gray hair that he combed over the bald spot on top of his head; his face was deeply lined by sun and age and reminded me of a hard maple coffee table that I owned. He frowned when he saw me approaching.

"My name's McKenzie," I said.

"Uh-huh. Miss said you might have some questions."

"You call Jenness Crawford 'Miss'?"

"The old woman was Ma'am; she's Miss. Whaddya need?"

"The night Tess Redding was killed . . ."

"Don't know she was killed," Mr. Doty said. "Don't know that. Miss has her ideas but the police think she's in the wrong, what I heard. Guessin' you're here to prove different?"

"Let's just say that Miss Crawford asked for a second opinion. The night Tess died . . ."

Mr. Doty pointed at the wall of the barn. Beyond the wall was a cabin at least twice the size of the one where Nina and I were staying.

"Me and the missus were sleeping," he said.

"The next morning . . ."

"The missus does cooking in the morning, mostly breakfasts for guests. And she does housekeeping, too. Been at it near fifty years. Been at it since before I was hired to take care of things. Was how we met, me and her, when I came to work at the castle. Was makin' a livin' doin' odd jobs for people hereabouts 'fore I got hired to do odd jobs here permanent. Couple weeks later, she gave me a jar of honey with the castle name on it. 'Don't say I never gave you nothing,' she said. We've been together ever since."

A little off topic, my inner voice told me. Yet I was experienced enough not to interrupt. One of the first things you learn about conducting interviews, once you get the subject talking it's a good idea to just let them talk until they say something interesting.

"Anyway," Doty said, "what happened, the missus was waiting for Ma'am; waitin' to serve her breakfast, only Ma'am doesn't show. That's not like her, Ma'am I mean. So the missus goes up to her room thinkin' something must be wrong and something was wrong, so she calls Miss and Miss sends the missus to fetch me. Miss was, oh she was pretty upset. Wanted to get inside that room awfully bad. Give me time, I coulda knocked the door down, no problem, but why you want to do that is what I told Miss. Get the ladder and climb up is what I told her. So, that's what we did. Came back to the barn, found a ladder, and dragged it around."

"Where was the ladder?" I asked.

Mr. Doty's expression suggested that the answer wasn't as simple as it should have been.

"Over here," he said.

Mr. Doty approached the entrance to the barn and hung a left. I followed him. He led me to the back of the barn. Hanging horizontally on storage hooks were three extension ladders. One was made of wood and looked as old as the castle. The other two were lightweight aluminum. The one in the middle extended twenty-two feet. I lifted it off its hook. I guessed it weighed about forty pounds.

"Not that one," Mr. Doty said.

"No?" I set it back on its hooks. The second aluminum ladder looked too small to reach the balcony, only about twelve feet. "Not this one?"

"The wood."

The wooden ladder looked as if it extended over thirty feet, still . . .

"Seems awfully heavy," I said.

"Over eighty pounds. What I meant by having to drag it. Leaning it up against the wall was a bitch."

I gestured back at the middle ladder.

"Why not use this one?" I asked.

"Wasn't there when I come for it."

"Where was it?"

"Halfway down the bank between the castle and the lake."

That caused me to pause for a beat or two.

(37)

"Did you leave it there and forget?" I asked.

"Mister, I take care of my tools. The ladder should have been here. Don't know why it wasn't."

"Did someone else on the staff borrow it?"

"No one says they did. Besides, anything needs fixin' 'round here, I'm the one who fixes it."

I lifted the aluminum ladder off its hooks and braced it against my shoulder.

"Show me where you found it," I said.

Mr. Doty didn't say a word. He turned and started back around the barn and I followed. The way the weight was distributed, carrying the ladder wasn't arduous in the slightest. We crossed the parking lot and followed the cobblestone path toward the castle before veering off. As we circled the castle Mr. Doty glanced over his shoulder at me.

"You 'kay?" he asked.

"Fine," I said.

"Word is they're thinking of tearing down the castle and building condominiums or some damn thing. Know anything 'bout that?"

I couldn't think of a good reason to lie, so I told him the truth.

"Right now it's just talk," I said. "It's the reason why the family is gathering, so they can talk."

Mr. Doty nodded his head as if he knew it all along.

"Hope that's all it is," he said. "Talk. Me and the missus hate to move, been here so long."

"I know that Jenness is lobbying hard to keep it from happening."

"Miss reminds me of Ma'am. Good people."

We soon reached the corner of the castle where Tess Redding's room was located except Mr. Doty kept walking until we reached the fence at the top of the bank. The fence was a little lower than chest high and consisted of three thick ten-foot rails

stretched between two four-foot-high posts, the sections running the length of the cleared property on both sides of the castle
to the trees. From a distance, it looked like one of those rustic
split-rail fences that you'd see cowboys leaning against while they
examine livestock and horses on a ranch. Up close, though, you
could see the careful prefabricated cuts and drill holes and the
bolts and nuts that held it all together. Beyond the fence, the bank
dropped at about a forty-five-degree angle for a good fifty yards
to Lake Anpetuwi. The bank was dotted with aspen, birch, pine,
and spruce trees and a lot of shrubs that I couldn't identify.

"Down there," Mr. Doty said. "About twenty, thirty feet. Reason I didn't see the ladder right off is that the Anpetuwi Lake
Association has this thing about clearing land along the lake-
shore. Don't want no lawns, don't want fertilizer running off
and polluting the lake. Don't want no erosion, neither. Ma'am
was okay with all that except, you look around the lake you see
people ignoring the rules all the time."

I turned my head to glance up at Tess's balcony.

"Let me try something," I said.

I carried the ladder to the castle, raised it so that it was verti-
cal, extended it, and rested it against the base of Tess's balcony.
I climbed the ladder without once looking down, scrambled over
the railing onto the balcony, stepped to the window, and raised
the sash. I crawled into Tess's room, counted to five, crawled out,
and lowered the window. I tried hard not to make any noise and
mostly I succeeded.

I climbed down the ladder, again without looking down,
pulled it away from the balcony, and collapsed it to its normal
length. I carried it to where Mr. Doty was standing at the top of
the bank, raised it above my head, and threw it over the fence
toward the lake. The ladder bounced on the ground, slid a few
feet, and came to a rest against a spruce tree about ten yards
away.

"Hey, man," Mr. Doty said.

I turned and glanced back at the balcony.

"Did you tell the cops about this?" I asked. "About finding the ladder?"

"No."

"Why not?"

"I didn't find it until way after they were gone. Besides . . ."

"Besides what?"

"They never asked."

THREE

Despite its modest population, the City of Redding was a big town in that it sprawled over sixteen-point-seven square miles that somehow included Lake Anpetuwi and the Redding Castle. I had to drive for nearly fifteen minutes, half of it along the meandering county road leading through the forest and the rest at fifty-five miles per hour on the highway, before I saw a sign that read WELCOME TO REDDING, GATEWAY TO THE WEST. I didn't know about that, but certainly the terrain had changed dramatically during the short trip. Gone was the lush forest, replaced by flat fields of corn, soybeans, sugar beets, and wheat stretching toward a hard blue horizon, the view interrupted only by the occasional farmhouse and a cluster of grain elevators rising up like the pillars of ancient Greek temples.

The county highway twisted and dipped and suddenly there was a river and a bridge and on the far side of the bridge there was a town that appeared like the setting for one of those Hallmark Channel TV movies where beautiful thirtysomething women and handsome fortysomething men fall in love without ever touching each other and nothing bad happens that can't be fixed with a smile and a heart-to-heart chat. Certainly the large number of people that I saw as I cruised down Main Street didn't seem overly concerned by anything in particular. Most walked in and out of any number of shops, cafes, and coffee-houses as if they had never heard of COVID-19 and its variants; nothing was closed, no one seemed to be social distancing, and only a precious handful wore masks.

The voice of my GPS system told me that my destination was on the right. If it hadn't I might have driven past the building that housed the Redding city offices without noticing it was there. The building was located near the center of town. It was two stories high and narrow and constructed of red brick that seemed as old as Redding Castle.

I parked the Mustang, stepped inside, and was greeted by a sign with two arrows. One arrow pointed left to Administration, City Clerk, Engineering Department, Finance Department, Human Resources, and Planning and Development. The other pointed right toward Mayor's Office, City Council, Parks and Recreation Department, Fire Department, and Police Department. That's when I realized that it wasn't just one structure. The city had repurposed several ancient downtown buildings to accommodate its offices, punching through their walls to create doorways. Such a vast improvement, I thought, over housing them all in one of those flat, pale brick, multipurpose monstrosities that most towns large and small seemed to favor.

I moved along quiet corridors, stepping from one building into the next until I reached the Redding Police Department. As I neared it, I found a wall with the names, ranks, and photographs of nineteen officers mounted on it. At the top was a face and name that I recognized.

"Are you kidding me?" I asked aloud.

A few moments later I was standing on one side of a bullet-proof partition and speaking to a young woman who was sitting at a desk on the other side and wearing a powder-blue mask.

"I would like to speak to the chief if she's in," I said.

"Do you have an appointment?"

"No, but I'm sure she'll be happy to see me. Just tell her it's McKenzie."

The woman left her desk, walked a few steps down a corridor, and entered an office. I couldn't see inside the office from where I was waiting but I could hear a voice shouting, "Are you kidding me?"

A moment later an African-American woman appeared in the doorway. She was wearing a dark blue uniform with an American flag and name tag over her right pocket and a gold badge pinned above her left. A tie that exactly matched her uniform was neatly knotted around her neck. The uniform matched her mask.

She looked at me.

I looked at her.

She started laughing.

She laughed as if I was the funniest thing she had seen in years.

"C'mon, now," I said.

"Let him in, let him in," she told her admin.

The admin pointed at her face. I pulled my mask from my pocket and put it on while she pressed a button that unlocked a secure door.

"Not my idea," she said when I stepped inside. "It's the government's."

A moment later, I was standing inside the office of City of Redding Police Chief Deidre Gardner.

"Hi, Dee," I said.

"McKenzie, what the hell are you doing here?"

"Me? What the hell are you doing here?"

Chief Gardner gestured at a chair in front of her desk.

"Sit, sit," she said.

I did. She sat in the chair behind her desk.

"I heard that you had been shot," Chief Gardner said. "LT said it was because you were kibitzing again."

"I got better."

"Glad to hear it, but is that why you're in Redding? You're kibitzing?"

"Answer my question, first. Why are you in Redding? The last time I saw you, what was it? A year ago? You were working a double homicide in North Minneapolis."

"A lot has changed since then."

"Tell me about it."

"It's a long story," Chief Gardner said. "I don't even know where to begin. George Floyd, I suppose."

"Yeah, that changed a lot of things."

"Another Black man killed by the white police, this time on film, nine minutes of film of a uniform kneeling on the man's neck; Floyd begging for his life, begging for his mother, screaming 'I can't breathe, I can't breathe.' On film. The protests that followed, the riots. They burned down the Third Precinct; the city just stood by and let them do it. Then people, the mayor, the city council started talking about defunding the police, abolishing the police. I didn't blame them. The MPD has always had a troubled relationship with the community, the Black community. Excessive force complaints every single day. Abuse. No one paying attention until Floyd; one of the reasons the city was forced to pay Floyd's family twenty-seven million bucks.

"You know, I went out on the street with the protesters. We're not supposed to do that. I wore a mask, not just because of COVID, but because I didn't want anyone to recognize me, other cops. I listened to what the protesters had to say. It was so demoralizing what they thought of us. The entire department was demoralized. Over one hundred cops left the force, some taking early retirement, some just walking away. Another one hundred and fifty took leaves of absence citing post-traumatic stress; a lot of them being crybabies. 'You're picking on me so I'm going home.' Others because they found it impossible to do their jobs knowing they wouldn't be supported if something bad happened, feeling the city had turned its back on them. That's nearly a quarter of the entire force, McKenzie. Meanwhile, people asking me, my people, Black people, getting into my face and asking—'Are you on their side or are you on our side?' Cops, also my people, asking the same question just as loudly, just as angrily—'Are you one of us or one of them?' My boss—LT." Chief Gardner snickered. "Lieutenant Clayton Rask. Commands the homicide unit in Minneapolis. You know that."

"Yeah."

"He kept saying 'Just work the job, just work the job' like if we ignored what was going on around us all of our problems would magically disappear. Like COVID. A couple of months later, while I was at my lowest, I saw a bulletin that said the City of Redding was searching for a new police chief. They wanted someone with the kind of experience that you can't get working along the South Dakota border and I thought if I could just get out of Minneapolis . . . McKenzie, all I wanted, all I ever wanted, was to be a cop."

"What did you do?"

"I applied; whaddya think? Not everyone gets lucky like you. I mean I'd be happy to track down a high-end embezzler in my free time, hand in my badge, and then sell him and his ill-gotten gains to an insurance company for fifty cents on the dollar. How much did you make doing that?"

"About two million after taxes."

"What are you worth now?"

"Five million give or take."

"The rich get richer."

"That's what my financial adviser keeps telling me."

"I applied for the job," Chief Gardner said. "That was on a Wednesday. By the weekend, I had changed my mind. I decided I was going to stay in Minneapolis. If I wanted things to be different, then I had to help make them different. Call it my MLK moment. But then the mayor called on Monday morning and asked me to come down here for an interview. Said they'd put me up overnight at the Redding Castle. Have you seen the castle?"

"I have."

"You're staying there, aren't you? You're here because of the old woman, aren't you?"

"Finish your story," I said.

"I thought, fine, I'll come down here. They were willing to talk to a woman about taking the top job; that told me something about the town. 'Course, I expected them to take one look at my Black face and nod and cajole and then send me on my way. It's happened before, people thinking I was a white girl. Does Deidre Gardner sound Black to you? Turned out, though, they knew exactly who I was. They had spoken to people. LT. Sonuvabitch never said a word to me about it. They offered me the job the next day. They called me on my cell early in the morning. I hadn't even left the castle yet to drive back to the Cities."

"You must have really impressed them."

"Yeah, but it turned out that the mayor and the city council also wanted to make a statement."

"That they were woke?"

"In a manner of speaking," Chief Gardner said. "A religious order had moved to town that calls itself the Sons of Europa; that worships Odin—"

"Odin? The Norse god Odin? Father to Thor, that Odin?"

"It wanted to build what it called a pre-Christian church in Redding, an assembly hall that'll attract like-minded Germans, Danes, Swedes, Norwegians, Finns—who else?—from Minnesota, the Dakotas, Iowa, Nebraska. They're going to call the church Tyr Haus. Tyr is the Norse god of war."

"Seriously?" I said.

"Unfortunately, they're not your run-of-the-mill pagans, either. The Sons of Europa proudly labels itself as a white man's religion that calls for the preservation of white families; that calls for north European descendants to preserve their ethnicity and combat white genocide with—and I'm quoting now—with 'cunning and physical skill.' The Southern Poverty Law Center has declared it to be a white supremacist hate group.

"When the natives heard they were coming—you need to remember, this was happening while people in Redding were watching the protests and riots in downtown Minneapolis on their TVs. Maybe the Sons thought that it would be a good time to move to rural Minnesota; that white people out here would embrace them and I suppose some did. But the majority—almost immediately a group formed calling itself Redding Against Hate—"

"RAH?"

Chief Gardner chuckled.

"RAH, yeah," she said. "That also told me something about the town. Anyway, the group was formed because, as people said, they didn't want Redding to become the center of hate in western Minnesota. People literally marched on city hall to make sure the Sons didn't get the permits they needed to rezone the property they had purchased from residential use to allow for assembly. Only the Sons haven't given up. They claimed the grand opening of Tyr Haus hasn't been canceled, it's merely been delayed. They're still handing out flyers. They're still recruiting followers. Meanwhile, the city council hired me."

"A Black female homicide detective from Minneapolis—yeah, that makes a statement."

"Sometimes I become so depressed by what I see happening in my country," Chief Gardner said. "And sometimes I don't. Which brings us back to you. Why are you here, McKenzie?"

"You were right before. I'm here because of Tess Redding."

"The woman woke up dead."

"Her granddaughter disagrees. She might have a point."

"That's crazy, bro."

I carefully recited everything I knew, starting with Jenness Crawford's suspicions concerning her own family and ending with my theory concerning Tess Redding's balcony and the ladder found halfway down the bank between the castle and the lake.

"Who are you?" Chief Gardner asked. "Jessica Fletcher?"

"A grievously underrated detective."

"I used to watch *Murder, She Wrote* when I was a kid. I knew even then that the show never came close to reality. For one thing, there wasn't anyone on it who looked like me. Only white people killed anyone on TV in those days, you know what I'm saying? I would have paid money, real money, if instead of confessing when Jessica explained in painstaking detail how the crime was committed, the suspect would have crossed his arms, looked her in the eye and said, 'Prove it, bitch. Prove it in court.'"

"Hey now, don't be calling Angela Lansbury names. The woman is a national treasure."

"She's from England."

"Okay, now you're just being mean."

"McKenzie . . ."

"Dee . . ."

"What do you want from me?"

"I want to read the incident report and the supplementals if there are any."

"No."

"Dee, if the case is closed, the records should be available to the public, am I right?"

Chief Gardner rolled her eyes and stared at her ceiling for a moment. I had the feeling she was no longer as glad to see me as she had been.

"Fine," she said.

The chief worked her computer, alternating between the keyboard and her mouse. Finally, she sat back.

"Here," she said.

I circled her desk and read what was on the screen over her shoulder. It didn't take long.

"I've seen more information on an excessive barking complaint," I said.

"With a barking dog there's a crime and a suspect. In this case, we don't have either."

"Jenness Crawford says—"

"I don't care what Jenness Crawford says. I tried to explain it to her as best I could; she just refuses to believe it. What am I supposed to do, McKenzie? Launch a homicide investigation because she doesn't like her family? The door was securely bolted; there was no forced entry . . ."

"The balcony—"

"Oh, puh-leez, Jessica. In any case, there was nothing unnatural about the way Mrs. Redding died. There was no sign of a struggle. There was no sign of violence inflicted upon her body. We should all die so peacefully."

"How 'bout an autopsy report?"

"McKenzie . . . all right, I'll play. But know I'm only doing this because you walked some of the same streets I did. C'mon."

Chief Gardner led me out of her office, telling her admin "I'll be back" as if there was a chance she might not be. A few moments later, we were on the sidewalk and heading north on Main Street. Chief Gardner removed her mask, so I removed mine.

"There's always talk about a resurgence, about the Delta variant and other variants that might follow, about remaining vigilant," the chief said. "Yet only a very few businesses in Redding still insist staff and customers wear masks and the county commissioners are dead set against mask mandates except in government buildings, not that everyone followed them in the first place. The divide was pretty much along party lines out here. If you were a liberal Democrat you wore a mask; if you were a conservative Republican you didn't. Most businesses, including the bars and restaurants, tried to follow the rules, partly because not infecting customers was good for their profit margins and partly because they could have been shut down and fined as much as twenty-five grand if they didn't. Even so, it seemed like a lot of people were looking to pick a fight over the mandates, you were either a sheep or a lemming, and the owners didn't want to put that on their employees. I didn't want to put that on my people, either, so we took a hands-off approach. We encouraged masks and social distancing, but we didn't demand. We warned people that they could be cited and fined a hundred bucks only we didn't write anyone up. That's the way the mayor and the city council wanted it and at the time I hadn't built up enough equity with them or the citizens to argue about it."

"You were trying to keep the peace," I said.

I didn't mean to be funny, yet Chief Gardner laughed just the same.

"I've been a cop for twenty years and no one has ever asked me to do that before," she said. "Mostly I just arrested people. But yeah, I tried to keep the peace. Turned out the county got away with it, too; the lack of enforcement. I mean if you think fifty-five hundred documented cases and seventy deaths is getting away with something."

"Seventy so far."

"Don't be unpleasant, McKenzie. Half the county still refuses to get vaccinated mostly because masks and social distancing and vaccines are intruding on the personal freedoms of hardworking 'Mericans; that they're interfering with their God-given right to be morons. Now we have the health people warning us about the upcoming flu season and what that might mean and people pushing back claiming it's all a government conspiracy. Welcome to the new normal."

"Do you like living in Redding, Dee?" I asked.

"I do. I wasn't sure I would. I'm a city girl, you know? I like clubs, I like music, I like to dance; I like to sit in the stands and root for my Lynx to win another WNBA title. I like to have my choice of restaurants serving every kind of food in the world. I like to stay up past ten o'clock. I even like the noise. People around here talk about how quiet it is like it's a wonderful thing. Silence makes me nervous. At least it did. I'm starting to get used to it. On the other hand—here, let me show you something."

Gardner didn't wait for a response. Instead, she took my hand and pulled me into the street. The traffic immediately stopped. Not only that, no one leaned on their horn or shook their fist or called us dirty names. One driver actually smiled and waved as we crossed over.

Gardner was laughing when we reached the other side.

"Imagine," she said. "Imagine growing up in a town where you don't have to look both ways before crossing the street."

I couldn't, but I wasn't trying very hard. That's because I was distracted by two women sitting close to each other, their heads nearly touching, as they spoke softly at a small table on the sidewalk just outside a coffee joint called Java House, a couple of paper cups with lids set between them. One was Olivia Redding, dressed in tight blue jeans, tight T-shirt, black knee-high boots, and an unbuttoned cable-knit sweater; her hair pulled into a ponytail. The other was at least two decades younger and dressed for work in an office. Olivia glanced at me as Gardner and I strolled by. Her body jerked upright as if she had been caught doing something illegal. I kept walking; pretending that I hadn't seen her.

My inner voice started reciting questions—*who was Olivia speaking to? Why did it trouble her to be seen with the woman she was speaking to? Where was Big Ben?* I ignored them all for the moment.

"What about being African-American in Redding?" I asked aloud.

"What about it?"

"It must be hard."

"No harder than being a sister in Minneapolis, in the Cities," the chief said. "People are probably just as racist out here, but they tend to keep it to themselves. Minnesota Nice. Besides, it's not like I'm alone. Redding has a population of just over eleven thousand. Six percent are African-American, five and a half percent Hispanic, five percent Asian—the numbers not hugely different from the rest of the state."

"Who knew Redding was so cosmopolitan?"

"Let's not get crazy. It has one—count 'em—one Asian restaurant, a Thai joint. So, are you going to tell me?"

"Tell you what?"

"Who the woman was that freaked when she saw you walking by."

"What makes you think it wasn't you dressed in your nice neat uniform that made her anxious?"

"Don't play with me, McKenzie."

I explained.

"So she's one of your suspects, huh?" Chief Gardner said. "A sixty-year-old woman dressing like she's twenty—sure looks dangerous to me."

"Where are we going, anyway?" I asked.

"We're here."

Unlike the rest of the town, Redding Memorial Hospital looked as if it had been built yesterday. It featured plenty of tan and beige brick, thick glass windows, thick glass doors, and pillars. Except for the fountain that the driveway circled, it looked as if it could stand up against a tornado.

The hospital was located at the intersection of Main Street and First Avenue and I told Chief Gardner, "Only small towns have intersections named First Avenue and Main Street. St. Paul doesn't. Neither does Minneapolis."

The chief gave me what I call the ignorance-apathy shrug, the one that said that she didn't know and she didn't care.

She led me to the front entrance to the hospital, through the lobby, and down a carpeted corridor to an office suite with a sign that read REDDING COUNTY MEDICAL EXAMINER AND CORONER. We were wearing our masks because several signs we passed said that we would be removed from the premises if we didn't.

The waiting room looked as if it had been furnished by the same guys who did the AmericInn hotels. Chief Gardner went up to the reception desk. A woman was bent over the bottom drawer of a file cabinet on the other side of it, showing us her behind.

"Boss in?" Chief Gardner asked.

The woman glanced our way without straightening up.

"Afternoon, Chief," she said. "Door's unlocked."

Chief Gardner rapped her knuckles on the receptionist's desk like she was sending a signal and moved to the door and pulled it open. She hung a right and marched down a short carpeted corridor to an office, its door also open. I followed behind.

"Hey, girl," the chief said.

A woman with long, straight hair that matched both the white linen lab coat and white mask that she wore was sitting behind a desk and reading a file. Her head came up. She was wearing reading glasses that she deftly removed and quickly set aside.

"Dee," she said. "What's up, babe? And who's this young man standing behind you?"

"Dr. Angelique Evers, this is Rushmore McKenzie. Don't ask him how he got his first name, he'll only tell you a long story that really isn't very funny. He has questions for you in your capacity as the Redding County medical examiner and not as the world's foremost authority on Elvis Presley and single malt scotch."

"Whaddya want to know, hon?"

"I want to know what killed Tess Redding," I said.

Dr. Evers glanced at the chief and made a gesture that asked, "Who is this guy?"

"Humor him," Chief Gardner said.

"What killed Tess Redding?" Dr. Evers repeated. "According to the death certificate, it was natural causes."

"Who made out her death certificate?"

"I did."

"What were those natural causes?" I asked.

"Could've been arrhythmias, stroke, undiagnosed congestive heart failure, respiratory arrest, various sleep disorders—shall I go on?"

"I was looking for something more specific."

"How 'bout old age?"

"Dr. Evers, did you perform—"

"I'm going to insist that you call me Angie because I don't believe you're nearly as rude as you sound or Dee here wouldn't be rolling her eyes the way she is."

I glanced at Chief Gardner, who was indeed rolling her eyes.

"My friends call me McKenzie," I said.

"Not Rushmore? Now I really do want to hear the story behind your first name."

"Angie, did you perform an autopsy on Tess Redding?"

"No, only an external examination."

"Why didn't you perform an autopsy?"

Dr. Evers glanced at Chief Gardner again before answering.

"Why would I?" she asked. "Listen, hon, in cases like this there usually isn't an autopsy. That's reserved for homicides, suspicious deaths, and unusual deaths of people who had no other health problems."

"Did Tess have health problems?" I asked.

"Not that we're aware of, but you need to remember—the woman was eighty-seven years old. A death like hers is usually due to cardiac arrhythmia, basically, an irregular heartbeat. Sometimes you can die in your sleep because of a massive stroke or a ruptured aneurysm. In those cases, the deceased usually will have complained earlier about symptoms like a headache or other pain. Tess didn't, at least that's what her granddaughter and her staff told me. 'Course, they also told me that she was one tough old bird; not prone to whining.

"In any case, when we found Tess she was curled up in a sleeping position, the blankets tucked neatly around her, no evidence of thrashing about. Her face was serene; her eyes were closed. By contrast, when death comes while not sleeping, there's a fifty–fifty chance the eyes will be open."

"What you're telling me—"

"What I'm telling you, hon, is that when a patient dies without any symptoms, absolutely and without question the most common reason will be cardiac arrhythmia, specifically ventricular fibrillation or pulseless ventricular tachycardia. Trust me, McKenzie; if you have to die, that's a great way to go."

"What about poison?"

Again Dr. Evers glanced at Chief Gardner, who was again rolling her eyes.

"Yeah, I don't believe it, either," she said.

"Did you perform a tox scan?" I asked.

"Why would I do that?" Dr. Evers said. "McKenzie, on average medical examiners perform autopsies in about a third of the cases that come to us. We run tests to determine the presence of toxins in even less than that. I mean, you'd have to give me a pretty good reason."

"Tess Redding's granddaughter believes that she was murdered."

"Since when?"

"What?"

"This is the first I've heard about it. She certainly didn't say anything like that to me when I was examining Redding or during the few days after we took possession of her remains."

"She didn't?" I asked.

"She asked me how her grandmother died, of course she did, and I told her. At the time she seemed comforted by what I told her. Now she's calling it murder? Honey . . ."

"First I heard about it was what?" Chief Gardner asked. "Three weeks after Tess's death? They were in the process of settling the old woman's estate. And Jenness Crawford gave me nothing to support her allegations except her unhappiness with her family."

"Is it possible to—" I began.

"Exhume the body?" Dr. Evers finished. "Dear heart, no. We don't do that here. It doesn't matter, anyway. Tess Redding's remains were cremated three days after she passed."

"On whose authority?"

"Her eldest son, Benjamin, who was also the executor of her estate. The family declined to hold a public funeral with half the town in attendance; there was still some lingering fear of COVID and large gatherings. Plus, I think they actually wanted to hold a small, private memorial service and the virus gave them an excuse. I was told that they scattered the old woman's ashes over Lake Anpetuwi."

I turned to look at Chief Gardner. She was leaning against the wall. She folded her arms across her chest, looked me in the eye, and grinned.

"Anything else you want to know, Jessica?" she asked.

A few minutes later, the chief and I were back on Main Street and walking toward the city's offices.

"Well, that wasn't as enlightening as I had hoped it would be," I said.

"What are you going to do, McKenzie? You can't go back to Redding Castle and tell your poor grieving friend that her aunts and uncles and her parents didn't actually conspire to murder her grandmother, can you? The woman will be heartbroken."

"All right, all right."

"You could tell her Tess's death was all part of a giant conspiracy and that the county medical examiner is in on it."

"That would mean that you're in on it, too."

"The sinister Black woman who appeared out of nowhere to wreak havoc across rural America—you could sell that."

"To whom?"

Chief Gardner gestured at the scene on the corner in front of us.

"To these guys, for one," she said.

I watched as a maskless young man offered flyers to the people walking past him. Some refused the flyers, some took them and immediately threw them away; others stopped to read them carefully. An older woman nimbly circled the young man with a digital camera as he made his pitch.

"I look around Redding and I see so much anger and divisive-ness," he said. "It saddens me. People like us were once the lead-ers of the free world; we were the role models, what everyone else aspired to be. Now we're called racists and bigots and are told we should be ashamed of our glorious past. Yet there is a new sun on the horizon, a sun that will bring light to these dark times."

Chief Gardner and I reached the corner and stopped. The woman with the camera gave a wave. The young man pivoted toward the chief and spoke directly to her.

"The Sons of Europa have followers everywhere across this great land; followers with the noble cause of rebuilding the future . . ."

Rebuilding the future? my inner voice asked.

"Where the sons and daughters of Europa, with the blessings of our holy Gods, will resume the path walked by our ancestors and once again take their rightful place as the leaders of the brotherhood of man . . ."

Isn't that a song from a Broadway musical?

"The Sons of Europa will show the way."

The young man thrust a flyer at Chief Gardner.

She smiled and shook her head.

"Trust me, Brian," she said. "I've heard it all before."

The woman with the camera took their photograph.

"I expect you to pick up the flyers that are littering the side-walk," Chief Gardner said.

She moved past the young man and continued down the street. I walked with her. Behind us I could hear the woman call-ing "Thanks, Brian" and then "Chief, wait up."

She caught us about a quarter of the way down the block.

"That's going to be a great photograph," she said.

"I don't suppose I could convince you not to print it," the chief said.

"I don't think so."

"Thanks, Barbie."

"C'mon, Chief." The woman tucked her camera in a bag. "I'm just doing my job."

"I know. Barbara, McKenzie; McKenzie, Barbara. Barbara is the owner of the *Redding Weekly Bulletin*."

"Owner, publisher, editor, news reporter, and chief bottle washer," Barbara said. "And you are?"

"McKenzie is an unlicensed investigator from the Cities." When Chief Gardner stopped walking we did, too. "You two should get together. I'd bet you'd have a lot to talk about."

"Such as?"

"That's one of the things you need to discuss and don't let McKenzie stonewall you, Barb. Toodles."

"Toodles?" I asked. "Is that street?"

The chief resumed walking to her office, leaving me standing in the middle of the block with Barbara, who had rested her hand on my wrist like she was afraid I'd get away.

"Dee," I called.

"Give me a shout before you leave town," she said without breaking stride.

"Dee."

"Enjoy yourself, Jessica."

FOUR

"Who's Jessica?" the woman asked.

"Apparently, I am. Listen, Ms. . . ."

"Finne. Barbara Finne."

"Dee is just messing with us."

"You know her well enough to call her Dee?"

"We knew each other in the Cities."

"Are you a police officer, too?"

"A long time ago."

"But not anymore? Did you retire?"

"Yes."

"Why?"

"Financial reasons."

"Now you're an investigator?"

"In a manner of speaking."

"What are you investigating?"

I took a deep breath.

"You're pretty good at this," I said. "Asking questions."

"Comes from about forty years of experience."

"All of it in Redding?"

"I started as a kid reporter working for the *Minneapolis Tribune*. When the *Tribune* merged with the *Minneapolis Star* and started cutting bodies I moved on to *The Evening Tribune* in Albert Lea, a small town on the border with Iowa. After that, I became a reporter and editor with the *Herald* in Grand Forks, North Dakota. When that was sold to a media conglomerate, I took a buyout and bought the *Redding Weekly Bulletin*."

"I thought small-town newspapers were in trouble," I said.

"As long as there are readers interested in what's going on in their communities, I believe newspapers will be around. We publish once a week, on Wednesdays, with a circulation of over 3,600 plus another 1,800 online subscriptions."

"Still, advertising revenue must be down."

"Redding is more fortunate than most towns in that we not only have the hospital; we also have several small manufacturing companies and other small businesses that support the community. 'Course, when COVID first hit, most of our retail advertising was pulled, which really hurt our cash flow. Now that things are loosening up a bit, we're getting some of that money back. Legal and public notices have helped, too; legal ads that must be placed by local government according to the law.

"At the same time, COVID was one of the reasons we're doing okay. COVID here in Redding was a vastly different story than in the Cities, than it is in Florida or California or Texas or the rest of the country. Plus, there's been the emergence of the Sons of Europa. And the death of Tess Redding and rumors that they're going to turn the Redding Castle into a commercial development. And the high school—half of our news is comprised of school functions such as sports, band concerts, or academic activities. You can't get that from the *Star Tribune* or anywhere else."

"I would think that the dependence people place on social media to get their news is only going to get worse," I said.

"A lot of information is almost instantly shared on apps like Facebook and Twitter and that has taken the thunder and lightning away from newspapers. So much of it is incorrect, though, or at least suspect. Newspapers have a great deal more credibility. People trust them; it's where they go to learn the truth." Barbara paused to take a deep breath. "McKenzie, you're pretty good at this yourself, asking questions."

"My experience, people love to hear themselves talk."

"Don't they, though?"

"You mentioned that there are rumors that they're going to turn Redding Castle into some kind of development," I said.

"Condos with a restaurant and retail space."

"Huh."

"Don't give me that, McKenzie. Huh?"

"There are questions I'd like to ask you."

"What a coincidence. There are questions I would like to ask you."

"My problem is that I don't want to see any of it in the Wednesday edition of the *Redding Weekly Bulletin*."

"Why not?"

"I'm not a public figure. I'm here for personal reasons."

"We can talk off the record," Barbara said. "For now."

"It's the 'for now' part that makes me nervous."

"McKenzie, does this have anything to do with Jenness Crawford suspecting that her grandmother was murdered?"

"Where did you hear that?"

"I have my sources."

"I bet."

"You'll notice though, that I haven't printed a single word about it nor will I unless official action is taken."

"Define 'official action.'"

"The chief brings someone in for questioning; someone is arrested. Unless that happens, it just idle gossip."

I gave it a few beats of thought before responding.

"Off the record," I said.

"For now," Barbara replied.

"Let me buy you a cup of coffee," I said.

Late afternoon and business at the Java House had slacked off. Barbara Finne and I were the only customers inside; ordering our coffees from behind a Plexiglas partition. The woman taking our order wasn't wearing a mask, though, and I could see her face. It was something I had missed during the pandemic, faces. At the academy, I was well trained in reading both facial expressions and body language; a practical and essential skill for any law enforcement officer. Because of the masks, I felt I was at a disadvantage.

"How's business?" Barbara asked.

"Good," the woman replied. "Much better than the last time we talked. Beverage sales have always been solid, except only a few of my customers were drinking them inside so I lost out on pastry sales. Now people are hanging around more, both inside and at the half-dozen tables on the sidewalk. Tell your readers that my raspberry white chocolate scones are back."

"What about the high school kids?"

"They came back the day they reopened the school, giving me a nice after-school rush like before; the kids hanging out. They don't wear masks, of course, but they never did except when you made them. Kids, you know; they think they're invincible."

The woman served our drinks in paper cups. I also ordered a couple of raspberry white chocolate scones to go just because. We grabbed a table on the sidewalk. I slid a scone toward Barbara.

"Thank you," she said. "You're a nice man."

"Hardly."

"I saw the tip you left."

I didn't know what to say to that, so I took a bite of the scone and washed it down with my coffee.

"Tell me about the plans for turning Redding Castle into a development," I said.

"I haven't seen any actual plans, yet I know that the city, the bank, and a local architect and developer are very keen on them."

"Isn't that a little presumptuous? Tess Redding isn't even cold in her grave yet."

"Not really. The project has been on-again, off-again since before the pandemic when Tess announced that she was going to sell the castle. The castle has such an iconic presence in our collective psyche that it was front-page news and it soon became a running story. What did it mean? Would someone buy the castle and keep running it the way it is? Would it be torn down? Would lake homes be built on the property? A commercial development? I don't think we went more than a couple weeks at a time without printing something about it. The story got a big boost when Tess announced that she had changed her mind; that the castle was no longer for sale. And another boost after she died. Now there's talk that her heirs will sell anyway, and we're back to wondering what that means.

"You need to remember that anything having to do with the Reddings is big news here. After all, the town was named after them. The county, too. When Madison Zumwalt won the state women's cross-country skiing championship I put her on the front page for two consecutive weeks. The fact that she's the granddaughter of Tess and Joe and the great-great-great granddaughter of John—that usually comes up around the third graf. Tell you what, McKenzie. Give me your email address. I'll send some of the stories I wrote about it and you can see for yourself."

I gave her my address. While Barbara was jotting it down, I glanced across the street just in time to see Big Ben Redding stepping through the doors of a red-and-white building that was built to resemble an old-fashioned steamboat. He stood at the top of a small concrete staircase and looked right and then left as if he was searching for someone.

Olivia Redding? my inner voice asked.

Seeing nothing that interested him, Big Ben skipped down the stairs to the sidewalk, turned, and followed it to a second, narrower sidewalk that ran between the red-and-white building and the large brick structure next door. He followed it and quickly disappeared from my sight. He had moved very well for a big man; there was a spring in his step.

"Barbara?" I asked. "What's that building across the street?"

She glanced over her shoulder.

"The Riverboat Hotel."

"It's a hotel?"

"Yes, why?"

"It doesn't look like a hotel."

"It's not a Hilton, but it'll do. It was built about one hundred years ago."

"Does it have a restaurant?"

"No."

"Interesting," I said, but what I was thinking—If he didn't go there to eat, why is Big Ben spending time in a hotel in the middle of an afternoon in downtown Redding?

I'll give you three guesses, my inner voice said.

Where is his wife? I wondered.

I'll bet you a nickel she isn't in the hotel.

"Huh," I said aloud.

"Okay, what does 'huh' mean this time?" Barbara asked.

"These scones are really good."

I took another bite and smiled to prove it.

"You haven't answered my questions, yet," Barbara said.

"Shoot."

"Why are you here? What are you investigating?"

My first instinct was to lie. I decided against it.

"You were correct before—Jenness Crawford was concerned about the timing of her grandmother's death. She asked me to look into it."

"Tess had named Crawford executive director of the castle two, three months ago," Barbara said. "She said, 'The torch has been passed to a new generation.'"

"Did she?"

"That's a direct quote, by the way. It's in the paper."

"Yes, well, for the record, all the evidence I've seen so far seems to prove beyond a reasonable doubt that Tess Redding died peacefully in her sleep after a long and fruitful life, so . . ."

"That's it?"

"That's it," I said.

"Why don't I believe you?"

"Because you have a suspicious nature."

"How do you know Jenness Crawford?"

"We met through my wife. Jen used to work for her."

"Where?"

"Rickie's. It's a jazz club in St. Paul."

"On Cathedral Hill," Barbara said.

"You've been there."

"I will on rare occasions visit the big city."

"I don't think of St. Paul or Minneapolis as a big city."

"You don't live a stone's throw away from the South Dakota border, either, in a town whose entire population wouldn't fill the Xcel Energy Center."

"True."

"I need to get going." Barbara stood. "It never fails. I have an entire week to put it together yet I'm always scrambling at the last minute to get the paper printed and delivered to the post office."

"Post office?"

"We don't use carriers. Instead, the *Bulletin* is mailed to our subscribers. I'll send you those stories."

"I look forward to reading them."

"How long will you be in town?"

"I haven't decided yet."

"You realize I'm going to check you out, right? You know I'm going to put something in the paper, right?"

"Not about Tess."

"Not about Tess."

"I admire your professionalism."

"We'll see."

Barbara walked away. I watched her go. As soon as she was out of sight, I cleared the table and crossed the street. Once again the traffic stopped for me.

Amazing, my inner voice said.

I walked to the staircase leading to the Riverboat Hotel and messed my hair for dramatic effect. I then dashed up the steps, yanked open the door and sprinted to the reception desk. I barely noticed the decades-old furniture and woodwork as I ran across the hardwood floor. A young woman gazed at me, an expression of anxiety in her eyes. I puffed at her as if I had been running for miles. She took several steps backward.

"I'm supposed to meet Big Ben Redding here," I told her. "But I'm way late."

The young woman was startled enough to provide me with information that she probably wouldn't have under normal circumstances, which was the entire point.

"Mr. Redding checked out ten minutes ago," she said.

"He checked out?" I pulled my cell phone from my pocket, again for dramatic effect, and made hand movements as if I were making a phone call. "No one tells me anything. Did his business associate leave, too?"

"She left a few minutes before he did."

I pressed the cell to my ear.

"Thank you," I said.

I moved quickly from the lobby and went outside again. Once I left the hotel, I slowed my pace and returned the cell to my pocket.

Mr. Redding checked out, my inner voice said. *Which means he checked in. Which means he wasn't visiting someone, someone was visiting him. A woman. Too bad you couldn't get a name without alarming the receptionist more than you already had.*

I stayed on the main sidewalk until I reached the second sidewalk as Big Ben had and followed it between the two buildings. It led me to a parking lot located directly behind the Riverboat Hotel. The lot contained half a dozen vehicles. I checked for a back door to the hotel and quickly found one.

Questions were raised—let's say, for argument's sake, that Big Ben had indeed been enjoying a little nonmarital afternoon delight. If he had parked in the lot, why didn't he use the rear exit to reach his vehicle? Why did he use the front door? Did he want to be seen? By whom? Or did the woman leave by the rear entrance and he didn't want to be seen with her? Or are you reading way too much into this?

Barbara Finne isn't the only one with a suspicious nature, my inner voice told me.

On the other hand, I reminded myself, Jenness Crawford said that Big Ben and Olivia had gone to town together. Only they hadn't remained together. I wondered why not. I wondered if either of them knew what the other was doing.

It was early evening when I returned to Redding Castle, yet because of daylight savings time, the sun was still high in the sky. I deliberately parked beneath one of four light poles stationed at the corners of the lot. It didn't take long to find the security camera that recorded the comings and goings of the castle's guests

I wondered if it was motion activated.

I wondered if the lights were motion activated.

I went looking for Mr. Doty. I found him inside the barn. I called to him from the doorway. He seemed annoyed to be interrupted from whatever it was he was working on.

"Don't know about cameras," he said. "Ain't my job. The lights, well we used to have them go on and off like you say, only there's an awful lot of critters about, raccoons and deer and such. It became a bigger pain in the ass jumpin' up to see what was moving about than just leavin' 'em on all night. Look close, though; you'll see they got them shields to eliminate light pollution, what Miss calls it. Lights shine on the parking lot but nowhere else so it ain't as much a bother to the guests."

"You wouldn't know when people come and go late at night then," I said.

"Depends. Sometimes they can get pretty loud. They're on vacation, know what I mean?"

I said I did and thanked him.

I began to cross the clearing toward the James J. Hill Cabin, careful to stay on or near the narrow cobblestone lanes. There were several hoses wound on reels, one I saw attached to the castle itself and several more attached to freestanding water spigots spaced a healthy distance apart. I was most interested, though, in the path lights that were spaced every ten yards or so. There seemed to be enough of them that even a first-time visitor could find his way around the castle grounds at night while minimizing the light pollution that Jenness seemed to be concerned about.

Are you still holding on to the idea of someone wandering about in the dead of night with a ladder? my inner voice asked.

Seems unlikely, I told myself. Still . . .

I continued on toward the cabin where Nina and I were staying. As I approached it, I glanced toward the cabin set nearest to us, the one named after General Oglesby, whoever the hell he was.

That's when I saw it, a figure, lying flat on his back on the grass.

He wasn't moving.

I stared for a moment.

"Hey," I called.

The figure still didn't move.

"Hey," I called again even as I started sprinting toward it.

As I drew closer I recognized the body of a woman.

"Miss?"

She didn't answer.

Details emerged as I approached her—five six, one hundred and thirty pounds, long brown hair streaked with gray, a long peasant blouse over blue jeans and sandals.

"Miss?"

I knelt next to her.

She looked up at me, shielding her eyes from the sun with the flat of her hand.

"What do you want?" she asked.

I stood and stepped away until we were a few feet apart.

"I thought you might be hurt," I said.

"Do I look hurt?"

"Ma'am, you're lying on the ground."

"Oh, now I'm a ma'am. A second ago I was a miss. What's that about?"

The door to the General Oglesby Cabin opened and a man stepped out. He looked to be about the same age as the woman—midfifties and wearing jeans and a flannel shirt—only he was smiling.

"Is the bad man bothering you, honey?" he asked.

Bad man?

"A woman can't just sit and meditate anymore without being accosted on the village green?" the woman said.

Village green?

"You're not sitting," the man said. "You're lying on the grass."

"I like to get as close to Mother Earth as possible."

"I'm sorry," I said. "I thought . . ."

The man waved his hand; the gesture telling me not to worry about it.

"When did you get back from town?" he asked.

Are you talking to me?

"Fifteen minutes ago," the woman said. "I was attempting to relieve my urban stress and then he arrived."

Urban stress? In Redding?

"Are you going to lie there all afternoon or do you want to go to the castle with me and see your niece?" he said.

"Jenness is a capitalist."

"We all have our faults."

"Excuse me," I said. "Are you Alexander Redding?"

"Yes, I am. But please, call me Alex."

I looked down on the woman who had made no effort what-soever to rise.

"Then you must be Jen's aunt Eden."

"How'd you know?" she asked.

"She told me you were coming."

"Are you a friend of Jenness?" Alex asked.

"I am." I gestured at the James H. Hill Cabin. "My wife Nina and I. My name's McKenzie."

"Nina," Eden said. "Do you call her ma'am?"

I gestured at the horizon.

"The sun was in my eyes so I couldn't see how young you were," I said.

Eden laughed at that and offered her hand to Alex. He helped his wife to her feet.

"Good one, McKenzie." Eden used her hands to brush her shirt and jeans both front and back. "So, should we be off to have tea with little Jenny; see if she's gained any weight since deciding to become a fat cat?"

Fat cat?

"Pleasure meeting you, McKenzie," Alex said.

"Likewise."

A moment later, I watched the two of them walking hand in hand across "the village green."

Nina was sitting at the small kitchen table and working with her laptop when I entered the cabin. She was wearing black-rimmed reading glasses and a short white terry cloth robe and nothing else that I could see; her hair was still damp from the shower.

"I like your outfit," I said.

"I should get dressed."

"Please, not on my account."

"There's coffee."

I went to the small coffeepot on the narrow counter and poured a cup.

"What are you doing?" I asked.

"Working."

"For who? Redding Castle or Rickie's?"

"Rickie's. By the way, I am so sore from bending over and kneeling and scrubbing and carrying stuff. That Jenness—I haven't worked so hard in my life."

"Never?"

Nina looked up from her computer.

"Not recently, anyway," she said. "You have emails."

"Can I use the laptop?"

"I need to finish this. Use your phone."

I went to the love seat set in front of the fireplace and stretched out, careful not to put my shoes on the cushion. I activated the email function on my phone—I usually keep it off except when far from home—and started browsing. I found six messages from Barbara Finne, all of them sent from the *Redding Weekly Bulletin* account. I read them in order.

FOR SALE, ONE CASTLE, SLIGHTLY USED

Redding Castle is now for sale according to Tess Redding, a fourth-generation member of the John Redding family that has owned the iconic lake home located on the eastern shore of Lake Anpetuwi since 1883.

Redding said the family made the difficult decision to close the castle and put the property up for sale during "many conversations" over the Christmas holidays.

Part of the reason for the closure is a decline in business during the past couple of years, Redding said.

"Also, I'm not getting any younger," she said. "And my

children all have lives of their own. None of them want to take over when I move on."

MAYOR, CITY COUNCIL UNITE IN
EFFORT TO SAVE REDDING CASTLE

Redding Mayor Matthew Abere and members of the city council were quick to react to news that Redding Castle, the iconic landmark located on Lake Anpetuwi since 1883, was up for sale.

"I'd say this would be a terrible loss to the community," Abere said. "If the sale goes through, I'd hope that the buyer would keep it open to the public."

"I'd really hate to see someone come in and destroy it," said City Councilwoman Brianne Halvorson. "People have really enjoyed seeing the facility because of its age and notoriety and its connection to the City of Redding for so long."

To that end, both Abere and Halvorson said the city would do "what it can" to keep it standing.

Redding Castle is well known throughout the state and helps bring people to the community, Abere said. It had been the "unofficial" headquarters for the Governors Fishing Opener three years ago.

SUN IS SETTING ON REDDING CASTLE

It's been said that John Redding chose the location for the iconic lake home that bears his name because of the amazing sunset.

Only now it appears that the sun will be setting on Redding Castle one last time.

Redding Mayor Matthew Abere said efforts to find a buyer who will keep it open as a resort hotel and restaurant have proved unproductive.

The problem lies in rewiring and bringing the building up to code, as well as other restoration challenges.

"The simple truth is that the castle needs a lot of work," Abere said. "And the cost necessary to restore the building is far more than buyers are willing to spend."

Redding Castle is listed on the National Registry of Historic Places. However, private property is not eligible for the Minnesota Historical and Cultural Heritage Grants program. Instead, they are mainly limited to tax breaks.

"That's just not enough," Abere said.

Tess Redding said that whatever happens to the castle that was built by her great-grandfather on Lake Anpetuwi will be up to the buyer.

REDDING CASTLE "CONDOMINIUMS"?

Although an offer has yet to be made for the property, plans are under way to demolish Redding Castle and replace it with luxury condominiums.

The effort is being spearheaded by Cassandra Boeve, owner of Boeve Luxury, LLC, a development firm located in Redding, and appears to already have the support of Redding State Bank as well as Mayor Matthew Abere.

"If we can't save Redding Castle, this is the next best thing," Abere said. "The project will create jobs and bring added tax revenue to the city.

According to sources, the project, tentatively called "Castles on Anpetuwi," will consist of a forty-four unit tower, ground-floor retail space including a coffeehouse and wine bar, and underground parking.

However, Tess Redding, a fourth-generation member of the John Redding family that owns the 137-year-old lake home located on the eastern shore of Lake Anpetuwi, says she has yet to hear from Boeve or anyone else connected with the project.

"Developers have called," said Redding, 87. "But not these people. This is the first I've heard of them."

The next piece came with a pic of Jenness Crawford and her grandmother; Jen hugging Tess Redding from behind, both of them smiling merrily.

REDDING CASTLE WILL STAY IN THE FAMILY

Plans to sell Redding Castle and its surrounding property have been put on hold, according to Tess Redding.

Instead, it will continue as a resort hotel and restaurant under the direction of Redding's granddaughter Jenness Crawford.

"My children and I had agreed to sell because business was in decline and because none of them wanted to take over management when I was gone," said Redding, 87.

However, she said that, under the direction of Crawford during the past year, the castle had already seen a sharp increase in business even during the height of the COVID-19 pandemic.

"Not only that, Jenness is family," Redding said.

Crawford is the daughter of Edward Crawford and Marian Redding Crawford. She is the great-great-great-granddaughter of John Redding who built the iconic lake home on Lake Anpetuwi in 1883.

There was one final newspaper article. It appeared with a note from Barbara Finne that read: "By the way, the following will appear in tomorrow's *Weekly Bulletin* unless you call me with a better story."

Another character has appeared in the ongoing saga to determine what is to become of 138-year-old Redding Castle.

Nina Truhler, owner of the renowned Rickie's jazz club located on Cathedral Hill in St. Paul, has been visiting the castle along with her millionaire husband, Rushmore McKenzie, as guests of Jenness Crawford.

Truhler and Crawford are close friends. Crawford worked as a manager at Rickie's before she was named executive director of Redding Castle months before the passing of her grandmother, Tess Redding.

McKenzie would admit for the record only that he and his wife were in town "for personal reasons." However, he spent a great deal of time exploring downtown Redding. He was particularly interested in learning about the Riverboat Hotel, asking if it had a restaurant.

He also expressed a keen interest in any information about any existing plans to transform Redding Castle into a commercial development.

At the same time, reliable sources report that Truhler spent hours Tuesday working with Crawford and the castle's housekeeping staff, going through each of the resort's rooms and cabins, as well as the restaurant and the lobby, becoming acquainted with nearly every aspect of the castle's business operations.

I started laughing.

"What's so funny?" Nina asked.

I rose from the love seat and crossed into the kitchen area. I gave her my cell phone.

"Read this," I said.

Nina's did, her eyes widening with dread.

"None of this is true," she said.

"Actually, if you read the piece carefully, you'll discover that every word of it is true."

"Except we don't want to buy the castle. Do we?"

"No, we don't. On the other hand, the piece doesn't actually say that we do."

"What will Jenness say?"

"That's a good question. I have another one for you, as well. Nina, I spent the entire day trying to re-create the crime. I met with the police chief, who, as it turns out, is a friend of mine, an expert homicide cop from Minneapolis. I met with the Redding County medical examiner, who seems very competent. I studied their reports. If Tess Redding was murdered, it was so expertly done that there is absolutely no way you could prove it. What's more, Jenness knows that. She knew it long before she called us."

"What are you asking?"

"Why exactly did she call us?"

FIVE

Nina claimed she had more work to do. I told her I was going to wander down by the lake while she did it. We agreed to meet near the patio at seven o'clock.

"I want to get a good seat for the sunset," she said.

I took my own sweet time crossing the clearing as I made my way toward Lake Anpetuwi, examining the grounds, fixing the location of the cabins and the parking lot and the barn and all that empty space between them in relationship to the castle in my head; imagining scenarios that involved silent, invisible killers.

Like ninjas, my inner voice said.

In real life, ninjas weren't all that impressive, I reminded myself. They're recognized as nearly mythological beings solely because of the movies, the same as Japanese samurai and Wild West gunfighters.

Uh-huh.

I leaned against the top rung of the wooden fence at the edge of the bank where the ground tilted down toward the lake, once again scrutinizing the area where Mr. Doty found the ladder. Someone had to put it there; thrown it like I had done. Who? Why? Questions without answers. I stared at Tess Redding's balcony while I asked them.

There's probably an embarrassingly logical explanation.
Probably, I told myself. I just wished I knew what it was.
Let it go, McKenzie.

Eventually, I wandered along the bank to the concrete steps that led down to the L-shaped dock. There were a number of kayaks and a couple of canoes tethered to it. There were also spaces for a paddleboat and a couple of fishing boats with motors, only those were being used by guests.

At the end of the dock were a couple of wooden benches that had been bolted to the deck. I sat on one of them and looked out at the calm, sun-dappled lake. It was much longer than it was wide; at least three miles by a half mile, I estimated. And quiet. In the distance I heard the murmur of a boat motor, yet that quickly faded away.

I could get used to this, I told myself—for about a week. Then I would start bouncing off the birch trees. Truth is I wasn't cut out for the lake life, or rural life, or any kind of life outside the city. I once owned a lake home about a hundred miles from the Canadian border. I loved going up there, yet not as much as I loved coming back. As idyllic and peaceful as it was, I always felt as if I was missing something back home. A ball game or a concert or art exhibit or new restaurant. Something. Still, I enjoyed the momentary pleasure of a soft breeze ruffling my hair and the warm sun caressing my face. I closed my eyes and embraced the silence.

It didn't last long.

The loud guttural sound of a horn started echoing across the water.

My eyes snapped open.

"What the hell?" I said.

"Haven't you heard that before?"

I spun off the bench and turned toward the unexpected voice. Eden Redding was on the dock and walking toward me.

"Miss Redding," I said. "You startled me."

"Not as much as that, I bet." She waved toward the lake. "The first time I heard it, I thought the end of the world was coming which, I guess, was the point."

The horn kept blaring.

"It reminds me of the horn they sound at Vikings football games whenever the team scores," I said. "Only multiplied by a hundred."

"It's called the Gjallarhorn, meaning resounding horn. Supposedly, the sentry that guards Asgard, the home of the Norse gods . . ."

"Odin, Thor . . ."

"Yes, yes. The sentry carries the Gjallarhorn and when the giants attack, signaling the beginning of the final battle when all of the cosmos will be destroyed, he's supposed to let out a blast from the horn to warn the gods, and all of humanity, really, that they're about to become extinct. These guys"—she gestured at the lake—"use it to tell their followers that dinner is served."

The horn ceased bellowing.

"These guys?" I asked.

"The Sons of Europa."

"The Sons of Europa have a place on the lake?"

Eden pointed.

"Just over—do you see where the stand of white birch trees is leaning over the water?" she asked. "They moved in—I want to say a year ago. The woman who sold the property to them didn't know she was dealing with the Sons, though. She thought she was just selling to some guy. It didn't become a big deal until the Sons tried to get the zoning law changed to turn the place into a church. Then it became a very big deal."

"I heard about that," I said.

"Tess, for one, was livid. I had never seen her so angry. Heck,

I've never seen her angry at all. Not in all the years I've been married to Alex, except for maybe that one time when Carly— never mind that."

"What did she do?" I asked. "Tess, I mean."

"She organized resistance."

"RAH?"

"RAH, RAH, RAH—you have to admit it makes for a nice chant. I was so proud of her. What was most fun is that she actually called me for advice. Me. I nearly dropped the phone. I don't think she was protesting against the Sons because she hated white supremacists so much as she wanted to keep them off her lake, still . . ."

"Tess foiled the Sons of Europa?"

"It wasn't just her but she was one of the ringleaders; the Redding name carries a lot of weight around here. She started a petition, collected letters from just about everyone who owned a place on the lake that she personally delivered to the city council, and she helped rally the townspeople. They held meetings on the patio. 'Course, this was before COVID."

"I bet that really upset the Sons," I said.

"Their argument was that the Redding Castle already existed on the lake as a hotel and restaurant so refusing their rezoning request amounted to discrimination against their church. Besides, they pointed out that federal courts have already ruled that you can't use zoning laws to zone out a religion. RAH, on the other hand, argued that there were laws on the books that make it illegal for any institution that proposes to exclude people on account of race to run an operation in the State of Minnesota. It looked like Redding and the Sons and were heading toward a very long, very contentious legal standoff.

"The city council, at the urging of its lawyers, found a way around it, though. They ruled that the castle had already existed as a hotel and restaurant before the City of Redding zoning laws were enacted, which allowed the castle to be grandfathered in, yet at the same time did not obligate the city to consider other zoning requests. And they argued that various covenants and other legal instruments specifically attached to the lake forbid what they called 'significant conflict activities' such as group gatherings, excessive parking demands, storage areas, and I don't know what else; there's like a dozen items listed. If the Sons decided to build their church in a different location within the City of Redding, the council said it would consider their petition when it was presented; so not actually forbidding their religion. I expected them to appeal only the Sons haven't yet. It's a small church. Maybe they don't have the money."

I pivoted toward the castle; gazed up at its turrets and steep gables and countless windows while letting Eden's remarks sink in. She seemed to know what I was thinking yet waited for me to speak.

"What'll happen if the castle is sold?" I asked. "I heard talk that a developer might tear it down and build a condominium-slash-entertainment center. Wouldn't the city council need to change the laws to allow for that?"

"I suppose."

"If the city changes the rezoning laws for the development, then it probably would be forced to accommodate the church."

"There's a downside to everything." Eden Redding moved to where a canoe was tied to the dock. "Do you want to see?"

"See what?"

Eden pulled the canoe until its hull was flush against the dock.

"The face of the enemy," she said. "C'mon. Get in. You take the back."

"I thought you were having tea with the little capitalist."

I climbed into the back of the canoe and settled on the seat. Eden climbed into the front and untied us.

"Don't think I don't love my niece because I do," she said. "I love her to death. Only you can tell she's a branch on the old John Redding oak tree. Besides, she and Alex are both speaking Redding now. It's a language that outsiders have difficulty grasping."

Eden pushed us away from the dock. I grabbed a paddle off the floor of the canoe and dipped it into the water. Eden took hold of the second paddle and did the same.

"I don't know anything about John Redding," I said.

"You haven't read the book?"

"Not yet."

We both pulled from the right side of the boat until I switched to the left to keep it moving in a straight line. When I did, droplets of water flew off the blade and showered the back of Eden's peasant shirt.

"You do know how to paddle a canoe, don't you?" she asked.

"I'll try to do better, miss."

I heard her chuckling.

"Good boy," she said. "Do you know who Horatio Alger is?"

"No, but I've heard the name."

"He was a hugely successful writer of young adult novels during the end of the nineteenth century. All of his books were about impoverished boys who rose from humble beginnings to greatness through good deeds and hard work."

"Is John a Horatio Alger story?"

"I think John's life was the template for all of the stories. Read the book."

I paddled; Eden navigated. Instead of cutting directly across the lake toward the Sons' place, we hugged the shoreline so she could show me the houses that had been built there. Some were old, some were new, most were large, and all of them looked expensive, although taken as a whole they paled in comparison to Redding Castle.

"It's kind of like an oasis," Eden said. "The lake and the forest, both surrounded on all sides by flat farm country. It's what makes it prime real estate. 'Course, over half of the people who live on the lake don't actually live on the lake. It's mostly summer homes, vacation homes for people living in the Cities. At least it used to be. See that house?"

Eden pointed at a large white structure with six pillars holding up a front porch that reminded me of a Southern plantation.

"It's owned by the executive vice-president of an investment bank," she said. "He used to come down here maybe a dozen times a year, if that. Now he lives here, at least for the time being. He started running his business from a guest room when COVID closed his offices and decided he liked it. Same with the woman next door. She's a Minnesota girl who managed the marketing department of a cosmetics company located in Atlanta, Georgia. When COVID hit, she moved back up here with her husband and kids; her family owns the house. Now she's running her department remotely; won't even consider returning to Atlanta. Not only that—I know her. She eats at the restaurant at least once a week. Last time I was here, she told me that the president of her company lives in New York and the head of the creative department lives in Sweden. How's that for working remotely?

"A lot of businesses started working that way during the virus. Now that it's behind us, sorta, many of them are making it permanent. They discovered that productivity actually increases when people work from their homes, who knew? Plus, it helps them reduce overhead; why pay high rents for office towers if you don't need them? The Target Corporation moved thirty-five hundred of its employees out of downtown Minneapolis last spring; how many other businesses have followed their lead since then? Which reduces travel time to and from offices, which reduces traffic congestion, which reduces pollution from cars and trucks—all good. Plus, remote work is starting to stimulate small towns and suburbs. They had been losing population because there were no jobs; because it was so hard to make a living out here. But now if you can work for 3M or Medtronic or General Mills or Cargill or Muehlenhaus and still live in Redding, why wouldn't you?"

"All of which makes transforming Redding Castle into luxury condominiums that much more attractive," I said. "That much more lucrative."

"The world is evolving."

"Capitalism at work."

Eden spun in her seat and glared at me. For a moment I thought she might try to whack me with the canoe paddle. Instead, she frowned and spun back.

"What pisses me off, is it's also allowing big business to drive wages down, too," she said. "Why pay a guy $200,000 to move to San Francisco when you can get away with paying half that if he works from Boise, Idaho?"

We paddled another quarter mile in silence. It was Eden who broke it.

"Anpetuwi," she said. "It's from the Dakota. Anpetu means daytime. Wi means sun."

"Daytime sun," I said just to prove that I was listening.

"Have you ever seen Lake Anpetuwi from the sky?"

"No."

"I have. It looks like a giant exclamation point, long and narrow with a small bay at the end that looks like a dot. The castle is located in the center of the dot. The great thing, though—the lake runs almost exactly east to west. The sun rises directly behind the castle and it sets directly in front of it and when the sunlight reflects off the lake, especially when it's calm, it's like fire rolling across the water until it reaches the castle."

"I saw it last night," I said.

"Spectacular."

"Yes."

"There. That's the headquarters for the Sons of Europa."

We were paddling past a stand of birch trees that were, in fact, leaning precariously over the lake. On the other side of them was a large, sprawling structure that looked less like a church than a two-story ranch house painted the color of the sky. The huge lawn surrounding it was expertly mowed and, unlike Redding Castle's, it rolled right up to the shoreline.

In front of the house was a gray polyethylene dock.

There was a man standing on the dock dressed in a white T-shirt and blue jeans. I placed him at about thirty.

He was cradling a lightweight AR-15 semiautomatic assault rifle.

"Heimdall," Eden said.

"His name is Heimdall?"

"Heimdall is the name of the sentry who guards Asgard; the one who's supposed to blow Gjallarhorn when all hell comes a knockin'. There's another one in the back standing guard where the driveway joins the road that circles the lake. Imagine taking a drive or a hike around the lake and coming across a guy with a machine gun."

We were about thirty yards from shore as we slid past Heimdall in the canoe. He watched us intently as if he half expected us to storm the beach. Eden called to him.

"Beautiful day, wouldn't you agree?" she said. "Perfect for a lynching."

Heimdall replied by gripping the AR more tightly.

Really, Eden? my inner voice asked. *Really?*

"Or maybe a cross burning later," she added.

I began to paddle faster.

Heimdall shouted at me.

"Hey, asshole," he said. "Better control your woman."

By her laugh, I guessed that Eden would have liked to see me try.

"You wouldn't know a real woman if she sat on your face," she said.

Heimdall didn't seem to have a reply for that.

I kept paddling, putting the dock behind us. Eden had to spin in her seat to look back at Heimdall.

"Does your mother know you're a racist prick?" she asked.

I was staring straight ahead so I didn't see his reaction, yet it was enough to make Eden laugh some more.

"Is that your IQ or the size of your dick?" she asked.

I continued to paddle, keeping the canoe in a straight line as we put more distance between us and the gunman on the dock. Even so, I half expected to feel the hard punch of a round as it tore into my back. Again.

We had paddled a good one hundred yards before I glanced behind me. The gunman was still watching us. I was surprised by how fast and shallow my breathing had become.

When did stuff like this start bothering you? my inner voice asked.

As if it didn't know.

I spoke aloud.

"Really, Eden?" I said. "Really?"

"You can't let people like him bully you. I don't care if he has a gun. That's just for show, anyway. He's just trying to frighten us; keep us in our place."

"I get that."

"He wants people to cower in fear before the mighty Sons of Europa."

"You think so?"

"I won't do it. You have to stand up for what's right. Always."

"Eden?"

"What?"

"You're starting to grow on me."

She thought that was funny, too.

We spun the canoe around and, ignoring the shoreline, paddled in a straight line back to the dock in front of Redding Castle. As we approached I could see Nina sitting on the concrete steps. She was wearing a bright yellow summer dress with spaghetti straps and a skirt that ended inches above her knees. I really liked that dress.

She rose from the steps and met us on the dock as we tied up.

"Hi," I said.

"Hi, yourself."

Eden and I scrambled out of the canoe. I offered her my hand, but Eden ignored it.

"That was fun, McKenzie," she said. "We'll have to do it again."

"Sure." I gestured at Nina. "This is my wife, Nina Truhler. Nina, this is Eden Redding."

"Jen's aunt," Nina said. She offered her hand and Eden shook it. "A pleasure."

"It's nice to meet you, too, ma'am," Eden said, emphasis on the "ma'am." "But I can't linger. I need to find Alex. I hope I get a chance to visit with you later."

Eden maneuvered past us on the dock and headed up the concrete stairs. Nina spoke quietly to me.

"Ma'am?" she asked.

I explained.

"Not the first time I've had to pay for your crimes," Nina said.

"I like her, though. Very much the militant liberal, always ready and willing to take a stand against racism, capitalism . . ."

"Do you think she'll vote to sell the castle to developers?"

"Oh, in a heartbeat."

I took Nina's hand and we climbed the concrete steps toward the castle. I didn't used to be a hand-holder; public displays of affection always embarrassed me a little, especially my own. Lately, though, I've discovered that my attitudes have been shifting. I blamed it on the pandemic.

We were two-thirds of the way up the stairs when Nina called, "Dibs."

"What?"

"I've checked it out," she said. "I think where we are standing now is the absolute perfect place to watch the sunset. Only it'll start going down in about fifteen minutes by my watch so you'll need to hurry."

"Where am I going?"

"To the bar. I need wine. Wine, I say. Something white and German. A Riesling or a Pinot Gris. Anything as long as it's not a Liebfraumilch."

"Coming right up."

I started climbing the remainder of the stairs.

"McKenzie."

I turned back.

"I'll drink a Liebfraumilch if that's all they have," Nina said.

I walked up the stairs to the bank, across to the patio and through the huge open doorway into the dining room. There was a small queue in front of the bar; a few customers wore masks, most did not. The bartender was masked though, so I put mine on out of simple courtesy.

When my turn came, I ordered a Summit EPA and "Whatever you have that's white and German."

The bartender poured what he called "A Silvaner."

"Some people call it Dracula wine," he said. "That's because it's very old, very pale, and is ruined when exposed to bright sunlight for too long."

The story bought him a nice tip, which was probably why he told it.

I turned and was making my way back to the patio when I was intercepted by Olivia Redding.

"I know you," she said. "You're here with Nina Truhler."

"Ms. Redding," I said.

She had changed her clothes. Gone were the tight T-shirt, jeans, and boots, replaced by a loose-fitting blouse with all the colors of autumn, a rust-colored skirt that reached to her ankles, and a matching shawl. Instead of a ponytail, her hair now fell around her shoulders. She still looked good, don't get me wrong. She also looked her age, though, and I wondered why.

Because she's not trying to impress you, my inner voice suggested.

"I saw you in town today," Olivia said.

"Oh? Why didn't you say hello?"

"I was with a friend."

"Did you grow up in Redding?"

"Goodness, no. I have never lived here. Ben and I met when he was playing football for the University of Minnesota. I was a cheerleader."

She said it with such pride that I felt compelled to stroke her ego; maybe earn a few brownie points.

"At the risk of sounding sexist," I said, "I think you could still dance with the U's Spirit Squad."

"What a charmer you are. I'm afraid I don't know your name."

"McKenzie."

"McKenzie, I noticed you were walking with Redding's police chief," Olivia said.

"Chief Gardner and I are old friends."

"Were you a police officer, too?"

"Yes."

"But not anymore?"

"I retired a few years ago."

"You're far too young to be retired."

"Now who's being charming?" I asked.

Olivia smiled for a moment, but then her mouth turned serious.

"I thought you might be talking to that woman . . ."

That woman?

"About Jenny's ridiculous and terrible and, quite frankly, extremely insulting theories about what happened to Tess," she said.

"Insulting?"

"She's accusing someone in her own family; her aunts, her uncles, my husband, even her own mother of murdering her grandmother. Wouldn't you find that insulting?"

"I haven't heard her actually accuse anyone," I said.

"Who else would have done it?"

"*If* Tess was murdered"—I emphasized the "if"—"there are any number of suspects."

"Like who, for example?"

"I've just learned that the Sons of Europa had reason to kill her."

"That's silly."

"Then there are the developers who had been planning to tear down the castle. They must have been pretty upset when Tess changed her mind about selling."

Olivia raised her voice sharply.

"That's outrageous," she said.

People who had ignored our presence before now had a

sudden interest in who we were and what we were doing. That didn't slow her down, though.

"How dare you say such a thing?" Olivia wanted to know.

"Just thinking out loud."

She leaned close to me. Her voice became a low hiss.

"Do everyone a favor, McKenzie. Keep your *thoughts* to yourself."

Olivia brushed past me and went to the bar. There were people still waiting in line, only she chose to ignore them.

"Amaretto," she said. "One ice cube."

"Mrs. Redding." The bartender spoke her name as if he was explaining why he was serving Olivia before his other customers. "Yes, ma'am."

Amaretto, one of the sweetest liqueurs I've ever come across, I told myself.

Now there's an angry drink, my inner voice said. *What does she pour when she's really pissed off? Mountain Dew?*

That's not the point.

What's the point?

She's barely annoyed when her own family is accused of murder yet goes off the rails when someone points a finger at developers? What's that about?

I returned to Nina. She was sitting on the concrete step where I had left her; hugging her legs against her body, her chin resting on her knees. I offered her the long-stem glass.

"Your Dracula wine," I told her.

"My what?"

I explained as I removed my mask and stuffed it in my pocket. Nina swirled the wine in her glass.

"I've never heard of that before," she said. "I wonder if I can do something with it; promote it on my drink menu. What do you think?"

I gave her my best Bela Lugosi impersonation—"I never drink . . . wine."

Nina stared at me for a few beats.

"I don't get it," she said.

"It's a line from the movie *Dracula*."

"Is that all you do when I'm not home, watch old movies and TV shows?"

"Sometimes I do favors for my wife's friends."

"Yeah, I deserved that."

"Speaking of which . . ."

I told Nina about my excursion with Eden Redding followed by my brief conversation with Olivia Redding.

"Huh," she said.

"My thoughts exactly."

"No one likes developers."

"Except developers and those who profit by them."

"Huh," she said again.

We sipped our drinks in silence until the bottom of the sun seemed to touch the top of the trees on the far side of Lake Anpetuwi. There was an explosion of light as the rays caromed off the calm water like it was a mirror, catching the breath of nearly everyone on the patio. The lake stopped reflecting the light, though, as the sun sank lower. Instead, it seemed to absorb it and then send it rolling down its length like a tsunami. I found myself fighting the urge to leap out of the way as the orange light funneled toward us, finally crashing against the shoreline and climbing the bank to the patio. It danced over us and around us until the top of the sun dipped below the trees and the light disappeared as if someone had slowly closed a dimmer switch.

Guests applauded.

Someone said, "Damn!"

Nina said, "I wonder what it's like to actually be on the lake when that happens."

"You might not see it when you're on the lake," I said. "Too close to the water."

"The people living in the houses on the two sides of the lake; they're not facing east or west. Do they see the same sunset that we do?"

"I don't know."

A heavy voice seemed to come from directly above us.

"They don't," it said.

I glanced upward. Big Ben Redding was standing on the staircase behind us, a drink in his hand, appearing from where I was sitting like one of those giants that Asgard seemed to be so terrified of. I stood so that my head reached his belt buckle.

"I grew up here," he said. "When I was a kid we explored all around the lake; there were only a few houses back then. And no, they can't see the sunset. Not the way we do. Ol' John Redding picked his spot very well. I'm Ben Redding, by the way."

"I'm McKenzie. This is my wife, Nina Truhler."

Nina was standing, too, and Ben leaned down toward her and offered his hand. His blue eyes seemed to sparkle as they met her blue eyes.

"My pleasure," he said.

Watch it, pal.

Nina shook his hand.

"A civilized gesture," Ben said. "So much better than waving or knocking fists and elbows, don't you think?"

"I do," Nina said.

I noticed Big Ben didn't offer to shake hands with me.

"My wife said you were here," he said. "Rickie's, right?"

"Yes."

Ben toasted her with the squat glass that he was sipping from and smiled. He never seemed to stop smiling.

"I love your club," he said.

"That's kind of you to say."

"Tell me you're doing all right during these difficult days."

"So far, so good," Nina said.

"I'm so happy to hear that, although I was wondering if things might not take a turn for the worse now that flu season is approaching. All the news media outlets seem to have different theories depending on their political affiliations."

"What do you do, Ben?" I asked. "Now that you're no longer playing football for the Gophers."

Big Ben chuckled.

"I rarely meet anyone who remembers me as number eighty-eight these days," he said.

I didn't have the heart to tell him that I knew only because Olivia Redding told me.

"Besides, my niece Madison is the family's sports hero now." Ben took a sip of his drink. "A much better athlete than I ever was. You know, I was on the last team to play in the old Brick House. Memorial Stadium. Junior year they moved us off campus to the Hubert H. Humphrey Metrodome in downtown Minneapolis. God, I hated that place. Artificial turf; everything artificial. Do you want to find a place to sit? Looking up at me and me looking down, that's not very comfortable, is it?"

Instead of going up to the patio, though, we went down to the dock, perching on the benches at the far end of it. The soft jazz played from the speakers on the patio seemed to sound much clearer down there. The moon and stars had yet to make an appearance and Ben gazed out at the darkness as if he were remembering something.

"So, what do you do now, Ben?" Nina asked.

"I'm almost embarrassed to say."

"Why?"

"Because so many people suffered terribly during the pandemic, businesses closing, yet we did great. My wife and I own Ben's Beez Honey."

"That's you?"

"That's us."

"I use your honey in my kitchen."

Ben raised his glass to her again.

"Another reason I hope Rickie's continues to do well," he said. "That's our market niche. A workhorse honey to be mixed with other ingredients. You'd hate to use the expensive, raw, super-special local stuff if people aren't going to taste it, right?"

"Exactly."

"How did you get into the honey business?" I asked.

"Almost by accident. What happened—I was drafted by the Buffalo Bills in '83. I won't tell you which round except to say it was in the double digits. Kay Stephenson was the new head coach. He didn't even know my name. Bob Zeman was the new defensive coordinator and linebackers coach. He kept calling me Reardon."

Big Ben Redding laughed as if it was all a wonderful joke, yet I couldn't imagine him thinking so at the time. He seemed to read my mind because he added, "It was a lot of fun while it lasted, but I didn't belong there. I knew that after the third day even though it took my coaches a couple of preseason games to figure it out. I just didn't have the speed you need to play at that level. Anyway, after I was cut, I came back home to Redding and looked around and asked myself, 'Now what?'

"It turns out that playing football in college doesn't prepare you to do much except play football in college; my degree was in communications and I hardly ever went to class. Then I thought—the one thing I enjoyed besides playing football was beekeeping. My sister Anna and I had built and maintained some colonies in a clearing in the woods behind the castle when we were kids. We had done pretty well, too. The year before I went to the U, we produced a little over one hundred and twenty pounds of honey. I won't bore you with the math, dry ounces versus fluid, but that came down to exactly one hundred and sixty-three eight-ounce jars; see, I remember the number. One hundred sixty-three jars of Redding Castle Honey that we sold for a buck fifty each mostly in the castle, but also at a couple of stores in Redding, too. You need to remember, back in those days a loaf of bread cost fifty cents, a pound of hamburger was a buck. You could buy a sixteen-ounce bottle of Coke out of a vending machine for a quarter. So, big money as far as me and Annie were concerned. I think our profit after expenses was about two hundred dollars. Woo-hoo!"

Ben started laughing again.

"How many pounds do you produce now?" I asked.

"Eight hundred and fifty thousand. 'Course, it's not all single origin. We own only about sixty-five hundred hives. We source most of our honey from beekeepers in North and South Dakota and also Montana, California, Minnesota, of course. We have a facility in Burnsville, just south of Minneapolis. I tell people that we employee 325 million honeybees.

"But that's what I mean by being a little embarrassed. Demand for honey is going up, pandemic be damned, partly because consumers recognize it as a healthy substitute for sugar and they don't mind paying a higher price for it. We, Americans I mean, consume an average of two pounds of honey per person each year. Last year Ben's Beez set a record; we moved over one-point-one million units."

"At a dollar fifty each?" I asked.

Ben laughed some more; he seemed like a happy fellow.

"We do a little bit better than that now," he said.

"Your plant is in Burnsville," I said. "Not Redding?"

Ben laughed again.

"Have you met my wife?" he asked. "Livy wouldn't be caught

dead living in Redding. See what I did there? Dead? Living? Oh, by the way, don't ever call her Livy to her face unless you can take a punch."

Ben rubbed his chin as if he had.

"Your wife wants to sell Redding Castle," I said.

"Who told you that?"

"Jenness."

"There are a lot of things that Olivia wants that she doesn't get. Jenny worries too much."

"Can I tell her you said that?"

"Now, now, now, McKenzie. You're not asking me to divulge how I'm going to vote, are you? I might be an old, beat-up football player who's had his bell rung once too often, but I'm not foolish enough to make a commitment before I hear what the developers have to say."

"I don't know about old and beat-up, Ben. You look like you could still play."

"Now you're just sucking up. But I like it, McKenzie. I like it."

We chitchatted for a bit longer. After a few minutes Big Ben glanced at his watch and excused himself.

"Better go find Olivia before she decides to find me," he said.

By the time he left, the night sky was filled with stars and the castle's lights were blazing in competition. It was easy to watch him climb the steps to the patio.

Nina lowered her voice so that only I could hear it.

"What you told me before, about seeing Ben outside the Riverboat Hotel in Redding—do you think he's cheating on his wife?"

"Time and experience has taught me not to jump to conclusions, even the most obvious ones," I said.

"Do you think he'll support Jenness just to infuriate Olivia?"

"Not necessarily. On the other hand, I don't think he'll vote against Jenness just to please her, either."

We crossed the length of the dock and started climbing the concrete staircase toward the patio and the music while we talked it over in hushed voices.

"I think Big Ben will vote against selling the castle," Nina said, "Carly is all for it; Jenness's mom will side with her and Eden—do you really think she'd sell?"

"If there's enough money on the table, yes, she'll turn capitalist, too, and argue how she's doing a favor for the environment and small towns and whatever. Seeing the way that she and her husband were together, I have to believe that Alex will vote whichever way she wants."

"According to my math, that's two to two."

"Leaving Anna Redding as the deciding vote."

"When is she supposed to arrive?"

I didn't have time to answer. We had reached the top of the staircase and I could hear Jenness Crawford calling to us.

"There you are," she said.

Jenness crossed the patio and took me by my wrist.

"Did you really paddle a canoe past the Sons of Europa?" she asked. "Did you really call them names?"

"Your aunt—"

"Eden told me what happened. She was laughing."

"At the Sons or me?" I asked.

"Both. Why would she do that?"

"From what little I know of her, I'd say she's not the kind of woman who likes to leave well enough alone."

"Dammit. I have enough problems without antagonizing the Sons. What next? Oh. Aunt Olivia said she saw you in town. She says you were walking with the chief of police."

"Deidre Gardner," I said. "Turns out we're old friends."

Jenness tightened her grip on my wrist and led me off the patio into the dark shadows surrounding it. Nina followed behind.

"What did she say?" Jenness asked.

I repeated everything that the chief and Dr. Evers had told me; I said I trusted their findings

"But the ladder," Jenness insisted.

"I don't have an explanation for that, yet."

"So, there's still a chance . . ."

"Jen, the day that your grandmother died, was any member of your family actually here; anyone besides you staying in the castle?"

"No."

"Okay."

Jenness hung her head and sighed. "I know, I know, I know," she said. "I suppose I should be glad that no one in my family is a murderer."

"I would be," Nina said.

"It's just that I heard that criminals aren't allowed to profit from their crimes."

"That's not quite how the law works," I said.

"And I thought . . . I'm grasping at straws, aren't I?"

So, my inner voice said, *you're a straw now?*

"I just want to save the castle so badly."

"I don't think this is the way," I said.

Jenness raised her head and grinned at Nina.

"I remember when I worked at Rickie's and all I had to worry about was making you happy," she said. "I thought that was hard. I had no idea."

Jenness spun around and headed back toward the patio. She called to us over her shoulder.

"Thanks, guys," she said. "We'll talk some more after I figure out what I'm going to do."

"Wait," Nina said. "Are you saying I'm hard to work for?"

Jenness didn't reply, but I was sure I could hear muffled laughter.

"I'm not hard to work for," Nina told me. "I might be—demanding, but I'm fair. Don't you think?"

"Thursday," I said.

"What?"

"Anna Redding is supposed to arrive Thursday."

SIX

Nina had threatened my life before we went to sleep and while I didn't think she would actually do the things to me that she promised she would do if I dared to wake her again "at the crack of dawn," I was careful to quietly slip out of bed the next morning.

"I need my beauty sleep," she told me in between the threats.

"No, you don't," I insisted.

Looking down at her after I donned my running shoes, shorts, and T-shirt, I decided that I was right and she was wrong, but since it was unlikely I'd survive the argument, I eased myself down the staircase and out of the cabin door.

I'm not usually an early riser, myself. I only get up at the crack of dawn when I'm preoccupied with a case and Jenness Crawford's certainly had me wondering as I stretched. I was no longer sure if we were brought there to solve the unlikely murder of her grandmother or if she expected Nina and me to help her save Redding Castle. And how would we do that? And did we want to?

After stretching, I began jogging along the narrow path that began near the James J. Hill Cabin and wound through the surrounding forest. There had been a carved sign posted where the path started that showed me where it ended behind the barn on the far side of the clearing. In between it meandered through the woods for three-point-five miles which were a little more than I usually ran along the Mississippi River back home. Because of my gunshot wound, I had been a little slow getting back into my regular workout routine and I could feel the ache in my legs after only a quarter mile. I tried to ignore it, asking myself what I was going to do next about Jenness.

Contact my financial adviser for advice, I decided.

When normal people get up, my inner voice suggested.

Along with the trees, I jogged past several clearings in the forest; large meadows adorned with assorted white, blue, pink, yellow, orange, and even purple wildflowers that I couldn't have identified at gunpoint. I was passing one of the meadows when I heard footfalls and a voice behind me.

"On your left," the voice said.

I immediately moved to my right, even as I turned my head in the opposite direction in time to watch a young woman with long legs and a golden ponytail lope past.

Madison Zumwalt glanced at me, kept running, and then glanced again. She was at least ten yards past me when she began to slow.

"You're McKenzie," she said. "You're Jenny's friend."

"I am."

"I saw you with her the other day. My mom says you're trying to help her."

"I am," I repeated.

"If you're a friend of Jenny's, then you're a friend of mine. I'm Maddie Zumwalt, by the way."

"Oh, I know."

"Jenny's been bragging me up, hasn't she?"

"Big Ben, too. Your family is very proud of you."

"Funny how that works. Last year at this time I was just

Maddie. Now I'm 'my daughter Madison,' 'my niece Madison,' 'my cousin Madison,' 'my friend Madison.'"

"Sociologists call it BIRGing—basking in reflective glory."

"I get that and I don't mind. Except, what'll happen if I lose?"

Good question, I thought, but didn't answer.

"Do you live in the castle?" I asked.

"Oh no, I live in town with Mom. I run here before I go to school sometimes because—you know what they don't have in the town of Redding? Hills and valleys or anything resembling an actual cross-country skiing trail. It's just so flat most of the time. I run here, not every day, maybe three, four times a week. The rest of the time I'm in town double-poling on roller skis and I swim, too, when the school's pool is open, because it increases my upper-body flexibility and it helps reduce back and shoulder and hip injuries. I try to get in at least five K—when I run, I mean—shower, grab breakfast. Mrs. Doty takes care of me. She makes these pancakes with fresh pineapple and coconut that's oh my God. At home I'd just grab a muffin or something and out the door. I don't have time to cook and Mom—the woman could screw up scrambled eggs. I do most of the cooking. Grandma Tess taught me a few things. She tried to teach Mom but apparently she couldn't be bothered. Why cook when you can toss something in the microwave for five minutes is the way Mom looks at it. Am I talking too much?"

"Not at all," I said. Although, I had to marvel at how effortlessly she spoke while running. 'Course, she had slowed down to match my speed, which meant she wasn't working very hard.

"*New friends can often have a better time together than old friends*. I learned that in school; we're studying F. Scott Fitzgerald."

I should hope so, my inner voice said.

"Livy says you're some kind of investigator," Maddie said.

"You call your aunt Livy?"

"Not to her face. Are you an investigator?"

"In a manner of speaking."

"You don't really think that Grandma Tess was murdered, do you? By someone in the family?"

"No, I don't."

But you've been wrong before.

"Jenny's just being melodramatic—that's what Livy and Mom say," Maddie told me.

"They might be right."

"I love Jenny. I love that she's trying to save the castle. I wish I could help her. Can I help her?"

"I heard that your mother wants to sell the castle," I said.

"Mom wants financial security. She's like Rosalind in *This Side of Paradise*. She thinks having enough money to live comfortably is more important than love. Love of family. Love of home. Love of a man. I've lived through three of her marriages. I disagree."

"Money will help you train."

"I'll be fine. I have two full-ride scholarship offers, one from St. Cloud State only two hours away and the other from the University of Colorado, where my aunt Anna went to school. I also have half-rides from Michigan Tech and Wisconsin–Green Bay."

"Which one will you accept?"

"Depends. If they sell the castle, I'll probably go to Colorado. If they don't, I'll go to St. Cloud. It'll be easier to come home from St. Cloud. This is home; not the houses where Mom's ex-husbands lived."

"Does your mother know that?"

"Not yet."

"Maybe you should tell her. It might change her mind."

"It won't but, you know what? Maybe I should tell her. Get the argument over with."

Maddie glanced down at the black band that she wore around her wrist.

"I'm way late," she said. "Have a good run."

With that, Maddie increased her speed until she was out of my sight.

About twenty-five minutes later, I reached the end of the line. I turned a gradual corner, labored up a hill, and there was the clearing with Redding Castle looming up like a mountain. I left the path and slowed to a walk as I circled the barn. Madison Zumwalt was already dressed for school and sitting on the concrete steps leading to the entrance of the castle. She was eating from a plate filled with pancakes and a banana.

Damn, she's fast, my inner voice told me.

I called to her as I walked past.

"Should you be eating like that after a hard run?" I asked.

She looked at me as if she felt sorry for me.

"Of course," she said. "You should eat within thirty minutes. Load up on carbs; keep your blood sugar levels steady."

I gave her a wave and kept walking.

You learn as you go.

I was soon passing the General Oglesby Cabin. Eden Redding had stepped outside alone and was starting to move through a series of poses that reminded me of an ancient Madonna music video but was really yoga. Instead of her usual loose-fitting attire, she wore leggings and a long fitted top that suggested she really was more of a miss than a ma'am. I gave her a wave, too.

Eden stared back at me like I was a large dog wandering around without a leash; like I was a potential danger to her. As I came closer she said, "Oh, it's you," and continued working through her yoga exercises.

Instead of being offended, I said "Good morning," and kept walking.

She couldn't recognize you from a distance.

I bet she wears contacts, I told myself.

I few moments later I was entering the James J. Hill Cabin. A voice called to me from the bedroom loft.

"McKenzie, is that you?" Nina asked.

"No, it's a sex-crazed maniac who wants to have his way with you."

"Even better."

"You should come down. We'll go have breakfast. Apparently, I should eat within thirty minutes of working out."

"Or you could come up here."

Man does not live by bread alone, my inner voice reminded me.

It was well past the thirty-minute mark when Nina and I finally sat for breakfast on the patio. Apparently, most of the other guests had already eaten because only a couple of the other tables were filled. I ordered the pineapple-coconut pancakes and decided that Madison was right, they were spectacular. Nina ordered banana french toast with pecans and rum-soaked raisins and proclaimed that the recipe was well worth stealing.

To give you an idea of how differently our minds work, though, Nina was wondering aloud if she should volunteer her services to Jenness again. Meanwhile, I was thinking that we seem to have a lot more sex while we're on vacation than we do when we're at home.

That's when Olivia Redding appeared at our table and tossed a folded copy of the *Redding Weekly Bulletin* next to my glass of orange juice. She was staring at Nina when she spoke.

"I didn't know that you were thinking of buying the castle," she said.

Nina and I both glanced down at the newspaper. The headline was clearly visible—*A New Suitor for Redding Castle?*

"Don't believe everything you read," I said.

Olivia turned on me.

"I'm sorry," she said. "Was I speaking to you?" When I didn't respond, Olivia turned her gaze back on Nina. "Well?"

"Don't believe everything you read," Nina said.

Atta girl!

"What does that mean?" Olivia wanted to know.

Nina pointed at the newspaper with her fork.

"Does it say that I'm thinking of buying the castle?" she asked.

"It implies."

"I don't care what it implies. What does it say?"

Olivia didn't reply.

"I came here to help Jenness," Nina said. "Don't you want me to help Jenness? She is your niece."

Olivia's harsh expression softened and a relaxed smile replaced her frown. The transformation was so quick and so complete that I didn't trust it for a moment.

"Of course I want you to help Jenny if you can." Olivia's voice practically dripped with sincerity. "And I apologize. I can't believe how rude I'm behaving. My only excuse is that since Tess passed, this has been the number one issue dividing the family: What to do about the castle? Everything else was easy; her investments, personal possessions. Tess was very clear about what she wanted done with those. But not the castle. Tess's children have been arguing about it ever since we got past the shock of her death. You're helping Jenny; of course you are. How are you helping her?"

"Among other things, recommending possible revenue streams to increase the profitability of the castle," Nina said.

"Such as?"

"Well, if you must know, she could stage outdoor concerts—jazz, rock, country western. She could host music groups from around the area, too; the high school. Hold the concerts in the clearing between the cabins. Another possibility is reviving the honeybee colonies. Redding Castle Honey."

Olivia looked up and away as if she had heard a particularly offensive obscenity.

"If I hear another word about Ben and Annie's fucking honey farm . . ." Olivia said.

Whoa.

"I'm sorry," Olivia added. "I don't know what's wrong with me today. Please, forgive me for disturbing your breakfast."

Olivia spun around. She walked fast enough to leave quickly yet not so fast that she looked like she was running and in the back of my mind I could hear my old baseball coach telling my teammates and me how to turn a double play—"Hurry, but don't rush."

"I don't think Olivia likes you," Nina said.

"I don't think she'll be visiting Rickie's anytime soon, either."

"I hate it when I lose customers."

"So, outdoor concerts?" I asked.

"Just popped into my head while she was standing there."

"Still, a good idea."

"Could be. Depends on logistics. Permits. Insurance. It's not like those old Judy Garland–Mickey Rooney musicals. 'We have the barn, we have the costumes; let's put on a show.'"

"I like that I'm not the only one who watches old movies."

"Ha." Nina gestured at the newspaper that Olivia had left behind. "I hate seeing my name in print."

"Actually, this is a good thing."

"In what way?"

"It gives us standing."

"What do you mean?"

"People still don't have to answer my questions, but because of the newspaper article they'll think they know why I'm asking them. It gives us credibility. I can walk into Redding City Hall now and say, 'Do I need a permit to hold a concert at Redding Castle?' Instead of asking 'Why do you want to know?' they'll be saying 'Oh, are you planning on hold a concert at Redding Castle?' Once you get people talking, it's amazing what you might learn."

"I'm starting to enjoy this, watching you work."

"Nick and Nora Charles, that's us."

Nina stared at me for a few beats.

"I'm supposed to know who they are, aren't I?" she said.

"Seriously? *The Thin Man*? Dashiell Hammett? William Powell and Myrna Loy must have played Nick and Nora in a half-dozen movies."

"Uh-huh."

"I'm going to make you watch that film tonight if I have to tie you to a chair."

"About that—have you noticed that we have sex more often when we're on vacation than we do when we're at home?"

After finishing breakfast, Nina went off in search of Jenness Crawford to ask if she required help. I decided to return to the cabin and call my financial adviser. Along the way, I noticed Eden Redding lying on the ground near the General Oglesby Cabin. She was still dressed in her yoga outfit. I called to her only she didn't reply.

Getting close to Mother Earth again, my inner voice suggested,

I kept walking, yet for some reason I couldn't get the woman out of my head.

"Eden," I called. "Give me a sign that you're okay."

Still no response.

All of my internal alarm systems began flaring at once. Time and experience had taught me to trust them.

"Eden?"

When she didn't answer, I began jogging toward her; half expecting her to pop up and admonish me for interrupting her meditation like she had the day before. Only when I reached her side, I found that her eyes were closed, her face was swollen, and she seemed to be having difficulty breathing. I knelt down next to her and placed two fingers against her carotid artery. Her pulse was too rapid to count.

I repeated Eden's name; patted her cheek like they do in the movies.

Nothing.

I shouted, or maybe it was a scream.

"Alexander Redding!"

Redding was standing inside the doorway of the cabin within an instant. Brief moments later, he was by my side, breathing as if he had run a hundred yards instead of ten.

"Eden, Eden," he said. "What happened?"

"I found her. She seems to be in some kind of shock."

"Oh shit, it is shock. Anaphylactic shock. I've seen it before."

"We need to get her to a hospital," I said. "Now."

The "now" and the way I said it, erased any questions or arguments Alex might have had. I gathered Eden up in my arms and lifted her off the ground. She didn't seem heavy at all as I carried her across the clearing to the parking lot, but by then I was so jazzed with adrenaline that I felt I could actually beat Madison Zumwalt in a cross-country skiing race.

My Mustang had all the latest electronics, so just stepping next to it with my fob in my pocket was enough to unlock the doors. I had Alexander climb into the backseat and together we nestled Eden next to him. A moment later I was behind the steering wheel and pressing the START button. The Mustang roared to life and we were off, driving the narrow winding road through the forest at a speed that invited disaster. Once we hit the open highway, I accelerated even faster, pushing the sports car well past eighty on the straightaways. The fifteen minutes it normally took to drive to town became less than ten. We passed an SUV; the driver flipped me the bird. I don't know why I thought that was funny, yet I laughed just the same.

Alexander spoke to me from the backseat. His voice was tinged with concern.

"This happened once before," he said. "Right after we were married. Eden hadn't known she was allergic to honeybees because she had never been stung by one before."

Honeybees! my inner voice repeated. *Damn!*

My right hand began to tremble on the steering wheel. I tried to ignore it.

"Was she stung at the castle?" I asked aloud.

"No, no. It was during a demonstration at Reconciliation Park in Mankato. A demonstration for Native American rights where they hung all those Dakota warriors. There were hundreds of people there, including cops and county deputies. A lot of back-and-forth, you know? People getting into each other's faces. Yet when she collapsed, it was a deputy that got Eden the medicine she needed to save her life."

He started laughing.

"That's funny?" I said.

"After the cops saved her, they arrested her; charged with disorderly conduct and failure to disperse. Please hurry."

A few minutes later, I skidded to a halt in front of the emergency entrance of Redding Memorial Hospital. We were sliding

Eden out of the backseat when a couple of the hospital's emergency staff appeared with a gurney as if they had been waiting for us.

"What do we have?" one of them asked.

"I think my wife's in anaphylactic shock," Alexander Redding answered. "I think she was stung by a bee."

Eden was placed on the gurney and they started pushing her toward the entrance to the hospital.

Alexander followed behind.

I watched them go, a feeling of terror deep in my stomach. *Stung by honeybees.*

A tech who had remained outside nodded at me with his chin. "Move your car," he said. "And get a mask.'

It took a few minutes to park the Mustang and a few more to work my way through the hospital to the emergency room. Every person inside Redding Memorial was wearing a mask, me included. I chatted briefly with a woman at the reception desk before I was directed to a room off a well-lit corridor. I fought the impulse to run to the room. Instead, I walked rapidly. *Hurry, don't rush.* I stepped inside and found Eden Redding sitting up in bed. Her yoga pants had been removed and an ice pack was resting on her thigh where, apparently, she had been stung.

Alexander was standing next to the bed and holding Eden's left hand. A device that resembled a white plastic clothespin was clamped to the middle finger of her right hand. The clothespin was attached to a white wire that ran to a monitor fixed to the wall above her head. A female doctor dressed in blue scrubs was reading the wavy red, blue, and white lines and the flashing numbers displayed by the monitor.

Eden looked up at me. I couldn't see her face behind her mask, yet I knew she was smiling.

"Well," she said. "That was terrifying."

Instead of being relieved, I was confused.

"You're all right?" I asked.

The sound of my voice and the expression in my eyes must have hinted at my confusion.

The doctor diverted her attention from the monitor to me.

"Are you McKenzie?" she asked.

I nodded.

"You got her here just in time," she said.

"I did?"

"We gave her a shot of epinephrine. Usually it doesn't take much more than a few minutes to counteract the allergic reaction, fifteen minutes tops. Given her condition when I first saw her, I thought that we might need to introduce intravenous fluids; perhaps even give her oxygen, yet that all proved unnecessary."

"I feel much better," Eden said.

"Your vitals are already very strong. Still, a close call, wasn't it? Listen, we'd like you to stay in the ER for a couple of hours in case one dose wasn't enough to reverse the allergic reaction. You might even consider staying overnight."

"I had a bad reaction to a bee sting once before," Eden said. "Epinephrine fixed me right up back then, too."

"You should carry an epinephrine sting kit," the doctor said.

"I did for years. An EpiPen. Only it happened so long ago, when I was stung, that I just fell out of the habit."

The doctor patted Eden's hand.

"Get back into it," she said. "I'll give you the names of a couple of providers I'd recommend before you leave."

"Thank you."

The doctor turned to exit the room but paused before she passed me. She rested a hand on my wrist.

"Well done," she said.

I nodded because I didn't know what else to do.

The doctor left.

Eden kept smiling at me behind her mask.

"I don't know how to thank you," she said.

"It was nothing."

"Nothing?"

"I didn't mean it that way. I meant—I'm happy I could help."

"I've been involved in social justice issues nearly my entire life—feminism, civil rights, multiculturalism. I've met people—the most helpful, the most heroic of them have always seemed to be most self-effacing. Why is that?"

"Because they don't think what they're doing is heroic? Just a guess."

"I'm grateful to you, McKenzie. I always will be."

"Do you guys need a ride back to the castle?"

"I've already spoken to my brother," Alexander said. "Ben will come get us when Eden is ready to leave."

"I'm sure the family is having a big laugh at my expense," Eden said. "Like the last time. Everyone thought that it was so funny; Ben and Annie. None of them could imagine being over twenty-five years old without ever having been stung by a bee."

"Well, you did live a sheltered life," Alexander said.

They both laughed at that; a private joke that I wasn't invited to share.

"Even Tess thought it was funny," Eden told me. "Once she knew I was going to be all right, anyway; making jokes about avoiding Ben and Annie's beehives; not eating the honey. I think the family was especially delighted that I was stung during a protest march. The big-city liberal socialist—that'll teach me."

"If that's what they thought, then they're all jerks," I said.

"Thank you for that, too, McKenzie."

"You're welcome."

We talked a little bit more after that, replaying the events of the morning, joking; coming down from the high. Eventually, I made my good-byes and turned to leave. Alexander intercepted me.

"McKenzie," he said.

I offered my hand; he gave me a hug.

"Thank you," he said.

"It was my pleasure."

I have to admit, I was feeling pretty good about myself as I approached the exit of the emergency room. The glass doors slid open. They weren't triggered by me, though, but instead by Barbara Finne, who was moving so fast when she entered the hospital that she nearly ran into me. She recognized me immediately and stopped.

"McKenzie," she said.

"Ms. Finne."

"Wow. I asked you for a story, but really."

"It's not my story."

She brought her hand up and slowly drew it above her head as if she was imagining the front-page headline on the next edition of the *Redding Weekly Bulletin*.

"Life of Redding heir saved by the quick thinking and fast driving of retired big-city cop," she said.

"A little clunky, don't you think?"

"It's a working title."

"Eden's fine, by the way."

"I know. I'm here to interview her."

"You seem pretty well informed." I glanced at my watch. "We couldn't have been here more than forty-five minutes."

"I have an army of news sources and like I said—anything to do with the Redding family is big news."

"Apparently, you have sources at the castle, too?"

Barbara tilted her head and gazed at me as if she was trying to figure out what I was talking about.

"Oh," she said. "Nina Truhler. So tell me, what did you think of my piece?"

"Nothing good."

"Come now . . ."

"I thought we had an agreement. Everything off the record."

"McKenzie, did I print a single word about what we discussed in private?"

"No, but you wrote that I was in town. You wrote that I was asking questions."

"What was I supposed to do, ignore what everyone else could see for themselves? People saw you talking to Chief Gardner; they saw you speaking with Dr. Evers. They saw your wife working in the castle. That wasn't off the record. Only what you said to me was off the record—for now."

"I suppose."

"Speaking of which . . ." Barbara dipped into the bag that hung from her shoulder and pulled out a notebook and pen. "Do you have anything to say for the record?"

"Not really."

"You saved a woman's life."

"No. The emergency room people saved her life. I just drove the car."

"More than that, I think."

"Honestly, Barbara, I'm just glad I could help out."

"I checked on you—remember, I told you that I would. Not just the internet, either. I made some calls to contacts in the Cities. It seems you make a habit of—what did you call it? Helping out?"

The words came to me—"Live well, be useful"—something I liked to say when people asked me why I did the things I do. Yet for some reason I couldn't bring myself to repeat them out loud to a reporter who would print them in a newspaper. Instead, I patted Barbara's shoulder and walked past her to the exit. The glass doors slid open again.

I heard her voice behind me.

"McKenzie, c'mon," Barbara said.

"You need to put on a mask."

And the glass doors slid shut behind me.

I climbed inside my Mustang and headed back to the Redding Castle at roughly the posted speed limit. I was halfway there when I realized I was actually rocking back and forth in my seat. My hands were trembling on the steering wheel. I knew why. Nervous energy. And not just because of the fast and furious drive to the hospital. I hadn't said anything to Eden and Alexander, and I sure as hell wasn't going to admit it to Barbara Finne, but I was frightened of bees. Make that terrified of bees. Way worse than my fear of heights. Ever since a swarm of them stung me sixteen times for the unpardonable act of hitting a hive with a football.

The hive had been part of an apiary, what they call a beeyard, located behind the house owned by Mr. Moseley, a friend of my father's. I was twelve years old and no, I didn't do it on purpose to see what would happen despite what my father might have suggested at the time. The way I remembered it, the honeybees rose up like a cloud in a Looney Tunes cartoon, formed a distinct arrow that was pointed directly at me, and swooped down. Still, it could have been much worse. Mr. Moseley had kept roughly three million honeybees. I could have been killed.

Eden Redding could have been killed, too.

People knew she was allergic to bees; her family.

Her enemies.

Hmm . . .

What? my inner voice asked.

I activated my on-board computer and asked aloud "What attracts bees to humans?"

The computer replied: *Bees are attracted to bright colors and certain smells. In most cases, they set their sights on flowers. However, they will investigate a human if you resemble a flower. Brightly colored clothing and sticky hands are perfect triggers for busy bees . . .*

"Sticky hands?"

I drove another half mile before I asked "How can I attract honeybees?"

In a very short time, a bowl of sugar water could attract hundreds of bees. Not only do these bees not visit and pollinate flowers, but the honeybees will store the sugar water in their hive along with honey essentially watering down the honey.

I pulled into the parking lot of the castle, shut down the car, and gave it a moment's thought before saying "Anything's possible" out loud. I exited the Mustang and began walking across the clearing. Jenness Crawford must have seen me through a window of the castle because the front door flew open and she dashed down the steps, intercepting me halfway to the General Oglesby Cabin.

She seemed genuinely concerned.

"Is Eden all right?" she asked.

"Yes. I just left her. She's fine. She actually seems very cheerful about all of this."

"What happened? I know you took her to the hospital; Alex called Ben and he told me, but what happened?"

I explained, starting with finding Eden lying on the ground and ending with my meeting with Barbara Finne.

"So, it's going to be in the newspaper," Jenness said. "That's great, just great. What else could go wrong?"

"It's not that bad."

"No, it's awful. Just damn awful. People are going to think we're overrun with killer bees; that'll be great for business. And Eden . . ."

"Eden is fine, I told you."

"Eden nearly died because she was stung by a bee. Now she's going to want to sell this place even more. Dammit."

Jenness turned and started beating a path back toward the castle. While she was going, Nina was coming. They spoke for a few seconds—nothing that I could hear—and when Jenness moved on Nina strolled to where I was standing. She didn't say a word until she wrapped her arms around me and hugged me tight.

"My hero," she said.

"I wish people would stop saying that."

"You saved another damsel in distress. How many is that now?"

"Who keeps track?"

"God, I love you so much."

"Now that's something I never get tired of hearing."

"What happened exactly?"

I told her.

"I get why Jenny's so upset," Nina said.

"I do, too, but honestly, you need to look at the bright side—no one died."

"So, there's that. McKenzie, I need to get back. I've been reviewing the castle's procurement procedures. So far they look pretty good to me. Damn, I'm so proud of you."

Nina spun and started moving back toward the castle. I called to her.

"Hey."

She looked over her shoulder at me.

"What?" she asked.

"Nothing. Just hey."

"I'll bring lunch to the cabin. We can eat alone—far from the madding crowd. Okay?"

"Okay."

I continued walking to the General Oglesby Cabin. It was about the same size as the one Nina and I had been using, except that it had a six-foot wooden porch and stained wood siding. The door was still open; Alexander Redding had left it that way when we carried Eden to my car that morning. I peeked inside and saw a black woodstove surrounded by rocking chairs. I closed the door and slowly circled the cabin twice without knowing what I was looking for.

Behind the cabin was a narrow dirt path that I followed to a clearing carpeted with yellow, white, purple, and blue wildflowers. In the center of the clearing I discovered the remains of Anna and Big Ben Redding's beehives along with a shack about the size of an outhouse that had been used for storage. It reminded me of the apiary at Mr. Moseley's house except it was considerably smaller and unkempt, as if the wooden hives had been standing idle for many years. I searched carefully for any sign of honeybees—trust me on that—yet discovered only a couple dancing around flowers far enough away that I was able to resist fleeing for my life.

I turned and followed the path back toward the cabin. Along the way, I found an empty white plastic tub; its blue label told me that it had once contained whipped cream. It was sitting just off the path near the edge of the woods. Given the pristine condition of the grounds, I was surprised to find it; I had seen no litter of any kind since I arrived at the castle.

I picked up the tub and sniffed the inside.

It smelled like plastic.

I ran my index finger along the inner edge and licked it.

It tasted like my finger.

Yet, I wondered—is it possible that someone deliberately attracted honeybees to Eden's cabin door using sugar water or some other enticement with the hope that one might sting and kill her?

Wait. What? First, a woman is murdered in her sleep in a locked bedroom and now a woman is assaulted by honeybees that were lured to her cabin? Do you know how insane that sounds?

Highly implausible, not insane.

Not even a five-time Tony Award–winning actress with six Golden Globes, plus eighteen Emmy and three Oscar nominations like, oh, I don't know, Angela Lansbury, could read that line with a straight face.

SEVEN

I didn't feel tired until I saw the rocking chair in front of the fireplace inside the James J. Hill Cabin. I set the plastic tub on the small kitchen table and sat myself in the chair, stretched out and closed my eyes.

It's not even noon yet, my inner voice reminded me.

"Must be all this fresh country air I've been breathing," I said aloud.

I started rocking up and down until I realized that I was in serious danger of falling asleep.

Can't have that.

I stopped rocking and sat up—*no rest for the weary*—and pulled my cell phone from my pocket. I scrolled through my contacts, found the name I was looking for, and tapped the icon. Like most people these days, I didn't know anyone's phone numbers except my own and the number for the house in St. Paul where I grew up when I was a kid.

I waited for a few moments until a woman's voice answered.

"Now what?" she asked.

"Why is it that every time I call, you make it sound like I'm imposing on you?"

"Because you are. I was sitting on the deck, drinking tea, enjoying the morning, and now this."

"Swear to God, H, if you hadn't tripled my money in the past eight years, I'd be annoyed."

"But I did and you love me so what do you want?"

I could picture the scowl on H. B. Sutton's face. Yet, despite her brusque manner she was actually quite pleasant to be around once you got to know her. Or, I should say, once she got to know you. I blamed her flower children parents for her reticence. They thought they were being cute when they named their daughter Heavenly-love Bambi. Instead, they doomed her to a life of teasing and mockery.

"Try growing up with a name like that, especially while wearing the peasant blouses and skirts my parents dressed me in, the flat sandals," she once told me. "Try going to high school or college; try getting a job; try being taken seriously by anybody."

When she reached an age where she could make her own decisions, she stopped using the name. She had once nearly been tossed out of grade school—grade school!—for refusing to answer to Heavenly-love during roll call. Instead she became H.B., or simply "H" to the few people she called friends.

H became an economist because money was one of the few things that everybody took seriously and eventually a financial adviser because she preferred to work alone. She lived on a houseboat moored to a pier on the Mississippi River next to Harriet Island in St. Paul because—well, that I could never quite figure out. Visiting her had always made me feel uncomfortable. Not as uncomfortable as heights or honeybees, still . . .

H called it "the earthquake effect." The idea that the deck is constantly shifting beneath our feet; that any unseen wave could make your world bob up and down. Some people find it very disconcerting, she once told me.

"Seriously, McKenzie, what can I do for you?" she asked.

"I want to talk about the hospitality industry."

"I told you before, the best thing Rickie's has going for it is its lack of debt . . ."

"I got that."

"Assuming customer expectations haven't dramatically changed, and I don't think they have . . ."

"H—"

"The economics will continue to improve as the pandemic fades and restaurants and clubs will regain the footing they lost."

"I'm not talking about Rickie's. Nina and I are all in on Rickie's no matter what, anyway."

"What are you talking about?" H asked.

"Hotels, resorts."

"Oh, they're screwed."

"Really?"

"I don't have the latest numbers in front of me, but I'd be willing to bet that over half of the hotels across the country are still at or below the threshold where they can break even and pay back debt. Drive-to leisure destinations with a strong weekend clientele . . ."

Like Redding Castle, my inner voice told me.

"Are faring better than the corporate-centered properties where attendance at weeklong business conferences constituted a major part of their profits, but all in all, it's a terrible time to be in that business. We've already seen a lot of properties pushed into foreclosure or some type of forced sale and I expect the trend to continue. In fact, I don't believe the industry will regain its pre-COVID numbers for at least another couple of years. Reuters predicts it'll take three, maybe four."

"What'll it take to stay alive until then?" I asked.

"Like I said—it's all about debt. In an environment of dramatically lower revenues, high fixed costs, less-than-optimal asset returns, and the need to conserve capital, hospitality organizations will need to determine which areas to prioritize and invest in. They will need to find the right balance between investment and conservation, one that achieves the highest ROI in the near to medium term."

"I'm not entirely sure what all that means . . ."

"The people who can keep paying their bills will survive; the ones that can't will die. McKenzie?"

"H?"

"You're not thinking of investing in a hotel, are you?"

"If I were, what would you say?"

"As your financial adviser, I would tell you that I don't recommend adding a hotel to your portfolio at this time. Listen, as with any major disruption like the one we're seeing in the hospitality industry, there will be opportunities to capitalize if you have the means to do so. At the moment, though, there are just too many unknown variables. Besides, you've never been that kind of investor."

"What about as my friend?"

"As your friend I'd say, Are you outta your damn mind? You'd be better off taking your money to Vegas and betting it on red."

"What if I owned a hotel, a resort really, and I had an opportunity to sell it for a big payday?"

"Take it."

"That's your professional advice?"

"Unless you're Nina and you built Rickie's from nothing and you love it like a child, then I'd tell you to hang on for dear life. Money is important, McKenzie, but it isn't always about money. You're an old movie guy. What's the line from *Citizen Kane*— 'It's no trick to make a lot of money if all you want is to make a lot of money'? Most people want something more."

"You've become a philosopher in your old age, H."

"Who are you calling old?"

I was deeply immersed in the book I found on top of the mantel above the fireplace—*Rolling Sunset: The History of Redding Castle*—when Nina burst through the cabin door.

"I have Dracula wine," she said. "And sandwiches. BLT for you and smoked turkey for me unless you want to trade."

"No, no, I'm good."

Nina set her bag on the small kitchen table and picked up the white plastic tub.

"What's this" she asked.

"A clue."

"A clue?"

"Or not."

"You know, the castle makes its own whipped cream."

"A clue then."

Nina stared at me for a moment as if she was waiting for me to explain only the more I thought about it the more silly it sounded, so I didn't say a word. Nina set the tub on the counter. I pulled up a chair as she distributed the sandwiches and poured the wine from a bottle she had opened before arriving.

"So, anything interesting happen since I saw you last?" Nina asked.

"Same old, same old. How 'bout you?"

"I might have found a way to save the castle or guarantee its destruction. It's a little unclear."

"Do tell," I said.

"I've been poring over Jenny's books. The castle has enormous fixed and variable costs—license fees, insurance premiums, property taxes, wages, payroll taxes, health care, utilities, cable, phone, what else? Food. Liquor. Right now she's not only generating enough revenue to remain afloat, she's making a small profit, except it's not going to be enough. Even during the best of times, Jen told me that winter was a slow period for the castle. Because of last year and the year she's having now, Jen hasn't been able to set aside enough money in a reserve account to get through it. It's possible to secure a line of credit from a bank, but the way things are, the interest rates would be unacceptable."

"H. B. Sutton said pretty much the same thing about the hospitality business in general," I said.

"When did you talk to H?"

"About an hour ago. Just so you know—she does not recommend that we invest in the castle."

"God, no," Nina said. "We have enough problems keeping our own business afloat."

I always like it when she says *we*.

"I'm beginning to think that's the real reason Jen asked us to come here," Nina added. "To convince us to invest. But what would we be investing in? It's not her castle. It belongs to the Sibs. She just works here. Fortunately, she doesn't need investors."

"She doesn't?"

"That's what I discovered. Honestly, I don't know why Jenness never saw it herself. She walks past it every day. I looked right at it myself and didn't see it. Neither did you."

"See what?"

"She has disposable assets that she can use to finance the castle until the hospitality industry fully recovers."

"What assets?" I asked.

"The art hanging in the castle's gallery. The Remington and Whistler and illustrations by Thomas Nast. It didn't occur to me until I saw an appraisal that Tess had commissioned years ago for insurance purposes. At the time, the Remington painting was valued at four hundred thousand dollars. The pastel by

Whistler—half a million. At least fifty thousand for the Nast. Plus the other art hanging on the walls, plus the piano, plus the chandeliers, plus the antiques, plus—the insurance company set the value at just under a million three. That's the appraised value. Who knows what it would all bring at auction. Probably a lot more."

"Wow."

"Wow is right," Nina said. "The Sibs, Jenness, they all grew up with this stuff. It never occurred to them to look at it as being more than just something their great-great-great-grandfather collected a hundred and fifty years ago. Either that or they just assumed that they were reprints, I don't know."

"Which raises the question—if some of the Sibs were willing to sell when their profit would be about $800,000 each, what will their attitude be if they suddenly realize it's at least a cool million?"

"Exactly the question Jenness asked. She sees the downside in everything these days. On the other hand, selling the Whistler alone, or just taking a loan out using it as collateral, would bring in more than enough for her to keep the castle going until life returns to normal."

"If the Sibs let her do that."

"A very big if. McKenzie, how is an empty whipped cream tub a clue?"

"Oh that. You'll think it's ridiculous."

"Try me."

I did.

"That is ridiculous," Nina said. "I mean, a honeybee hit man?"

"It's possible. Bees tried to kill me once."

"So I've been told—how many times?"

"It was a traumatic and emotional experience that I'm still struggling to cope with, thank you for your sympathy."

"Forget the honeybees for a minute. What would you have done if Eden had been struck by lightning?"

"I would probably have searched for a lightning rod," I said.

"It's kind of like cloud-watching, isn't it? Eventually, we always see what we're looking for."

"It's why innocent people sometimes go to prison."

"I think it's time we went home, McKenzie. Don't you? We're not accomplishing anything here and I worry about being away from Rickie's for too long."

"We could be back in Minneapolis in three hours."

"No, not yet. I promised I'd give Jenness all of my recommendations for the castle this afternoon; I've been keeping notes. Besides, I'd like to see that sunset one more time."

"Tomorrow then. First thing in the morning?"

Nina nodded and gathered up her sandwich wrapper.

"I need to get back to the castle," she said. "What are you going to do this afternoon?"

"Drive into Redding and say good-bye to my pal Dee."

"Meet me on the steps in front of the castle before sunset? If not sooner?"

"Sounds like a plan."

I took my own sweet time driving into Redding, actually staying within the posted speed limit for a change. The sun was shining, the birds were singing, it was seventy-five degrees in the shade without a cloud in the sky, and the entire world seemed bright and carefree—unless you looked closely. Then you could see the masks some citizens wore against the pandemic and the kid on the corner handing out flyers promoting racism and the dueling campaign signs espousing conflicting political views that allowed for no compromise and you'd realize how deceptive appearances could be.

I parked in front of the Redding city offices. Instead of going inside, though, I sat in the Mustang and sent a text.

"Busy?"

Less than a minute passed before Redding Police Chief Deidre Gardner replied—"30 mins."

"Java House?"

"C U there."

I left the Mustang and crossed Main Street. I was disappointed that there was no traffic to stop for me. Two blocks later, I reached the coffeehouse. A woman, both of her hands supporting a cardboard tray containing a half-dozen cardboard coffee cups with plastic lids, was using her shoulder to force the door open. I took hold of the handle and pulled.

"Got it," I said.

"Thank you," she answered.

She maneuvered past the sidewalk tables and the patrons sitting at them and turned up the street, her back to me. At no point did she see my face. Yet I had recognized hers instantly. She was the fortysomething woman that Olivia Redding had been conspiring with when Chief Gardner and I walked past the very same coffeehouse the day before. She was now wearing a white blouse, black pencil skirt, and black heels; her auburn hair bobbed up and down on her shoulders like gentle waves beating against the shore.

I decided to follow her; perhaps learn who she was because—well, because that's what I do.

The woman moved up Main Street and I thought she might be heading for the hospital. A block short of it, though, she hung a right and crossed the street. I was a couple of hundred yards behind her and not too worried that I would lose her in the bustling traffic because there wasn't any—until she rounded the corner of another one of Redding's ancient buildings and disappeared from my sight. My first thought was that she had made me. I moved quickly up the sidewalk and crossed the street myself, careful not to break into a full run for fear of attracting attention. I hugged the brown brick wall of the corner and glanced down the street she had taken. She was still moving unhurriedly toward her destination, wherever that was. I continued to follow.

The woman finally stopped. While hugging the cardboard tray to her chest with one hand, she tentatively reached for a door handle with the other. I nearly jogged to her side to help, yet restrained myself. Finally, she opened the door a half foot, caught the edge of it with the toe of her shoe, and used her now free hand to steady the tray. Using her foot and hip, she pushed open the door wide enough to slip inside. I kept moving forward, pretending to window-shop. When I reached her door I slowed considerably.

There were large windows in the front of the building that she had entered; it looked less like an office than a retail store. Inside, I could see the woman, her back to me still, as she distributed the coffee cups to five people who had gathered around her, keeping one for herself. They all appeared younger than she was except for an attractive woman sitting behind a reception desk who was at least a decade older, maybe more, with dusky red hair streaked with silver. When the tray was empty, the woman thrust it at the chest of a young man a full foot taller than she was. He took the tray and grinned and I was left with the impression that next time it was his turn to get the coffee.

The woman disappeared down a narrow corridor; I never did see her face except for the brief glance I had at the coffeehouse. The others quickly followed her, leaving only the receptionist. She saw me standing outside the window and smiled as if she was used to seeing strange men standing outside the window and looking at her. I gave her a nod and continued walking.

Instead of returning to Java House by the way I came, I decided to circle the block so that the receptionist wouldn't see me again. The last thing I needed was to be accused of stalking even though, technically, that's exactly what I was doing. As I strolled, I accessed the search app on my cell phone, typing in the name I saw printed on the glass door—Boeve Luxury, a Development Company.

The moment its website popped up on my screen, I remembered where I had seen the name before—a piece printed in the *Redding Weekly Bulletin* that Barbara Finne had sent to me, the one reporting that Boeve Luxury wanted to demolish Redding Castle and replace it with a tower of condominiums.

I perused the website. The "About Us" link told me that Cassandra Boeve had started her company nearly a decade earlier after spending the previous ten years working for a couple of fairly well-known architectural firms in the Cities, including one that had helped build Target Field for the Minnesota Twins. She was best known for designing luxury homes; there were photographs of three of them located on Lake Anpetuwi alone. She also developed an eighteen-unit apartment building in Willmar and a small retail complex in Marshall, both Minnesota towns less than an hour's drive from here. Yet she had built nothing that was nearly the size and scope of the project that she had proposed to replace Redding Castle.

Castles on Anpetuwi would have been a big step up for her, I told myself. I bet it broke Boeve's heart when Tess Redding announced that the castle was no longer for sale; that it would remain in the family. Although I suspected that she was somewhat less than teary-eyed when she learned later that Tess had died.

Oh, I don't know, my inner voice said. *Maybe that's why she was having coffee with Olivia Redding—she was expressing her condolences.*

The page designated "People" showed me photographs of Boeve and the rest of her staff along with their names, official titles, and résumés. The person I labeled as a receptionist was actually a "Principal—Office Administrator." Her name was Veronica Bickner and her résumé stated that she was a Redding native with a bachelor's degree in business administration from what was then called Mankato State University but was now known as Minnesota State. Before that she was elected "Prom Queen" of Redding High School Class of 1980.

Principal—does that mean she owns part of the business or that her job is to watch over the children?

Chief Gardner had already arrived at the Java House by the time I returned; she was standing near the door with her hands on her hips and looking around as if she had lost something. She saw me crossing Main Street. This time there was traffic and it actually stopped for me.

"There you are," she said. "I thought you blew me off."

"Never."

"So, where were you? What were you doing?"

"Buy you a cup of coffee, Dee?"

"Evading the question, that sounds promising."

Chief Gardner and I stepped inside the coffeehouse. The woman who served us must have remembered me from the day before, or at least she remembered my tip, because she was quite solicitous. Which earned her another big tip.

After we were served, the chief and I retired to an open table on the sidewalk where we sat facing the street. The kid, I remembered his name was Brian, was still attempting to pass out flyers on behalf of the Sons of Europa and not having much luck. Given the population of the town, I decided that he had probably already accosted everyone there was to accost.

"So, Jessica, have you broken the case yet?" the chief asked.

"Really? Is that going to be a thing, now?"

"I kinda like it. I thought I'd call LT and tell him you have a new nickname."

"Please don't."

Chief Gardner chuckled at that.

"Do you have anything new to report?" she asked.

I flashed on my theory that Eden Redding was a victim of attempted murder by honeybees and decided that there were some things that, once spoken aloud, a guy simply could never live down; that would follow him forever.

"Nothing at all, Dee," I said.

"Dammit, I was looking forward to being shown up by you."

"All right, all right. I just wanted to say good-bye. Nina and I are going home tomorrow."

"I've never met the woman, but she must be a saint being married to you."

"People keep saying that."

"Is it true that you were married in the Winter Carnival Ice Palace?"

"I know a guy."

"Bet you do."

"Dee, what can you tell me about a woman named Cassandra Boeve?"

"I can tell you that I work for her."

"Don't you work for everyone in Redding?" I waved a finger at her. "You can't give me a ticket; my taxes pay your salary."

"Except in Boeve's case, she's a member of the Redding City Council. She voted to hire me. Very enthusiastically, too."

"Being on the council—isn't that a conflict of interest?"

"Why? Because Boeve wants to buy Redding Castle and turn it into condominiums?"

"You know all about that?"

"I read the *Weekly Bulletin*, too, McKenzie."

"I followed her from the Java House to her office on Second Avenue."

"Why would you do that?"

"Because she's the woman that Olivia Redding was having coffee with yesterday when we walked by."

"I know."

"If you knew, why didn't you tell me?"

"Why didn't you ask, Jessica?"

I ignored the dig.

"Don't you think that it's interesting that she and Olivia were meeting?" I asked.

"That a woman who wants to buy some property was talking to a member of the family that owns the property? No, not particularly. Besides"—the chief took a long pull of her coffee—"there could be another reason for the meeting."

"Such as?"

"You're a baseball guy. What would you say if I told you that Cassandra Boeve was a switch-hitter; that she batted from both sides of the plate?"

I took a sip of my own coffee while I absorbed that tidbit of information.

"Do you know that for a fact?" I asked.

"I'm a seasoned investigator."

"Do you think that she and Olivia play on the same team?"

"It's possible. Why not?"

"For one thing, Olivia is at least twenty years older than Cassandra."

"Oh, puh-leez, McKenzie! Would you even think that if she were an older man hitting on a younger woman?"

"Probably not."

"Well, then."

"It would also explain why Olivia had dressed to look younger."

"Of course, there's another, even more reasonable explanation for why they were together."

"Such as?"

Chief Gardner leaned close to me and lowered her voice. "They're friends sharing a cup of coffee like, you know, you and me." She brought an index finger to her lips. "Shh."

"No, that can't possibly be it," I said.

Chief Gardner began to laugh and then I laughed, too. Nina was right about cloud-watching.

"Fucking Nazi!"

The slur started on the corner across the street and seemed to spread through Redding like ripples from a pebble someone tossed into a pond. Everyone within earshot turned to look as an older man dressed the way you'd expect a farmer to be dressed pushed young Brian with both hands, hitting him high in the chest. Brian deliberately put his hands behind his back as if he were afraid he might accidentally retaliate against his attacker. The old man pushed him again. And again. Until Brian tripped and fell backward; his flyers flew from his hand and littered the wide sidewalk.

"Is it starting already?" Chief Gardner asked.

I didn't understand the question; didn't have time to answer it, anyway.

The chief rose from the table and dashed across the street—without looking both ways first. I followed.

The old man was hovering above Brian and shouting.

"My father was killed fighting you fucking Nazis," he said. "You think I'm going to let you take over my town?"

He looked as if he was getting ready to use his boots when Chief Gardner put a heavy hand on his shoulder and pulled him back.

"Mr. Sorteberg," she said. "Mr. Sorteberg, what are you doing?"

"Look at that, look at that." Sorteberg pointed at an image printed on Brian's flyers. "What they call a *sonderrad*. It's a symbol of the fucking Nazis, just one step below the swastika."

"Stop saying that," Brian said.

He scrambled up from the sidewalk. I could have helped him, yet I didn't. Once standing, he clenched his fists. Chief Gardner moved between him and the old man.

"We're not Nazis," Brian said. "The Sons of Europa support strong white families, that's all. We're trying to protect white people."

"Listen to this shit," Sorteberg said.

Brian pointed at him.

"He should be arrested," he said. "He should be arrested for assault."

"You started it," Sorteberg said.

"That's a lie."

"Stop it, both of you," Chief Gardner said.

"You saw what he did. He pushed me, but I never pushed him back, I never raised my hand, you saw."

"Brian . . ."

"Brian? Brian? He's Mr. Sorteberg, but I'm Brian?"

"Mr. Hermes, then."

"Who's side are you on?" Sorteberg asked. "Calling this Nazi mister? You were appointed by the city and you can be un-appointed."

"Stop it."

"You don't tell me—"

Chief Gardner raised her hand like she was drawing a gun and pointed a finger in the old man's face.

"I said stop it," she said.

She turned to face Brian Hermes.

"And you . . ." she said.

"I didn't do anything wrong," Hermes said.

I recited from memory—"Whoever commits an act knowing or having reasonable grounds to know that it will, or will tend to, alarm, anger or disturb others or provoke an assault or breach of the peace, is guilty of disorderly conduct, which is a misdemeanor."

They all stared at me.

"Ninety days or a thousand-dollar fine or both," I added.

"That's crazy," Hermes said.

"I can arrest you both and let a judge decide what's crazy," Chief Gardner said. "Or I can let you both go your separate ways."

"He attacked me," Hermes said.

"Think about it—do your people want this to happen?"

"He doesn't have any people," Sorteberg said. "His family's disowned him."

"Shut up," Hermes said.

"You broke your mother's heart."

"Shut up, shut up."

"Get out of here—*Mr.* Sorteberg," Chief Gardner said.

Sorteberg snorted, actually snorted.

"I'll remember this, Chief," he said.

He spun on his heels and walked away. Chief Gardner turned to face Hermes. His eyes were wet and shiny.

What Sorteberg said about his mother must have really hurt, my inner voice decided.

"Mr. Hermes," the chief said. "You, too."

Hermes nodded.

"And pick up your damned flyers."

Chief Gardner and I turned to recross Main Street. This time the traffic didn't stop. An SUV nearly hit us; Chief Gardner was both surprised and angry yet did not voice her feelings.

"You said, 'Is it starting already?'" I reminded her.

"Did I?"

"When you saw Sorteberg shoving the kid."

"McKenzie, I have this ache deep in my stomach that won't go away. It tells me that this is going to get much worse before it gets better, assuming it ever gets better. The Sons claim that they have seven hundred followers scattered over fifteen states; that's the number they gave out. I bet six hundred and eighty are from outside Redding who don't give a damn about Redding or the people who live here. The twenty who do live here—we're going to have our own little race riot, sure as hell. It's just a matter of time."

By then we had reached the Java House. The owner had already cleared our half-finished coffees off the sidewalk table.

"So, tell me, Dee," I said. "Why exactly did you leave Minneapolis again?"

EIGHT

Eden Redding was holding court from a lawn chair set near the General Oglesby Cabin, her husband by her side. Two other people were sitting and one was standing in a half circle around her. As I walked near, I heard a woman say, "I keep searching the sky for honeybees. I'm amazed that you would even step outside much less sit in a chair not far from where you were stung."

"He who is not every day conquering some fear has not learned the secret of life," Eden said.

There was a pause in the conversation as if her audience was confused by Eden's remark.

Carly Redding was the person standing at the edge of the circle.

"Is that another one of those pretentious quotes you like to drop on us community college grads?" she asked.

"You say that like you're embarrassed," Alex Redding said. "You could have gone to the U like the rest of us. Or the University of Colorado like Anna."

"Then I would have turned out like the rest of you."

"Ralph Waldo Emerson," I said.

They all turned to look at me.

"The quote," I said. "Ralph Waldo Emerson."

"McKenzie," Eden said.

She rose from her chair and quickly bisected the circle to reach me.

"Let me guess," Carly said. "You went to college, too."

"As a matter of fact, I'm a Golden Gopher like your aunts and uncles."

"McKenzie," Eden repeated as she hugged me. "Thank you, again."

"Are we going to do this every time we meet?"

"Probably. By the way, you were right, it was Emerson."

Eden took my hand and pivoted back toward the others. Everyone was watching us except Carly, who found something in the woods to fix her attention on.

"This is McKenzie," she said. "He's the one who saved my life."

"I didn't actually save your life," I said.

"You got her to where it could be saved," Alex Redding said. "In the nick of time, the doctor told us." He also rose from his chair and crossed to my side. He didn't hug me, though, merely shook my hand.

The woman who was speaking when I first arrived also rose from her chair. The man sitting next to her stood as well.

"You seem to be doing a lot for the Redding family," the woman said. "First Jenny and now Eden."

"Actually, my wife is helping Jenness. I'm just hanging around, enjoying the castle."

"Enjoy it while you can," Carly said.

She continued to stare into the forest and for a moment I wondered if she was attempting to conjure a swarm of honeybees. I dismissed the idea when I realized that, when it came to the castle, she and Eden were on the same team.

The woman offered her hand and I shook it.

"I'm Jenny's mother." There was a tinkle of pride in her voice as if it was something she enjoyed saying. "I'm Marian Crawford. Please call me Mari. This is my husband, Edward."

He looked me in the eye and gave me a Minnesota Nice head nod; the one that said we're all in this together; there's no need to talk about it.

"Ed," he said.

"Ed," I repeated.

"Aren't we all just the best of friends now?" Carly said.

"Ms. Zumwalt," I said. "We've never been formally introduced."

"I know who you are."

"I know you, too."

The remark seemed to surprise her and not in a good way.

"What do you know?" she asked.

"Only what Maddie told me."

"Oh, okay." The defensiveness I had detected in her voice and body language softened as if she knew that her daughter would never speak ill of her. "When did you see Maddie?"

"This morning. We were both jogging around the castle."

Carly nodded as if it all made perfect sense to her.

"Apparently, it's one of her favorite things to do," I added.

"I am sorry about taking that away from her, but we can't have everything."

"I'll be sorry to see the old place go, too," Mari said. "We've had many, many wonderful times here."

"Speak for yourself," Carly said.

"Wait," I said. "Mari, are you voting to sell the castle, too?"

"Did Jenny tell you about the vote?"

"Yes, but she thinks you're on her side."

"I'm sorry."

I noticed, though, that Mari didn't explain exactly what she was sorry for.

"The money's just too good to pass up." Ed draped a strong arm around his wife's shoulder and gave her a squeeze. "Don't mean we don't love Jenny. Don't mean we don't appreciate what she's tryin' t' do. You know, McKenzie, we're farmers." He spoke with the same pride that Mari had for their daughter. "We have close to five hundred acres northwest of town; a little more than most. We do a little better than most, too. Netted over eighty thousand last year, a good year; mostly soybeans and corn, some beets."

"How much of that was in government handouts?" Carly wanted to know.

Ed glared at her like she had called him a particularly dirty name.

"Wouldn't be a problem if the government would just stay out of it, let the free market swing." Ed returned his gaze to meet mine. "But they're making it all political. Gotta punish China, gotta punish the EU; all those tariffs ends up punishing us. Russians invaded Afghanistan back in '79 . . ."

"Here we go," Carly said.

"Jimmy Carter enacted a grain embargo in response." Ed's voice grew in volume and intensity. "What did the Russians do? Started getting their grain from Argentina, Brazil, Canada even; started growing it themselves in the Ukraine. Here, prices plummeted. Thousands lost their farms. Thousands. My old man, he'd tell you he was lucky t' stay on his feet back then; one of the lucky ones. And that market, the grain market, it never went back to what it was."

"Honey," Mari said.

Ed gave her a slight smile and a head nod.

"What I'm sayin' . . ." Ed's voice returned to his just-folks roots. "The money from the castle and them paintings . . ."

Jenness must have told them about her plans for the artwork, my inner voice decided.

"That'd be a nice somethin' to hold on to in case history repeats itself."

"Yeah, I get it," I said.

"You know farming?"

I flashed on what H. B. Sutton had told me earlier that morning about Rickie's.

"I know about hanging on to what you love," I said.

Ed gave me another Minnesota Nice head nod, this one telling me that we understood each other.

"Jenness will understand, too," Eden said. All that time, she had continued to hold my hand.

"I don't know," Mari said. "She's a lot like you. She's fierce when it comes to something that she believes in and she believes in the castle."

"She'll get over it," Carly said. "Everyone will. We'll tear it all down and forget it ever existed."

"Why do you always have to be such a—" Alex said but didn't finish.

"Such a what?"

"Never mind."

"What?"

"This is where we grew up," Mari said. "This is where our parents grew up and grandparents and all the Reddings for over one hundred and thirty-five years. How can you be so—"

Mari didn't finish, either.

"What?"

"Such a bitch," Eden said. "Everyone bites their tongue around you because they don't want to make you angry, but you're always angry. Why is that?"

"Maybe it has something to do with my childhood," Carly said.

She turned and marched off toward the castle, got halfway

there, paused, and veered off to the parking lot instead. Moments later, she climbed inside a car, started it up, and drove off.

"What a pill," Alex said. "How is it possible she and Maddie are so different? Carly is angry at everyone and everything. But her daughter—Madison might be the most competitive person I know and that includes Big Ben and Anna . . ."

Everyone laughed except me.

"Yet she's also one of the kindest people I know," Alex added.

"It's this place," Mari said. "The castle. And us. Madison told me once that Carly never behaves like this at home; that she's not like this anywhere else except here, except around us. It's as if she reverts back to when we were kids and we didn't have time for her, when we were always ignoring her or telling her how dumb she was."

"That was Ben and Anna."

"We didn't exactly rush to her defense, though, did we?"

"That's because they were calling us dumb, too," Alex said.

"True."

"Still doesn't explain Maddie."

"Tess," Mari said.

They all nodded in agreement and smiled, too, as if that one word said it all.

"Tess," Mari repeated. "I can't say she was a great mother to Carly because I think she was exhausted from raising children by the time she came along. But she was a terrific grandmother to Maddie."

"And Jenny," Ed said.

Eden gave my hand a shake and released it.

"McKenzie," she said. "Now you know that the Reddings are just as messed up as any other family you've ever come across. Maybe just as messed up as yours."

"I was an only child," I said.

"That must have been nice," Alex said.

"Hey," Mari said and gave him a shove.

"I wonder what John Redding would have thought about all of this," Eden said.

"And all the Reddings that came after him," Alex added.

"About Jenness," I said. "It's none of my business, I know, but you really ought to tell her your plans."

Mari looked away while Ed stared directly at me.

"Do you have children?" he asked.

"No."

"Uh-huh."

His meaning was clear—if I didn't have children myself, I certainly had no right to tell others how to raise theirs.

"It's like I told you before," I said. "I know about hanging on to what you love."

Ed looked away. A moment later, his head turned and he gave me another Minnesota Nice nod, this one telling me that I had made a good point.

"Nothin' for sure yet," he said. "If the offer ain't what we expect, we'll see."

"He's right, though," Mari said. "We should tell her."

"We'll see," Ed repeated.

No one had much to say after that until Alex announced, "I need a beer." His wife and in-laws decided they required refreshments as well.

"McKenzie, care to join us?" Eden asked.

"Thank you, but I have much to do," I said.

It wasn't true. It was just that I had had enough of the Redding family to last for a while.

I returned to the James J. Hill Cabin. There was half a bottle of Dracula wine left over from lunch and a copy of *Rolling Sunset:*

The History of Redding Castle. I sat in the rocking chair in front of the fireplace and indulged in both. About an hour later, Nina arrived.

"I thought you'd still be in town," she said.

"Dee and I ran out of things to say to each other. How 'bout you? I thought you'd be longer, too."

"I was giving Jenness my recommendations for making the castle more profitable when she announced that there didn't seem to be much point."

"Uh-oh."

"She had a long conversation with her parents before our meeting. Apparently, it didn't go well."

"They're voting to sell the castle."

"You knew?" Nina asked.

"I met them about an hour or so ago. They said it was just too much cash to pass up in these uncertain times. For what it's worth, H.B. would have advised them to take the money, too."

"I feel sorry for Jenness."

I held up the book for Nina to see.

"John Redding wouldn't have," I said. "He'd have been on the side of the developers."

"Do we have any wine left?"

I handed the bottle to her. There was a little less than a full glass remaining. She drank it straight from the bottle.

"Tell me," she said.

"John was an entrepreneur. Or an opportunist. Depends on your point of view. Oh, by the way—General Oglesby Cabin? It was named after Richard Oglesby who became a major general in the Civil War and later governor of Illinois. He was at the battles of Fort Henry, Fort Donelson, Corinth, Shiloh. His men loved him. Called him 'Uncle Dick.' One of his men was John Redding. Only Redding wasn't a frontline soldier. He was

Oglesby's quartermaster. His job was to get what the soldiers needed, when they needed it and where they needed it."

What I told Nina—John Redding grew up poor on a farm in Decatur, Illinois, the hometown of Uncle Dick. He left school to start clerking in a dry goods store at age twelve; apparently he was the only person the store's owner trusted to measure out the whiskey, rum, and wine for his customers. He worked his way up the ladder, changing jobs frequently, eventually becoming a supervisor for a general merchandise firm with stores scattered throughout the West, including one in St. Paul, where he became friendly with the Gunderson family. That becomes important later.

Eventually, the United States went to war with itself. Redding was drafted; "conscripted" they called it back then. He immediately began looking for someone he could hire to take his place; something you could do in those days. Only Uncle Dick stepped in. Oglesby had been appointed to lead the Eighth Illinois Volunteer Infantry Regiment and he needed a quartermaster. He knocked on Redding's door, so to speak, and that was that.

Meanwhile, the Dakota War of 1862 took place in Minnesota; this was only four years after it had become a state. The Dakota, also known as the Sioux, fought for all the reasons you'd expect Native Americans to rise up against the people who forced them onto reservations—the corruption of Indian agents, broken treaties, theft of Indian land, the cutting off of food and the money to buy it. When told that the Dakota were starving, one agent said, "So far as I am concerned, if they are hungry let them eat grass or their own dung." Of course the Dakota went to war; you would have, too.

The Dakota attacked settlers up and down the Minnesota River valley in the southwestern portion of the state, killing 358; they nearly burned New Ulm to the ground. The Minnesota Volunteer Infantry was soon formed and marched on the Dakota.

After much fighting, the Volunteers captured 1,600 Dakota, including women, children, and elderly men in addition to warriors. A military tribunal sentenced 303 to be executed, except President Abraham Lincoln stepped in and commuted the sentence of 265 of them. That left thirty-eight Dakota men to be hanged in Mankato—the largest mass execution in United States history.

The majority of the Dakota were expelled from Minnesota; most fled to the northern plains of what was then the Dakota Territory or Canada's Northwest Territories. At the same time, most of the white settlers had abandoned their homes and farms in the Minnesota River valley and fled east toward the Cities, leaving the area largely unoccupied.

When the Civil War finally ended, Colonel John Redding was left to wonder what to do with himself; somehow supervising someone else's general stores no longer appealed to him. It was about then that he received a letter from his good friends the Gundersons, who urged him to come for a visit. While he was in St. Paul, two things occurred that changed Redding's life. Thing one—he became reacquainted with Emily Gunderson, who had grown from a lanky child to "the most beautiful creature these war-weary eyes had ever beheld," John wrote in a letter. They were soon married. He was thirty-six. She was seventeen.

"Of course she was," Nina said.

Thing two—he met a fur buyer he had known before the wars. The American Fur Company had become very profitable while purchasing furs from the Dakota and white trappers around the Minnesota River valley, except the buyer told Redding that the business had all but disappeared following the uprising. If he had learned nothing during the Civil War, Redding had learned that one man's misfortune was another man's opportunity; H. B. Sutton had basically told me the same thing that morning.

"Let me guess," Nina said. "He took Horace Greeley's advice and went west to grow with the country."

"Oh, boy did he."

Redding took Emily to a settlement that was little more than forty people living in a half-dozen buildings at the intersection of the only two main roads in the area. He built a store. He began selling agricultural equipment to the farmers who returned to the valley. He worked with his pal James J. Hill to build a railroad to Redding from St. Paul.

"By the way, they had changed the name of the place to Redding a couple years after he arrived," I told Nina. "Redding insisted."

The railroad brought civilization to southwestern Minnesota. And more settlers. And more profits. The community grew larger and larger. Redding's stores grew bigger and bigger. He began buying and hauling grain. He began buying farms and flipping them. When his neighbors became more prosperous, he started a bank. And when he convinced Hill to extend the railroad to St. Cloud and to Watertown and Sioux Falls, South Dakota, ka-ching, ka-ching, ka-ching.

"My point is, if John Redding were alive today, he'd be the one trying to turn the castle into a tower of condominiums," I said.

"He became rich," Nina said.

"One of the wealthiest men in Minnesota."

"What happened to his money?"

"The Great Depression happened to his money. 'Course Redding had passed about fifteen years earlier and wasn't there to see it. His kids did as well as they could, only the family's wealth was tied too closely to many agricultural concerns and agriculture cratered. The bank failed, too. The Reddings went from the top one percent to the top ten percent, which was still pretty good but not what it was."

"And now the castle is all that's left of John Redding's legacy," Nina said. "The castle and his art collection."

"Easy come, easy go."

The remainder of the afternoon was spent mostly in kayaks with Nina and me enjoying the weather and each other's company as we paddled along the shoreline past the public boat landing up to the compound owned by the Sons of Europa. The same "Heimdall" was standing guard on the same dock dressed in the same white T-shirt and blue jeans and cradling the same AR-15 lightweight semiautomatic assault rifle.

"Good afternoon," Nina said to him as we slid past him. "Beautiful day, isn't it?"

He watched her carefully—I would have, too—before shifting his eyes to me. I gave him the Minnesota wave, which means I raised my hand slightly, my index finger extended as if I was going to point at something without actually pointing at anything.

He didn't react to either of us.

We kept paddling, moving a few hundred yards past the Tyr Haus before Nina said, "You know, I had never seen a person carrying a gun in real life until I started spending time with you."

"You're welcome," I said.

"I guess he's a guard, but what is he guarding against?"

"The giants."

"What giants?"

I explained about Asgard and the Gjallarhorn.

"Ragnarok," Nina said.

"You know about Norse mythology?"

"I saw the movie. Help me, but I liked Tom Hiddleston playing Loki more than Chris Hemsworth playing Thor."

"I noticed that you gravitate toward the bad boys."

Nina glanced over her shoulder at me and grinned.

"I'm pretty sure, though, it won't be the giants who destroy the world," she said. "It'll be the little people. They have less to lose."

We reached the midway point along the south shore when Nina decided we should paddle across the lake to the north side and follow it back to the castle. She was anxious that we didn't miss the sunset, yet I was sure we still had plenty of time and paddled slowly.

"It occurs to me, that after Ragnarok the world is supposed to be reborn rich and fertile," Nina said. "Plus, it'll be repopulated by two human survivors. Like Adam and Eve."

"Is that what they said in the movie?"

"My point—we should practice."

I started paddling faster.

Except practice was delayed by yet another spectacular sunset and dinner. Afterward, Nina took my hand.

"There's something I want to do," she said.

Instead of leading me to the James J. Hill Cabin as I had hoped, though, she took me inside the castle and guided me to the second floor. Minutes later we were standing inside the art gallery. Nina ignored the Remington, Whistler, and Nast illustrations, as well as the dozen cameos and small wall art pieces, and strode directly to the century-old Steinway grand piano. Standing above the keys, she took a deep breath, and began playing a few bars from a song I didn't recognize.

"Listen to that," she announced. "It's tuned. I didn't think it would be."

She sat on the piano bench and began playing. I thought she might play some jazz, but she chose Claude Debussy's "Clair de

Lune." At home when she played, I would grab a huge pillow with the logo of the Minnesota Twins, crawl under the piano, and listen. Only we were in a public space, after all, so I sat—oh so gently—on a love seat that might have been an antique. Nina went from Debussy to Tchaikovsky's "Waltz of the Flowers" before segueing into "Over the Rainbow" and my favorite song, "Summertime."

I didn't speak. I never spoke when Nina played, not even when she said things like "That doesn't quite work, does it?" or "What if I tried this?"

She started playing "Someday My Prince Will Come," laughed at herself, and switched to "'Round Midnight" by The- lonius Monk.

A woman stepped into the gallery and faced Nina and the piano. She was tall and thin with the stern expression of a no- nonsense high school algebra teacher and the posture of a ma- rine sentry and I thought: she's the one who should be guarding Asgard.

Nina spoke while she played.

"Am I disturbing you?" she asked.

"Not at all," the woman said. "I know that some people like that kind of music."

A smile tugged at the corners of Nina's mouth, yet she refused to let it form.

The woman turned her attention to the Remington. She leaned in close like an art critic examining the brushstrokes. After a few moments, she spoke as if she was expecting us to cherish every word.

"I always appreciated his sculptures more than his canvases," she said. "They're more naturalistic and rely less on the ethno- graphic realism found in his paintings."

Whatever that means, my inner voice said.

By then Nina had moved seamlessly into one of Chopin's

nocturnes. I had no idea which one; the man wrote twenty-seven. The woman straightened, closed her eyes, and tilted her head to the right as if she was remembering something. A slight smile formed on her lips, yet it quickly disappeared when she opened her eyes and saw me watching her.

"The love seat you're sitting on is over three hundred years old," she said.

"And still comfy," I said.

She stared for a moment and I honestly didn't know if she was trying hard to keep from smiling or screaming. She turned her attention to the Whistler. Once again she seemed incapable of keeping her opinions to herself.

"To his critics," she said, "Whistler's compositions seemed empty, his brushstrokes slapdash. I disagree, but perhaps I am unduly prejudiced, for his brushstrokes have always reminded me of my own fingerprints."

"Oh, were you busted?" I asked.

Sometimes you just can't help yourself, can you, McKenzie?

"Was I what?" she asked. "I will have you know, young man, that I was fingerprinted in accordance with the demands of the education department for which I was briefly employed while attaining my doctorate degree."

"Where did you go to school? Sing Sing?"

The woman glared at me as if her fight-or-flight response was fully engaged; she didn't know if she should tear me a new one or leave. While she was considering her options, Jenness Crawford came through the door and paused as she listened to the music.

"You play so well, Nina," she said. "You should play professionally. Everyone says so."

"I did when I was a kid; helped pay my way through college."

"Why did you quit?"

"I had just too many other things to worry about."

"Like Erica," Jenness said. "And the club."

Nina shrugged and continued to play.

"You should go back to it, playing professionally, I mean. Don't you think so, Anna?"

Anna Redding. The college professor. She's early.

The woman shrugged the same way Nina had and turned to stare at the Whistler some more.

"Have you met my friends?" Jenness asked. "This is Nina Truhler. I used to work for her. She taught me everything I know." She pointed at me. "This is McKenzie."

Anna nodded at us, yet did not speak.

"This is my favorite aunt, Anna Redding," Jenness said. "Dr. Redding."

"A pleasure," I said.

Nina kept playing the piano.

I stood up.

"Jenny, I'm afraid I've been sitting on your three-hundred-year-old love seat," I said.

"That's what it's for." Jenness turned back toward her aunt. "Nina and McKenzie have been trying to help me keep the castle operating."

"Unsuccessfully, it would seem, based on what you told me when I arrived," Anna said.

Wow.

Nina's response was to immediately switch from Chopin to a boogie-woogie number made famous by Meade Lux Lewis called "The Fives."

"Must you?" Anna said.

"I'm sorry," Nina said. "Was I being rude?"

"Like I told you, Anna," Jenness said. "These are my friends. And Nina's recommendations would work wonders if only the Sibs would allow me to implement them."

Nina slid effortlessly into the very slow, very romantic "I Can't Get Started (with You)." I always admired how she did that, moving from one song to another, one tempo to another, without ever taking her fingers off the piano keys.

"Obviously, a new strategy is required," Anna said. "Wouldn't you agree?"

"Do you have one?" Jenness asked.

"Let's just say I know my brothers and sisters and their spouses a little better than you do."

Whatever that means, my inner voice said.

Jenness gestured at the art gallery, yet I think she meant to include all of Redding Castle.

"I can't believe they want to give this up," she said.

"Dear girl," Anna said. "Dear, dear girl. We give up nothing. Come."

Anna Redding walked out of the art gallery as if she was marching down to the Army recruiting center to sign up. Jenness glanced at us, shrugged, and followed her aunt out the door.

Nina stopped playing.

"Any requests?" she asked.

I sang the lyrics from a song recorded by the Animals in the sixties—*We gotta get out of this place, if it's the last thing we ever do.*

"I don't know that one. How 'bout . . ."

Nina began playing the 1920s foxtrot "Ain't We Got Fun."

Eventually, we made our way back to the James J. Hill Cabin, where Nina asked if I was going to tie her to the chair and make her watch *The Thin Man* as I promised that morning.

"I'd be happy to tie you to the chair, but we don't need to watch the movie," I said. "We could do other things."

"No, I want to see it. I've been thinking about it all day."

"You have not."

"Seriously, can we get it on the computer?"

Yes, unfortunately, we could.

We laid next to each other on the love seat while we watched. My arm was around her shoulder; her head rested against my chest. It would have been perfect, except Nina had questions.

"Would the police really let Nick do all those things?"

"Shh."

"The actress playing Dorothy, isn't she the same one who played Jane in the Tarzan movies?"

"Shh."

"This doesn't make any sense. Why would Nick and Nora . . . ?"

"Shh."

When the film was over—"Actually, that was a lot more fun than I thought it would be. Should I tell you my favorite line?"

"Please."

"After Nick solved the murder, after he was nearly killed solving the murder, and Nora wrapped her arms around him . . ." Nina wrapped her arms around me. "And she said, 'I'm so glad you're not a detective.'"

And she kissed me.

And we made our way up the narrow staircase to the loft bedroom.

And we turned off the lamps.

And a light like the flames from a fireplace shimmered through the windows and danced against the walls.

"What is that?" Nina asked.

I quickly went down the stairs and pulled opened the cabin door.

"McKenzie?" Nina said.

"Someone erected a cross in the clearing and set it on fire."

NINE

On that Thursday morning in September in Minnesota, the sun rose at exactly six fifty-five. Chief Deidre Gardner had arrived twelve minutes before that time. She parked her black-and-white SUV in the lot and crossed the clearing to the bench where I was drinking coffee from a cardboard cup. The creases on her uniform shirt and slacks looked as if they could cut butter.

She stopped about twenty feet short of me and stared down at the partially burned wooden cross that was lying on the grass, much of it covered in sand. About two feet of it was still sticking out of the hole where it had been erected; the smooth surface on top of the wood showed where the chain saw had done its work.

I couldn't imagine what thoughts were dancing through her head and didn't dare ask.

Chief Gardner moved to the bench and sat next to me.

"Where's Holzt?" she asked.

"Restroom. Be nice to him. It's been a long night."

"You're here alone?"

"After we put out the fire, there wasn't much to do except throw accusations around. Your officer did what you told him to do. He shooed everyone back to their cabins or rooms and secured the scene."

"Everyone but you?"

"Phillip and I are friends now."

Chief Gardner continued to stare at the cross.

While we sat, a woman, Mrs. Doty I presumed, emerged from the cabin that she shared with her husband on the far side of the parking lot near the barn. She crossed the lot and followed the cobblestone path toward the entrance to the castle. She seemed to be watching us, yet that didn't slow her pace. The front door opened just as she reached it. Officer Holzt stepped across the threshold and held it for Mrs. Doty, who quickly disappeared inside. The officer closed the door and crossed the clearing to where Chief Gardner and I sat. He had a cardboard cup identical to mine and offered it to his boss.

"Coffee, Chief?" Holzt asked. "One sugar, one cream, right?"

Chief Gardner accepted the coffee.

"Thank you," she said. "That was very considerate."

"Suck-up," I said.

Holzt smiled in agreement.

"What else have you got for me?" the chief asked.

"Not much," he said. "Jimmy took about a hundred photos. He left at two fifteen. The fire department packed up and drove off ten, fifteen minutes earlier. I made sure everyone else left the area at around the same time. Since then I've been standing guard waiting for daylight. Waiting for you. Your friend McKenzie here has been keeping me company most of the night."

"What about the cross?"

"What about it?"

"What's it made of?"

"Well, Chief—wood."

"What kind of wood? Oak, maple, aspen, birch? Did someone cut a tree down and put it together in their backyard, or is it treated wood from a sawmill or lumberyard? What's holding it together? Nails? Bolts? Wire? Kite string? How heavy is it? Could one person have put this up or did it require two or more?"

Holzt knew that he was being tested and wasn't doing very well. He straightened and said, "I don't know."

Chief Gardner threw him a safety line.

"Is that because you didn't want to contaminate the crime scene?" she asked.

He refused to accept it.

"No, ma'am," he said. "I didn't think to look."

"Look now."

Holzt was clearly surprised by the instruction.

"Don't you want to have the sheriff's crime scene people look at it first?" he asked.

Chief Gardner gestured at the cross.

"Go 'head," she said.

Holzt bent to his task and examined the cross closely, brushing off the sand where it was in the way. I expected him to give us a running commentary, only he didn't. Instead, he took his time, keeping his thoughts to himself until they were fully formed.

"The base and the arms of the cross are both about four-by-six inches 'round and ten feet long," he said. "They look from a distance like they were carved with an ax, only they weren't. Up close you can see how it was trimmed by a saw; you can see the notches and the drill holes at each end. I'd bet the wood came from a lumberyard. Also, the base and arms are held together with two bolts and nuts set diagonally."

Holzt lifted the cross and rested it on his shoulder.

"It's not that heavy," he said. "I think one person could have done this, except . . ."

"Except what?" Chief Gardner asked.

"Except it's too cumbersome for one person to carry for any distance. Whoever put this up must have dragged it here."

"From where?"

The officer carefully returned the cross back to nearly exactly where he found it and began examining the ground around it.

"There's . . ." Holzt stooped to a spot near where the hole had been dug. "There's groove marks, ruts; I don't know what else to call them. Here in the ground."

"Where did they come from?" Chief Gardner asked.

Her officer pointed more or less at the corner where the parking lot met the road that led to it.

"That way," he said.

"Be sure."

Holzt began to follow the trail across the clearing toward the spot he had indicated. He moved slowly.

"He's all right," I said. "Idealistic. Wants to be a good cop. Thinks he's making the world a better place."

"You two must have had a nice long talk last night."

"You'll notice he's not behaving like you're punishing him or like he's doing you a favor; humoring his bitchy boss."

"Like you said, he's all right but young; has a lot to learn."

"Didn't we all?"

"Don't we all still?"

"You're not bringing in the county sheriff's department?"

"Have you met the sheriff? He's a glad-handing good-ol'-boy politician knows as much about law enforcement . . . He calls me Dee Dee. I'll call him for manpower if I need it, but not expertise."

Holzt followed the ruts the cross had made in the ground when it was dragged across the clearing to an area near where the large carved rock welcomed visitors to Redding Castle. He examined the ground and the asphalt driveway, yet appeared to find nothing. He rested his hands on his hips and looked up. Something caught his eye. He lowered his arms slowly and took several steps toward the parking lot while he continued to look up. He stopped, glanced right and left; examining the lights that hung from the poles located on each corner of the lot.

"He sees it," I said. "He's coming toward us. Look how happy he is. He wants to earn your respect and admiration. Uh-oh, he's slowing down. He's unsure now. Wait for it."

Officer Holzt returned to where we were sitting on the bench.

"The ruts ended at the corner near the rock," he said. "I saw some scuff marks on the asphalt that could have been made by dragging a piece of wood, yet nothing else caught my eye. If I had to guess, I would say that someone drove the cross to the castle in the back of a pickup truck; the arms and legs are too long for a car or SUV. He parked at the foot of the parking lot and dragged the cross to this spot. He dug a hole, slipped it in, lit it up, and ran like hell the way he came."

"What else?" Chief Gardner asked.

Holzt was staring at me when he said, "There's a security camera mounted on a pole with a good view of the parking lot. We should examine the footage, unless someone already has."

Chief Gardner turned to look at me, too.

"Yeah, about that," I said. "I studied the video late last night. Footage gives us nothing, I'm afraid. It recorded a couple arriving at the castle at exactly ten oh-two P.M. There was no other movement at all except for a rabbit at about midnight until the fire department arrived, followed by Phillip here, and later by Officer Overvig."

"I'll need to look at it myself," Chief Gardner said.

"Of course."

"So, Phillip, what does that tell us?"

"The security camera? It tells us that whoever burned the cross knew that it was there and was careful to avoid it."

"How would they know that?"

"They've been here before," Holzt said. "Guest, staff, someone who had dinner in the restaurant or ordered takeout—anyone who drove into the parking lot and knew what to look for."

"I know your shift ended a long time ago, Phillip, but I need you to write a sup for me. Include anything and everything that comes to mind. Leave a hard copy on my desk."

"Yes, ma'am." Holzt started walking away. He stopped and returned to his chief.

"Since I'm already collecting OT—Chief, how 'bout I check with the Home Depot and Bickner's Lumberyard, see if they sell this kind of wood; see if they remember who they sold it to recently."

"Good idea."

"I could also reach out to Marshall or Willmar; see if they have anything for us."

"Let's keep it in the family for now."

"Yes, ma'am."

"Phillip? Good job."

Holzt touched his fingertips to his eyebrow like he was giving a salute.

"Ma'am," he said.

Chief Gardner and I watched him walk off to his own SUV and drive away.

"McKenzie?"

"Dee?"

"I have eighteen full-time officers under my command and only a couple of them with investigative experience and they . . . they have a lot to learn, too. I hope to change that. In the meantime, I'm hiring you as a consultant; I'll have my admin deliver a contract."

"How much does the Redding Police Department pay its consultants?"

"In your case—about the price of a large coffee at the Java House."

"I don't know, Dee. I was planning to go home today."

"I'll throw in some scones. Listen. From now on you'll call me Chief Gardner, especially when we're interviewing witnesses."

"Yes, Chief."

"I don't need to explain why, do I?"

"No, Chief."

"You'll remain by my side while we're conducting the investigation. You will listen. You will observe. You will not ask questions or make comments unless it's to point out something that I've missed. Think of me as lead and you as secondary."

"Okay."

"I'll take whatever you can give me, McKenzie, but basically you have one job and one job only—keep me from fucking up. Some asshole burned a cross in my city. My city, McKenzie. This is my city now and I'm taking this a little personally and not just because it's my city. Do you feel me?"

"Yes."

"We're going to solve this BAM. What I want from you . . ."

"Make sure that 'by any means' doesn't actually mean 'by *any* means.'"

"I'm four at the moment. I'm ten-four. Make sure I stay that way; don't let me tune up any uncooperative racists."

"Witnesses."

"Isn't that what I said?"

"Yes, Chief."

Chief Gardner stared at the fallen cross some more.

"Tell me everything you saw, everything you know."

"You want it with or without adjectives?"

"Talk like I'm LT and you want to impress me."

So, I did . . .

I yanked open the cabin door. I saw the burning cross. I started running toward it. I have no idea why. It's not like I had a plan.

Nina called me out over it later.

"I remember thinking," she said. "I remember thinking at the time that most people would have called the fire department, called the police. Not my guy. Oh, no. How long ago did they shoot you? Five months? Well, it's nice to know that you're still the man I married for better or for worse."

"I was a cop for a long time," I told her.

"You've been not a cop for a long time, too."

"My old man, he used to say, 'Once a marine, always a marine.'"

"How many beaches did he storm after he left the service?"

"I don't think he ever stormed a beach, even when he was a marine. I don't think he ever set foot in a landing craft except maybe during training."

"You're missing the point."

"No, I'm not. I'm just trying to change the subject."

That was later, though. At the time I was running toward a cross burning in the middle of the clearing behind Redding Castle. I didn't have a plan until I did. The clearing was dotted with water spigots. Attached to the spigots were garden hoses wound on reels that were used to water the grass. I grabbed the one closest to the cross, turned on the water, and began dousing the flame up the ten-foot high trunk and across the ten-foot arms. There was a loud sizzling sound and the distinct odor of gasoline. I didn't think the water was doing much good.

I glanced around me as I used the hose. I had lost track of time by then, yet I remember looking at my watch just after the movie ended that Nina and I had been viewing. One ten. Exactly. I figured it was now pushing one twenty, maybe one twenty-five, and all of the cabins were dark with only a few lights showing through the windows of the castle. I wondered if I could get the fire out and the cross down before anyone noticed.

Footfalls on my right caused me to turn my head away

from the flames. I didn't see him until he entered the circle of light—Mr. Doty. He wasn't wearing a shirt, which reminded me that I wasn't wearing shoes. He was carrying a chain saw; a small one used for trimming trees and not for cutting them down. He fired it up and I remembered thinking, "The noise . . ."

Mr. Doty notched the cross as close to its base as he could get without burning himself and then cut from the other side.

Maybe the chain saw sounds louder than it actually is because you're listening so intently, my inner voice suggested.

Lights appeared in the cabin windows—one, two, three, four—almost like they were in sync. More lights appeared in the castle.

Or not.

The cross fell and lay flat on the grass. Mr. Doty took the saw and ran back toward the barn on the far side of the parking lot. I continued to douse the gas-soaked wood with the hose.

Cabin doors flew open. People began venturing outside; moving timidly toward the flames. On its back, the cross didn't appear nearly as impressive; it looked more like a grass fire. Mr. Doty appeared again. He was pushing a wheelbarrow filled with sand. The fire was beginning to die out. He used a shovel to spread sand on the wooden beams. That finished the job, leaving nothing but smoke to fill the air.

"What's going on?" someone asked.

"It that a cross?" asked someone else.

A small crowd gathered to stare, but its attention was drawn away from the smoldering wood to the parking lot. The City of Redding Volunteer Fire Department appeared, sirens terrifying any small animals that might have been nearby; its cherries and berries bouncing red and blue lights against the trees. It was followed by a black SUV with POLICE printed on the white doors in large block letters and CITY OF REDDING printed in small type below it.

"This ain't good," Mr. Doty said.

"No," I said.

They were the only words that we shared during the entire incident.

The firefighters didn't see a fire to fight and the police officer didn't see anyone to serve or protect, just a bunch of people standing around in the dark; the only light coming from the cabins and the castle and the tiny lamps that followed the cobblestone paths. They came toward us just the same.

Officer Phillip Holzt—I learned his name later—glanced down at the smoldering cross, looked up at the people gathered around it, put his hand on his hips, and said in a perfect British accent, "What's all this then?"

"He did not," Chief Gardner said.

"Swear to God."

"Don't play, McKenzie. Tell the story straight, c'mon now."

More people appeared, moths drawn to a flame even though the flame was out. Jenness Crawford was among them, dressed in gym shorts and a T-shirt and nothing else. The expression on her face was a mixture of shock and rage. She was about to speak, only before she could Nina stepped in front of her and rested her hands on the young woman's shoulders. I found out later what she said.

"Everyone's watching you. Your guests; everyone. They'll be frightened if you're frightened. They'll be calm if you're calm. They'll behave how you show them to behave."

Jenness stepped out of Nina's grasp and moved to the cross. She spoke as if she was amused.

"Mr. Doty, it's a little early for this, isn't it?" she said.

Mr. Doty was clearly confused.

"Miss?" he said.

"In the past we got pranked when high school was ending, not when it was beginning."

"Yes, Miss," Mr. Doty said.

"It's COVID," Nina said. "School closed a couple months before graduation. Now they're open again. Kids are restless."

A firefighter nudged a wooden beam with his boot as if searching for a spark that he could extinguish. By then a second officer had arrived—Jim Overvig.

"Don't do that," he said.

"Why not?" the firefighter asked.

"It's evidence. This whole area is a crime scene."

"It's not a crime scene," Jenness said. "It's a prank. I'm wondering if this one is better or worse than the time they toilet papered, what was it? Twenty trees? Worse, I think. I'm sorry, everyone. I'm sorry that your evening was disturbed. I would recommend that you all go back to bed. That's what I'm going to do."

"Bullshit."

The obscenity came from the edge of the small crowd. It came from Eden Redding. By the way, nearly everyone was half-dressed or wearing robes and pajamas. Eden was fully clothed.

"Was she?" Chief Gardner asked.

"Bullshit," Eden repeated. "This wasn't some schoolyard prank. This was a deliberate act of racist violence and you know it."

"I know nothing of the kind, Aunt Eden." Jenness emphasized the word "aunt" as if she wanted her guests to believe that they had walked into a family dispute. "In any case, we can talk about it in the morning."

"We'll talk about it now." Eden walked up to Officer Holzt and stood directly in front of him. "I demand that arrests be made."

"Who do you want me to arrest?" Holzt asked.

"You know goddamn well who. The Sons of Europa."

"Ladies and gentleman," Officer Overvig said. "I need you to clear the area. Please. There's nothing to see anymore."

A couple of guests did exactly what he asked and returned to their cabins and rooms. The rest remained to watch the show.

"Ma'am, unless there's concrete evidence . . ." Holzt said.

"How much more evidence do you need and don't call me ma'am."

That's when Olivia Redding entered the fray.

"Really, Eden," she said. "Must you? Can't you put off your rabble-rousing until the morning?"

Big Ben Redding stood with his arm around his wife's shoulder. They looked regal.

"Regal?" Chief Gardner said. "How were they dressed?"

"Robes, pajamas, slippers," I said. "Big Ben's hair was neatly combed; Olivia had lipstick on."

"Like they were expecting to be seen?"

"Just like."

Big Ben stepped forward. His size gave him a take-charge vibe.

"I agree with my niece," he said. "There's nothing to be gained by standing around in the dark. We can sort it all out in the morning."

That's when I gestured Holzt aside. He was young, mid-twenties, I guessed. So was Overvig and I thought, of course you put your rookies on third shift.

"Call your boss," I told him.

"Sir . . ."

"Call Dee. Tell her what's happening. Tell her that I'm here."

He did.

"I think it was using your first name that prompted him to do what I asked," I said.

"None of my officers call me Dee or Deidre," Chief Gardner said.

"What do they call you?"

"Chief."

"Not boss?"

"What happened next?"

"Your officer did what you told him to do."

Holzt stood more or less in the center of the crowd and raised his arms. Like his colleague, he spoke formally.

"Ladies and gentlemen," he said. "We need you to clear the area. Please do so immediately. Thank you for your cooperation. If this is a prank, we'll deal with it. If it's not, we'll deal with that, too. Please go back to your cabins, go back to your rooms. We may contact some of you tomorrow. If not, I hope you enjoy the remainder of your stay in Redding."

Holzt turned to the volunteer firefighters.

"You guys take off, too," he said. "Thanks for coming."

He next spoke to Officer Overvig.

"The boss says she wants photographs and lots of them," he said.

"See, they do call you boss," I said.

"Not to my face," Chief Gardner said.

The guests all left the scene; so did Mr. Doty, pushing his wheelbarrow back to the barn. So did the firefighters. Overvig started taking his pictures. The Reddings remained, however. They gathered in a tight circle to talk it over. I kept my distance with Holzt. Nina, God love her, stood close enough to listen to what was being said.

She told me later that Eden blamed the burning cross on the Sons of Europa. She called it "an attack on civilization."

Jenness blamed Eden. She called it "an attack on Redding Castle" that was prompted by Eden's hate-mongering.

"What hate-mongering?" Chief Gardner asked.

I explained about our canoe trip past the Sons' dock the evening before.

"So, you're thinking it was an act of retaliation," the chief said.

"I'm not thinking anything," I replied. "Just stating the facts, ma'am."

In her defense, Eden told Jenness that we must all confront injustice wherever we find it; that Jenness should know that.

Big Ben said that up until now the Sons had left the Reddings alone, even though Tess had personally rallied the town against them; that she was the one who started RAH.

Alex Redding took his wife's side.

Olivia said that the Reddings in general and her in particular didn't need all this drama in their lives and the cross burning was just another good reason to sell the place. She said she was sure that "Little Carly"—she actually called her sister-in-law "Little Carly"—would agree.

Jenness said, "No."

Olivia told Jenness, "You don't get a vote."

Eden announced, "But I do."

Big Ben said that he didn't think they were accomplishing as much as they might and, "We can all get together and talk about it in the morning. It'll be better in the morning."

"Screw you, Ben," Eden said. "Screw you all." She stalked off toward her cabin, Alexander following close behind.

"Please," Jenness said. "Everyone, please."

Big Ben patted her arm and said, "We'll talk tomorrow."

He and Olivia returned to the castle.

That's when Anna Redding spoke up; Nina had no idea how long she had been standing near her and she was startled.

"An opportune transpiration, would you not agree, Ms. Truhler?" she said.

"Opportune, Ms. Redding?"

"As I intimated earlier, I know my family; I understand my family. These happy events can only strengthen my niece's position."

"Happy? That's an odd choice of adjective."

"Not at all, Ms. Truhler. Not at all. Ah, yes, and for future reference, I prefer the title 'doctor.' I am quite sure that I earned it."

"I'm sure you did, Dr. Redding."

Jenness heard her aunt's voice; found her standing in the darkness.

"Oh, Anna," she cried. "I don't know what to do. When word of this gets out it'll ruin everything."

"Shh, my dear."

Jenness rushed into the older woman's arms. Anna Redding hugged her and smoothed her hair as a mother might console a heartbroken child.

"It's going to be all right, dear," she said. "I know it doesn't seem like it at the present time, yet it will. You'll see. Come. Come inside with me."

Anna led Jenness back to the castle.

Nina moved to where I was standing.

"Walk me home," she said.

I did. Along the way we had a brief conversation about how we weren't actually going home today.

"It'll be like rats deserting a sinking ship," Nina said.

Shortly after, I put on my shoes and returned to the cross and Officer Holtz. We took turns getting each other coffee from the urn set in the lobby for the castle's guests. Sometime during all of that, I snuck into the castle's computer room and reviewed the security footage.

"Okay, Chief," I said. "I told you my story. Now tell me yours."

"What do you mean?"

"The City of Redding Volunteer Fire Department, your

officers—let's say the cross was set on fire just before I saw it. Or it could have been burning for some time; it doesn't matter. When I got there, everything was quiet. The cabins, the castle—not a creature was stirring, not even a mouse. That was at one twenty, maybe one twenty-five tops."

"Your point?"

"The City of Redding is a good fifteen minutes away from the castle even if you drive like a maniac. I know, because I have. Plus, there's the time it takes for the volunteers to assemble. Yet they arrived at just about the same time as everyone else in the castle figured out what was going on. Call it one thirty."

"Call it exactly one thirty-four according to the fire department's log."

"When was the 911 call made?" I asked.

"One oh-six."

"So, you got the call before everyone else in the castle knew what was happening."

"Convenient, wasn't it?"

"Chief, who called it in?"

"The county's 911 operator told me the caller ID didn't list a name; that it read 'wireless caller.'"

"But there was a number."

"Of course."

"Well, then."

"We're working on it. What do you think, Jessica? This is the movies? TV? Everything happens instantly?"

"I wish you would stop calling me that."

Especially not in front of Madison Zumwalt, I thought, as I watched her approach from the parking lot. She was dressed for running; her long hair in a ponytail.

"Hey, Chief." She spoke like they were old friends, reminding me again that it was a small town. "McKenzie."

"Madison," Chief Gardner said.

Maddie gestured at the sand-covered wooden beams lying on the grass.

"So, it's true then," she said.

I glanced at my watch.

"News travels awfully fast in Redding," I said.

"Olivia called Mom early this morning. Mom was really angry that she woke her up until she found out why Livy was calling. Now she's happy. Sometimes I wonder about Mom. Do you know who did this?"

"Not yet," Chief Gardner said.

"Mom says it was the Sons of Europa. Or maybe she was just repeating what Livy told her, I don't know. Whoever it was, Mom acts like they did us a favor. Like I said, sometimes I wonder about her. McKenzie, are you going to run today?"

"I don't think so."

"Well, okay. I'll see you guys later. Pancakes in twenty?"

"We'll see."

Madison started walking toward the beginning of the forest trail near the James J. Hill Cabin. By the time she reached it, she was in a full stride.

"The girl runs a five K in twenty minutes—for exercise—do you believe that?" I asked.

Chief Gardner leaned against the bench and closed her eyes.

"Maddie's very fast," she said.

"I wonder how long it takes for her to ski five K."

"I think it depends on the snow and weather conditions."

"Are you a snow skier, Chief?"

"No."

"Skater?"

"No."

"Why do you live in Minnesota?"

"Because it's home."

"When do we go to work?"

"In about two minutes."

"Where do we start?"

TEN

I called Mr. Doty's name. His reply came from deep inside the barn. Chief Gardner and I followed his voice until we found him sitting on a wooden stool in front of a workbench, the bench and the walls in front of it filled with all manner of hardware and tools that were as neatly sorted and arranged as the medical devices in a surgical suite.

"Mr. Doty," I said. "This is . . ."

"You be chief of police," he said.

"That's right," Chief Gardner said.

"We ain't got no other Africans on the force I know of; figured it must be you."

"African-American."

Mr. Doty nodded his head and gestured more or less at the front of the barn.

"Gotta be pretty upset what happened," he said, "because, you know, history and stuff."

"I am."

"Don't know what to say."

"You're a hero."

"Am I? Don't see why."

"In the middle of the night you cut down a burning cross with a chain saw and doused it with sand."

"Don't make me no hero."

"How did the cross get there, do you think?"

Mr. Doty stared for a moment as if he was unsure what he was being asked.

"I don't know," he said.

"Did you see anything?"

"Naw."

"Hear anything?"

"Naw. I don't think so."

"You don't think so?"

"Kinda confused by it all."

"When did you go to bed?" the chief asked.

"Ten. Ten thirty. Don't stay up, me and the missus, like we used to."

"McKenzie saw the cross burning a little before one twenty A.M."

"Saw him out there with the hose; knew it wasn't going to do much."

"You arrived just moments later with a chain saw."

Mr. Doty nodded some more and sighed. The sigh sounded like "Yeah."

"But you said you were in bed at ten thirty," the chief reminded him.

"I was."

"How did you see McKenzie?"

"Through the window."

"What made you go to the window?"

"I don't know."

"You don't know?"

"Somethin' woke me. I don't know what it was. You asked if I heard anything. I don't know. Didn't open my eyes and go 'What was that?' Just opened 'em. I opened my eyes and somethin' told me to go to the window. I went to the window. I saw what I saw."

"What did you do next?" the chief asked.

"I put on my pants and shoes and ran out t' the barn t' get a saw. I knew McKenzie's hose wasn't gonna do nothin'."

"Did you stop to call 911?"

"No."

"Why not?"

"Didn't occur to me. 'Sides, me 'n McKenzie, we had it figured out."

"Did Mrs. Doty call?"

"No. She didn't—I didn't wake the missus. It was the volunteers what woke her, the fire department. Them sirens. They shouldn't a done that; use them sirens. No need to wake everyone. Bad enough I had t' use the chain saw."

"After you cut down the cross . . ."

"I went back to the barn to git some sand," Mr. Doty said. "Then I come back. McKenzie done a better job than I thought wit' the hose by then; didn't need to use the whole wheelbarrowful."

"Did you see anyone?"

"No, like I said."

"I meant earlier. Someone walking about who shouldn't have been here. A stranger, perhaps?"

"Chief of Police—this is a hotel, a resort, 'kay? Restaurant. All we got is strangers. You don't know that?"

"Could someone have driven into the parking lot without you knowing? Someone in a pickup truck, perhaps."

"I guess, yeah. I don't guard the parking lot."

"You live next to it."

"I told McKenzie just the other day, 'kay? People come here, mostly they're on vacation. Sometimes they make a lot of noise and I hear 'em. Sometimes they don't make no noise and I don't even know they're there. Last night, you asked 'bout last night,

(180)

a couple, younger couple, I heard 'em laughin'. Was 'bout ten. They parked their car and I heard 'em laughing and then they went into the castle and I didn't hear nothin' until—until whatever it was made me git up and go t' the window. Don't know what else you want me to say."

"Okay."

"We good here, Chief of Police?"

"My name is Deidre Gardner."

"I know your name."

"You seem upset, Mr. Doty."

"Well, it's—it's a bad thing what happened, don't you think?"

"Yes, I do. Thank you for your time."

I couldn't let it go at that, though.

"Mr. Doty." Both he and Chief Gardner looked at me as if they were surprised to see me standing there. "Mr. Doty, the wooden beams that were used to make the cross . . ."

He nodded his head as if he had been waiting for the question.

"You saw it, too, didn't you?" he said.

"Yes."

"Wasn't gonna say nothin' 'less you brought it up; 'less someone brought it up."

"Why not?"

"It looks bad."

"Yes, it does."

"See what?" the chief asked.

"I've been thinkin' 'bout it all night," Mr. Doty said.

"Me, too," I told him.

"See what?" Chief Gardner asked again.

"Over here," Mr. Doty said.

He rose from the stool and led us to a corner of the barn. Stacked into the corner were a half-dozen ten-foot-long rails and three four-foot-high posts, all cut to build a rustic-looking split-rail fence identical to the one that ran along the length of the castle's property, the fence that kept visitors from tumbling down the steep bank into the lake.

"My extras," Mr. Doty said.

"Are any planks missing?" I asked.

"I don't think so."

"Are you telling me this is the wood that the cross was made from?" Chief Gardner asked.

"Don't know if it was my wood," Mr. Doty said. "Coulda been the same wood come from somewhere else. I mean, my wood—it all seems t' be here far as I can tell. Built that fence long time ago; built it four, five years ago. Didn't have no reason to replace any of the sections since then."

"Could someone have put the cross together in the barn without you knowing about it?"

"I checked my tools, my drill and wrenches; even looked over my long bolts and nuts. Everything's where it's supposed to be; don't look like no one touched it. Gas I use for my machines; can't say anyone's touched that, neither."

"That doesn't answer my question."

"I want t' say no."

"You want to?" Chief Gardner said.

"I didn't hear anyone take my ladder night Ma'am died, too. I don't know. Drill doesn't make that much noise when you think about it. If the doors were closed, I don't know."

"Mr. Doty, what will you do if the Reddings decide to sell the castle?"

He stared at the chief, his jaw set as if he was afraid of opening his mouth; of saying something that would get him in trouble.

"You would be out of a job, wouldn't you," the chief added. "Both you and Mrs. Doty."

Mr. Doty stared some more; his breath became labored.

The chief stared back; she was breathing normally.

The waiting game.

I stepped in again.

"We know you've thought about it from what you told me the other day," I said.

My words seemed to break the tension.

Mr. Doty was talking directly to me and not the chief.

"Yeah, we thought about it," he said. "'Course we thought about it, me and the missus. Decided if the castle goes, then we'll go, too. Missus has people up near Alexandria. Go up there; get a small place on a lake or somethin'. Can't stay here in Redding. Too flat. Nothin' to do. And we got money, if you think that's a problem. We'll both get the max from social when we apply and we have money saved up; the missus took care of our investments, IRAs and such. We'll be fine."

"Glad to hear it."

Mr. Doty turned back to look at the chief.

"But you're wrong," he said. "What you're thinkin'."

"What am I thinking?" Chief Gardner asked.

"That I did something. That I—burning crosses, that can only hurt the castle. Why would I want that? Castle's been my home, me and the missus, fifty-some years."

"Why didn't you tell me about the wooden beams, that the cross was made of the same wood you have here in the barn? Why didn't you tell me the moment I walked through the door?"

"Cuz, Chief of Police, I knew you'd blame me."

"Most people are blaming the Sons of Europa."

"Yeah, I heard Miss Eden sayin' that last night. That don't make no sense to me, neither. Them Sons—I don't necessarily support keepin' someone outta church cuz of skin color, you know? But show me one racist thing they done. They ain't done nothin' I know of."

"Till now."

"You don't know that. You don't know they did this."

Geez, Mr, Doty, my inner voice said. *You don't support the Sons of Europa, do you?*

"You're right," the chief said. "I don't know."

"I'm more worried 'bout kids cookin' meth in the woods than I am of those people. You should be, too."

Chief Gardner pulled a white card from her pocket. I didn't see what was printed on it. I assumed it was the logo of the Redding Police Department and her phone number. She gave it to Mr. Doty.

"If you think of anything else that you might have forgotten to tell me, you'll call, won't you," she said.

Mr. Doty nodded yet he didn't put much effort into it.

The chief turned to leave. Mr. Doty called to her.

"Hey," he said. "The cross, the mess on the ground—Miss is kinda anxious that we clean it up. That okay?"

"Go 'head."

Mr. Doty nodded some more.

Once we were clear of the barn, Chief Gardner spoke without looking at me. I didn't know if she was angry or not.

"You were going to tell me about the wooden beams, weren't you?" she said.

"I was curious to hear what Mr. Doty would say about it."

"That doesn't answer my question."

"I knew about it because just yesterday I was leaning on the fence that it was used for."

"McKenzie?"

"Yes, I was going to tell you about the wooden beams."

"When? At the end of the episode when Jessica explains whodunit?"

"I should have told you sooner."

"Like immediately, goddammit."

Yeah, okay, she's angry, my inner voice said.

"I'm sorry," I told her.

"Anything else you'd like to share, now is a good time."

I flashed on Eden and the honeybees.

"You know everything I know," I said.

"What a depressing thought."

"Mr. Doty called you African."

"I've heard worse."

"Chief of Police."

"To some people I don't have a name, only a function. If I worked in a restaurant, he'd call me 'waitress.' If I was in a department store, he'd call me 'girl.' In Minneapolis, I was 'detective' even to some of the people I worked with. You can't let it get in your way."

We knocked on the doors of each of the cabins that ringed the clearing of Redding Castle. The guests were divided into two distinct groups. The first was outraged by the cross burning and saw it as yet another example of the great divisions that existed in our country. The second group seemed amused as if it were simply an odd thing that occurred while they were on vacation and they couldn't wait to tell their friends about it. No one, however, testified that they saw or heard anything until Mr. Doty fired up his chain saw.

Eventually, the chief and I reached the General Oglesby Cabin.

"It was the Sons of Europa," Eden Redding said. "I know it."

"How do you know it?" Chief Gardner asked.

"I saw him."

"Who?"

"Heimdall."

"Heimdall?"

"The guard. McKenzie knows who I mean."

Eden explained about our canoe trip past the dock in front of the Sons' compound. Her version was a little more colorful than mine.

"I saw him," she added. "Heimdall. Last night. I got out of bed and went to the window and I saw the cross burning and I saw a man running away from it and it was Heimdall. I could see his face because of the flames."

"You saw him clearly?" the chief asked.

"Yes."

"You're willing to testify to that?"

"Yes."

I couldn't let that slide, though.

"Eden," I said.

"What?"

"You wear contacts, don't you?"

"What?"

"You wear contact lenses . . ."

"So what?"

"Do you wear them when you go to bed?"

"Of course not."

"When you got out of bed last night, did you put them in before you looked out the window?"

Eden hesitated before answering.

"My eyesight isn't that bad," she said.

She had been unable to recognize you from a much shorter distance when you were crossing the clearing the day before, my inner voice reminded me. *In broad daylight.*

"Do you need to wear contacts or glasses when you drive?" I asked.

Eden didn't answer.

"It's an easy thing to check," I said.

"Yes, I need to wear contacts when I drive," Eden said. "That doesn't mean anything. I saw him clearly. It was Heimdall."

"Okay."

"Whose side are you on, McKenzie?"

"He's only asking what a prosecutor or defense attorney would ask," Chief Gardner said. "It doesn't mean we don't believe you."

"I know what I saw."

"You're convinced that the Sons of Europa are responsible for all of this."

"Who else?"

Eden explained in detail that Tess Redding was instrumental in quashing the Sons' plans to build a church on Lake Anpetuwi; that she had organized resistance against them.

"They wanted revenge on the family," she added. "It's as simple as that."

"Ms. Redding . . ." the chief said.

"Please, call me Eden."

"Eden, thank you."

"And you're Deidre if I'm not mistaken."

"Chief Gardner when I'm working."

"Of course, of course."

"What did you do when you first saw the cross burning?"

"I got dressed. I was going to go out and see if I could help put it out, but I saw that McKenzie and Mr. Doty had it under control. When everyone else gathered around it, so did I."

"Did you think to call the police, the fire department?"

"No, I didn't. I assumed that McKenzie or Mr. Doty or someone else had already done that. That was foolish of me, wasn't it?"

"Not necessarily," the chief said. "Someone did call the police and fire departments. Last night, though, you told my officer . . . What did you say?" The chief made a production of pulling her notebook from her pocket and consulting it, even though I knew that she hadn't written anything down since she arrived at the castle. "You said, 'This was a deliberate act of racist violence' and you demanded that 'arrests be made.' Yet you didn't mention seeing Heimdall running away to Officer Holzt. Why not?"

"I didn't have the chance. Your officer, as you call him, was trying to get everyone to leave the crime scene and my family . . . My family greatly disappointed me."

"I understand," Chief Gardner said. "About families, I mean. McKenzie, you were with Eden in the canoe when the two of you paddled past the Sons of Europa's dock, correct? Do you think you can identify this Heimdall person?"

"Yes, Chief."

"I think we'll go have a chat with him."

"Yes, Chief."

"I'll be happy to go with you," Eden said.

"It's best that you remain here," the chief said. "I would appreciate it you didn't tell anyone else what you saw until we get this sorted out."

The chief gave Eden a business card and was about to leave when Eden spoke up.

"I can't promise that, Chief, promise not to tell people what I saw. I told my husband last night—if Tess were here, she'd be organizing a protest. She'd be mobilizing RAH against these, these white supremacists. Since she's not here, I have put it upon myself. I've already started contacting people. Resistance is essential, don't you see? What the Sons did—this cannot stand. It will not stand. Not in Redding."

"Unofficially, I wish you well," Chief Gardner said. "Officially, I'm telling you to make sure your protest is peaceful. I mean it. Keep it peaceful and you'll have no trouble with me."

"It will be as peaceful as the Sons of Europa allow it to be."

"The Sons carry ARs," I said.

"Right is on our side."

Okay.

Apparently, one of the people Eden contacted was Barbara Finne. She had parked her car in the lot and was crossing the clearing as Chief Gardner and I made our way toward the castle. She called our names. Instead of continuing to where we were walking, though, she halted at the spot where the cross had been set afire. Mr. Doty had cleaned up the mess as best he could, only one could easily see the outline of the wooden beams burned into the grass.

Barbara took her digital camera from her bag and started taking pics.

"I guess now is as good a time as any," the chief said.

"To do what?"

"Explain ourselves to the media."

We altered course and made our way to where Barbara was kneeling on the grass and attempting to take a photo that would show both the imprint of the cross and the castle in the background.

"Barbara," the chief said.

"Chief," Barbara replied. "I'm told that the Sons did this."

"No, someone said that they suspected that the Sons of Europa were allegedly responsible for this crime, yet we have uncovered no evidence at this time to justify those accusations. However, our investigation is ongoing."

"Do you have any other suspects?"

"I have no comment on that at this time."

Barbara kept circling the burned grass with her camera. She spoke in a voice that was less than respectful.

"Have you interviewed any witnesses?"

"I have no comment on that at this time."

"Honestly, Chief, I expected a little more from you seeing as how you're an African-American and a burning cross has always been a symbol of hate and intimidation directed at both your people and mine."

"Your people?"

"I'm Jewish."

"I didn't know that."

"Some would prefer that I wear the Star of David wherever I go."

"What do you want me to say, Barbara? I'm going to find out who did this. I am going to make it my mission in life. And then—"

I quickly flashed on the instructions she had given me earlier that morning. "Chief," I said.

Chief Gardner spun toward me. Her face was angry, yet it quickly softened. She even smiled.

"As I was saying, I am going to find out who did this." The chief turned back to Barbara. "And let the law take its course. In the meanwhile, our investigation . . ."

"Is ongoing. I get it."

Barbara slid her camera back into her bag and retrieved a tan reporter's notebook and pen.

"What about McKenzie?" she asked.

"He has been retained by the City of Redding Police Department as a consultant."

"May I interview him?"

"Not while he remains a consultant for the City of Redding Police Department."

"I'm told that he was the one who first discovered the burning cross and took steps to knock it down."

"Who told you that?"

Barbara studied the chief for a moment as if she was considering whether or not to answer.

"No one in the police department," she said.

"That's something anyway."

"You know I'm going to work this story like it's my path to a Pulitzer, right, Chief?"

"I know."

"I hope we'll still be friends when it's over."

"Print the truth and we'll still be friends," Chief Gardner said.

"The problem with the truth is that even two conscientious and scrupulous people might not always agree on what it is."

"Do the best that you can."

"You, too."

The chief and I made our way to the castle. As we walked, I threw a glance over my shoulder. Barbara was moving in a straight line to the General Oglesby Cabin. Eden was standing in the doorway waiting for her.

"At least you have a week before the story blows up," I said.

"What makes you say that?"

"The *Weekly Bulletin*—it's weekly."

"Barbara sends what she calls a 'daily briefing' by email to all of her subscribers when she has a breaking story like this."

"Meaning it's already blown up."

"Thank you for that, by the way."

"What? Keeping you from going off in front of Barbara?"

"No, for the intel about Eden's eyesight."

"Yesterday I was a lot closer to her than Heimdall would have been, yet she didn't recognize me."

"I'm thinking that Eden might have seen exactly what she wanted to see."

"If she saw anything at all," I said.

"Heimdall. If only."

"Hmm?"

"Idris Elba played Heimdall in the movie *Thor: Ragnorak*. I would love to interrogate Idris Elba."

"There's only one thing to do in the meantime. Buy you breakfast, Chief?"

All of the tables on the patio facing Lake Anpetuwi were empty except for those on the far side that had been commandeered by the Redding siblings. A woman was clearing one of them when we arrived.

"Too late for breakfast?" I asked.

She smiled brightly as if a cross burning in the clearing behind the castle had happened so long ago that it wasn't worth remembering.

"It is," she said. "I'm sure we can manage something, though. Morning, Chief."

"Just coffee for me," the chief said.

I held up two fingers.

"The same," I said.

"Sure thing," the woman said.

"Miss?" I asked.

"Sir?"

"Do you have any of that sticky pudding?"

"We do."

"A small portion." I was looking at the chief when I added, "Just enough to keep body and soul together."

"Coming right up," the woman said.

She scurried away, leaving us alone with the Reddings. They were watching us now, a suspicious expression on all of their faces except for Anna's. She seemed amused.

"Well?" Olivia said.

Chief Gardner pulled a chair away from a small table and sat down.

"Ms. Redding?" she asked.

"What are you doing about all of this?"

"Our investigation is ongoing."

Carly Redding moved a few paces away so that she was standing apart from her brothers and sisters.

"What the fuck does that mean?" she wanted to know.

"C'mon," Big Ben said. "There's no need for that kind of talk. What's wrong with everyone this morning?"

"The Sons of Europa attacked the castle last night and I want to know what the chief of police is going to do about it," Olivia said. "Is that too much to ask? I don't think so."

"Neither do I," Marian Redding said. I hadn't seen her at first. Unlike the other Reddings, she was still sitting and without her husband by her side she seemed smaller.

"We do not know for a fact that the Sons committed this atrocity," the chief said.

"Eden saw them," Carly said. "Are you saying she's a liar?"

"Our investigation is ongoing."

"You are calling her a liar."

"I heard an interesting tidbit of information this morning; perhaps the chief did, as well." Anna slowly took a sip of coffee from a china cup and deliberately placed the cup on a matching saucer that she held in her hand, making sure she had acquired everyone's attention before continuing. "I heard that the wooden beams used to make the cross came from our own barn."

For a few beats, the Reddings seemed genuinely dazed by their sister's remark. Big Ben clenched and unclenched his fists as if he was contemplating punching her out. It was Carly who broke the silence.

"What the fuck?" she said.

"I heard that it was the same wood that we had used to build the fence."

Anna waved more or less at the lake as if the gesture alone would tell her audience exactly which fence she was referring to.

"That's a stupid thing to say," Big Ben told her. "Why would you say that?"

"Mrs. Doty told me." Anna smiled. "Unlike you, I actually converse with the help. In any case, if she told me, it stands to reason she might have told others."

"That's crazy," Olivia said.

"Yes, Livy, it is in a word, crazy."

Olivia glared at her sister-in-law. I didn't know if she objected to the evidence Anna had presented or to her use of Olivia's hated nickname.

Anna leaned far enough forward in her chair to set her cup and saucer on the small table in front of her.

"Everyone here knows their way around the castle, of course, as well as the barn," she said.

"What is that supposed to mean?" Alex asked.

"Just a fact worthy of consideration, wouldn't you agree, Chief Gardner?"

"Our investigation is ongoing," the chief said.

"Jesus Christ," Carly said.

The waitress who had taken our order took that moment to serve the coffee and my sticky pudding. She must have been able to accurately gauge the mood on the patio because after setting a tray between the chief and I, she swiftly departed without a word.

"It would be helpful if all of you would tell me exactly where you were last night," Chief Gardner said.

It was a simple question, easily answered. Carly was in her bed in Redding, Marian was in her bed at her farm just outside of Redding, Alex was in bed with his wife Eden in the General Oglesby Cabin, Big Ben and Olivia were sleeping in their room in the castle, and Anna was reading in Jenness Crawford's room. No one heard or saw anything before the fire department arrived—except for Eden.

"She claimed she clearly saw that guard, that sentry that she called out on the Sons' dock two days ago," Alex said. "She must have told you?"

"She did," the chief said. "We'll be speaking with the Sons next."

"I should hope so," said Carly. "This is a fucking catastrophe."

"We need to sell this place, the sooner the better," Olivia said.

"*We could never learn to be brave and patient, if there were only joy in the world*—Helen Keller," Anna said.

"Another Redding quoting shit," Carly said.

"We'll get to the bottom of this soon enough, right, Chief?" Big Ben said. "Until then, I think we should all just relax."

"You fucking relax," Carly said.

She used that line to depart on.

"What a pill," Alex said after his sister was gone.

The remaining Reddings reseated themselves at their patio tables and resumed talking as if Chief Gardner and I were no longer there.

"I wonder how poor Jenny is taking all this," Marian said.

"I don't know," Big Ben said. "I haven't seen her this morning. Have you?"

Marian shook her head.

"She's probably curled in a ball somewhere and weeping her eyes out," Olivia said.

"Don't say that," Marian said.

"Not to worry," Anna said. "I often hear casual mention of this or that gene skipping generations. This is nonsense, of course. Genes do not disappear and then reappear in later generations. However, the expression or manifestation of genes—traits, if you will—can skip generations under some circumstances."

Alex placed both hands on his head as if it suddenly hurt.

"What are you talking about?" he asked.

"I'm suggesting that our darling Jenness more strongly resembles old John Redding than we do. She is not weeping, as Livy suggests. Oh no. I'll wager she is in her office at this very moment, in deep consultation with her mentor, both recognizing the question in front of her and taking the necessary steps to answer it."

Consulting with her mentor, my inner voice said. *I was wondering what Nina was up to.*

Olivia shook her head.

"I asked you, please, not to call me Livy," she said.

While the Reddings talked it over, I finished both my coffee and the sticky pudding. Nina was right—it tasted exactly like the recipe she served at Rickie's.

Chief Gardner ignored her coffee, however. Instead, she slipped her cell phone from her pocket and set it faceup on the tabletop. She removed her notebook, consulted a page, and tapped the phone number that was written there on to the keypad of her cell and hit CALL.

A moment later, we both heard the ringtone of a cell phone calling to its owner from the far side of the patio.

"Clever girl," I said.

Olivia Redding reached into her pocket and pulled the phone out. She read the caller ID. I had never seen the color leave someone's face so quickly. Give her credit, though—she didn't panic; didn't even glance toward our table. Instead, Olivia told her family, "Excuse me," and pivoted in her chair so that her back was to the Reddings and us. She swiped right and pressed the speaker of her cell against her ear.

"This is Olivia Redding," she said.

Chief Gardner spoke quietly.

"We can speak privately or we can speak publicly, you decide," she said.

"What would we talk about?"

"The reason I have your cell number."

Olivia rose from the table and smiled.

"I need to take this," she told her family. "I'll see you all later."

Olivia spoke calmly as she crossed the patio.

"Yes, we can talk," she said into the phone. After she entered the castle, putting walls and distance between her and her family, she added, "Meet me in the art gallery."

ELEVEN

I was ready to rush right up there; taking the steps two at a time. Chief Gardner, though, preferred to keep Olivia waiting and wondering. She sipped her coffee as she explained herself to me.

"The thing about the phone number of the wireless caller who contacted 911 this morning—it had a 952 area code," she said. "We both spent enough time investigating crimes in the Twin Cities to know that 952 is attached to the suburbs southwest of Minneapolis. That's as far as I took it, deciding to wait for the cell phone provider to give us a name and address. Yet it occurred to me while watching the Reddings squabble that one of them might have made the call. Except, Redding's area code is 320; that excused Carly and Marian. The area code for Mankato where Eden and Alex Redding live—507. Marshall, where Anna Redding teaches, is 507, too. That left Olivia and Big Ben. I bet they live on Lake Minnetonka."

"Edina, actually."

"Ah, one suburb too far."

"You're a clever girl," I repeated. "LT would be proud."

Chief Gardner finished her coffee.

"Think we've given Livy enough time to worry herself into an anxiety attack?"

"Oh yeah."

Only Olivia wasn't anxious, at least she didn't appear to be.

We found her in the art gallery leaning against the windowsill and staring more or less at the spot in the clearing behind the castle where the cross had been set afire. She began speaking as we entered the room, not even bothering to look at us. Her voice had a certain melancholy tinge to it as if she had made a decision and wasn't particularly happy about it.

"I don't know what to tell you," she said. "Or if I should tell you anything. Yes, I called 911 this morning. I had hoped to remain anonymous, not that it matters. It should have occurred to me that you could easily trace the phone number back to me; I don't know why it hadn't. Not that that matters, either."

"You witnessed a crime," Chief Gardner said. "That's what matters."

"I did what was expected of me, too. I reported the crime, which I am not legally obligated to do." Olivia turned her head to look at Chief Gardner for the first time. "Am I?"

"No."

"Nor must I voluntarily provide information that I might have about a crime to the authorities. Correct?"

"You understand your rights."

Olivia turned her head to gaze out the window some more.

"I was pre-law at the University of Minnesota. What do you think, McKenzie? Pretty good for a cheerleader, don't you think?"

"You didn't become a lawyer?" I asked.

"No."

"What happened?"

"Ben happened. Ben's Beez happened. We won't talk about that."

"Ms. Redding, you saw the fire long before anyone else did," Chief Gardner said.

"Did I?"

"By fifteen minutes or more. I'm very concerned about those fifteen minutes."

"I wish I could help you, Chief."

"You called it in at exactly one oh-six A.M."

"I didn't know the time."

"Where were you when you first saw the fire?"

"Here. In this room."

"Were you alone?" I asked.

Olivia smiled slightly and moved from the window to the love seat that I had used the evening before. She sat down, leaned back against the cushions, and stretched her legs straight out.

"Yes, I was alone," she said.

"Where was Mr. Redding?" the chief asked.

Olivia closed her eyes and sighed. For a moment, I didn't think she would answer.

"In our room, sleeping," she said. "I slipped away without him knowing. Since we seem to be heading in that direction, no, our marriage is not what it could be. He's cheated on me so many times it's almost become a running gag."

"Have you ever cheated on him?" I asked.

"Not at first, but after I realized that he wasn't going to change no matter how often he promised, yes, I did, every chance I got."

Olivia's eyes snapped open and she leaned forward on the love seat.

"You want to know why I was in this room last night?" she asked. "I've decided it's time to put an end to this silly farce, as much fun as it's been, and make no mistake, McKenzie, Chief, it's been an enormous amount of fun being married to Big Ben Redding. Especially since I decided, like him, to ignore the conventions of an honorable marriage. The truth is we never should have married. We should have remained roommates instead; business partners; friends with benefits. That's pretty much how we've lived for the past four decades anyway. Only I don't want to become a casualty of old age; have Ben come to me one day and say he's trading me for—what? What's the rule? Divide your age by half and add seven years and . . . I don't know."

I flashed on Cassandra Boeve and the time I saw her and Olivia sharing coffee.

"You could do the same thing," I said.

"Now there's a thought, McKenzie. Don't think it hasn't crossed my mind, either. Only that's not why I was in this room last night; that's not what I was thinking. I was sitting here, in this very spot, and wondering if it was possible after I leave Ben for me to get my hands on this glorious artwork. The Reddings, even Tess; they grew up with all of this hanging on the walls and never once realized its true value, not aesthetically or monetarily. Only I did."

"Jenness is convinced that you hate this place."

"No, no, I love it. I don't care for the City of Redding, but this place—I remember the first time I saw Redding Castle, the first time Ben brought me here. It was our junior year at the U. My family had been so upset that I would blow off Christmas with them to spend it with my boyfriend's family instead. But my God, the place just took my breath away. It was like walking into Charles Dickens's *A Christmas Carol* without the ghosts, well, except for Carly. When he was drafted by the Bills, Ben and I actually talked about me living here and visiting him in Buffalo during the season. Best-laid plans."

"Now you're lobbying to sell it," I reminded her.

"Community property," Olivia said. "My share of Ben's Beez and half of his share of Redding Castle will fund a very comfortable retirement. Besides, after Ben and I split, I don't think I'll be welcome here. Anna already wants to drive a stake through my heart."

"Any particular reason?"

"I broke up the team. She and Ben were pretty tight when they were kids; almost inseparable. You can still see it, sometimes; the connection. But then Big Ben went to the big city and saw all those big-city lights and became a big man on campus—it was just too big for Anna to compete with. When he brought the cheerleader home—that was inexcusable. I was warned, too, by his siblings and a few old friends. Ben had dated the Redding High School prom queen—they held the prom in the castle—and I was told that Anna had done her very, very best to sabotage their relationship, so watch out they told me. What really irked, though, was when Ben and I built Ben's Beez."

"Why?"

"Anna wasn't invited along for the ride. Apparently, it was her idea to start the beehives behind the castle when they were teenagers and when Ben decided to make it his life's work without her—Ben had planned on calling it Redding Castle Honey; that's the name we had used in all of our business plans. He wanted to print an image of the castle on our labels; use it for marketing and sales. Anna just flipped out. You'd have thought she took lessons from Carly. She actually threatened to sue us. So, Ben's Beez Honey."

"Ms. Redding," Chief Gardner said.

"Yes, yes, you want to know about last night."

"You said you were sitting here."

"Yes, and while I was sitting here, I saw shadows dancing on the wall and red light reflecting off the window glass. My first thought was that the castle was on fire. I got up, looked out the window, and saw the cross burning."

"Did you see anything else?" the chief asked.

"No."

"Did you hear anything?"

"No."

"The sound of a truck engine, perhaps?"

"No. Sorry."

"What did you do?"

"I watched it burning and wondered 'what the fuck?' Excuse my language; I was channeling Carly for a moment. I called 911 and told the operator what I saw."

"Why didn't you give your name?"

"You'll laugh at me."

"Not even if I thought it was funny," the chief said.

"I was afraid everyone would blame the messenger. As McKenzie pointed out, I've been lobbying hard to sell the castle. If I was the one who pointed out the burning cross, I felt some people, my family, might think that I had put it there."

"What did you do after you called 911?"

"I went back to our room, slipped into bed, and waited for the sirens. When they arrived, I acted as if I was as surprised to hear them as Ben."

"Now you're using the burning cross to bolster your argument to sell the castle," I said.

"Makes me look bad, doesn't it? But something else I learned in pre-law—according to the Supreme Court, it's not illegal to burn a cross unless it's carried out with the intent to intimidate an individual or group."

"Ms. Redding, did you burn that cross?" the chief asked.

"No, I did not. There are some lines even I won't—step over."

"Do you know who burned that cross?"

"No, I do not."

"While burning a cross might not be a crime, under Minnesota law, lying to police is considered obstruction of the judicial process, which means you'll face an obstruction of justice charge."

"A misdemeanor offense punishable by up to ninety days in jail and fines up to one thousand dollars. I'll take my chances."

We left Olivia Redding sitting on the love seat in the art gallery. A few minutes later, the chief and I were leaning against the fence at the top of the bank overlooking Lake Anpetuwi. I pointed in the general direction of the compound occupied by the Sons of Europa.

"What good reason do I have for going over there?" the chief asked.

"You have a witness who places Heimdall at the scene."

"A witness whose testimony could very well be self-serving."

"Welfare check. You knock on the door and inform the Sons that you're concerned because they've been accused of setting fire to a wooden cross at Redding Castle."

"What I'm most concerned about is that I'll be accused of allowing my personal beliefs to *color* my professional judgment. Yes, that was a pun."

"I hadn't noticed."

The chief's cell phone rang. She answered it.

"This is Chief Gardner."

The volume was high enough that I could hear Officer Holzt speaking.

"Chief, Phillip Holzt here. I have a couple of things for you, some that you'll like and some that you won't."

"What things?"

"I went over to Home Depot. They don't sell anything like the wooden beams that the cross was made of. But Bickner's Lumberyard does. It fact, Bickner himself told me it was a big seller for them; a lot of the area farmers who have livestock or just want to enclose their property use the fencing and some people with big yards do, too. The thing that you're not going to like—news about the cross burning is all over town. Bickner had heard about it before I got there. When I asked about wooden beams, he put two and two together and got twenty-two. He walked me right over to an area in his yard where they store that stuff and I found the exact same beams that the cross was made from. Bickner also went out of his way to tell me that he sold two bundles of—it's called Western Red Cedar, by the way—he sold two bundles to the Redding Castle five years ago. He also said— Chief, he said he sold a quarter bundle of the exact same wood to Conrad Fredgaard last spring right after COVID hit."

"Is he sure?" the chief asked.

"He's sure. Bickner said he'd be happy to dig out copies of the receipts for us if we want."

"Thank him for me. And Phillip, ask him to produce the receipts not just for Fredgaard, but also for the castle and all of his other customers."

"I already have him working on it. According to Bickner, though, we're talking at least a couple of dozen people in the past two years alone."

"Phillip, you're doing a great job."

"I'll get the receipts."

"Thank you, Phillip."

The chief deactivated her phone and put it in her pocket.

"Who's Conrad Fredgaard?" I asked.

"He's the 'lawspeaker' for the Sons of Europa."

"Lawspeaker—does that mean what I think it does?"

"I'll drive."

It took us ten minutes by car to reach the compound owned by the Sons of Europa; Madison Zumwalt probably would have reached it in half that time running through the forest. We parked on the edge of a paved county road named Lake

Anpetuwi Boulevard that circled the lake. The boulevard seemed to work as a dividing line. There were plenty of small and medium-sized homes on the side of the road that hugged the forest yet none of them were nearly as large or palatial as those on the side that hugged the shoreline.

We walked to the entrance of the Sons' driveway. It was blocked both by a long wooden gate that swung inward and a man dressed in camo and cradling an AR-15 semiautomatic assault rifle. There was a sign fixed to the gate. It read TYR HAUS.

"Halt," the sentry said. "Who goes there?"

"Are you kidding me?" I asked.

The chief flashed me a look that was a combination of surprise and annoyance.

"I'll be good," I told her.

"Good morning," she told the sentry. "City of Redding Chief of Police Deidre Gardner to see the lawspeaker."

"He's been expecting you." The sentry leaned on the gate and gave it a shake as if he wanted to make sure it was latched. "He said you're supposed to wait here."

The chief nodded.

The sentry turned and marched down the driveway. It was long and curved; I couldn't see the house or the lake from where we were standing. Several times as he walked, the guard threw a glance at us from over his shoulder. I waved at him.

"Stop it," the chief said.

"This so-called lawspeaker is fucking with you."

"Did you think he wouldn't?"

"Have you noticed the wooden fence along the property?"

"I've noticed."

Conrad Fredgaard kept us waiting for a good ten minutes. When he finally did appear, he was accompanied by the sentry. Unlike the sentry, though, Fredgaard was wearing jeans, a button-down dress shirt, and a black sports jacket. He had dark hair and dark eyes and if you had told me he was a descendant of ancient Romans instead of Vikings, I would have believed you.

Fredgaard strolled up to the gate. The sentry halted several steps behind him and assumed a parade rest position, his left foot twelve inches to the left of his right foot, his weight equally distributed on both feet, his right hand holding the rifle, the butt of the rifle touching the ground with the muzzle inclined forward and his left hand behind his back.

That's what I like to see in my church, my inner voice said. *Paramilitary training.*

Behind them, far down the driveway, I could see Heimdall peeking around the curve like a child wondering what it is that he wasn't supposed to see.

I bet he was told to stay out of sight.

"Chief Gardner." Fredgaard spoke with the practiced confidence of someone who worked in public relations. "I expected to be confronted by you long before now."

"Oh?"

Fredgaard held up his cell phone. There was an image on the screen, only it was too far away for either Chief Gardner or I to clearly see.

"The *Redding Weekly Bulletin* is accusing us of a despicable act. Should I read the headline and subhead? 'Burning cross found in backyard of Redding Castle. Redding heir blames the Sons of Europa.'"

"I am sorry about that," the chief said.

Fredgaard studied her face for a moment.

"I believe you are," he said.

"I'm sure that the article doesn't say that the City of Redding Police Department is holding you responsible."

"It says your investigation is ongoing."

"I would like to speak to the member of your church that the Redding heir claims she saw at the castle last night."

"I don't know who that would be."

Nice try, Chief.

I pointed at Heimdall, who was still standing at a distance and watching us while pretending not to. Fredgaard's gaze followed my finger. Anger flashed across his face when he saw Heimdall, yet only for a moment. He glanced at me, at the chief, and back at Heimdall. He was one of those guys you could actually see thinking. He waved Heimdall forward. Heimdall was clearly reluctant to join us and stopped next to the sentry. I noticed a bandage on his left hand.

"Good afternoon," the chief said.

Heimdall didn't reply.

"You must forgive Brother Marcus," Fredgaard said. "He is observing a period of silence and is not allowed to speak."

"That's inconvenient."

"I can see how you might think so."

"How long is this period of silence to last?"

"I'm not sure."

"Uh-huh. As the news article claims, I have a witness who places him at Redding Castle at approximately one twenty this morning."

"I have eight witnesses who will testify that he was here at one twenty this morning."

"Including yourself?"

"Yes."

"Brother Marcus," the chief said. "I'm afraid I don't know your last name."

Fredgaard pressed his index finger against his lips and said, "Vow of silence, remember? His name is Marcus Kohn, only he doesn't need to tell you that, does he?"

"Not even if he's suspected of a crime?"

"Brother Marcus is not legally required to answer your questions. Even if you arrest him, he is not legally required to answer your questions whether he has an attorney present or not."

"Hey, Marc," I said. I pointed at his left hand. "I notice you're wearing a bandage. You didn't have that when I saw you last night around seven."

Heimdall—yes, I knew his name, yet I always thought of him as Heimdall—glanced at his hand like it was the first time he saw it. So did Fredgaard.

"Did you burn yourself?" I asked.

Heimdall didn't answer.

"*Mr.* Kohn"—Chief Gardner emphasized the "mister"—"you do have the right to remain silent. I have rights and responsibilities as well. Must I exercise them?"

Again, a momentary flash of anger colored Fredgaard's face and yet again, he quickly brought it under control.

"Show them," he said,

Heimdall seemed confused.

"Show them your hand," Fredgaard said.

Heimdall hesitated for a long moment before stepping forward. He slowly unwrapped the gauze bandage around his left hand, and when finished, held his hand up for us to see. There was a single straight cut that ran the length of his palm.

"Brother Marcus took part in a blotting ceremony last night," Haugen said. "His vow of silence is an integral part of it."

"Blotting ceremony?" the chief asked.

"Blot is the term for a ritual blood sacrifice to our sacred gods of Asgard. Adherents, like Brother Marcus, will cut themselves and allow their blood to drip into the land as a gift to them or to strengthen their connection to them or to seek divine inspiration from them. In many ways, it is similar to Roman Catholics who fast or deprive themselves of some small pleasure or indulgence during their time of Lent."

Fredgaard seemed happy with his explanation because he was smiling when he finished. Chief Gardner was not smiling, however.

"A witness identifying your man isn't the only reason I'm here," she said.

"No?"

The chief walked over to the edge of the driveway where the gate met the rustic-looking split-rail fence—an exact duplicate of the one found on the bank at Redding Castle.

"Is this supposed to keep people out?" she asked.

"It merely marks our property," Fredgaard said. "There are ordinances dictating the kind of fences that can be constructed on the lake."

"No ten-foot-tall cyclones topped with barbed wire, huh?"

"We are a church—"

"With armed guards."

"Chief Gardner—"

"The wooden beams used to make this fence are identical to the ones used to make the cross that was burned at Redding Castle."

Instead of anger, the expression that flashed oh so briefly across Fredgaard's face was one of surprise. Once again, he recovered quickly.

"The wood was purchased at Bickner's Lumberyard," he said.

"We know."

"Bickner has sold the same wood to many other customers."

"We know."

"Will you be interrogating them as well, Chief Gardner?"

"Yes."

Fredgaard had nothing to say to that. Behind him a man, half walking, half jogging, approached with a phone in his hand.

"I'd like your permission to come inside your fence and look around," the chief said.

"Do you have a search warrant?" Fredgaard asked.

"No, I do not."

"You're not likely to get one, either, are you, Chief Gardner? Not without probable cause."

The man said, "Lawspeaker," yet Fredgaard shrugged him off.

The chief leaned against the fence and crossed her arms over her chest. She gestured at Heimdall with her chin.

"You don't think I have probable cause?" She gave Fredgaard a broad smile; a smile bordering on laughter. "I was with the Minneapolis Police Department for many years before I came here, most of them in homicide; that's no secret. What I always found amusing during my time there was the number of suspects who quoted the law at me; who thought the law was like a pair of handcuffs or something that they could somehow use to keep me from learning the truth. McKenzie, you knew me back then. How often did that work?"

"Well, there was that one guy—no, no, now that I think of it, he's doing life at the Minnesota Correctional Facility in Oak Park Heights."

"Do you think you can intimidate me?" Fredgaard asked.

"Lawspeaker," the man said again.

Fredgaard spun toward him.

"What?"

The man showed him what was on the screen of his phone. Fredgaard read it and wrapped his arm around the man's shoulder.

"I apologize for shouting," he said.

"'S okay," the man said before retreating back down the driveway. Heimdall glanced around, didn't see anyone holding up a stop sign, and decided to follow him. The sentry remained at parade rest.

"It seems that there is to be an emergency meeting of the Redding City Council this evening," Fredgaard said. "We shall answer your charges . . ."

"I haven't charged anyone with anything yet," the chief said.

That caused Fredgaard to pause as if he was replaying the entire conversation in his head.

"That's true," he said.

"At the same time, I've noticed that you haven't denied responsibility for the burning cross."

"We will make our thoughts known at the city council meeting tonight."

"There will be protestors," the chief said.

"We do not fear them."

Chief Gardner gestured at the AR-15 the sentry was holding.

"My concern is that they will fear you," she said.

"We shall arrive unarmed to the lion's den." Fredgaard smiled his PR smile as if he was pleased by his reference to Daniel. "And we shall be judged blameless."

The chief bowed her head at him.

"Lawspeaker," she said.

Fredgaard smiled some more and retreated down the driveway back toward Tyr Haus.

The parking lot was full when we returned to Redding Castle and the long driveway leading to it was lined with cars. Many of the owners of the vehicles were gathered near General Oglesby Cabin; Eden Redding stood in their midst. Others, however, were lined up outside the front entrance to the castle.

Chief Gardner halted her SUV in the center of the lot.

"I need to get back to the house," she said.

I reached for the door handle.

"Wait," she said.

I waited.

"What do you think?"

"Are you asking for my expert opinion, Dee?

"I am."

"Thank you. I think burning a cross in the Reddings' backyard is an astonishingly counterproductive thing for the Sons of Europa to do. It can only galvanize the town against them." I gestured at the crowds. "Which apparently, it has. You said yourself, the Sons is still a small organization; only a few hundred supporters scattered over a dozen states. One of the reasons they want the church on the lake it to help attract followers; don't you think? A pretty, tax-free setting where like-minded racists can meet and shake hands and hug each other in solidarity. Once they build a significant membership, God knows what they'll get up to. For now, though, it's all about ingratiating themselves with the community; it's all about making friends."

"Are you saying that you don't think the Sons did this?"

"I'm saying it would be stupid of them if they had."

"Both you and I have seen stupid before," the chief said.

"Yes, we have."

"Which raises a simple question—if the Sons didn't do this, who did?"

At that moment, the crowd surrounding the General Oglesby Cabin began cheering. We could easily hear them inside the SUV.

"I keep asking myself, What would Jessica Fletcher do?" I said.

"Probably throw it to a commercial break. Listen, McKenzie, I need a pair of eyes at the meeting tonight; someone to surveil the crowd. I probably won't get much chance to do it myself. My experience, the people who commit hate crimes take great pride in their work. They might not want to go to jail, but at the same time they want you to know what they did and why they did it.

Take those idiot insurrectionists who stormed the U.S. Capitol in DC. They posted their crimes on Facebook for God's sake, on Instagram. So, watch carefully and hope our suspect—whoever that is—tells us everything we need to know."

Anna Redding struck me as a woman who never smiled unless she was greatly pleased. I found her sitting at a patio table sharing a glass of wine with Jenness Crawford and Nina. She was smiling like she had just won the lottery. I heard her speaking as I approached.

"Enjoy the moment," she said. "You must, you simply must. At the same time, I caution you not to take too much comfort in it. I am reminded of what occurred in England after that nation broke away from the European Union. A cheesemaker of whom I am familiar lost nearly 350,000 pounds in export sales in a single calendar year. He shared his sad tale on Twitter and that prompted a frenzy of nationalistic cheese-buying by his fellow countrymen. His in-country sales increased over nine hundred percent. Except shouting 'Buy British, buy British' proved to be an unsustainable business model. It bought him time to determine how to best regain his European customers post-Brexit, yet that was all. Time. Now you have time. You must use it wisely."

"I understand," Jenness said.

"Hi," I said.

I rested my hand on Nina's shoulder. Her hand came up to cover mine.

"McKenzie, there you are," she said.

"Ah, yes, McKenzie." Anna continued to smile. "Have you and Chief Gardner solved the riddle of the burning cross?"

She makes it sound like a Hardy Boys novel, my inner voice said. *Or Nancy Drew.*

"The investigation is ongoing," I said.

"Pity."

"You're not acting like it's a pity."

"I have a fondness for the law of unintended consequences."

"We've booked every table in the dining room for at least the next three weeks," Jenness said. "We've booked every room and cabin for every weekend until Halloween; I have only a few Monday, Tuesday, and a couple of Wednesday rooms open. All of this in just the past few hours. People have heard what happened and they're rallying around us. It's fantastic. My takeout orders—I can't even keep up."

"Jenness was able to contact all of the employees that she was forced to lay off and asked them to come back at least part-time," Nina said. "She might need to hire more."

"Aunt Anna says this is not sustainable," Jenness said. "She's probably right; she usually is. If we can maintain this volume of business through November into the Christmas season, though—Christmas has always been a big holiday for us—we'll not only survive the winter doldrums, we'll be in a position when spring arrives to duplicate the revenues the castle enjoyed pre-COVID. We can return Redding Castle to the heights it enjoyed when my grandmother was young. With the suggestions Nina made—concerts at the castle—there's no reason why we can't do even better than that."

"What about—" I brought my hand up like I was stopping traffic when, in fact, I was merely stopping myself. "That's great news. I'm so happy that something good has come of all of this."

Anna chuckled; it didn't sound as if she did it a lot.

"McKenzie is trying not to be a downer," she said. "Isn't that what the kids say? Downer?"

Maybe when you were a kid.

"He's concerned about the vote my brothers and sisters and I are expected to take tomorrow to determine the future of the castle," Anna said. "I, for one, am confident of a positive outcome.

Jenny, you will be stating your case after the Sibs have heard the developer's presentation and no doubt they will be excited by the prospect of unexpected riches. They will also be made aware of the enormous amount of work that lies before them. I shall see to it. We are, after all, selling a great house that needs to be emptied. A liquidation sale of its contents will be required and that's only the beginning. You, on the other hand, are asking for nothing from them save patience. At the risk of repeating myself, concentrate solely on the potential profitability of the enterprise for I do not believe my brothers and sisters will be swayed by family history. Do not show weakness or concern. Leave it to me to remind them that if the gods of commerce should conspire against you, Redding Castle and Lake Anpetuwi will retain their value. They are not going anywhere."

"Thank you," Jenness said.

Anna reached across the table and squeezed her niece's hand.

"Now I shall get out of your way," she said. "Back to work, you two. Make me proud."

All three women rose as one. Anna went one way and Jenness went another. Nina said, "I'll be there in a second."

When we were alone, she wrapped her arm around mine.

"What's going on?" she asked.

"What do you mean?"

"You're smiling too hard. You only do that when something's bothering you and you don't want people to know."

"I'm happy that things seem to be turning around for Jenness and the castle. I will be genuinely ecstatic if the vote goes her way tomorrow. I'm just trying to wrap my head around Anna's remark concerning the law of unintended consequences."

"What about it?"

"What makes her think they were unintended?"

TWELVE

Finding a parking space proved difficult. I ended up near the hospital and had to walk several blocks to the Redding city offices. Along the way, I encountered a surprising number of citizens gathered in small groups and hanging around the entrances to the coffeehouses and restaurants and bars; about ten percent of them wore masks. There were City of Redding police officers and county sheriff's deputies, too, a few chatting with the citizens while others stood apart and watched. Their voices were muffled in some cases, subdued in others. No one was shouting, no one was cursing; no one sounded angry. The loudest sound I heard as I made my way down Main Street was nervous laughter. It was as if everyone was waiting for something to happen.

The atmosphere was much the same inside the ancient brick buildings that hosted the city offices, although the number of people tightly gathered in the enclosed area increased the volume. Plus, there were signs and placards. Most supported RAH, yet a few suggested to me that the Sons of Europa had its followers as well.

RACISM IS NOT WELCOME HERE was met with ALL ARE WELCOME HERE.

SAY NO TO HATE SPEECH was held across the corridor from THE FIRST AMENDMENT IS FOR EVERYONE.

My favorite sign was written in crayon on cardboard and held aloft by a kid who looked like she should be at home studying for tomorrow's geography quiz—LIFE IS TOO SHORT FOR THIS ****.

*Whatever this **** is,* my inner voice added.

Some people had already claimed seats inside the city council chambers, yet most had remained in the corridor outside the entrance while waiting for the meeting to commence. About half the audience refused to wear masks despite the government edict. Eden and Alex Redding were among those that did. Eden seemed to be giving a speech, or at least a pep talk, to a dozen people who all leaned in close to hear what she was saying while Alex smiled like a proud parent.

On the other side of the corridor, I saw a maskless Conrad Fredgaard speaking to a smaller knot of people that included Brian Hermes, the kid with the flyers. Heimdall was nowhere to be seen. However, two men who I branded as bodyguards stood behind Fredgaard, although the way they moved suggested to me that instead of hiring professionals, the lawspeaker had simply picked the two biggest guys in his haus and hoped for the best.

What caught my attention and held it, though, was the woman who was hanging on to Fredgaard's arm. She was in her early thirties, tall and slender with the blondest hair and bluest eyes I had ever seen; her eyes were even bluer than Nina's, which I didn't think was physically possible. She wore a plaid knee-length dress, black high-heel boots, and a pouting expression, and I thought, my goodness, Fredgaard, in what Nordic prop shop did you find her?

My attention was wrenched away, however, by a woman's giddy laughter. I turned my head just in time to see Big Ben Redding sweep a woman half his size off the floor. He held her in his arms as if he was presenting her as a gift; she wrapped her arms around his neck as if she didn't want to be let go. Olivia shook her head at the two of them and gestured at the floor. Big Ben released the woman and, once standing on her own two feet, both she and Olivia hugged. That's when I recognized the woman—Veronica Bickner, who was the office administrator and principal of Boeve Luxury, a Development Company.

"Pathetic, isn't it?" Anna Redding said.

I flinched at the sound of her voice; surrounded by people and noise she still managed to startle me.

"I didn't see you there," I said.

"No one sees me there." Anna pointed in the general direction of Big Ben. "I find this incomprehensible." She spoke as if she didn't care to hear my opinion; only wished to voice hers. I gave it to her, anyway.

"To the untrained eye, they look like people who are happy to see each other," I said.

"Given the distressing circumstances that prompted this gathering, I would suggest that their behavior is indiscreet to say the least, never mind that the story of Big Ben and the small-town girl he left behind, that he keeps leaving behind, is a tale best played out in private."

"Girl he left behind?" I asked.

"Repeatedly."

"Ms. Redding—"

"Dr. Redding."

"Dr. Redding, would you please explain?"

You know you want to, my inner voice added.

"They were together all through puberty and high school or are those two events interchangeable?" Anna asked. "Ronnie gave him her virginity the night of their senior prom, in the castle no less, or so rumor has it. Ben moved on afterward, of course he did, moved on to the cheerleader of all people, leaving Ronnie alone and heartbroken. She actually worked at the castle for a time, hoping, I'm convinced, that Ben would come back to her. She purchased an inexpensive bungalow about a half mile from the castle, not actually located on the lake, yet near it, on the wrong side of the street, possibly for the same reason.

"McKenzie, when you're a woman living in a small town, back in the early eighties at least, you did one of two things after you were graduated. You either left to go to college or you stayed and became married. Ronnie eventually married Dave Bickner, who was the son of the man who owned the lumberyard and the second-most-eligible bachelor in Redding after my brother. She was quite lovely in those days."

"Still is," I said.

"Possibly. For twenty-five years she and Dave sustained an unremarkable and childless union; him working at and eventually inheriting the lumberyard; her helping out in between classes at Mankato State University where she attended part-time. That is, until ten years ago, when she abruptly sued Dave for divorce. A small town, McKenzie, yet no one saw it coming. Instead of spousal support, Veronica demanded a onetime lump sum payment for her years of marital servitude that she immediately invested in the development company founded by her niece, becoming an active junior partner."

"You're talking about the company that wants to buy Redding Castle. Which means Veronica has as much at stake in tomorrow's vote as anyone."

"More, I would think."

"Why more?"

Anna took on the stern air of a teacher exasperated by a dull student.

"Have you not been listening to me?" she asked.

It took a few beats before I replied—"The girl Ben keeps leaving behind."

"Exactly. Ben and Ronnie's liaison has continued down

through the decades. Ben comes home, he spends time with her; he leaves. She seems satisfied by this arrangement. I cannot imagine why. I would find it unfulfilling if not disrespectful. In any case, if the Sibs vote to sell Redding Castle, Ben will no longer have a home here to come back to, will he? Ronnie will at last be forced to say good-bye to him finally and forever. Poor thing."

Yeah, I can tell you're brokenhearted at the prospect.

"Do you think Olivia is aware of their relationship?" I asked aloud.

"Yes, McKenzie, I believe Livy is aware."

I glanced at the two women. Olivia and Veronica were behaving as if they were the ones who had been classmates back in the day.

"If that's true, then Olivia is a very open-minded woman," I said.

"I often ridicule her because she deserves it, yet time and experience has proven to me that she is both shrewd and endowed with strength of character. For all of his outsized charisma, do you honestly believe Ben is capable of building and maintaining a company as successful as Ben's Beez Honey? It has taken the two of them together. Right brain and left brain. I'll leave it to you to decide which is which. In any case, I believe their business partnership has precedence over their personal relationship."

"I was told that you continue to resent the fact that Olivia married your brother; that you're jealous of their business success; that it was you who kept them from using Redding Castle as the name and trademark for their company. 'Course, that's none of my business."

"Spoken like a pulp-fiction detective, McKenzie. And yes, it's none of your business. Excuse me."

I watched as Anna started to merge with the surrounding

throng of people. She managed to take half a dozen steps before turning back to face me.

"I love my brothers and sisters," she said. "I celebrate their every achievement."

She spun around once more and walked away.

"What was that about?" Barbara Finne wanted to know.

I was startled again.

"I wish people would stop sneaking up on me," I said.

Barbara's response was to gesture more or less in the direction that Anna had gone.

"The Redding siblings are in conflict," I said.

"Are you still on the clock, McKenzie?"

"I am."

"So I can't ask any questions on the record."

"I wish you wouldn't."

"How 'bout deep background?"

"You're assuming I know something worth talking about. I really don't."

"You know that the Reddings are in conflict."

"I don't think that's news."

"Now that's news," Barbara said.

"What?"

Barbara pointed at the entrance to the city council chambers where Chief Deidre Gardner in her perfect blue uniform was talking to a man who seemed as round as he was tall and who was wearing a white and brown uniform that resembled a basket of unfolded laundry. The badge he wore actually had his name embossed on it.

"The chief and the sheriff speaking in a civil manner," she said. "Let me get my camera."

Barbara wasn't kidding. She dipped into the bag draped over

her shoulder, produced an electronic camera, and took a couple of pics.

"I'm told that he insists on calling her Dee Dee," I said.

"She calls him 'Doogie.' His real name is Doug Housman."

"They don't get along, I take it."

"That's because Doogie is prejudiced against women and Dee Dee is prejudiced against incompetence." Barbara returned the camera to her bag. "He's a lousy sheriff, yet a great politician."

"Looking at him, I assume the sheriff's department doesn't have any physical fitness requirements."

"It does—for everyone but Doogie."

"It's good to be king."

"McKenzie, have you spoken to Conrad Fredgaard?"

"I was present when Chief Gardner spoke with Conrad Fredgaard, if that's what you're asking."

"Did he deny having anything to do with the cross?"

"No."

"He wouldn't deny it when I spoke with him, either," Barbara said.

"His followers want him to have done it; if he denies it they'll be displeased. Everyone else wants him to have done it, too, only if he admits it, they'll put him away. There is power in silence."

"My impression is that he's waiting to take his spot at center stage."

"There's that, too."

"Here we go."

The crowd began to filter into the city council chambers. Barbara and I were caught in the rush. The blonde I had seen earlier brushed past me, pulling Conrad Fredgaard by his hand.

"This way, Daddy," she said.

They pushed their way to the front of the crowd. Barbara glanced at me.

"Daddy?" she asked.

"I think it's an honorary title," I told her.

There were seats for about eighty people divided in two sections; the rest of us stood along the walls; again, only about ten percent wore masks. A microphone was mounted on a stand in the empty aisle between the two sections. Eden and Alex Redding stood close enough to the microphone that they could reach it in a hurry. Big Ben, Olivia, and Veronica Bickner had found seats in the back. Anna Redding was seated near the back door.

The family that sits together . . . my inner voice said.

At the front of the chambers was a long table that curved inward. Mayor Matthew Abere sat at the center of the table. I knew it was him because of the engraved sign he was sitting behind. On his right was Brianne Halvorson, whose name I recognized from a newspaper article that Barbara Finne had sent me. On his left was Cassandra Boeve. There were two other council members and at the end of the table was a man whose sign identified him only as CITY ATTORNEY. Three people working video cameras moved among the crowd. Two of the cameras were pointed at the council members; the third at the audience. My impression was that the proceedings were being broadcast live on a public access cable channel.

All of the government employees wore masks except when they spoke, which I thought kind of defeated the purpose.

Mayor Abere used a wooden gavel to call the meeting to order.

"We all know why we're here," he said after he removed his mask. "To discuss the incident that occurred at Redding Castle, a place that is dear to all of our hearts. But please, please let us be civil to each other, I beg you."

He wanted to say more, only Councilwoman Halvorson interrupted.

"I would like to say that the City of Redding condemns all

racism and all hate speech in all of its hideous forms now and forever," she said.

Some members of the audience applauded. Abere glared at her as if to ask, "Are you done now?"

She wasn't.

"I would like to hear from Chief of Police Deidre Gardner," Halvorson said. "Chief, what can you tell us?"

The chief rose from her seat and moved to the microphone. I knew her well enough to read her body language; she clearly didn't want to be there. Yet she stood straight and spoke confidently.

"Officers of the Redding City Police Department responded to a 911 call made from Redding Castle at one thirty-four this morning," she said. "A wooden cross had been set on fire in the clearing behind the castle. By the time my officers arrived, however, the cross had been cut down and the flames extinguished by members of the castle's staff. My officers secured the scene and we have been gathering evidence and conducting interviews ever since. Beyond that, I can only tell you that at the present time our investigation is ongoing."

"Bullshit."

The obscenity came from a woman at the far side of the room who was sitting directly in front of Eden Redding. Most of the people in the chambers turned to look at her. The chief did not.

"Watch your language; we're on TV," Cassandra Boeve said. "Children might hear."

She was ignored.

"Why the hell won't you tell us the truth?" the first woman asked. "Why won't you tell us that there was an eyewitness; that the witness saw a member of the Sons of Europa set fire to the cross?"

"Chief?" Councilwoman Halvorson asked. "Is that true?"

"It would be improper for me to comment on an ongoing

investigation," Chief Gardner said. "I'm sure the city attorney would agree."

The city attorney didn't reply. He looked as if wished he was anyplace other than where he was.

"If you know who did this, why don't you say so?" someone else yelled.

"Chief, if you know something . . ."

"It would be improper . . ."

"Sheriff Housman," Mayor Abere said. "What can you tell us?"

The sheriff rose from his seat as if he expected to hear applause. He did not move to the microphone, but turned to the crowd and spoke in a voice meant for a baseball stadium and not a small room.

"Dee Dee has refused to allow me access to the investigation," he said. "She claims"—he quoted the air—"that it is her job."

"The City of Redding has jurisdiction," the chief said.

"This thing is too big for you."

The chief refused to reply.

"Did you hear me?" the sheriff asked. "I should be in charge here."

"What about that?" Mayor Abere asked.

"It is the city's jurisdiction," the chief repeated.

"But you're not doing anything?" someone yelled.

"Our investigation is ongoing."

"I think we need to have a vote right here and now," said Councilwoman Halvorson. "A vote of no confidence in Chief Gardner."

There was a murmur of approval.

"That's not necessary, is it?" Cassandra Boeve asked.

"I think it is," Halvorson replied.

More murmurs.

"Councilwoman Halvorson," the chief said. "It is this council's privilege to dismiss me anytime it likes. But know this, I will not be bullied into committing an illegal or unethical act. I have too much respect for the badge I wear and the city that gave it to me. It is the reason why I have carried a signed but undated letter of resignation in my pocket since the day I was sworn in. Tell me—does anyone here, anyone, believe that they are more outraged by this crime than I am? Does anyone here believe that they want to see justice done more than me? Anyone? Our investigation is ongoing. When it is completed, I will present all evidence to the city and county attorneys and to no one else. Are there any other questions?"

There weren't.

"Thank you," the chief said. She sat down and stared straight ahead. Her hands were clenched; her fingernails digging into her palms. Anyone else would believe that she was furious. I knew that she was working hard to keep from laughing.

The room quickly returned to the business at hand—calling each other names. Eden Redding began the proceedings.

"We have no words that can possibly express our outrage at the Sons of Europa's unquestionable embrace of racism, of pure bigotry," she said. "There are no words that can adequately state our anger over the fact that our ancestral home of Redding Castle was made a victim of their hate."

Others chimed in.

"You can't just bar people from practicing whatever religion they want or saying anything they want as long as it doesn't incite violence."

"A burning cross is violence."

"The community should be open-minded and respectful to all."

"A whites-only religion? That's what they're preaching? Puh-leez."

"I for one don't see a problem with it."

"White separatism is white supremacy, there's no two ways about it."

"RAH, RAH, RAH—they call themselves Redding Against Hate, but they're the ones who are being hateful. They're the one calling people names, not the Sons of Europa."

"They're just repeating what their so-called ancestors said— white is right."

"This is hurting our hearts and the so-called anti-hate group is to blame."

"Don't forget, the Sons held a food drive during the pandemic."

"White supremacists with great PR."

Finally, Conrad Fredgaard rose from his seat and strolled slowly to the microphone. The way the blue-eyed blonde stared at him, her hands clasped together beneath her chin, you'd think she was expecting him to announce that he loved her more than life itself and they were moving to Aruba. The chamber grew quiet. A cameraman moved in for a close up.

"I am Conrad Fredgaard, lawspeaker for the Sons of Europa Tyr Haus. This council knows me. You citizens of Redding know me. We have been here before, labeled as racist, condemned as evil, simply because we have chosen to honor and respect the culture and ethnicity of our Northern European ancestors. Yet we have not committed a single act or voiced a single opinion to invite these insults and condemnations. A cross was burned at Redding Castle. It was a disgusting, despicable, heinous crime. A false flag act committed by those who seek to vilify and slander our name simply because we wish to gather together and celebrate as the descendants of Anglo-Saxons, of Lombards and Goths, and of Vikings, a name this great state has chosen to bestow on its professional football team. Yet we will not point fingers. We will let you decide among yourselves who has the most to gain by burning that cross, by attempting to stop us from preserving the heritage, and the customs, and the bloodlines of our forefathers."

There was a murmur at the word "bloodlines."

Barbara leaned close to me.

"He didn't deny it—again," she said.

"I noticed."

"You're white supremacists," Eden Redding said.

"That is not true, Ms. Redding," Fredgaard replied. "We are not white supremacists. We are white separatists. There is a difference. We do not hate others. We do not place ourselves above anyone or any group or any religion. We support Black Lives Matter. We abhor the violence inflicted on Asian-Americans and the lie that they are somehow responsible for the coronavirus. We applaud the hashtag MeToo movement. At the same time, we do not ask you to support us. We ask only that we be left alone to worship our gods and practice our religion as we see fit. We seek only to preserve our white heritage. We want our white children to grow up to be mothers and fathers of white children of their own. We wish to protect white people from the threat of extinction."

Fredgaard turned and looked directly at the woman who had called him "Daddy." Many people in the audience did the same.

"We want a thousand years from now, ten thousand years, a hundred thousand years from now, for there to be white people with blond hair and blue eyes walking among us," he said.

For a moment, there wasn't a word uttered by anyone in the chamber. Finally, the young girl I had seen earlier holding the LIFE IS TOO SHORT FOR THIS **** sign bowed her head.

"Sweet Jesus," she said.

"That was exciting," I said.

Chief Gardner leaned back in her chair and swiveled it about while she gazed at the ceiling of her office.

"The Sons are all about preserving blue-eyed blonds," she said. "Who knew?"

"They are an endangered species."

"I remember reading a sci-fi novel when I was a kid—*The Lathe of Heaven* by Ursula K. Le Guin. In it there was this guy who could change reality with his dreams and one night he eliminated racism by dreaming everyone gray."

"Light gray or dark gray?"

"Light gray."

"Well."

"Maybe Fredgaard read it when he was a kid, too, and it messed him up. Now he's terrified of turning gray."

"Dee, do you really have an undated letter of resignation in your pocket?"

She laughed at the question.

"I suppose I should write one in case somebody demands to see it. Do you have anything for me?"

"No. If our cross burner was there tonight, he kept his ID to himself."

"McKenzie, do you think Fredgaard was telling the truth; that it was a false flag operation?"

"'Course it was. The question is—whose flag? I thought burning a cross in the castle's backyard was a dumb move; only seeing Fredgaard in action tonight—you might argue that the Sons did it so they could proclaim their innocence, condemn their foes, and extol their religion in front of the city council and a live audience, not to mention public access TV; maybe generate a little sympathy and support for his church. Good PR, baby."

"I'm so tired that actually makes sense to me."

The chief and I walked out of the Redding city offices together. The streets were quiet.

"No fires," I said. "No protestors overturning cars or looting businesses. Apparently, cooler heads have prevailed."

"Thursday night in Redding. It's ten P.M. Do you know where your children are?"

"In the woods cooking meth?" I asked.

"Ah, Mr. Doty. I was wondering if he could be a supporter of the Sons of Europa. Or an actual member. Or if he just likes burning crosses."

"So was I. He wasn't there tonight, though, if that matters."

"'Course, he could be a legit guy who's just worried about kids cooking meth in the woods."

"Aren't we all?"

Behind us a door closed. There was the sound of footsteps and a voice.

"Chief."

We turned to see Barbara Finne moving toward us.

"Girl, don't you ever go home?" the chief asked.

"Don't you?"

"I am home. It's right where I'm standing. I'm thinking of getting a lounge chair."

"Somehow I can't picture you sitting in a lounge chair."

"What? Black people can't lounge?"

"About that."

"Forget it, Barbie. I have nothing to say to the press."

Barbara slipped her bag off her shoulder and thrust it at me.

"Hold this," she said.

I did.

Barbara wrapped her arms around Chief Gardner and hugged her tight.

Ten seconds later, she released the chief and took back her bag.

"Thank you," Chief Gardner said.

"Wait 'til you read what I have to say about Doogie and the city council; you'll thank me even more. Good night, Chief. Good night, McKenzie."

We watched as Barbara walked up the street and disappeared around a corner.

"I don't know why she did that," the chief said.

"It's just a guess, Dee, but she must think you're pretty good copy."

The chief went her way and I went mine with the promise that we would talk soon. I headed up Main Street. Not for the first time, I was impressed by how quiet it was. I could actually hear the conversations of people I couldn't even see, although I was unable to understand what they were saying. A pair of voices became more distinct, though, as I approached the intersection with Second Avenue. Two women.

"Where's Ben?" one asked.

I stopped in my tracks.

"Where do you think?" the second answered. "Do you believe we drove separately by accident?"

"I, for one, am glad you did."

I hugged the redbrick wall of a building, hiding myself in the shadow I found there. The voices sounded like they were coming from right around the corner.

"My aunt, though," the first woman said. "I love her so much. I doubt I'd even have my business if it wasn't for Ronnie, but my God, what is wrong with her?"

"Ben. He's like an addiction. Trust me, I know."

"But you're over him."

"I am."

"Now if we can only get my aunt to go cold turkey."

"After the vote tomorrow."

"Ben promised Ronnie that he would vote to sell the castle to us."

"I don't believe him. He's just saying that to make her happy while he's in Redding. It won't matter, though. Carly, Marian, and Alexander will carry the vote."

"You're sure?"

"As sure as I can be. Still, you need to make a wow presentation to guarantee Mari and Ed. Good enough so they'll feel justified in turning against Jenness; so good they'll be convinced they don't have a choice."

"I was heading to my office to work on it when I saw you."

"Did I distract you?"

"A little bit."

"Well, now it's time for you to get back to work, young lady."

"You could come with me."

"Work not play."

"Livy . . ."

Livy? my inner voice asked. *You get to call her Livy?*

"Livy, you really wouldn't mind moving to Redding, would you?"

"It's not where you live; it's whom you're living with that matters."

They stopped talking. I pushed myself away from the building and walked a half block back down the sidewalk as quietly as possible. I gave it a half beat and resumed walking forward again, this time as noisily as possible. I even started to whistle "Summertime."

The voices remained silent.

I crossed Second Avenue, fighting my curiosity with all my might; keeping myself from even glancing down the street toward Boeve's office.

A couple of blocks later, I found my Mustang. I started it up, and drove down Main Street. I slowed as I crossed Second Avenue; looking intently. The street was empty.

* * *

While I was driving to the castle, my cell phone pinged the arrival of a text message. I read it off the display on my dashboard.

"The bar is open."

I found Nina sitting at a small table on the patio of Redding Castle. Her eyes were closed and she seemed to be listening to the music being piped over the invisible speakers, a Canadian songbird named Emilie-Claire Barlow singing "Dream a Little Dream of Me" in French.

There were two glasses on the table, a wineglass and a squat glass filled with a dusky-colored liquid. I sat at the table. Nina seemed to know I was there without opening her eyes.

"The Dracula wine is mine," she said. "I ordered you some Knob Creek smoked maple bourbon."

"You are my favorite person in the entire world, thank you."

"She's very good."

"Hmm?"

"Emilie-Claire. She's a very good singer. I wonder if I can book her. Hey, I saw you on TV."

"How'd I look?"

"Engrossed."

"I was waiting for someone to jump up and scream, 'yes I did it, I burned that cross and I'm glad, do you hear, ah-ha-ha-ha-ha-ha.' Imagine my disappointment."

"Probably it would have been better if someone had."

"Oh?"

"Things have taken a turn."

"In what way?" I asked.

"Jenness and I and some of the staff were watching cable access while we were taking care of business. Apparently, we weren't the only ones because right after the council meeting broke up the phone started ringing. At least a half-dozen people canceled their dinner reservations."

"Let me guess, Conrad Fredgaard's line about letting the

viewers decide who had the most to gain by burning that cross resonated with some folks."

"It kind of threw Jenness. Now she's wondering what tomorrow might bring."

"Me, too."

"This trip hasn't turned out to be much of a vacation, has it?"

"You're not having fun?"

"Whatever happens tomorrow," Nina said, "one more sunset and we're out of here. Deal?"

"Deal."

THIRTEEN

The day passed slowly. Nina had once again been recruited to serve the Redding Castle. Meanwhile, I was left to my own devices. I went for a run in the morning, yet did not encounter Madison Zumwalt or Eden or any of the other Reddings. Later, I kayaked around the entire lake.

I passed the compound owned by the Sons of Europa again. A new sentry had been posted on the dock. It occurred to me as I slid past him—he actually smiled and gave me the Minnesota wave—that he wasn't there to frighten his neighbors after all. He was there to protect himself and the rest of the Sons from his neighbors. Think about it—he wouldn't need to stand guard if he and the Sons weren't being threatened, would he? Therefore, standing guard proved that they were being threatened. Simple cause and effect. It was one of the psychological tactics used by manipulators to ensure obedience by their followers, which made me both respect and dislike Conrad Fredgaard all the more.

When I finally returned to shore, I found Nina taking a break on the patio. She told me that two more people had called to cancel their reservations, but that all of the vacated spots had been snapped up by customers from an ever-expanding waiting list.

"So, there's that," she said.

I continued to wander about the property, even drifted behind the General Oglesby Cabin to check out the old honeybee hives again. Apparently, Mr. Doty was doing the same thing. He had opened the door to the battered shack and was looking inside when I arrived. He closed the door and gave it a shake as if he were half expecting it to fall down.

"They don't build them like that anymore," I said.

"Prefab crap," he said. "Was here before my time."

"Yet it's still standing."

Mr. Doty shook his head as if he couldn't believe it.

"Them hives . . ." He moved to one and gave it a rap with his knuckles. "I don't know. Miss wants to know what I think; if all of this can be fixed back up, but I don't know. I think she should talk to Miss Anna is what I think. Miss Anna knows bees."

"Not Big Ben?"

"He's a seller, not a worker." Mr. Doty chuckled to himself. "Queen bee not a worker bee. Miss Anna was the worker; did all the learnin' 'bout how to do what needed to be done. 'Sides, Miss Anna don't live so far away she can't help out if we need it; give us instruction. So, Chief of Police—what she gonna do about the cross, you know?"

"I haven't heard."

"She still thinks it was me, don't she?"

"I haven't heard," I repeated.

It wasn't the answer Mr. Doty wanted to hear. He stared at me for a few beats, the muscles in his jaw pulsating as if he had something to say. Apparently, he thought better of it, though, because he moved swiftly past me and up the narrow path that led through the band of trees back toward the castle.

I lingered in the meadow to survey the small sea of yellow, white, purple, and blue wildflowers spreading out before me. At least until I caught sight of a few honeybees floating dangerously close by and I decided that that was enough nature for today.

It was nearing two in the afternoon when the SUV arrived. Olivia Redding must have been expecting it because she was waiting in the parking lot. Cassandra Boeve and Veronica Bickner were both greeted with handshakes, not hugs, and I was wondering if that was for the benefit of anyone who might be watching, like, I don't know, me.

The rear hatch of the SUV was opened and Cassandra and Veronica slid out what looked like a two-foot-high model mounted on a three-foot-square base covered by a white sheet. Olivia helped by grabbing up a black leather art portfolio and a stand used to display the visual aids that were carried inside the portfolio. Together, they walked slowly to the entrance of the castle, Cassandra and Veronica behaving as if one false move would invite catastrophe. I was standing inside the lobby and watching through a window. When they reached the door, I opened it and held it open as they passed through.

"Need any help?" I asked.

Cassandra gazed at me, an expression of alarm on her face.

What? Are you afraid I'll peek under the sheet? my inner voice asked.

"We're fine," she said.

"This way," Olivia said.

The women climbed the carpeted stairs, heading for which room I couldn't say. I wasn't invited to the presentation; only the Sibs.

"I'm afraid we're going to have to wait a while before you can begin," Olivia said. "Turns out Carly is going to be late. I don't know why. Probably getting another tattoo on her ass."

A short time later, the three women appeared on the patio. They secured an empty table and beverages were ordered and served. I sat close enough to them that I could overhear their conversation while pretending to fiddle with my cell phone.

Only they didn't talk about the upcoming presentation or the events of the past twenty-four hours or even their own personal relationships. Instead, they discussed the education system in general and Redding High School in particular and how important it was for students to have a normal, uninterrupted school year. It reminded me of conversations I've had with my closest friends where hockey and baseball were usually the major topics because what else were we going to talk about, our hopes and dreams?

Eventually, Big Ben Redding appeared. He moved to where the women were sitting and, without asking for permission, pulled a chair from a nearby table and joined them. They didn't seem to mind. All three women smiled as if there was no one else they would rather talk to and I flashed on what Anna Redding had told me about Big Ben's "outsized charisma."

"We're still waiting on Carly," he said. "My guess, she's either having her hair done or she's cleansing her karma."

"How do you clean your karma?" Olivia asked.

"You sever ties with toxic people, take responsibility for your mistakes, and perform actions that nourish the spirit," Veronica said. "Also, you have to forgive people. That last part's the hardest."

"You sound like you speak from experience," Ben said.

"It's a small town, there's not a lot to do."

I was trying hard not to laugh for fear that they would discover that I was eavesdropping. They might have figured it out anyway.

"McKenzie," Ben said. "How often do you cleanse your karma?"

"At least twice a month whether it needs it or not," I said.

That brought a small chuckle from everyone except Cassandra Boeve.

"You're McKenzie?" she asked.

"I am."

"I read in the *Bulletin* that you were interested in buying the castle."

"If I may quote my wife—"

"Nina Truhler?"

"Don't believe everything you read."

Cassandra nodded as if she thought that was sound advice. By then Eden and Alexander Redding had joined the group.

"I thought we were meeting upstairs," Alex said.

"Carly," Olivia said as if her name alone explained everything.

"What a pill," Alex said.

Eden bent down to my chair and gave my shoulders a hug from behind.

"McKenzie," she said.

She kissed my cheek and then rubbed it to remove the lipstick stain she put there.

"Eden, we need to stop meeting like this," I said.

Cassandra and Olivia glanced at each other and quickly looked away, indicating if only for an instant that they shared more than business.

"How goes the battle against the forces of evil?" Ben asked.

"If more people would join the battle there might be less evil to fight," Eden said.

Olivia wagged a finger at her.

"Good point, SIL," she said.

Eden's eyes widened as if the abbreviation for sister-in-law was a term of affection that she didn't often hear.

"Where's Carly?" This time the question came from Marian Crawford. She stood in the middle of the patio, her hands on her hips, and swiveled back and forth like she was trying to remember where she had set her bag. "I told her I could give her a ride."

"I think she wants to make a grand entrance," Ben said.

"As usual," Anna Redding said.

She moved past Marian and claimed a small table off to the side of where Ben, Olivia, Cassandra, and Veronica were sitting, angling her chair as if it was her job to chaperone the table.

"I take it Ed's not going to make it?" Alex asked.

"He's at home getting ready for the harvest," Marian said. "The GDUs are higher than normal for this time of year and if the weather holds, he said he wants to be in the fields early, as early as tomorrow. There is much to prepare, he says."

"What are GDUs?" I asked.

"Growing degree units," Anna said. "They're used to calculate the amount of heat needed for corn and soybean plants to reach maturity over time."

"If you're so smart, Annie, why are you teaching at some small-town college?" Carly said.

She was standing in the doorway between the castle's dining room and patio. Her hair was styled, her makeup expertly applied, and she was wearing a tailored short-sleeve dress with a round neckline and swinging skirt; white polka dots shimmered against the glossy, wine-colored fabric.

"SMSU is an integral component of the Minnesota State College and Universities System, not that you would know," Anna said.

"You look nice," Marian said.

"We're about to win the lottery," Carly said. "I thought I'd dress for the occasion. The rest of you look like you're getting ready to work the fields with Ed."

"Only if I get to drive the tractor," Olivia said.

"Combine," Marian said.

"Combine," Olivia repeated.

"Well, let's get to it," Ben said. "Are you ready?"

Cassandra nodded that she was. Everyone stood.

"Care to join us?" Eden asked.

"I'd love to," I said.

"No," Anna said.

She moved directly to the entrance of the castle as if she intended to lead the way. Carly jumped in front of her. Eden patted my shoulder.

"Sorry," she said.

Eden joined the parade into the castle. Big Ben remained behind as if it was his job to herd stragglers. Veronica Bickner entered the castle right before him. Ben caressed her round behind with his big hand. Veronica gave him a hard look with an expression that I translated to mean "I want you to keep doing that, only not now."

A moment later, I was alone on the patio. Yet only for a moment. Jenness Crawford emerged from the castle followed by Nina. Jenness didn't speak a word. She quickly moved across the patio, down the concrete steps to the lake, and along the dock to the benches at the far end of it. She sat and stared at the water.

"Moment of reckoning," I said.

Nina took the chair next to mine.

"Jen didn't want to come out on the patio while the Boeve crew was here for fear of saying the wrong thing," she said. "She's feeling very anxious."

"I get that."

"What do you think?"

"If I were a betting man . . ."

"And you are."

"I'd wager that Jen's going to ask you for a job by the end of the evening."

My opinion was reinforced ninety minutes later when the Redding siblings gathered on the patio again. They were smiling and nodding their heads and chatting as if they all actually agreed on something for a change.

"That was an excellent presentation," Big Ben said.

"Thank you," Cassandra Boeve replied.

"Yes, excellent," said Marian.

"Thank you."

"Four-point-six million dollars," Carly said. "More than I expected."

The figure caught the attention of two couples sitting at a table not far from where I was. A woman bent her head to the others and mouthed the words, "What did she say?"

"Shh," Alex said.

"And don't forget the artwork," Carly said.

"Shh."

"It's not a secret, is it?"

"For the time being it is."

"Besides, we don't need you shouting our personal business across the patio," Anna added.

"Fine," Carly said. "But I'm going to tell Maddie."

"Maddie's family," Alex said, as if that made all the difference in the world.

"Jenness hasn't made her presentation, yet," Anna said.

"Puh-leez," Carly said.

She produced her cell phone and crossed the patio to make her call.

"I should pack up my things," Cassandra said. "Get out of the way."

"I'll help you," Olivia said.

The offer was met with a broad smile.

"I hope to hear from you soon, Mr. Redding," Cassandra said.

"Are we going to start that again, Cassie?" Big Ben asked. "I'll call you tonight one way or another."

He was smiling. Which caused both Cassandra and Olivia to smile. Surprisingly, Veronica was not smiling. At least I was surprised. When Cassandra and Olivia left the patio, she followed dutifully behind as if she had nowhere else to go.

"I'm guessing it went well," I said.

Eden Redding took a chair at my table. There was a pitcher of Summit Ale and a couple of glasses in front of us. I didn't ask for the extra glass when I ordered the pitcher. The waitress just assumed I wouldn't be drinking the entire thing alone. Silly girl. 'Course, Nina had been sitting with me when I placed the order. That was immediately before she returned to the James J. Hill Cabin to work remotely on her own business instead of the castle's, for a change.

Eden gestured at an unused glass.

"Help yourself," I said.

She filled the glass with beer and drank half.

"How'd it go?" I asked.

"Carly thinks she's about to become a millionaire."

"Is she?"

"After everything is settled and the art is sold, it'll probably be closer to a million and a half."

"That's a lot of money."

"Plus it'll be considered part of our inheritance from Tess's estate, so we won't need to pay taxes."

Eden drank the rest of the beer and set the glass down.

"I need to think," she said.

Eden rose from the table and crossed the patio. She ended up leaning against the fence at the top of the bank and looking out at Lake Anpetuwi. Alex joined her there.

After a few minutes, Olivia returned to the patio.

A few minutes later, Jenness Crawford appeared.

"I'm ready," she said.

"Good." Big Ben moved to her side and turned to face the patio. "Everyone?"

"Let's get this over with," Carly said.

An hour later, the mood had changed dramatically.

I was still sitting at my table and reading a Jess Lourey novel on my phone when Olivia Redding stalked across the patio toward a small table at the far end. A waitress approached almost immediately. Olivia barked out an order before she came within ten feet.

"Amaretto," she said. "One ice cube."

By the time Olivia's drink was served, Eden and Alex had appeared. They were both carrying beverages in their hands; apparently they had stopped at the bar before stepping outside. They settled at a table as far away from Olivia as possible while still remaining on the same patio.

Next came Carly. She seized a spot directly between them, her gaze shifting from Olivia on her left to Eden and Alex on her right.

"What. In. The. Holy. Fuck?" she said.

"Watch your language," Alex said.

"Fuck you," was Carly's reply. "You just pissed away one and a half million dollars. Are you fucking insane?"

"I explained my reasons," Eden said.

"Who gives a shit about the goddamn Sons of Europa? They're assholes."

"Someone has to stand up to them."

"It doesn't have to be fucking us. And you." Carly turned her wrath on Olivia. "What the hell is going on with you?"

"Shut up, Carly."

"Don't tell me to shut up. Tell your prick husband."

Olivia rose from her table and crossed the patio. When she was within striking distance, her hand came up and caught Carly flush on the jaw. Carly's head snapped back. She fell off to her side, yet managed to maintain her balance. Her own hand came up to caress her face. The look of fear in her eyes—I didn't know if it was caused by the blow itself or by how quickly Olivia had delivered it.

She's hit people before, my inner voice told me.

I came out of my seat and rushed between them, feeling very much like a referee at a hockey game.

"Whoa, whoa, ladies," I said.

"You hit me," Carly said.

"You're lucky I don't kill you," Olivia replied.

"Kill me?"

Carly leapt toward Olivia, hands extended. Olivia went into a defensive stance, her elbows tucked in; her knuckles facing the sky.

Yeah, she knows how to fight.

I managed to keep between the two women.

"Ladies, ladies," I chanted. "Calm down."

"McKenzie." Anna was standing in the doorway with Marian Crawford and Jenness. "Surely you must know that the worst thing you can tell someone in the throes of strong emotions is to calm down. It sounds like you're dismissing the reasons they're upset in the first place. I say, let them fight."

Olivia spun around and marched back to her table.

"If you were anywhere near as smart as you think you are, Annie, you'd stop talking and listen once in a while," she said.

"Hear, hear," Eden said.

The expression on Anna's face reminded me of the one on Carly's right after she was slapped.

"I don't mean to divide the family," Jenness said.

"The family was divided long before you were born," Alex said.

"Saving the castle—it should help keep us together."

"Let's hope so," Big Ben said.

He squeezed past the trio standing in the entrance and started moving in a straight line toward Olivia. Carly pulled his arm.

"Why?" she asked. "Just tell me why. Speak to me like—like I'm a stupid child and all of you are trying to humor me."

Big Ben wrapped his little sister in his enormous arms and pulled her close.

"I'm sorry," he said. "I am so sorry for the way I treated you when we were young; the way we all treated you. We should have done better. We should have—we should have done for you what we're doing for Jenny now. We should have given you a chance. That's why I voted against the development. I wanted to give Jenness her chance to make the castle pay. If she can't—the castle's not going anywhere, like Anna said. The property, Lake Anpetuwi, it isn't going to lose its value. If anything, it will only increase in value. Give Jenness six months to see if she can save the castle. One hundred and thirty-eight years it's been the family home. My God, it must be worth it, don't you think?"

"No, no, no." Carly pushed herself out of her brother's arms. "You said you should have given me a chance when we were young. Give it to me now. Do you know what I can do with one and a half million dollars?"

"You mean besides squander it?" Anna asked. "Sex, drugs, rock 'n' roll?"

Carly spun toward her older sister. I couldn't see her face; only her hands as they clenched and released. A moment later, Carly pushed past the trio still standing in the doorway and disappeared inside the castle.

"Carly, Carly," Marian called. There was no response. "Why did you say that?"

"Olivia's right," Big Ben said. "You're not very smart, Anna. You just have a lot of letters following your name."

Anna's response was to turn around and disappear inside the castle, too.

"I didn't want this," Jenness said. "I just wanted—I wanted to do what Tess asked me to do when she first hired me. Save the castle."

"Oh, honey." Marian ran her hands up and down her daughter's arm, and then pulled her close. "It'll be fine, you'll see."

"Dad isn't going to like this."

"It'll be fine."

And they, too, disappeared inside Redding Castle.

Ben moved next to the table where Olivia was sitting. She pretended not to see him standing there.

The volume of the music piped onto the patio suddenly seemed to increase—Ray Charles singing "It Had to Be You"— and for a moment I actually wondered if Big Ben had a remote in his pocket or if it only sounded louder because we were watching so intently. He offered Olivia his hand as if he were asking her to dance.

"They're playing our song," Ben said.

"Since when?"

"It could be our song if you let it."

"You've shared yourself with too many women, Ben."

"Yet I always come back to you. Truth is, I never actually leave. Besides, what about all those men—and women—that you've dallied with?"

Olivia's response was to sip more of her drink.

Big Ben continued to offer his hand.

"You weren't really planning to live in Redding, were you?" he asked.

Olivia shook her head.

"No," she said. "At least not anymore."

"Well, then?"

Olivia rose slowly from her seat and took Ben's hand.

"Why are we married, anyway?" she asked.

"For fun and profit," Ben answered. "But mostly for the fun."

At first, they stood apart as they swayed to the music. Only, as the song continued, they moved closer and closer until there wasn't any distance between them at all. They danced as one while Duke Ellington covered "I Got It Bad (and That Ain't Good)" and slid into full swing mode for "On the Sunny Side of the Street" by Louis Armstrong, two well-matched partners who anticipated and complemented each other's moves, both of them laughing. I didn't know if they loved each other, yet watching them dance it was clear to me that they *liked* each other immensely; that they reveled in each other's company, even when they slow danced to Earl Hines's piano version of "Blues My Naughty Sweetie Gave to Me."

"Hey, Ben?" Alex called from the edge of the patio. "Who's going to tell Boeve?"

Ben and Olivia stopped dancing.

"I guess I should," Ben said.

"No," Olivia said. "I should."

"Are you sure?"

"Yes. I suppose now's as good a time as any, too."

"I could go into town with you."

"No, I'll see you later."

"When?"

"Ben, this is going to be either a very short conversation or very long. You know what I mean."

"Good luck."

"I could say the same thing to you. Don't you have a call to make?"

"She'll get over it."

"We'll see."

All of the Reddings finally abandoned the patio. As if on cue, other guests began to fill it, claiming tables in anticipation of the setting sun. Nina appeared and seized the vacant chair next to mine.

"I am both shocked and a little dismayed," she told me.

"Why?"

"My staff seems to be running my business very well without me. My assistant manager actually told me to relax, they had this."

"I heard that you're not supposed to tell people to relax."

"What should you tell them?"

"Have a drink?"

"Sure."

I signaled a waitress and ordered Dracula wine. While she was waiting to be served, Nina asked, "So, anything interesting happen while I was gone?"

The water on Lake Anpetuwi at 11:00 P.M. was as smooth as glass, a pitiful cliché, of course, but appropriate when you consider how still and tranquil it was. Nina and I had commandeered kayaks and paddled a few hundred yards from the shore so she could show off her knowledge of the constellations to me, especially the water constellations.

"There's Capricornus, the sea goat," she said. "You can see Pisces the fish and over there, that's Aquarius, the water bearer. You can barely see it because it's so dim but—can you see where I'm pointing?—that's Piscis Austrinus, the southern fish."

No, I couldn't see where she was pointing. I could barely see her. The night sky might have been filled with billions upon billions of stars, as Carl Sagan once said, but it was also moon-free at that time in September. What's more, nearly all of the lights belonging to the homes located on Lake Anpetuwi had been extinguished including most of the lights in Redding Castle; the lake and shoreline were virtually invisible. There was one light glowing over the castle's patio and another much weaker lamp posted at the foot of the concrete staircase leading to the lake, although I suspected they were placed there less for illumination and more as a beacon that would allow late-night adventurers, like Nina and I, to find our way back home.

Yet, while I could make out only a dim outline of Nina and her kayak, I could see the planet Mars exactly where Nina had said it would be—I knew it was Mars because it was red—and Saturn to the right of Mars and the great star Antares—at least I think it was Antares—below and between them. Together the three bodies completed a triangle. I asked if it had a name.

"I think they just call it the Triangle," she said. "It'll disappear when winter comes."

After a few more pleasant moments of drifting together on the lake in the dark, we began to paddle toward the lights. When we were close enough, I used the flashlight on my cell phone to get ourselves onto the dock in one piece and secure the kayaks.

"I'm almost sorry that we're leaving in the morning," Nina said. "I like it here now that there's no drama."

From the castle I heard a distinct pop.

"What was that?" Nina asked.

It was followed by two more pops in quick succession.

I was looking at my cell phone so I knew the exact time—11:17 P.M.

"Is someone shooting off fireworks at this time of night?" Nina asked.

"They're gunshots," I said. "Stay here."

I started sprinting up the concrete steps toward the sound. I could hear Nina behind me.

"Here we go again."

I dashed up the steps, across the patio, and into the castle. I stopped in the lobby and listened hard for any kind of signal that would tell me where to go. I heard it in Jenness Crawford's voice.

"Ben, Ben!" she shouted. "Olivia?"

I climbed the stairs and moved quickly down the second-floor corridor. Jenness was dressed as I had seen her two nights before in gym shorts, a T-shirt, and nothing else. She was standing outside her grandmother's bedroom now used by her aunt and uncle. I watched her pound on the door.

"What's going on?" she asked. "Ben? Let me in. Please."

"What happened?" I asked.

"I don't know. I heard loud voices and then I heard— McKenzie, I thought they sounded like gunshots."

"I heard them, too."

"I can't get in." For the first time, I noticed that she had a large ring of keys in her hand. "The room is locked from the inside like—like when Tess . . . McKenzie, what should I do?"

"Stay here," I said.

I quickly made my way back down the corridor to the stairs leading to the lobby. I found Nina in there.

"Dammit," I said. "I told you to stay on the dock."

"You didn't actually think I would, did you?"

I shook my finger at the lobby floor.

"Stay down here," I said.

"Sure."

I moved through the front entrance and ran in the direction

of the barn. On the way, I thought I might be better off if I searched halfway down the bank in front of the castle, only this time I found the twenty-two-foot aluminum ladder exactly where it was supposed to be, hanging from hooks on the side of the barn.

I pulled it off the hooks and headed back toward the castle. I was no longer running; a forty-pound ladder is apt to slow you down.

I circled the castle until I found Tess's balcony. I extended the ladder and propped it up against the railing. I climbed it—without looking down—and hoisted myself over the railing onto the balcony. I went to the window. It was closed. I slid it open and climbed inside the room.

His body was the first thing that I saw, lying on the floor next to the bed. He was wearing pajamas beneath a knotted robe; his clothes soaked in blood. I moved to his side and placed two fingers against his carotid artery. It was a useless gesture, just the same. Big Ben Redding was dead. You could see it in his opened, unblinking eyes.

FOURTEEN

Jenness kept pounding on the bedroom door, only now it was my name that she chanted.

"McKenzie, McKenzie, are you in there?"

I went to the door. The dead bolt was firmly in place. I unlocked the door and deliberately opened it only a couple of feet. I didn't want Jenness to get past me; I didn't even want her to see inside. I squeezed out of the bedroom and shut the door behind me.

"What is it?" she asked.

Nina was standing behind her. I was actually relieved that she had refused to listen to me because I knew what was going to happen next.

"Hang on to yourself, sweetie," I said. "There's no easy way to say this. Big Ben has been shot. He's dead."

"No." Jenness attempted to get past me; tried to get inside the room. "No, no."

I kept her out.

"I'm sorry," I said. "I'm so, so sorry."

"Let me in."

"I can't, sweetie. It's now a crime scene. You don't want to see him anyway."

Nina moved up behind the young woman and wrapped her arms around her. She spoke softly.

"Jenny," she said. "Jenny, we need to leave here."

"But Ben . . ."

"Jenny?" I asked. "Did you see anyone after you heard the shots? When you went into the corridor, did you see anyone?"

"Not now," Nina said.

"Yes, now."

"What?" Jenness asked. "See anyone? No, I . . . No, no I didn't . . . I heard voices. I heard shouting and then . . . This can't be happening."

"Jenny? Where's Olivia?"

That caused her to stiffen and for a moment her mouth hung open.

"You don't think . . ." she said.

"Where is she?"

"I don't know. I haven't seen her since—since right after my presentation."

I nodded my head. That was a signal to Nina. She used her hands on Jenness's shoulders to spin the young woman around and guide her down the corridor. It wasn't an easy task. There was weeping and at one point I thought Jenness's legs would buckle beneath her. Beyond that, there didn't seem to be any other movement in the castle; if anyone heard the shots and Jenny's pounding, they didn't think to investigate.

I pulled my cell phone from my pocket and called Chief Gardner. She answered on the third ring. She knew it wasn't a social call. In Minnesota, you don't call someone after 10:00 P.M. unless there's a problem.

"What is it?" she asked.

"Dee . . ."

I told her what I had found and how I found it. She must

have put me on speakerphone because her voice became tinny-sounding and the volume went up and down as if she was moving around the room. Getting dressed, I guessed.

"I need you to secure the crime scene until I get there," she said.

"I will."

"I'll call the county's forensic unit and my investigators, the ME—hell, I'll bring everybody. McKenzie, you said the door was latched from the inside?"

"Yes."

"Like with Tess?"

"Yes. I had to . . . Ah, dammit!"

"What is it?"

I didn't answer. Instead, I went back inside the bedroom, the cell phone in my hand. I searched the walk-in closet and the enormous bathroom; I even peeked under the bed—something I should have done immediately after I discovered Ben's body. I found nothing except for a .32 wheel gun that had been discarded next to the open window. It had not been there when I first arrived, I was sure of it.

I heard the chief's voice over my cell phone speaker.

"McKenzie, what's going on?" she asked.

"I'm sorry, Dee."

"What happened?"

"I made it possible for the killer to escape."

That caused Chief Gardner to pause for a few beats.

"Dee?" I asked.

"Please, McKenzie, don't do anything else until I get there."

Chief Gardner and her people arrived without lights or sirens. They moved through the castle and its grounds quietly and professionally. I doubted that any guests would even know they were there until they woke in the morning.

The chief and I chatted quietly in the corridor, trying to stay out of the way of the county sheriff's department's forensics people who were doing their thing inside Big Ben's bedroom. The unit was called the "Investigative Division" even though it consisted of only two people.

I was once again giving the chief a step-by-step recitation of my activities, this time on the record; Officer Phillip Holzt was standing behind the chief, listening intently and taking notes.

"I'm sorry," I said for probably the twentieth time.

"I don't get it," Holzt said. "Sorry for what? It sounds to me like you did everything right."

"The door was locked from the inside," Chief Gardner reminded him. "The killer shot Ben and went to the door to make his getaway; that's my guess. Only Jenness Crawford was on the other side of it. The killer threw the dead bolt, keeping Jenness outside but also locking himself in. The killer remained trapped in the room until McKenzie put the ladder up and climbed through the window. The killer probably hid in the closet. When McKenzie left the room, when he went into the corridor, closing the door behind him, the killer went out the window and down the ladder, leaving the gun behind."

"Yeah, but how was McKenzie supposed to know that?"

"I used to be a professional," I said.

"Instead of a kibitzer," the chief said. "On the other hand, if you had discovered the killer, you probably would have been shot, too."

Again, my inner voice said.

"You're just trying to make me feel better about myself," I said aloud.

We were interrupted by a heavy thud, thud, thud that turned out to be Sheriff Douglas Housman marching down the corridor toward us, his weight making the corridor shake. He was followed closely by the Redding County medical examiner. Somehow I didn't think they had come together.

"Dee Dee, what do you think you're doing?" the sheriff wanted to know.

"Hello, Sheriff," the chief said. She gave a brief nod to Dr. Angelique Evers and gestured toward the door of the bedroom. Dr. Evers slid past her and stepped inside.

"You call my people out on a murder investigation without telling me," Sheriff Housman said. "Without asking for my permission? Who do you think you are?"

"I know how you like to go to bed early and since it's my jurisdiction . . ."

"You use my people it becomes my jurisdiction."

"Never going to happen."

"You don't talk to me like that, woman. I'm the county sheriff."

"How many murders have you investigated, Doug?"

The chief said "Doug" yet I heard "Doogie." I gestured toward the door to the art gallery behind me. Chief Gardner nodded her head even as she spoke to the sheriff.

"A double homicide six years ago," she said, "and you botched it. If it wasn't for the Bureau of Criminal Apprehension covering your ass the suspect would have walked. How many votes would that have cost you? In Minneapolis, I investigated as many as forty murders a year. A year. My clearance rate was ninety-three percent. You are not taking jurisdiction, Doug. Don't even think about it."

"I'll pull my people off."

"You do that. I'll call the BCA in Willmar and ask them to process the crime scene instead and you can explain why to the media and to the voters. Tell them why I was forced to go out-side the county for assistance. Are you feeling me? Look, Doug, you want everyone to think that you're large and in charge, I get that. So, tell them you're running a multi-department investi-gation, 'kay—just thinking? Tell them that it's such a heinous crime, the killing of a Redding heir in the Redding Castle, that you personally formed a joint task force to guarantee that justice will be served. I'll even make sure you're there when we make an arrest. Hell, I'll let you make the arrest. Just get out of my way."

I don't know what the sheriff had to say to that. I stepped inside the art gallery and immediately heard a loud whooshing sound as if all of the air was being sucked out of the room.

Moments passed, yet I didn't move.

Finally, Chief Gardner entered the art gallery.

"It's all about PR with Doogie," she said.

Dr. Evers followed behind her.

"This is going to be an easy death certificate to write," she said. "Let me know when you're done, Dee, and I'll have my people remove the body. I'll perform the autopsy tonight and give you a detailed report—what?"

The chief was staring at me staring at the wall.

"McKenzie, what is it?" she asked.

"Look around," I said.

"At what?"

"I don't see anything," Dr. Evers said.

"That's the point," I said.

"The paintings," Chief Gardner said. "The Remington and Whistler, they're gone."

Jenness was sitting on a sofa in the castle's enormous lobby. She was still dressed in gym shorts and a T-shirt. Her face was streaked with tears, yet she wasn't crying now. Nina was seated next to her; her hand resting on Jenness's shoulder. She looked as if she had been crying, too.

Chief Gardner had waited until Dr. Evers and her people removed Big Ben's body. Afterward, she went straight to where Jenness was sitting and knelt in front of her. She took the young woman's hands in hers.

"I'm sorry," the chief said. "I'm going to be asking a lot of you at the worst possible time. I wish I could leave you alone to mourn your uncle only I can't."

Jenness nodded her head as if she understood, yet I doubted that she did.

"Tell me what you heard," Chief Gardner said.

"I told McKenzie."

"I know. Tell me."

Jenness did, explaining how she had been watching TV when she heard loud voices raised in argument coming from the room next to hers—the room that Big Ben and Olivia had shared.

"You heard Ben's and Olivia's voices?" the chief asked.

"They were very loud and I was afraid they would disturb the other guests, not on this floor because the only two guest rooms are on the far side of the castle, but above them and . . ."

"Ben and Olivia's voices?"

"Yes, I told you. They were coming from the room, oh, I get it. The voices. I heard the voices only I—I didn't know what they were saying and, I guess, I can't say for certain that they were Ben's or Olivia's. Is that what you want to know?"

"Yes."

"If it wasn't them, who could it be?"

"You heard the voices . . ."

"I heard the voices and then I heard the gunshots. McKenzie says he heard them, too, only they didn't sound like—they didn't explode like they do on TV or in the movies. I mean they weren't as loud. When I heard them I jumped out of bed. I was in bed, and I went out of my room into the corridor and over to Ben's room right next to mine and I knocked on the door. And I called his name. And Olivia's. I was—I know it sounds silly now, but I was concerned about the noise. I didn't become frightened until—until I started pounding on the door and no one answered."

"Could anyone have left that room without you knowing?"

"I don't see how. I got out of bed so fast after I heard the shots and there was no one in the corridor."

Chief Gardner was gazing at me when she said, "Okay."

So as not to appear like a complete putz, I decided to enter the fray, so to speak.

"What about the servant stairs?" I asked.

"No," Jenness said. "I would have seen if someone was using them. I would have heard."

"Servant stairs?" the chief asked.

"I'll tell you later," I said. "Jenny, where's Anna? She was staying in your room, wasn't she?"

"She's in the kitchen now."

"Now?"

Nina nodded.

"She was coming through the door of the castle at the same time that we came down to the lobby earlier," she said.

"Why wasn't she in the bedroom with you?" I asked.

"I was watching TV," Jenness said. "Watching TV on my computer. Anna said if I was going to watch TV, then she would come downstairs to read even though I told her I'd be happy to wear headphones."

"How long was she gone before you heard the voices arguing?" Chief Gardner asked.

"An hour maybe. I wasn't paying attention to the time."

"For the record," Anna said. "I didn't hear or see a thing."

Anna moved across the lobby more or less from the direction of the kitchen. She was carrying a mug of hot chocolate topped with mini-marshmallows on a tray. She set the tray on a table next to the sofa, picked up the mug, and handed it to her niece.

"I don't think this is going to help," Jenness said.

"It can't hurt," Anna told her. "My mom, your grandmother, was very big on treating trauma with hot chocolate."

Jenness took a sip and winced slightly at an unexpected taste.

"It's spiked with peppermint vodka." Anna said. "That was something else she used to add once we became of age."

Jenness took a long pull of the drink. Anna sat next to her and wrapped her arm around her shoulder as if she was claiming her niece away from Nina. She was wearing pink satin pajamas beneath a matching robe and slippers. I could see the bottom of one of her slippers when she crossed her legs. If they had been outside, I couldn't tell.

"You left the bedroom because you wanted to read," Chief Gardner said.

"Yes," Anna said. "I like it quiet."

"Where did you go?"

"Down here."

"Where?"

"Here, here, in the lobby." Anna twisted on the sofa and pointed at a corner of the lobby behind her where two stuffed chairs and a small table were located. The lamp on the table was lit.

"I was catching up on my Louise Erdrich," she said.

"Did you hear the shots?" the chief asked.

"No."

"Did you hear your niece pounding on the door?"

"No."

"Anna," I said. "When I came into the lobby, you weren't here."

"I went for a walk," she said. "I guess I missed all the excitement. By the time I returned, Jenness was here with . . ."

She wagged a finger at Nina as if she had misplaced her name.

"Awful late to be going for a walk," Chief Gardner said.

"Not really. It was a very pleasant evening and up until an hour ago I would have said perfectly safe. I wished to observe the night sky. Saturn, Mars, and Antares are particularly bright this time of year."

"While you were down here, before you went on your walk, did you see anyone enter or leave the castle?"

"No, but you don't need to take my word for it." Anna pointed behind Chief Gardner and me at a camera positioned very near the castle's reservation desk. "Surely, the security camera is working."

"We'll examine the footage in a minute. Ms. Redding—"

"Dr. Redding."

"Dr. Redding, have you seen your sister-in-law lately?"

"Olivia?" Anna's hand came up to cover her mouth. She spoke into her palm. "I hadn't thought of that."

She slowly removed her hand.

"I have not seen Olivia since immediately following Jenny's presentation late this afternoon," Anna said. "I am aware, of course, that she and Ben were not in agreement concerning the future of the castle."

"You can't possibly believe—no, no, it's not true," Jenness said.

"There's a very good possibility that this incident has nothing to do with the sale of the castle, but rather—" Chief Gardner said.

"Incident?" Anna said. "Is that what you label it?"

"The artwork in your gallery," the chief added. "When did you last see it?"

"What do you mean?" Jenness said.

"The Remington and Whistler are missing."

Anna was on her feet so quickly you'd think she won a chance to play *The Price Is Right*.

"They can't be," she said.

"And yet they are," I told her.

Anna made to cross the lobby and dash up the stairs. Chief Gardner blocked her path.

"The gallery is a crime scene," the chief said. "My people are processing it now. I'll let you know when you can go back into the room; back into Ben's bedroom."

"Yes, of course."

Anna reclaimed her seat next to Jenness.

"What a waste," she said.

"Waste?" asked Chief Gardner.

"If they're not recovered, I mean. Both paintings are irreplaceable."

"So is Ben," Jenness said.

"Of course he is, dear. Drink your chocolate."

Chief Gardner needed Jenness's help compiling the names, addresses, and phone numbers of every single person who had visited Redding Castle in the past week including guests, staff, and delivery people as well as family members. She didn't require her help in accessing the footage taken by the security cameras in the lobby, restaurant, and parking lot, though, only her permission. The chief and I studied every second of video even as she downloaded copies. We saw Anna descending the stairs with her book in hand and crossing the lobby toward the chairs and table she had pointed to earlier. The way the camera was set, though, we couldn't actually see her sitting in a chair. She came back into frame fifteen minutes later and we watched as she walked out of the front door, again with her book in hand. The time stamp read 10:37 P.M.

The chief rewound the video, stopping it when Anna first came into view.

"Ten twenty-three," she said.

"So, Anna leaves the bedroom at ten twenty-three, spends a grand total of fourteen minutes reading, and then steps out at ten thirty-seven, exactly forty minutes before I heard the gunshots."

"We see her again entering the lobby at eleven thirty-four, just as Jenness and—that's Nina, your wife?"

"Yes."

"She's lovely."

"Even under the worst conditions," I said.

"So much better than you deserve."

"True, very true."

"Anna's late-night stroll lasted forty minutes."

"Seems long."

"Especially in thin pajamas and a robe. How cold is it?"

The face of my cell phone displayed the time, date, and temperature. I tapped an icon to refresh the image.

"Fifty-four degrees."

"If it was February, kids would have been running around in shorts," the chief said. "In September—I don't know."

"Perhaps she wasn't outside all that time."

Chief Gardner had put the footage from the parking lot back on the monitor and let it run.

"Anna didn't come back into the lobby," she said. "We don't see her in the restaurant or parking lot. We don't see anyone until you arrive in the lobby at eleven eighteen."

"Wait," I said. "Go back."

"What?"

"The parking lot footage, go back."

The chief reversed the image on the screen.

"Okay, wait, wait, wait. Now go forward. Watch this area here." I pointed at the upper part of the screen. "Did you see that?"

"Yes."

Chief Gardner reversed the image and let it run it forward again.

"There seems to be movement only we can't make out what's moving," she said.

"There's no moon tonight and the light from the parking lot doesn't touch this area. Jenness uses shields to reduce light pollution."

"It could be a deer."

"Hell, it could be a bear."

"It's moving fast, whatever it is. What's the time?"

"The stamp reads ten twenty-six."

"Three minutes after Anna moves into the lobby and eleven minutes before she leaves it, not that that matters."

"It does matter. Come with me, Chief. I want to show you something."

I led Chief Gardner up the staircase to the second-floor corridor and down the corridor toward the art gallery and Big Ben's bedroom. The Investigative Division was packing up its gear.

"You have the weapon?" the chief asked.

"We have the weapon," replied the head of the team.

"You have the vic's phone?"

"We have his phone."

"I don't know which is more important."

"I'll tell you as soon as I find out. We should have at least a prelim in the morning."

"I'd like to see your case report before the sheriff does," Chief Gardner said.

"I can't promise that; you know how he is. I do promise you'll get the real goods. I won't hold anything back just to please him."

"Thank you."

"Thank you, Chief. It's a pleasure to work with professionals. Off the record, if you decide to run for county sheriff, you'll have my vote."

"Thank you."

The specialists sealed the bedroom and the art gallery with crime scene tape and retreated down the hallway toward the lobby.

"What do you want to show me?" Chief Gardner asked.

I nudged the wall at the end of the corridor, listened for a distinctive click, and swung the wall open, showing the chief that it was actually a door. Beyond the door was the white staircase.

"What do you know?" she said. "A secret passageway."

"They call it the servant stairs," I said. "It's not a secret, though. I was told that the family and everyone who has ever worked at Redding Castle knows about it."

"Where does it lead?"

"Spirals down to the kitchen."

"Have you used it?"

"No."

"Let's go."

"You first."

"Ha."

We descended the staircase to the kitchen, swinging open the door at the bottom. It looked just like any other door that you've ever seen; there was nothing secret about it.

The kitchen was large and impossibly clean; when the chief snapped on the lights, I had to shield my eyes from the reflection off the counters and the large stainless steel refrigerator and range. There were three additional doors in the kitchen. One led to a pantry, a second, much larger door, led to the dining room, and a third door on the far side of the kitchen led outside. Chief Gardner crossed over to it. It was unlocked. She yanked it open.

"Now we know how the artwork was smuggled out," she said.

"It would have been a tough haul down the stairs. The Remington was about three feet by four and a half. The Whistler was only a little bit smaller."

"Two thieves?"

"Two trips?"

"Three trips. The thief was returning to the art gallery for the Nast illustrations. Ben Redding discovered the thief. The thief forced Ben at gunpoint back inside his bedroom and one thing led to another."

"That's one theory."

"I'm open to suggestions."

"Two separate crimes?"

"I would prefer one. We find the paintings, we find the killer."

"The FBI has a rapid deployment Art Crime Team in Milwaukee. I know the agent in charge."

"Of course you do. That would suggest, though, that the thief was a pro; that he already had a fence or a buyer lined up before he made his move."

"Whoever did it knew enough to avoid the cameras in the lobby and parking lot."

"Except art thieves don't shoot people. It makes prominent artwork impossible to sell. It's one thing to buy hot, it's another to buy bloody."

"A spontaneous act then."

"Who do you know who wants the art and might be stupid enough to steal it?"

"Olivia Redding?"

"She doesn't strike me as stupid."

"It's her husband that Dr. Evers is slicing up as we speak."

"I hesitate to send out a BOLO until I know more. You said she lives in Edina? I'll reach out to the EPD and have them surveil her house in case she goes home."

"I think I might know where she is."

"Well, by all means, Jessica, lead the way."

Cassandra Boeve's enormous home looked as if it had been built and artfully displayed solely to flaunt her architectural skills to potential customers. It was located just south of downtown Redding in a large, flat, open field with nothing to distract the casual observer from its railed rooftop balcony called a "widow's walk," high windows, arched doorways, sunporch, multilevel patios, and three-car garage attached to the house by a breezeway. Much of the house was hidden from view at that time of night, especially after Chief Gardner flicked off the headlights of her SUV, yet I saw enough of it to make me feel as though I should wipe my feet.

The chief and I left the SUV on the concrete driveway and followed a narrow sidewalk made of fitted flagstones to the porch. I did wipe my feet on a welcome mat as the chief pressed the doorbell.

"This is the part of the job I hate the most," she said.

I agreed with her.

There were a few lights burning inside the house, yet at two in the morning, we didn't expect anyone to be awake.

Chief Gardner pressed the doorbell again. A moment later we heard a woman's voice.

"Who is it?"

The chief identified herself even as the porch light flicked on and a shadow passed over the spyhole. A moment later, the door was pulled open and I recognized Cassandra Boeve. She was wearing a dark blue robe that extended to her ankles that she tightened when she saw us, her makeup was smeared, and her hair disheveled and my first thought—she hadn't been sleeping when we rang the doorbell.

"Councilwoman Boeve, may we come in?" the chief asked.

"Chief Gardner, yes, of course." Cassandra opened the door wide enough for us to pass through. "What is this about? It's awfully late."

I could identify only two rooms from off the foyer, both with high ceilings and plenty of dark wood. To the right was a living room built for entertaining large parties and to the left was a dining room where the same large parties could eat without being crowded together.

"Councilwoman, we're looking for Olivia Redding," the chief said.

"Oh? What makes you think she's here?"

"Cassie." Olivia appeared from around a corner. Her robe was pink and thin and ended above her knees; she seemed only slightly as disheveled as Cassandra, making me think she had time to comb her hair. "Ben would never have sent them if it wasn't important." She moved closer to us. "What's happened? Another cross burning?"

"Ms. Redding, I'm Deidre Gardner, chief of the City of Redding Police Department."

"I know. I saw you at the city council meeting last night. What happened? McKenzie?"

The chief stepped forward.

"Ms. Redding, I regret to inform you that Ben Redding was shot and killed tonight at Redding Castle," she said.

"Oh no, no, no, no," Cassandra chanted.

Olivia said nothing. She stared at the chief as if she had heard a strange sound that she was having difficulty comprehending.

"Ms. Redding . . ." the chief said.

Sounds started coming from Olivia's mouth, vowels and consonants that formed no words. At the same time, she waved a hand behind her as if she were searching for a chair. She started to sit even though she couldn't find one. The chief and I both moved forward, catching her before she fell. We managed to half drag, half carry her to a sofa inside the living room. Once Olivia was seated, Cassandra pushed between us and wrapped her arms around her friend.

Olivia stared at the woman as if she didn't know who she was.

"I should, I should—there's something I should do," she said. "Something . . ."

"Oh, Livy . . ."

And Olivia Redding melted into a sea of tears before my eyes.

I admired Chief Gardner's patience. She had many questions to ask, yet waited until Olivia was more or less in a frame of mind to answer them. Many minutes passed and several glasses of water consumed. Cassandra had offered her friend something harder to drink, yet Olivia had refused.

"I need to keep my wits about me," she said.

More minutes passed.

"Do you know who did this?" Olivia asked.

"Not yet," the chief replied.

"Where was he shot?"

"In your bedroom."

Olivia shook her head.

"Why am I not surprised?" she said. As the words came out of her mouth, though, she closed her eyes and gritted her teeth as if she felt a sudden pain that she was trying to power through.

"Do you know who could have shot him?" the chief asked.

"You mean besides me?"

"Ms. Redding . . ."

"No, I don't. I know members of my family were upset that he voted against selling the castle, but that was . . . I don't know."

"You were upset that he voted against selling the castle," I said.

"Yes, but I had always known that he was going to. I've known since the subject first came up after Tess died. Ben wanted a reason to keep coming back home to Redding and the castle gave him that. Without the castle, what was he going to do? Stay on the farm with Marian and Ed?"

"Ms. Redding, where were you tonight?" the chief asked.

Olivia nodded at the question as if she had been expecting it.

"Here, with Cassie," she said.

"All night?"

"From about—when did I arrive? Five thirty?"

"Yes," Cassandra said. "Before six, anyway."

"You never left the house?" the chief said.

"No. Except . . ."

"We went to dinner," Cassandra said.

"When? Where?"

"It was late."

"I came here around five thirty and told Cassie what happened with the castle vote," Olivia said. "She was very upset as I knew she would be. It took a while before we were able to . . . We talked it over, talked about how six months from now everything could change. The possibility that Jenny would fail—that made us feel better. Gave us hope for the future. And then we made love. Afterward, we went to a Pheuxn Café for some Thai food. After that, we came back here and made love again."

"You can check with the restaurant," Cassandra said. "They know me there."

Chief Gardner didn't say if she believed their alibi or not, but I knew that she would verify it one way or another, of course she would. She'd call on the restaurant. If it came to it, she would get a subpoena for Olivia's and Cassandra's GPS records.

"Do you know who could have been in that bedroom with Ben?" the chief asked.

"Honestly, Chief, your guess is as good as mine," Olivia said.

"Do you know if he had any enemies in Redding?"

"I want to say no. For all his faults, and his faults mostly affected me, Ben was a very likeable guy."

"You want to say no, but you won't?"

"It was Ben who burned the cross behind Redding Castle."

"What? No," Cassandra said. "He couldn't have."

"I saw him," Olivia said. "I had been sleeping. He woke me when he tried to slip out of the bed unnoticed. Ben was not the most graceful of men except when he was dancing or playing ball. I didn't say anything at the time because I didn't want to have that conversation again. Besides, I had spent part of the afternoon with Cassie—and Ben probably knew it, so—so I pretended I was asleep. After he left, I couldn't go back to sleep, though. My mind was too busy wondering who he was going to meet. A guest in the castle? It was possible. Ben made friends easily, you see. I even considered the possibility that he had arranged to meet Eden. He had spoken of her earlier that evening in somewhat admiring terms, both he and Anna. He said he liked her fierceness and fearlessness. He actually used those words. He liked that she could be inspired to do most anything for a just cause.

"Eventually, I went to the art gallery like I told you, Chief. I saw the flames like I told you. I saw Ben, which I didn't tell you. He didn't look up at the window and wave, yet it was easy enough to identify him after—forty-two years we've known each other. I called 911, refusing to give my name. Now you know why. After Ben made sure the cross was burning properly, he went back inside the castle. I returned to the bedroom and crawled under the sheets. A few minutes later, Ben climbed into bed with me and we both pretended we were asleep until we heard the sirens."

"Why?" Chief Gardner asked. "Why would he do such a terrible thing?"

"He did it to manipulate Eden. He didn't tell me that; it's just my guess. He needed an argument powerful enough to convince Eden to vote against her own best interests, against all that money. The burning cross—her vote wasn't so much against selling the castle to Cassie, it was a vote against the Sons of Europa. And it gave Ben the majority."

"You told me that Eden was going to vote in favor of my offer," Cassandra said.

"I told you what you wanted to hear. I told you what I wanted to happen."

"You lied."

"I didn't . . ."

"You never intended to sell the castle to me, either, did you? Did you?"

"Cassie . . ."

"If you had wanted it to happen, you would have said something about the burning cross. You would have told people; told the police what you saw that night. You would have told me. Why didn't you?"

"I couldn't do that to Ben."

"You said you loved me, only that's not true."

"Yes, it is."

"I see it now. You've never loved me. You just used me the same way Ben used Aunt Ronnie."

"I love you more than I have words to say."

"No. It's all a lie. You were never going to move to Redding to be with me; that was never going to happen, was it? Was it?"

"I can't run Ben's Beez from Redding."

Cassandra closed her eyes, shook her head, opened her eyes, and stalked out of the living room without uttering another word, disappearing into her enormous house.

"I need to return to the castle," Olivia said. "McKenzie, I don't think I can drive. Would you . . ."

"Yes, of course," I said.

"Give me a moment to get dressed."

After she left the room, Chief Gardner glanced at her watch.

"I need to get back to the house," she said. "And then I need to get some sleep. You, too. Tomorrow is going to be a busy day."

"I take it I'm still working as a consultant for the City of Redding Police Department. You know, I have yet to see a contract."

"It's in the mail. McKenzie, I had a thought while Olivia was telling us about Ben and the cross. Could someone else have seen him besides her?"

"You mean Mr. Doty?"

"I never liked that he didn't have a reason for getting out of bed at one thirty in the morning."

"I never liked that he stood up for the Sons of Europa when everyone was blaming them for burning the cross."

"Do you think he was holding out on us?"

"We can ask."

Olivia appeared in the living room five minutes after Chief Gardner left. She was dressed now in tight jeans and boots and a red cable knit sweater with one shoulder cut out; not the same clothes she had been wearing on the patio when she had danced with her husband. Her hair was combed, her makeup neatly applied. She slung her bag over her shoulder and went to the door. Her hand was on the knob.

"Cassie!" she shouted. "Cassie, I do love you. I will always love you. Please understand."

Cassandra Boeve didn't reply.

"Good-bye, Cassie."

Olivia opened the door and we stepped out onto the porch.

"It never would have worked, anyway," she told me. "I'm too old for her."

Olivia led me to her car, a BMW hybrid, and pressed the key fob in my hand, although it probably wasn't necessary. It would have started with her holding it just as well as me. We eased backward out of Cassandra's long driveway to the street and started making our way through downtown Redding toward the castle.

Olivia didn't have anything to say until she did. Her words came out in a torrent. Ben was this, Ben was that; their marriage was a sham except for when it wasn't. She brought both her legs up and kicked the dashboard while she chanted obscenities in time to the kicking.

She became quiet again and stayed quiet until I drove the BMW into the parking lot of Redding Castle. After turning off the car, I gave her the key fob. She squeezed it in her hand as if it was a precious gem she was afraid to let slip from her grasp.

"I loved him so much," she said.

The tears began to flow again.

We stayed in the car for a long time.

I tried to remain quiet when I entered the James J. Hill Cabin, yet managed to wake Nina just the same. Either that or she was waiting up for me. She descended the stairs from the loft bedroom.

"How did it go?" she asked.

"I don't believe Olivia Redding killed her husband, if that's what you mean. Or Cassandra Boeve."

"That's not what I meant."

"I'm fine," I said.

"Are you?"

"I am and just so you know—I'll always be fine because no matter what happens, no matter what tragedies I visit, I always have you to come home to."

"Sometimes you say the most romantic things."

FIFTEEN

It was late in the morning when I received a text from Chief Gardner—"Mr. Doty first."

I wandered across the clearing behind the castle, finally taking a seat on a bench not far from where Big Ben Redding had burned his cross. We are none of us just one person, but rather many different people depending on the circumstances. Ben had been a good man until he wasn't, well-liked by the people who knew him; a serial philanderer, true, yet also a sports hero, an entrepreneur, a businessman; funny and pleasant; he made me smile. Yet the majority of people would always remember him now as the despicable jerk that burned a cross in his own backyard. Probably, he deserved it, too. What was it Shakespeare wrote? *The evil that men do lives after them; the good is oft interred with their bones.* I thought it was sad just the same.

When Chief Gardner's black-and-white SUV entered the lot, I left the bench and walked to where she had parked. I made a production of looking at my watch while she exited the vehicle.

"What?" I asked. "Did you decide to sleep in this morning?"

"You should have my problems, McKenzie, you really should. Have you seen Mr. Doty?"

"No."

Chief Gardner started across the parking lot toward the barn. I joined her.

"How's the mood in the castle?" she asked.

"Everyone's behaving like someone died, Jenness especially."

"Any ugly rumors I should know about?"

"I overheard a couple on the patio blame the Sons of Europa."

The chief stopped walking.

"I wish to God it was them. Nothing would give me greater pleasure than frog-marching Lawspeaker Fredgaard and his entire racist, terrorist cell into a courtroom. Only they're going to come out of this looking like some damn victim-hero; a martyr to the cause of white supremacy. Fucking Ben Redding, what was he thinking?"

The evil men do, my inner voice said.

"I take it you don't think the Sons are involved in Ben's death," I said aloud.

"I'll tell you why later. Mr. Doty first."

We found Mr. Doty sitting on a high stool in front of his workbench surrounded by his tools. Only he wasn't working, just sitting there, as if the tools were talking to him, telling him stories.

I said, "Good morning, Mr. Doty."

He ignored me.

"Chief of Police," Mr. Doty said. "Been waitin' on you."

"Oh?"

"Come to arrest me, ain't cha?"

"Have you committed a crime?"

"No."

Chief Gardner moved to the workbench and leaned against it so she could look him directly in the eye.

"It's time for the truth, Mr. Doty," she said. "Don't lie to me again."

"Truth and nothin' but the truth."

"That's right."

"I didn't lie to you before."

"I asked if you knew how the cross got there; you said you didn't. That was a lie."

"Ma'am, you don't know . . ."

"We know about Ben Redding."

Mr. Doty stared like he was playing Texas Hold'em and wondering if the chief was bluffing.

"Did you help him build that cross?" Chief Gardner asked.

Mr. Doty stared some more.

"Mr. Doty . . ."

"No, ma'am. Didn't help. When I found him in the barn; I heard a noise, knew someone was about, so I come down and found him." Mr. Doty pointed toward the corner where the extra wood was being stored. "He had already doused the cross with gasoline time I got here. Tried to talk Mr. Ben out of it, I did; told him this was a bad thing he was doing. Mr. Ben said he was saving the castle. He asked me if that was a bad thing. I said no, it wasn't only—you gotta remember, Chief of Police, I worked for Mr. Ben. Technically, I work for all them Reddings, not just Miss. Been workin' for 'em since they was just little kids."

"You cut the cross down and smothered it with sand."

"That was only after McKenzie here got involved. Mr. Ben said he wanted to make a statement. I figured by then the statement had already been made whatever that was supposed to be. Am I in trouble?"

"Last night . . ."

"Chief of Police, I ain't got nothing to do with that, I ain't lyin'."

"Where were you last night at about eleven fifteen?"

"I was in my cabin." Mr. Doty tapped the top of the workbench. "I was in bed." He tapped it again. "That ain't no lie. You can ask the missus." He tapped the bench a third time. "I heard McKenzie here. Went to the window when I heard 'im around the barn." Another tap. "I saw him hurrying off with the ladder. I told myself, whatever it is I ain't involving myself this time. Whatever the Reddings are up to is on them. That's a fact." He emphasized his last statement with an even louder tap.

"Did you see anyone besides McKenzie?"

Mr. Doty didn't answer.

"Did you see anyone on the grounds besides McKenzie?" Chief Gardner said.

"Not then," Mr. Doty replied.

"When?"

"Hour before McKenzie I saw someone. I was getting ready for bed."

Make it ten thirty, my inner voice said.

"What did you see?" Chief Gardner asked.

"Over there." Mr. Doty gestured more or less at the edge of the clearing. "Where the woods meet up with the driveway."

The chief was thinking the same thing I was; I could see it in her eyes. The shadow we had spotted on the parking lot security footage.

"What did you see?" Chief Gardner asked.

"At first I thought it was a deer," Mr. Doty said. "Then I saw her face clear. It was Miss Carly."

It wasn't difficult to learn that Carly Zumwalt lived in a house located two blocks from Redding High School. Chief Gardner took us there in her SUV. Along the way I quizzed her about how she knew that the Sons of Europa had nothing to do with Big Ben Redding's murder.

"I spent most of the morning meeting with my nerds," the chief said. "In Minneapolis, a murder investigation is just a job. Ballistic experts, fingerprint analysts, forensic pathologists, evidence technicians—I don't care how dedicated they are, how conscientious, they're all just doing their jobs and when you're investigating fifty murders or more a year, it gets treated like a job. Out here, though, where you have one homicide in a decade, it becomes a very big job. Everyone gets excited. Everyone wants to do their best. It hasn't been twenty-four hours yet and I already have a ballistics report. Ben was shot with by a .32-caliber handgun purchased in 2001 by Joseph R. Redding."

"Joseph Redding?"

"Tess's husband; he passed in 2004."

"Do you think the piece was left in the room he shared with his wife; the room where Ben and Olivia were staying?"

"That's just one of the items on the long list of things we don't know. Anyway, my guys . . ."

"Your guys?"

"I think of them as my guys now, screw the sheriff. My guys said the gun was wiped down. However, they were able to lift a partial off the end of the barrel. They're running it through the FBI's fingerprint database as we speak."

"The Integrated Automated Fingerprint Identification System," I said. "You'd think they'd come up with a catchier name."

"Whatever they call it, nearly a third of the population is in there for one reason or another, so fingers crossed. What else? Angie, Dr. Angelique Evers, told me that Big Ben had sexual congress—her words, not mine—with an unidentified female almost immediately before he was killed. She swabbed his dick and found plenty of woman jizz—my words, not hers."

"DNA from the fluid?" I asked.

"In the Cities, I've seen DNA tests take as long as fourteen days to go from the crime scene to a reliable profile. What'll you bet I get mine within seventy-two hours? I might even get it sooner than that. This afternoon. Angie says she has friends."

"What about Ben's cell phone?"

"My new best friend in the county's Investigative Division says they haven't unlocked it yet."

"The slacker," I said. "What's he been doing for the last"—I glanced at my watch—"twelve hours?"

"I know, right? He told me he'd call as soon as they have access. I'm very curious to learn where Ben's been in the past couple of days and who he's called."

"Have you cleared Olivia?"

"Yes. Her and Boeve. The old man at the Thai restaurant says they make a nice couple."

"Maybe Olivia can unlock the cell for us."

"Something to consider."

By then we had arrived at Carly Zumwalt's house. There were two cars in the driveway of her three-bedroom split-level and I assumed that one of them belonged to Madison. I had hoped that she wouldn't be home, except it was early afternoon on a Saturday in Redding, Minnesota. Where else would she be?

Chief Gardner knocked on the door. It was Madison who answered it. She looked as if she had been crying and for a moment I was relieved. I'm sure the chief was, too. Explaining to someone that their loved one had died, much less that they had been murdered, was the worst duty a cop can perform.

"Morning, Madison," the chief said.

"Chief. McKenzie."

"I am so sorry for your loss."

"Thank you."

"Madison, we would like to speak to your mother."

Madison moved to keep us from entering the house.

"She's not home," she said.

"Isn't that her car in the driveway?" the chief asked.

"What I meant is that she's not home to visitors. She's still in bed."

"Awfully late in the day."

"She—she isn't feeling well."

"Do you know what happened to your uncle?" the chief said.

"Yes. I can't believe—it's a terrible thing."

"Madison, it's important that we speak to your mother."

"I told you, she's sick. Why do you need to talk to her, anyway? She didn't do anything."

"Madison . . ."

"She was here all last night."

"I need her to tell me that."

"She's sick, I told you."

"What she means is that I'm hungover," Carly said. She appeared behind her daughter. She was wearing a sweatshirt and pants that announced her allegiance to the Redding High School Red Hawks; her hair and face, especially the eyes, suggested that she had been awake for approximately thirty seconds.

"Let them in, Maddie," she said.

"Mom . . ."

"It's all right."

Madison opened the door wide and moved out of the way. The chief and I stepped inside. Madison closed the door and leaned against it as if she couldn't wait to open it again.

"I'm sorry that you're not feeling well," Chief Gardner said.

Carly moved deeper inside her house and we followed.

"A self-inflicted wound; that's what Ben would say," she told us. "You shouldn't feel sorry for people who hurt themselves, he would say."

"When did you last see your brother?" the chief asked.

"On the patio right after Jenny's presentation. McKenzie was there. He'll tell you. I was pissed off because Ben and Annie and Eden—don't think for a second it was Alex; Eden does all the thinking in that family; she's had him by the balls for years. Decades. They voted against selling the castle. Even Jenny's mother knew it was a good deal, yet they decided against selling. Cheated me out of one and a half million dollars."

"Mom," Madison said. She moved to a stuffed chair and sat on the edge. "Mom, you talk too much."

"I'm not saying anything that they don't already know," Carly told her. "Anyway, McKenzie heard what they said to me, what Annie said to me. I just—I just couldn't deal with them anymore so I walked out. I haven't seen any of them since."

"You heard what happened to your brother?" the chief asked.

"Last night. Jenny called. She said—she said I should know." Carly looked for a chair, found one, and sat down. "Someone murdered my brother. Probably . . ."

"Probably?"

"Ben slept around. Everyone knew it. Livy knew it. My first thought was to blame her, only he's been doing it for so long and she's been doing it, too, so . . . They had an open marriage, I guess. I tried something like that myself with my second husband. It didn't work out. Besides, Ben—he wasn't that bad a guy."

Carly lowered her head and covered her eyes with her hand. If we had left her alone with her grief she might have started crying. The chief didn't have time for that.

"Madison said you were here all night," she said. "Is that true?"

Carly looked up at her daughter; I couldn't read her expression.

"That's right," she said.

"All night?" Chief Gardner asked.

Carly took her time replying as if she was weighing the consequences of her words.

"No," she said. "I went to the liquor store for a bottle of vodka. We were out."

"When?"

"I don't remember exactly."

"Give me an estimate."

"Ten, ten thirty."

"How long were you gone?"

"Ten minutes. Fifteen. The store is like a mile and a half from here."

"How did you pay?"

"What?"

"How did you pay for the vodka? Cash? Check?"

"Credit card."

"You know we can check with the liquor store; we can check with the credit card company."

"Go 'head."

I was watching Madison fidget throughout the exchange. *She seems awfully anxious,* my inner voice told me.

"Did you go back to the castle?" Chief Gardner asked.

"No, why would I?"

"When you went to the liquor store . . ."

"I said no."

"You're saying that you went directly to the liquor store . . ."

"Yes."

"And you came directly back home . . ."

"Yes."

"And the entire trip took ten, fifteen minutes."

"That's right."

"Ms. Redding, I have a witness who places you at the castle no later than ten twenty-six P.M."

"That's bullshit."

"I have video showing . . ."

"That's bullshit," Carly repeated. "I was nowhere near the castle last night."

I watched as Madison ground her fingernails into the palms

of her hands. Unlike Chief Gardner, I didn't think she was doing it to keep from laughing.

She's trying to keep from screaming.

I took a chance.

"For the record," I said, "Big Ben was killed at exactly eleven seventeen P.M."

Chief Gardner's head snapped toward me. Her eyes suggested that I was insane.

Madison looked at me, too. Her eyes expressed surprise.

"What did you say?" she asked.

"I said your uncle was killed at eleven seventeen. Exactly."

"Oh God, oh God, Mother." Madison slipped off her chair and knelt on the floor. She used her hands to steady herself. "I thought . . . Oh, my God."

"Maddie . . ."

"She was here. She was here at eleven seventeen. She came through the door—it was a quarter to eleven. I know it, I know it. I swear it's true."

Carly came off her chair and knelt next to her daughter.

"Maddie, what are you saying?" she asked.

"You were here when Ben was shot. You were here. You couldn't have . . ."

"Oh, Maddie, you thought I killed your uncle? How could you think that? What is wrong with you?"

"Me? What is wrong with you? You said you could kill them all. You said you wanted to kill them all. Your brothers. Your sisters. For what they did to you, you said. And then you left. You drank and drank and then you left and you were gone for over an hour. An hour. Then Jenny called and said—what was I supposed to think?"

"You're supposed to think that I'm your mother. You don't accuse your mother of murder."

"She didn't accuse you," I said. "She was trying to protect you at considerable risk to herself. Let's move on. Let's talk about that missing hour. The hour you spent at the castle."

"I wasn't at the castle," Carly said.

"Yes, you were."

I glanced at Chief Gardner. She waved her hand as if she was giving me the floor.

"It's an interesting problem," I said, "from a legal standpoint, I mean. The paintings that were stolen . . ."

"Paintings?" Madison said. "What paintings?"

"Jenness didn't tell you?"

"She told me about Ben and I—I don't know if she said anything about paintings. I just—I just lost it, I guess."

I had eyes on Carly, yet I spoke directly to her daughter.

"The Remington and Whistler were stolen last night just before your uncle was killed," I said. "They were removed from the art gallery and taken down the back stairs, the servant stairs. For argument's sake, let's say they were stolen by your mother here. Technically, twenty percent of the paintings belong to her; that's what I meant by a legal problem. 'Course, if she had just moved them from one room to another inside the castle, of which she also owns twenty percent, it's not actually stealing. She could argue that she was moving the paintings to protect them from vandals or something. Or simply that she thought they looked better hanging somewhere else. No harm, no foul. If, on the other hand, she had put them in the trunk of her car and drove home with the idea of selling them without the permission of her brothers and sisters, her co-owners, now we're talking burglary in the first degree punishable by as many as twenty years in prison—if your mother's brother and sisters choose to prosecute. Do you think they would choose to prosecute your mother?"

"I didn't steal the paintings," Carly said. "Go 'head and check the trunk of my car if you want."

"Where are they?" Chief Gardner asked.

Carly stared for one beat, two, three, four . . .

For chrissake, my inner voice said. *We're giving you an out. Take it.*

"I put them in the shack for safekeeping," Carly said.

"What shack?" I asked.

"Behind the Oglesby Cabin."

"Where the honeybee hives are?"

"Yes."

"Tell me about this," the chief said.

"It's like McKenzie said, I wanted to protect them from vandals, you know, because of the cross burning and all that. The Sons of Europa."

She doesn't know that Ben burned the cross.

"At ten thirty at night?" Chief Gardner asked.

"They burned the cross at night."

"When you were at the castle, did you see anyone?"

"No."

"Did you hear anyone?"

Carly didn't reply.

"It's important, Ms. Zumwalt," the chief said.

"If you know something that can help about Uncle Ben," Madison said.

"I heard someone, I don't know who," Carly said.

"Where?"

"On the servant stairs. McKenzie guessed right, I took the paintings down the servant stairs . . ."

"So you didn't need to pass the security cameras in the lobby," Chief Gardner said.

"Because it was easier; an easier trip to the shack. Do you want me to . . ."

"Keep talking."

"I don't need to answer your questions, you know. I didn't do anything wrong."

"Mom," Madison said.

"I'm sorry," the chief said. "Please continue."

"I took the paintings down the stairs and out to the shack one at a time," Carly said. "They weren't heavy, but they were bulky and I didn't want to damage them. The third time—after I put the Remington and the Whistler in the shack I went back for a third time for the Nast illustrations and some of the other things and I heard—there was someone at the top of the servant stairs. They seemed to be having trouble opening the door like they couldn't find the latch. So, I left. I ran across the clearing to the edge of the woods . . ."

"Outside of camera range," Chief Gardner said.

"Where I parked my car on the road leading to the castle instead of the lot because I didn't want to take up a space that was reserved for a guest."

"Good answer," I said.

Chief Gardner looked at me as though she didn't agree.

There were more questions and answers after that, only they didn't amount to much. Finally, we left. Neither Madison nor Carly led us to the door. Before I closed it myself, I heard Madison speaking to her mother.

"I think you should know, I decided to take the scholarship offered by the University of Colorado," she said.

I had traveled between the City of Redding and Redding Castle so often in the past few days that I was beginning to feel like a yo-yo. We had escaped the downtown and were back on the highway before Chief Gardner spoke to me.

"A perfectly good felony bust shot to hell," she said, although her voice suggested that she wasn't particularly disappointed.

"You wanted to recover the paintings; we're recovering the paintings."

"If they're where Carly says they are. Besides, we would have recovered them sooner or later, anyway. That woman wouldn't have lasted five minutes in an interrogation room."

"What would arresting her have accomplished except screwing up her family even more than it already is? Screwing up Madison? Besides, I wasn't kidding. There really are issues involving possession to consider."

"That's not for you to decide. Or me. It's the county attorney's job. My job . . ."

"Is to keep the peace?"

"All right, all right."

"Look at it this way, Dee—we're closer to learning who shot Big Ben."

"Oh, we are, are we?"

"We're eliminating suspects."

"Yeah, we only have about twenty left. By the way, how did you guess that Maddie was protecting her mother?"

"Body language."

"Angela Lansbury would be proud."

"I like to think so."

"Imagine thinking that your mother committed murder."

"Imagine deciding to cover for her."

"I hope Maddie does make it to the Olympics; I really do."

We parked in the castle's lot and walked side by side across the clearing toward the General Oglesby Cabin. Eden Redding came out to meet us.

"McKenzie," she said. "Where were you?"

Was she looking for you? my inner voice asked. *Do you care?*

"Not now," I said aloud.

The chief and I moved past her.

"Where are you going?" Eden wanted to know.

I turned toward her and pointed.

"Stay here," I said.

I had no reason to be angry with her; she hadn't burned the damned cross, after all. Yet I was. Go figure.

Chief Gardner and I gained the dirt path and followed it through the collar of trees to the large meadow behind it. The chief was in the lead. I stopped when I saw a few honeybees hovering above the flowers. The chief glanced over her shoulder at me.

"What is it?" she asked.

"Nothing," I told her.

The chief moved past the dilapidated hives to the shack and pulled on the door handle. The door was sealed by a hook and eye latch. She unlocked it and pulled, again. The door swung open and I watched as the chief placed her hands on her hips and stared inside.

This time I was the one who asked, "What?"

"I'm not an art person," Chief Gardner said. "But locking paintings in what amounts to little more than an outhouse . . ."

"I don't know. Have you seen what they're hanging at the Walker Art Center these days?"

I rounded the chief's shoulder and peeked inside the shack. The two paintings were leaning against the wall; they had barely fit inside.

"Despite the problems we'd have prosecuting Carly, I'm still tempted to call the crime scene guys," the chief said.

"They're busy."

"So they are."

The chief reached inside and pulled out the Whistler. I took the Remington.

"Try not to drop it," the chief said.

I was more concerned about tearing the canvas with a branch from a tree or shrub as we carried the paintings along the narrow path back to the clearing. Eden was waiting for us at the end of the path; Alex Redding had joined her.

"What the hell is going on?" Eden asked. "Where did those come from? Chief? McKenzie? Where did you find them? Were they stolen? Answer me."

"It would be improper of me to comment on an ongoing investigation," Chief Gardner said.

We continued across the clearing. As we approached the castle, Jenness, Nina, and Barbara Finne emerged to join the parade. Jenness seemed concerned that we were carrying a million dollars' worth of fine art like they were flat-screen TVs that we bought on sale at Kmart. Barbara catalogued them with her camera. Nina was grinning as if this was just another day in her life.

"Where did you find those?" Jenness wanted to know.

"I'll explain later," the chief said.

"May I have a word with you, Chief?" Barbara asked.

"Later."

Instead of heading for the front entrance to the castle and its lobby, Chief Gardner deliberately went around to the back and entered through the kitchen. I followed closely behind her. Once inside the kitchen, she moved to the door that opened on the servant stairs and began to climb them. The stairs were very narrow and it was tough going while carrying the paintings. When she reached the top, she fumbled for the latch.

"I can't open it," the chief said.

I was directly behind the chief. Jenness was behind me. The stairs were so narrow that she couldn't push past us to unlock the door.

"About halfway up on the right side of the door, there should be a handle," she said.

"I can't see it in the dark," the chief said. "Oh wait . . ." I heard the door click open. "I got it."

Chief Gardner passed through the doorway and carried the Whistler down the corridor to the art gallery. The door was shut and yellow crime scene tape blocked her path. She rested the painting against the wall, removed the tape, opened the door, and carried the Whistler inside. She didn't attempt to mount it; merely leaned it against the wall under the space where it had been hanging. I did the same with the Remington.

"Safe and sound," the chief said. "Although, when you think about it, the castle's security is a joke. If I was an insurance company, I'd be very upset. Might even raise my rates."

We stepped back into the corridor. It was crowded with Eden, Alex, Jenness, Nina, and Barbara. Questions came to us from all sides, mostly concerning how the paintings got from here to there and back again. Chief Gardner's answers remained vague. I said nothing at all, although I did give Nina a wink. She smiled and shook her head as if to say "Really, McKenzie?"

"Carly," Eden announced. "It was Carly, wasn't it? She killed Ben and stole the paintings because we voted against selling the castle."

"No." It was the only definitive answer that Chief Gardner had offered. "She did not."

"Prove it."

"I already have."

"I don't believe you."

"I do," Anna said. "It is a pity, though."

I was startled yet again by her presence. She seemed to possess an uncanny facility for appearing seemingly out of nowhere.

"What does that mean—a pity?" Eden asked. "Do you want her to be guilty?"

Apparently, she's willing to accuse her sister-in-law of murder, yet is outraged when someone else does, my inner voice said.

"Don't you?" Anna asked. "William of Occam relentlessly

wielded the proposition that the simplest of theories should be preferred to the more complex. It would be so much simpler if we could hold Carly responsible, wouldn't it? So much more convenient. No one likes Carly."

"No one likes you, either," Alex said.

"Please stop," Jenness said.

"I wear my detractors like a medal," Anna said.

"You are your own hero—I'm sure that's what you tell yourself when you're all alone and you're always alone, aren't you, Annie? That's because you're such a pill."

"Stop it," Jenness said. "Just stop it. You people make me want to cry and I am so tired of crying."

She pushed past the small crowd and moved down the corridor. Nina gave me a shrug as if to say "this is my life now" and joined her friend. Anna allowed them both a healthy head start before following. Eden and Alex waited until she was nearly to the staircase before they trailed in her footsteps. Barbara Finne remained behind.

"Deidre," she said.

"Barb."

"I would like to interview you on the record."

"I have nothing to tell you right now."

"The sheriff has been doing a lot of telling; I just want to make sure I get the facts straight."

The chief rubbed her eyes and face as if the few hours of sleep she had the night before weren't nearly enough.

"What did Doogie have to say?" she asked.

"He said he has faith in you."

"Whaddya know, Dee," I said. "You've made a friend."

"He said that after he assembled the county-city joint task force, he personally put you in charge of the investigation because of your many years of experience investigating homicides for the Minneapolis Police Department."

"Meaning he'll get the credit when we make an arrest and I'll get the blame if we don't," the chief said.

"He said he expects an arrest within twenty-four hours."

"When did he say that?"

"Eight twenty this morning."

I glanced at my watch and did the math.

"So you have eighteen hours and forty-two minutes left," I said. "Easy-peasy."

"Barbara," the chief said. "When this is over I promise I will give you a very long interview on the record. You can ask me anything you want."

"I look forward to it."

"In the meantime, what do you have for me?"

"What do you mean?"

"Who have you interviewed? What did they say?"

"I'm not sure it's proper for you to ask me that," Barbara said. "An impartial press . . ."

"Girl, help a sister out. I only have eighteen hours . . ."

The chief looked at me and I looked at my watch.

"And forty minutes," I said.

"Eighteen hours and forty minutes to solve the case," the chief said. "How time flies when you're having fun."

"I spoke to Ed and Marian Crawford before I came out to the castle," Barbara said. "They're heartbroken but they have a harvest to worry about, that's what Ed told me. Rain in the long-term forecast; no time to waste. He also has an alibi."

"You asked for an alibi?"

"No, Ed sort of volunteered that he and Marian were in Willmar last night for a dinner put on by the Kandiyohi County Corn and Soybean Growers Association."

"Okay."

"I interviewed Eden and Alex Redding at length, too. They said that they were asleep when the murder took place."

A likely story, my inner voice said.

"They're claiming that the timing makes the Sons of Europa a likely suspect in the murder of their brother," Barbara added.

"Swell," I said.

"But they're also willing to give the justice system time to act before they make any accusations."

"Swell, again." I said.

"Do me a favor, Barb," Chief Gardner said. "When you send out your daily briefing, don't mention the Sons."

"Is there a good reason for that?"

"Yes."

"But you're not going to tell me what it is."

"With a little luck, we'll be able to do that interview before you go to press next Wednesday."

"I'm going to hold you to that, Chief."

"By the way, have you seen Olivia Redding?"

"She was in the computer room off the lobby a half hour ago. She's refused to answer my questions, too. She said if there's anything I need to know, I should ask the chief of police."

SIXTEEN

Chief Gardner and I found Olivia Redding in the cramped room behind the reservation desk working a computer and her cell phone simultaneously—Barbara had not been allowed to accompany us. Olivia gave us a wave that basically indicated, "I'll be with you in a moment," even as she spoke into the phone.

"I understand," Olivia said. "No, I understand. I appreciate everything that you're doing. Okay. Okay. I'll talk to you soon." Olivia set her phone down and tapped the end call icon. "First guy I'm going to fire. I've been on the phone all day; sending emails. There's so much to do. Lawyers. Most of the people at the company have been cooperative, sweet even. Some have decided that now's their chance to take advantage of me."

She was wearing the same tight jeans and boots from the evening before along with a sweatshirt bearing the name and illustration of Redding Castle. For the first time since we met, she looked old.

"Ms. Redding, I need your help," the chief said.

"I was going to say the same thing to you. I've been talking to a funeral home about conducting services maybe here, maybe the Cities, both—I haven't decided. I'm told that it will be some time before Ben's body is released for burial."

"We need to give the medical examiner time to finish her work," the chief said. "A couple of days at least. I'm sorry."

"I understand." Olivia chuckled; if you can call the strained sound she made a chuckle. "I've been saying that a lot lately. I understand. I wish it were true. You said you needed my help?"

"Is it possible for you to unlock Ben's cell phone for us?"

Olivia chuckled again.

"No," she said. "One thing Ben and I never shared, that we never left unattended for the other to find, was our cell phones. Certainly we never told each other our passwords and unblock patterns. You must think we had an appalling marriage."

"No," I said. "Unconventional, maybe, but . . . I saw you dancing together."

Olivia stared long enough at me that I thought I might have said something awful.

"I forgot what I was going to say," she told me. "Oh, Chief, you sealed my bedroom. It's a crime scene. I understand—there's that word again. Except, can I go up there and get some clothes; some other things? You can come with me to make sure I don't do anything wrong."

"I need to contact my office," the chief said. "McKenzie will go with you."

"Thank you."

I tore the yellow crime scene tape from the bedroom door and opened it. Olivia moved past me and went directly to the walk-in closet, being careful not to look in the direction of the bed or the spot on the floor next to the bed where Ben had fallen. I did, though. There wasn't much to see except for the bloodstain on the hardwood floor.

That's never coming out, my inner voice told me.

I listened as Olivia packed a bag behind me.

"I'll just be a moment," she said.

I moved to where I thought the killer must have stood when he fired the three rounds into Big Ben's chest; even brought my hand up as if I was holding a gun.

He must have known his killer well to allow him—or her—to get that close.

"Just a sec," Olivia said.

She moved from the walk-in closet to the bathroom. I heard her opening cabinets.

I turned from the bed and looked toward the bathroom. There were chairs arranged in front of the fireplace that stood between me and the bathroom. On the cushion of the chair closest to the bathroom door was a copy of a hardcover novel.

The Round House by Louise Erdrich.

"Olivia," I said. "Is this yours?"

She came out of the bathroom.

"What?" she asked.

I pointed at the book.

"No," she said. "That's not mine or Ben's. I've been meaning to read it, though. Why?"

"Just wondering," I said.

After making sure she had what she needed, I shooed Olivia out of the bedroom. As she was moving down the corridor, I called Chief Gardner. She answered her cell phone almost immediately.

"McKenzie," she said.

"You need to get up here."

A few minutes later, Chief Gardner came through the door, carefully closing it behind her. I was standing in the center of the bedroom. I was about to speak; only the chief demanded silence by pressing her index finger against her own lips. She also stepped into the center of the room and spun slowly, taking in everything around her. She did this for several minutes before she sighed dramatically.

"All right, dammit," she said, "what did we miss?"

I pointed at the copy of Louise Erdrich's novel sitting faceup on the cushion of the chair in front of the fireplace. The chief stared at the book until its significance became clear to her.

I started to speak, again.

"Shh," the chief said. At the same time, she pulled her cell phone from her pocket and tapped a couple of icons, including speaker. I could hear the phone ring; heard it quickly answered.

"City of Redding Police Department, this is Officer Phillip Holzt."

"Phillip . . ."

"Hi, Chief."

"Phillip, I need you to do something for me; I need you to do it now."

"Yes, ma'am."

"The county's Investigative Division took God knows how many photographs and video of the crime scene at Redding Castle last night. They should be uploaded in the case file. Pull them up for me."

"Yes, ma'am."

The chief told her officer what she was looking for. It took him several minutes to locate it.

"Yes," he said. "A book on the chair cushion."

"Enlarge the image; tell me what's on the cover."

"It's gray with what looks to me like chunks of wood floating around and the words 'A novel, Louise Erdrich, *The Round House.*' Why is that important?"

"Chain of custody. Thank you, Phillip. I'll talk to you later."

The chief moved swiftly from the room. I lingered long

enough to restore the yellow crime scene tape and rushed down the corridor. I caught up with her just as the chief was entering the computer room. It was vacant. Olivia must be off changing clothes, I decided. Chief Gardner worked the computer until we found the footage from the security camera taken the previous evening.

"I have copies at the house, but I don't want to take the time . . ." She ran the video forward until the time stamp read 10:23 P.M. "Here's Anna entering the lobby. She's carrying a copy of *The Round House*."

"She said she went to the lobby to read," I reminded the chief. "She said she was catching up on her Louise Erdrich."

Chief Gardner fast-forwarded the video until the time stamp read 10:37.

"Here she is leaving the lobby with her book in her hand," she said.

Again, the chief fast-forwarded the video, slowing it to real time at 11:33. The seconds ticked off. We saw Nina helping Jenness down the stairs and to the sofa. We saw Anna Redding entering the lobby at nearly the same time. She moved toward Jenness, her hands extended, as if to ask what had happened.

Her hands were empty.

"I'll be right back," Chief Gardner said.

It took her only a few minutes to walk to her SUV, open the truck, and remove a nine-by-twelve-inch clear plastic evidence bag with write-on panels for chain of custody information. She returned to the castle and made her way back to Big Ben's bedroom. At this point, I was just following her around.

Once inside the bedroom, she filled in the write-on panel, moved to the chair, and very carefully placed the book inside the evidence bag. She sealed the bag and held it up for me to see.

"Where's Anna Redding?" she said.

"You're asking me?"

"Let's go get her."

"No, wait."

"For what? McKenzie, the timing works perfectly. Anna leaves the lobby at exactly ten thirty-seven. With her book. She circles the castle, goes through the kitchen, climbs the servant stairs, and knocks on her brother's door. With her book."

"Why sneak around?"

"Because she doesn't want anyone to know that she's sleeping with her big brother, that's why. Ben lets her in. They screw each other's brains out for a half hour. They get into an argument. Anna shoots him with her father's gun. That's at exactly eleven seventeen, forty minutes after she left the lobby. Only Jenness Crawford is so quick to the bedroom door that Anna can't get out. Next we see you entering the lobby at—I have eleven eighteen—you go upstairs and two minutes later come back downstairs, exiting the lobby at eleven twenty to search for a ladder. You find a ladder, use it to climb into the bedroom; you find Ben dead, and go through the door into the corridor. Let's say ten minutes from start to finish. Make it fifteen just to be generous. At eleven thirty-two, Anna sees her chance and escapes down the ladder, leaving her book behind. She circles the castle and comes through the lobby entrance empty-handed at exactly eleven thirty-four. Sure looks guilty to me."

"Why are you in a hurry, Dee?"

"Haven't you heard? I have less than twenty-four hours to make an arrest."

"You don't give a damn about the sheriff and his schedule, cut it out."

"McKenzie . . ."

"You told me not to let you fuck up. You told me that was my one and only job."

"You think I'm wrong about this?"

"No, I don't, but you have time to make sure. Anna Redding

isn't going anywhere. Your guys running fingerprints; checking on DNA—let them do their jobs before you do something you might regret."

"Like what?"

"Like arresting the wrong suspect. You know how that always complicates the prosecutor's case when it gets to court."

Chief Gardner took a deep breath. She never struck me as someone who counted to ten, yet it was a good ten seconds before she spoke.

"All right," she said. "I'll hold off for now."

"On the other hand, I didn't say we shouldn't hear what the woman has to say, you know, in the natural course of our ongoing investigation. Just don't arrest her."

"Not even if she confesses, like they do on *Murder, She Wrote*?"

We found Anna Redding sitting outside on a bench with a nice view of Lake Anpetuwi, although she seemed much more interested in the screen of her cell phone. I sat on her right side. Chief Gardner sat on her left. Given the circumstances, most people would have found our abrupt appearance disconcerting. Anna behaved as if she had been expecting us. She spent a few moments signing off her phone and placing it into her pocket before she spoke.

"Chief Gardner, McKenzie," she said. "To what do I owe the pleasure of your company?"

"We have questions," I said.

"I thought I explained myself at length last night. Or was it early this morning?"

Chief Gardner produced the copy of Louise Erdrich's book.

"Oh, you found it," Anna said.

She reached for the book. The chief pulled it back.

"Where was it?" Anna asked.

"In your brother's bedroom," I said.

"How did it get there?"

"That's what we would like to know," Chief Gardner said.

"I'm afraid I can only speculate," Anna said.

"Feel free," I said.

"Clearly you believe that finding my book there proves that I'm responsible for my brother's demise. I assure you, I am not. I took the book with me when I left the lobby last night to search the night sky. After some time passed, I went into the kitchen for a glass of water. I set the book on the counter. After enjoying my drink, I went back outside, leaving the book behind. Later, when I returned to the kitchen to procure hot chocolate for my niece, I noticed that the book was missing. How you came to find it in my brother's bedroom, I cannot say. Perhaps Ben came downstairs for a drink of water, as well, spied the book and took it back upstairs with him. Perhaps someone else discovered the volume and took it upstairs when he—or she—went to visit my brother. Are there any other possibilities?"

"Yes," I said.

"Such as?"

"Dr. Redding, you were outside for a long time last night," the chief said. "Considering how you were dressed . . ."

"I'm a Minnesota girl born and raised," Anna said. "The cold doesn't bother me. I recall a period when I was performing as a field experience student, a student teacher if you will, as part of my degree program at the University of Colorado. My charges would often marvel that I would be comfortable wearing little more than a sweater while they were bundled in their heavy winter garments."

"You said you saw no one entering or leaving the castle."

"I doubt those were my exact words, yet they convey my meaning. If I may be allowed, you people . . ."

You people? my inner voice asked. *Really?*

"You seem to have embraced the hypothesis that someone in the Redding family is responsible for my brother's death." Anna pointed at the evidence bag in Chief Gardner's hand. "That I am responsible. You are greatly mistaken. I recommend instead, that you concentrate your suspicions on individuals outside the family."

"Such as?" I asked.

"I suggested a possible suspect at the city council meeting Thursday night."

"Veronica Bickner?"

"You said it yourself, McKenzie, as a principal of Boeve Luxury, Veronica had as much at stake in the vote to sell the castle as anyone. The vote went against her. Given her on-again, off-again relationship with my brother, I would not be surprised if your evidence technicians discovered her fingerprints all through Ben's bedroom. In fact, I am convinced of it."

"We'll see," Chief Gardner said.

"If there's nothing else . . ." Anna stood; she gestured at the evidence bag on the chief's lap. "I look forward to the return of my property."

Anna strolled back toward the castle while the chief and I remained on the bench.

"Oh, she's good," I said. "You're not going to trip her up during a Q and A."

"You don't think, McKenzie, that she might actually be innocent, do you?"

"I think we're going to need more than the book to prove that she isn't."

Chief Gardner's response was to pull her cell phone from her pocket and make a call. I heard only her side of the conversation.

"Dr. Evers please . . . Chief of Police Deidre Gardner . . . Angie . . . Yes, it's me. The DNA from the fluids on Ben Redding's dick . . . I get that it takes time. What I want you to do is match it against Ben's DNA . . . To find out if he had sex with his sister . . . I know it's messed up. Angie, I don't have to tell you to keep all of this to yourself, do I? . . . The sooner the better . . . You're the best."

The chief put her phone away.

"Any thoughts, Jessica?" she asked.

"Three things. Four, actually. First—Carly told us that she heard someone at the top of the servant stairs trying to work the latch; that's why she took off before clearing out the art gallery. Second—Veronica Bickner worked at the castle when she was a kid, so she probably knew about the servant stairs, if in fact, she had climbed them. Three—I'm curious to learn why Anna is so convinced that we'll find Veronica's fingerprints in Ben's room. It's almost as if she knew she was there."

"What's the fourth thing?"

"I wish you'd stop calling me Jessica."

"Help me close this case and I'll call you any damn thing you want."

The first thing that made me go "hmm" was the realization that Veronica Bickner's home was only a ten-minute walk through the woods from Redding Castle. I knew this, of course. Anna told me just before the Redding City Council meeting that Veronica had purchased a bungalow on the wrong side of the street that circled Lake Anpetuwi, only it didn't register until we called her up on my phone's maps app. The second thing was when she met us at her door wearing a black nightgown and matching robe. She didn't say "hello" or "good-bye" or "come in" or "go to hell," but left the door open and walked back inside the house without any of us uttering a word.

The chief and I glanced at each other, a "what's all this then?" expression on our faces, and entered the house cautiously.

We found Veronica sitting on a sofa in her small living room, her legs tucked beneath her. She was sipping from a clear glass tumbler. There was orange juice in the glass and ice and from the glazed expression on her face, a lot of something else as well.

"Mrs. Bickner," Chief Gardner said.

"Did you come to tell me he's dead? I already know. Cassie called this morning." Veronica lifted her glass to us. "Can't you see? I'm in mourning."

"Were you with Ben last night?" the chief asked.

Veronica nodded her head.

"For the last time," she said. "Every time I was with Ben Redding I thought it would be for the last time and now . . ."

Veronica took another pull of her drink. I stepped forward and took the glass from her hand.

"What are you doing?" she asked. "I need that."

The bungalow was small; it was very easy for me to find my way to the kitchen. Veronica chased after me and watched as I poured the drink into the sink, rinsed the glass, and filled it with cold water.

"Is this a police thing?" she asked. "Am I under arrest?"

"No, ma'am," Chief Gardner said. "You are not under arrest. We have questions we'd like to ask, though."

I tried to hand the glass back to Veronica. She shook her head and refused to accept it.

"I don't want it now," she said.

"Please," I said.

"Fine." Veronica took the glass and drank the water down in one go. "Happy?"

I took the glass from her, refilled it, and handed it back.

"Are you my mother now? McKenzie, right? I don't need a mother. I need . . ." Veronica wrapped her arms around herself, barely holding the glass upright; her mouth twisted in a painful-looking grimace. "I need . . ."

"Mrs. Bickner," the chief said.

"I need to sit down. Sit down before I fall down."

Veronica moved to her kitchen table, pulled out a wooden chair, and sat. She held the water glass in front of her with both hands.

"When Cassie told me what happened, my first thought was that Olivia did it," she said. "But Cassie said that was impossible. They were both eating pad thai at the time."

Veronica drank half of the water.

"You went to see him last night," Chief Gardner said.

"Yes, although no one was supposed to know that. It was supposed to be a secret, like everybody didn't already know that we'd been having an affair for the past forty years. Like Olivia didn't know. I'm sleeping with Ben while she's sleeping with my niece. It sounds like a plot to an adult film, not that I watch adult films."

Veronica finished the water and handed me the glass. I took it, refilled it, and handed it back.

"Thank you," she said.

"You went to see him last night," Chief Gardner repeated.

"Yes. Didn't I tell you that? Ben called me. He called me twice. The first time was about six thirty. He called to say that the Reddings had voted against selling the castle to me and Cassandra. Ben didn't say that he cast one of the votes against us, but I knew he had. I knew because of the way he tried to sugarcoat it; saying how we'd still be able to see each other now when he came back to visit the castle. He was talking about Christmas, for God's sake; how we always met for Christmas. I was angry. I own twenty percent of Cassie's business. This deal would have made me rich. I might even have become as rich as Ben. I told him that we were through, finally and forever. I told him not to call me again. And I hung up.

"He called back at about ten o'clock. Of course I answered

the phone. I always answered the phone. Ben said that it looked like Olivia's meeting with Cassandra was going to last all night. I said in that case . . ." Veronica laughed at herself. "I had no pride and no shame when it came to Big Ben Redding. None. I said, in that case, he should come on over. This is where we've been meeting ever since I bought the house ten years ago. Only he said I should go to the castle like I used to when we were teenagers, him sneaking out or me sneaking in. Like on prom night."

The chief read the same chapter in the interrogation manual that I had; the one that insisted once you managed to get a suspect talking, you let them talk, which explained the angry glare she flashed at me when I interrupted.

Only I had to ask—"Mrs. Bickner, did you ever meet Ben in town?"

"Oh, no, no, no," Veronica said. "It's a small town, McKenzie. Reputations are easily ruined. Ben said he didn't care about his, but he cared deeply about mine. We were always very careful when we were in town together."

Chief Gardner tried to get Veronica back on track.

"Ben called you at ten o'clock," she said.

"A little after," Veronica replied. "He told me to come over to the castle. He told me to sneak up the servant stairs like I did when—it must have been decades since I last did that. So, I walked over, walked in—the Reddings never locked their doors. I went up the stairs

"Mrs. Bickner, did you happen to see a book lying on the kitchen counter?" the chief asked.

"No. Do you think I turned on the lights and made myself a sandwich? Besides, I didn't go there to read. I went directly to the servant stairs." Veronica chuckled. "I had forgotten how to unlatch the door. I must have spent five minutes before I figured it out. Once I did, I slipped into the corridor—it was exciting, like when I was a girl. I knocked on Ben's door and he let me in and it was the same as it had always been with us—me and him and nothing else in the world for nearly an hour. And then I told him . . ." Veronica laughed some more. "I told him if he thought I was going to spend the night he was crazy. I was still mad at him. I got dressed, which didn't take long; I was wearing what I'm wearing now. You know what Ben did? He dressed, too; put on his robe. He said he might take a walk in the woods later. I said not to let the big, bad wolf get him. Then I left the castle, walked home, and waited for him. I waited all night. Only he never came."

Veronica drank more water.

"When did you leave the castle?" the chief asked.

"I don't know. Eleven o'clock? I know it was ten after when I got here and the castle is only ten minutes away. Chief Gardner, I didn't kill Ben. I loved him so much."

The exact same words that Olivia used, my inner voice reminded me.

We spoke for another twenty minutes before Chief Gardner was satisfied. She thanked Veronica for her time and we left the bungalow. We were following the path back toward Redding Castle when the chief remembered why she was miffed at me.

"The question you asked her about meeting Ben in town, what was that about?" she asked.

Before I could answer, the chief's cell phone rang. She read the caller ID before answering it.

"Chief Gardner." She listened for a moment, said, "Hang on for a sec," and put the phone on speaker. "Go 'head."

"I said I didn't send the DNA samples to the county," Dr. Angelique Evers told us. "I have a male friend . . ."

"Male friend?" the chief asked.

"You don't think I can have a male friend?"

"It was just the way you said it."

"He's a forensic scientist who works out of the FBI's resident agency in Mankato. He did a rush job as a favor to me. He thinks I'm gorgeous."

"We all do, Angie."

"Anyway, your DNA samples—siblings share about fifty percent of their DNA, half siblings, uncle, aunts, nieces and nephews about twenty-five percent, first cousins twelve-point-five percent and so on all the way down to sixth cousins who share zero-point-zero-one percent, which they don't."

"Who don't?"

"Ben Redding and his lady friend. There is no genetic relationship between the two samples at all except that the pattern of SNPs indicate that both subjects are approximately eleven percent Welsh. What are the odds?"

Chief Gardner thanked Dr. Evers for her time and hung up the phone.

"What did I tell you about getting my samples early?" she said.

"Ben didn't sleep with Anna. After talking with Veronica Bickner, I didn't think he did."

"I don't know why I'm relieved, but I am. You were right about not slapping the cuffs on her. Except the book . . . How else could it have gotten in the bedroom? Veronica said she didn't touch it."

"Print the book."

"Duh, Dick Tracy."

"In the meantime . . ."

"Would you rather be a Jessica or a Dick?" the chief asked.

"Do I have a choice?"

"Just this once."

"Ben Redding spent time with an identified female at the Riverboat Hotel in Redding on Tuesday afternoon. I saw him leave the hotel while I was chatting with Barbara Finne. I confirmed later that Ben had checked in and checked out; the woman he had arranged to meet left just a few minutes before he did."

"That's why you asked the question? If he wasn't meeting Veronica . . ."

"Who was he meeting?" I asked.

"You know what? I'm still going to call you Jessica. Tracy had the toys, but Jessica had the brains."

"Is that a compliment?"

Back to the City of Redding; I was pretty sure I could have made the drive with my eyes shut by then. The chief and I got lucky twice. The first time was when we found an empty parking spot directly in front of the Riverboat Hotel. The second time was when we discovered that the young woman I had spoken to on Tuesday afternoon was working the reservation desk.

"May I help you?" she asked.

She spoke cautiously. I think she was intimidated by Chief Gardner's immaculate uniform.

"Do you remember me?" I asked.

"I'm sorry, no. Should I?"

"Last Tuesday, I asked about Big Ben Redding . . ."

She stared for a moment and smiled.

"You were late for a business appointment," she said.

"Only Ben had left just before I arrived."

"I remember."

"You said his business associate—a woman—had departed just before he did."

"You're the one who said it was his business associate. I figured it was his date. I mean, think about it."

"What was her name?"

"I have no idea."

"You didn't ask her name?" Chief Gardner asked.

"Why would I?"

"She came into the hotel . . ."

"Mr. Redding was waiting for her in the lobby. They embraced and went up the stairs together. Two hours later, they came back down the stairs. She left the hotel by the rear entrance. He checked out and left by the front door. Then this gentleman came in. That's it."

"You don't know who the woman was," the chief said.

"It's not that small of a town. I mean, I knew Ben Redding. Everyone knew Big Ben Redding. Only not the woman. Does this have anything to do with him getting shot?"

"Hang on a sec," I said.

I took my cell phone from my pocket and searched for a website. After I found it, I searched the site until I located a pic and filled my screen with it. I held the phone up so that the desk clerk could get a good look.

"Yeah, that's her," she said.

"Are you sure?" the chief asked.

"Yes."

"Are you absolutely sure?"

"Yes, I am absolutely sure."

"I might need you to make an identification in court."

"Yeah, well, I mean, if I have to."

A minute later, the chief and I were standing on the sidewalk next to my Mustang.

"You know, the most common motives for murder are money, jealousy, and vengeance," Chief Gardner said. "In this case we might have all three."

"It would seem so."

"Dammit, it shouldn't take more than two hours to run fingerprints. Why the hell haven't I heard anything yet?"

"It's the weekend," I said. "There's probably a backlog. I remember one case I worked, it took three days."

"You're not making me feel better, McKenzie."

"The prints might not even be in the system."

"Shh, God might hear you."

"Although . . ." I accessed the same website on my cell as I did in the hotel and after perusing it for a moment, switched to another site. The chief watched me do it.

"Yeah, they should be there," I said.

"So, what's the holdup?" she asked.

"If you're so worried about meeting the sheriff's deadline, I have an idea."

"I don't want to hear it."

"Okay."

"What is it?"

SEVENTEEN

It was early evening and the castle's guests had yet to gather to witness the rolling sunset. However, the patio was filled with Reddings. I pretended to be surprised to see them there.

"What's going on?" I asked.

"Perhaps you would care to inform us," Anna said.

She was sitting alone more or less in the center of the patio as appropriate to the clan's new matriarch—the king is dead, long live the queen. On her far right sat Carly. Near her, but not with her, sat Marian. Eden and Alex had claimed a spot two tables away. Olivia sat alone on the left next to a table occupied by Jenness and Nina. Everyone looked serious except Nina, who was smiling as if this was the most fun she ever had. She actually winked at me.

Would you stop it? my inner voice said.

"I came for the bourbon," I said aloud.

A waitress appeared and I ordered a double of maple-flavored Knob Creek, no ice.

"May I?" I asked and sat at Anna's table without waiting for her reply.

"The chief of police asked us to meet her here," Marian said.

"She did?"

"Just a little while ago."

"Where's Ed?"

"On the combine."

"Why did the chief ask to meet us?" Olivia asked.

"Convenience, I suppose. Last I heard, she was asking a judge to issue a warrant for the arrest of the person who murdered your brother. Probably, she doesn't want the suspect wandering off."

"Does she think it's one of us?" Marian asked.

"I honestly don't know," I said.

"I thought you were helping," Eden said.

"There's help and then there's help. I'm not actually a police officer, remember? Legally, there are things I'm not allowed to do."

"Like arrest anyone," Nina said.

She smiled at me. I smiled back.

"Among others," I said.

"Veronica's not here," Anna said.

"She's not?"

I pretended to look around even as the waitress set my drink in front of me. I made an effort to pay except Jenness announced, "On the house." The waitress smiled and moved away. I promised myself I'd give her a nice tip the next time I saw her.

"It was Veronica, wasn't it?" Anna asked. "Veronica Bickner."

"We don't think so," I said.

"But her fingerprints . . ."

"You were correct, Dr. Redding." She seemed pleased that I used her title. "Mrs. Bickner did spend the evening with your brother, leaving behind her fingerprints and other—identifying characteristics. Plus, she readily admitted to having an affair with your brother since they were in high school together . . ."

"The whore . . ."

"There's no need for that," Olivia said.

"You're a whore, too."

Olivia stood and for a moment, I thought she would march across the patio and smack Anna upside her head. Only Nina stood and blocked her path. She leaned in and whispered something to her that I couldn't hear and Olivia resumed her seat.

"In any case," I said, "Mrs. Bickner left the castle a good fifteen minutes before Big Ben was shot."

"How do you know?" Anna said.

"There was a witness."

"I didn't . . ." She checked herself. "I didn't know that."

"It doesn't matter, anyway. In the murder business, we always talk about motive, means, and opportunity. Yet none of that means squat without specific evidence tying the suspect to the crime."

"Is there any specific evidence?" Alex asked.

"Dr. Redding mentioned fingerprints. It turns out the suspect screwed up."

"How?" Anna asked.

"Whoever wiped off the handgun before dropping it next to the bedroom window missed a spot." I held my thumb and index finger an inch apart, my hand pointing downward like I was holding something scummy. "At the tip of the barrel."

"Whose fingerprints are they?" Carly asked.

"Eden."

"Me?"

Eden Redding seemed genuinely shocked that I had called on her.

"Your fingerprints are on file, aren't they?" I said. "Because of your numerous busts for disorderly conduct, violating curfews, failure to disperse, resisting arrest during your many protests against social injustice."

"I've never resisted arrest."

"You said that you saw Heimdall burn the cross the other

night; you organized protests against the Sons of Europa because of it. Except it wasn't Heimdall, was it?"

"I saw someone."

"It wasn't Heimdall. It wasn't the Sons of Europa."

"Who was it?" Jenness asked.

"Eden?" I asked.

She refused to answer.

"Stop playing games, McKenzie," Alex said.

"Dr. Redding," I said. "Who did Eden see Wednesday night?"

"It was Ben," Olivia said.

"That's not possible," Eden said.

"Dr. Redding," I said. "Is it possible?"

"Why are you asking me?"

"Just seeking a second opinion."

"Ben did it to influence Eden's vote," Olivia said.

Eden dropped her head into her hands.

"What have I done?" she asked.

"What you've always done," I said. "You took a stand against injustice. That you were lied to is on the liar, not you."

"McKenzie, I didn't kill Ben."

"I know; you were asleep at the time."

"How can you be sure of that?" Anna asked.

"If Eden had been awake, she would have noticed Carly carrying the Remington and Whistler paintings past her cabin on her way to the honeybee shack."

"It was Carly all along," Eden said. "I knew it. I just knew you stole the paintings."

"Oh, relax," Carly said. "I was just storing them for safekeeping."

"That's garbage," Alex said.

"It was Carly who killed Ben," Eden said.

"No," I said. "Carly was in Redding when the crime took place. Same with Olivia."

"I told you," Carly said.

"Who then?" Eden asked.

"Marian," I said.

"But—but I was in Willmar," she said. "You can check."

"The chief did. She's very thorough. But please . . ."

"Talk straight, McKenzie," Alex said.

I think he's starting to get annoyed. They all are. Better start wrapping this up.

"Marian," I said aloud. "After Tess died, you helped clean out her room."

"Yes."

"Did you happen to come across a .32-caliber handgun that had been owned by your father?"

Marian's eyes grew wide.

"Joseph bought it in 2001, just a few years before he passed." I said. "Pretty sure Tess kept it, though. When you were cleaning out her room . . ."

"It was in the drawer of the nightstand next to the bed," Marian said. "I didn't touch it. I hate guns. I said . . . Anna was with me. I told her to get rid of it. She—she laughed at me and said I was a little coward."

"I said you were acting unduly frightened as a child might; that's not the same thing," Anna said. "Language matters."

"Dr. Redding," I said.

"I put the gun with the other personal possessions that we took out of my mother's room. I have no idea what happened to it after that. That's what you wish to know, correct?"

"Motive, means, opportunity."

"I'll play your silly parlor game," Anna said. "What was my motive?"

"Jealousy, to start with."

"Jealous of whom?"

"Olivia, Veronica—who else was Ben sleeping with besides you?"

I heard a collective gasp from the other Reddings. Anna's response was to actually snort at me.

"That's very uncivilized," I told her.

"It's what you deserve for that filthy accusation."

"Ben spent the better part of Tuesday afternoon with a woman at the Riverboat Hotel in Redding."

"What of it?" Anna asked.

"We showed the desk clerk a photograph. This photograph." I held up my cell phone for Anna to see; her pic filled the screen. "It was taken off the staff and faculty page of the Southwest Minnesota State University website."

Anna stared at her pic for a few beats more and glanced at the rest of the Reddings.

"Why would you drive forty minutes to meet your brother in a hotel room for two hours and drive forty minutes back home, and return to the castle the very next day as if nothing happened?" I asked.

"If you had asked me in private, McKenzie, I would have told you the truth. We met to discuss the future of the castle without the distraction and near hysterical input of our younger siblings."

That actually sounds plausible, my inner voice admitted.

I kept pushing.

"You left Jenny's bedroom," I said. "You heard someone fumbling with the latch to the door leading to the servant stairs . . ."

"What I heard," Carly said.

"You hid in the art gallery," I added. "That's why you were upset when you learned that the paintings had been stolen. You were in the gallery and you hadn't noticed. That's because you were so intent on watching Veronica Bickner sneak to Ben's door and knock softly. He let her in and you went

(321)

down to the lobby. Eventually, you left. You were gone for forty minutes. Did you stay outside all that time or did you wait in the kitchen until Veronica went home? Doesn't matter. Immediately after she departed—you were the witness I mentioned earlier, by the way—after she departed, you climbed the servant stairs and went to Ben's room. You confronted him. I don't know what was said or why. I don't care. I do know that you shot him three times in the chest. Before you could leave, though, Jenness was at the door. You locked her out, at the same time locking yourself in. When I came through the window, you seized the opportunity to escape, climbing down the ladder, circling the castle, and coming through the door just in time to comfort your niece. The timing is well documented."

"What complete and utter nonsense."

Anna was standing now. I stood with her.

"You left your book in the bedroom," I said. "That is also documented."

"I explained the book."

"Now explain the gun."

"I told you what I did with the gun. Determining how it came to be found in the bedroom is your job, not mine."

"Explain your fingerprints on the gun."

"You're bluffing, McKenzie. Unlike dear Eden, I'm not a criminal. My fingerprints are not on file."

"Yes, they are. You mentioned it the other night in the art gallery when you were examining the Whistler. Remember? At the University of Colorado you had to submit your fingerprints in order to work as a student teacher in the Colorado Department of Education. It was part of your degree program. They were forwarded to the FBI's database along with forty million other employment-related fingerprints."

"That was nearly forty years ago."

"And yet fingerprints never change."

Anna didn't have a ready reply to that one. Her silence was punctuated by the sound of a police siren. It seemed very near.

Nice touch, Deidre, you clever, clever girl.

"They're coming for you, Anna," I said aloud.

"That's *Doctor* Redding to you. And let them. I do not fear the police. Perhaps they will believe me when I testify that the fingerprints found on the gun must have been left there when I handled the weapon over a month ago."

Also quite plausible. You're in trouble.

She knew it, too. Anna smiled at me; smiled as if she had won something and leaned in close, so only I could hear her voice.

"Despite your filthy mind, I didn't kill my brother because of some incestuous sex fantasy or because he might reveal my involvement in the cross burning. That's why you'll never convict me. You're not intelligent enough to ascertain why I actually did it, why I smiled when I did it, are you?"

"I don't need to be," I whispered back.

My words didn't faze her one bit. Anna straightened up and smiled some more. She spoke loud enough for everyone to hear.

"What do they say on TV?" she said. "This is a bum rap."

"Did you get all that?" I asked.

Chief Gardner stepped onto the patio followed by Officers Phillip Holzt and Jim Overvig; they had been hiding in the dining room.

"I got it," she said. She held up a recording device as proof.

"What is this?" Anna asked.

I pulled a tiny transmitter from beneath my collar and showed it to her.

"It's a wire," I said. "You would know that if you actually did watch a lot of TV."

"When you get to prison, ask if they show reruns of *Murder, She Wrote*," the chief said.

Officer Holtz pulled Anna's arms behind her back and put the cuffs on her.

"You're under arrest," the chief said.

"Where's Doogie?" I asked.

Chief Gardner's reply was to smirk as she started reading Anna her rights from a laminated card that she held in her hand—"You have the right to remain silent. Anything you say can be used against you in court . . ."

The Reddings were all standing. They watched us as if in a trance; as if they were waiting for someone to explain what they were witnessing.

"I have nothing to say," Anna said.

"That's okay," the chief told her. "You've said enough. McKenzie?"

"Dee?"

"It's always a pleasure to watch Jessica Fletcher at work."

"I hate you, Dee."

"We'll talk soon."

"It better be soon. I'm going home. I mean it this time."

There was plenty of commotion on the patio as Chief Gardner and her officers escorted Anna Redding out of the castle. Voices were raised. Questions were asked. I answered some and ignored the rest. Eventually, I made my way across the patio to where my wife was standing. We wrapped our arms around each other.

"What did you tell Olivia to keep her from punching out Anna?" I asked.

"I told her that you knew what you were doing."

"So, you lied."

"Why did Anna do it? Do you know?"

"My guess—all these years Anna never forgave Ben for stealing her honeybees and she remained jealous of his women. When she realized, while watching the prom queen from the art gallery, that things would never change, she finally took her revenge."

The three most common motives for murder, my inner voice said.

"McKenzie?" Nina said.

"Yes, dear?"

"I'm so glad you're not a detective."

JUST SO YOU KNOW

The reason it had taken the FBI so long to process Anna Redding's fingerprint was because it was smeared—not the print lifted from the gun, but on the original card where they had rolled her left forefinger when she was in college. Her prints were taken again, of course, after she was booked, and the ridge patterns matched the partial perfectly. It was because of the gun, because Anna had deliberately carried it into the bedroom with her that night, that the county attorney charged her with murder in the first degree, which carried a life sentence. Smart woman that she was, Anna pled down to second degree and is now serving seventeen years, eight months at the Minnesota Correctional Facility in Shakopee.

The Redding Castle collapsed, both figuratively and literally. I don't think it was the murder that did it, but the revelation that Big Ben Redding was responsible for burning the cross on his own property, at Anna's urging it was later revealed. Nina and Jenness had devised a marketing plan that would rebrand it from "Historic Redding Castle" to "Infamous Redding Castle" using the family's history as a draw, not unlike the Glensheen mansion in Duluth. Only the Sibs would have nothing to do with it. Truth be told, I don't think that Jenness's heart was in it, either. I knew this because she and Nina kept in touch and Nina told me everything.

The remaining four Reddings—Olivia inherited Ben's share; Anna was legally forbidden to profit from her crimes—voted to sell the castle and all of its property to Cassandra Boeve. Cassandra had attempted to renegotiate at a lower price; only Olivia stepped in, reminding her that she wasn't the only developer in Minnesota, "Just the prettiest."

I couldn't help but laugh when Nina told me that.

"I don't know why I like her so much; why I liked Big Ben," I said. "They set a very bad example."

Nina's response was to point two fingers at her eyes, then mine, then hers, then mine again.

The luxury condominiums went up quickly after Cassandra bulldozed the castle. She also built a restaurant that offered live music six nights a week. She called it "Redding's" and hired Jenness to run it, offering her a percentage of the profits as well as a salary. Olivia was there for the grand opening. Nina said that Jenness said that Olivia and Cassandra kept their distance most of the evening, yet somehow managed to end up dancing together by closing.

Having voted to change the zoning laws to accommodate Castles on Anpetuwi, the Redding City Council felt compelled to approve the Sons of Europa's request to turn its house on the lake into "a gathering place," Cassandra casting the only dissenting ballot. Except it never happened. That's because the church soon went bankrupt.

According to Chief Gardner, Lawspeaker Fredgaard's amazing blue-eyed blonde wasn't just arm candy; she was an accomplished con artist and embezzler who made off with the Tyr Haus funds. Fredgaard tried mightily to inspire his small group of followers to refinance the church, only the money didn't come in. His mortgage and other bills did, however. He ended up selling Tyr Haus to—wait for it—Eden Redding, who turned it into the headquarters of a nonprofit group that supported social justice causes throughout southwestern Minnesota.

As for the aluminum ladder found lying on the slope outside Tess Redding's balcony—I never did learn how it got there. One of life's many mysteries. Oh, well . . .